SF
COOK
PORT
Port of Shadows
The Ch
Compa
Cook, Gle
P9-CSE-574
DEC 2 6 2018
DISCARDED
Public Library

TOR BOOKS BY GLEN COOK

THE INSTRUMENTALITIES OF THE NIGHT

The Tyranny of the Night

Lord of the Silent Kingdom

Surrender to the Will of the Night

In Working God's Mischief

An Ill Fate Marshalling

Reap the East Wind

The Swordbearer

The Tower of Fear

THE BLACK COMPANY

The Black Company (The First Chronicle)

Shadows Linger (The Second Chronicle)

The White Rose (The Third Chronicle)

Shadow Games (The First Book of the South)

Dreams of Steel (The Second Book of the South)

Chronicles of the Black Company
(comprising *The Black Company*, *Shadows Linger*, and *The White Rose*)

The Books of the South (comprising *Shadow Games*, *Dreams of Steel*, and *The Silver Spike*)

Return of the Black Company (comprising *Bleak Seasons* and *She Is the Darkness*)

The Silver Spike

The Many Deaths of the Black Company (comprising *Water Sleeps* and *Soldiers Live*)

Bleak Seasons (Book One of Glittering Stone)

She Is the Darkness (Book Two of Glittering Stone)

Water Sleeps (Book Three of Glittering Stone)

Soldiers Live (Book Four of Glittering Stone)

Port of Shadows

Ingram $26 10/18

PORT OF SHADOWS

Glen Cook

A TOM DOHERTY ASSOCIATES BOOK
New York

HURON PUBLIC LIBRARY
521 DAKOTA AVE S
HURON, SD 57350-2797

This is a work of fiction. All of the characters, organizations, and events portrayed in this novel are either products of the author's imagination or are used fictitiously.

PORT OF SHADOWS

Copyright © 2018 by Glen Cook

All rights reserved.

A Tor Book
Published by Tom Doherty Associates
175 Fifth Avenue
New York, NY 10010

www.tor-forge.com

Tor® is a registered trademark of Macmillan Publishing Group, LLC.

The Library of Congress Cataloging-in-Publication Data is available upon request.

ISBN 978-1-250-17457-4 (hardcover)
ISBN 978-1-250-17456-7 (ebook)

Our books may be purchased in bulk for promotional, educational, or business use. Please contact your local bookseller or the Macmillan Corporate and Premium Sales Department at 1-800-221-7945, extension 5442, or by email at MacmillanSpecialMarkets@macmillan.com.

First Edition: September 2018

Printed in the United States of America

0 9 8 7 6 5 4 3 2 1

COPYRIGHT ACKNOWLEDGMENTS

Portions of this work, in somewhat different form, have appeared previously.

The chapter "Tides Elba" initially appeared in the anthology *Swords & Dark Magic,* edited by Jonathan Strahan and Lou Anders, HarperCollins, 2010. Preceded by a limited-edition hardcover from Subterranean Press.

The chapter "Smelling Danger" initially appeared in the anthology *Subterranean: Tales of Dark Fantasy 2,* edited by William Schafer, Subterranean Press, 2011.

The chapter "Bone Candy" initially appeared in the anthology *Shattered Shields,* edited by Jennifer Brozek and Bryan Thomas Schmidt, Baen Books, 2014.

PORT OF SHADOWS

PROLOGUE

I was permitted to record the following but do not doubt that the pertinent Annals will disappear and be read by none forever whilst those of us who lived it forget every instant of love and horror.

It started in humanity's bleakest hour, as the Domination staggered toward its demise. I know these things only through a windfall blessing: Resurrectionist fugitives who fled from Honnoh early took the relevant documents with them, only to give them up in transit. Unable to decipher them myself, I passed them on to Charm.

Some generous spirit there returned a translation copy, that was, for sure, edited, censored, and bowdlerized, but, even so, was one that offered a skeleton on which I could flesh out a pragmatic phantasm of the truth.

1

Once Upon a Time, in Dusk

The night was silent but for the clop of hooves on wet cobblestones. A sliver of moon winked at the world from behind straggler wisps of cloud, silhouetting the grim spires of Grendirft. No light shone anywhere from that fortress.

The air was still and nearly chill now that the rain had gone away. A hint of corrupting flesh tainted the air of imperial Dusk.

It was not yet late enough in the season for many insects.

The black coach stopped, its right side wheels a yard from an unguarded drop-off into a moatlike canal that existed to carry off wastes rather than to present a defensive barrier. A waste chute debouched into the canal just yards upstream from the coach.

The driver tied off his reins. He climbed down. He assumed a stiff parade rest at the canal's edge, but after a brief wait he turned, opened the coach door, and retrieved a boat hook. He now held that tool like it was a pole arm.

A corpse made a small plop as it hit the water. Momentum brought it to the surface where the coachman waited. He did not have to use the boat hook.

He pulled the girl from the canal carefully. She was slippery. The rain had freshened the water, so her brief immersion did not gift her with the sewer perfume she might have acquired on another night. She wore nothing. Any abuse she had suffered was not obvious. She was fifteen at the oldest. She did not weigh much. The coachman had no trouble getting her into his vehicle. He wrapped her in blankets and propped her in a corner. She looked like she was sick or drunk or asleep when he finished.

"You down there! What are you doing?"

That demand came down from eighty feet above.

The coachman's heart, thumping already, now hammered although he knew no one could get down from there in time to identify or stop him. He had gone through this in dry runs a half dozen times. This was the first time he had been noticed.

He kept the coach moving sedately while departing the area. It was unlikely that anyone would check why a coach had been standing beside the waste canal, despite it being about the time when the Dominator's henchmen disposed of the used-up virgin of the night.

Dusk's gates never closed. What fool would invade the capital of the Domination, especially when the dread lord of the empire was in residence? No one living owned that much audacity.

The coachman was remarkable in having shown the daring he had.

There was no cause for the guards at the Jade Gate to disrupt his departure. A small donative did, however, change hands. That was customary. In return the soldiers were entirely cursory in their inspection.

The coachmen explained, "That's my daughter. Fourteen and blind drunk, to my shame. But you can't help loving them, whatever they do."

The younger soldier chuckled. "See what you got to look forward to, Jink?" he told his companion, then said, "Jink's got him three daughters coming up."

Jink said, "They hit eleven, they go into a cage until I get them married. You probably ought to put yours on a chain," he told the coachman. "Go on, now."

The coachman climbed back up, snapped his reins, heaved a sigh of relief, and got his team moving.

He was racing time.

The girl would not last long.

2

Long Ago and Far Away: Sometimes Called Bathdek

Excitement began to stir inside Grendirft when the Lord Chamberlain discovered that tonight's visitor to the Dominator had been disposed of as if she was a common used-up diversion instead of one of the Senjaks. The men responsible were new. They had not been trained before being put to work as replacements for predecessors who had descended the waste chute themselves because of their stupid actions.

The Lord Chamberlain battled terror that had him on the verge of tossing up everything he had eaten all week. He maintained just enough control to report the disaster to the girl's next-oldest sister, Bathdek.

"Perhaps He became a little inappropriate. He has had some difficulty keeping hands off . . ." Shift blame as much as possible. He might not have long to live, otherwise, and the death he was likely to die would be neither gentle nor swift.

Bathdek's voice was chill. "I understand. It was sure to happen to one of us." She had survived visits with the Dominator herself. The madman was less aggressive with her and her other sisters, who did not fit His preferences as well as Dorotea. "He killed her?" That might cost the mad emperor everything. "And He disposed of her as if she was one of His nameless night toys?" She was almost too outraged to be enraged. "That doesn't seem like something He would do even when He was drunk on poppy milk."

The Lord Chamberlain promised, "I will recover her body."

"You most certainly will. We will need a body next time He demands her company. Else we could all become victims." All predicated on the assumption that He was so far gone that He would not recall the killing.

Her fear was like none that she had known before. If the mad emperor abandoned His compact with the Senjaks, the family might not survive. Nor would He, afterward. He might be the monster sorcerer of all time but He could not stand against the enmity of all the world without the support of the people who had brought Him to absolute and total dominion.

Again the Lord Chamberlain promised, "I will find her. I will bring her back." It should not be that difficult. The body would be in the waste canal.

But her body was not in the waste canal.

Several bodies were in the canal, human and otherwise, floating or not, but none were that of the youngest Senjak sister.

The Lord Chamberlain's panic level was historic. And it became contagious.

3

In Modern Times: Tides Elba

We were playing tonk. One-Eye was in a foul mood. He was losing. Again. Situation normal, except nobody was trying to kill us.

Elmo dealt. One-Eye squeaked. I peeked at my cards. "Another hand so damned bad it don't qualify as a foot."

Otto said, "You're full of shit, Croaker. You won six out of the last ten."

Elmo added, "And bitched about the deal every damned time."

"I was right whenever I dealt." I was right again, too. I did not have a pair. I had no low cards and only one face card. The two in the same suit were the seven and knave of diamonds. I do not have years enough left to fill that straight. Anyway, we all knew One-Eye had a rare good hand.

"Then we should make you full-time dealer."

I shoved my ante in. I drew, discarded, and threw my hand in when it came to me.

One-Eye went down with ten. The highest card he had was a three.

His leathery old black face ripped in a grin absent an adequate population of teeth. He raked in the pot.

Elmo asked the air, "Was that legitimate?" The gallery numbered half a dozen. We had the Dark Horse to ourselves. The place had become the Company watering hole in Aloe. The owner, Markeg Zhorab, had mixed feelings. We were not the kinds of guys he wanted hanging around but because we did his business was outstanding.

Nobody indicted One-Eye. Goblin, with his butt on the table next over, reminded Elmo, "You dealt."

"Yeah, there's that."

One-Eye has been known to cheat. Hard to manage in a game as simpleminded as tonk, but there you go. He is who he is.

"Lucky at cards, unlucky at love," he said, which made no sense in context.

Goblin cracked, "Hire yourself some bodyguards. Women will tear down doors to get to you."

A wisecrack from Goblin usually fires One-Eye up. He has a hair trigger. We waited for it. One-Eye just grinned. He told Otto, "Deal, loser. And make it a hand like the one Elmo gave me."

Goblin said something about Missus Hand being the only lucky lady in One-Eye's life.

One-Eye went on ignoring the bait.

I began to worry.

Otto's deal did not help.

One-Eye asked, "You know how we run into weird customs everywhere we go?"

Elmo glared holes through his cards. He grunted. Otto arranged and rearranged his five, meaning he had a hand so bad he did not know how to play it. One-Eye did not squeak but kept on grinning. We were on the brink of a new age, one in which the black devil could win two in a row.

Everybody checked Goblin. Goblin said, "Otto dealt."

Somebody in the gallery suggested, "Maybe he spelled the cards."

That rolled past One-Eye. "The weirdest custom they got here is, when a girl loses her cherry, from then on she's got to keep all the hair off her body."

Otto rumbled, "There's some grade-two bullshit if I ever heard any. We been here three months and I ain't seen a bald-headed woman yet."

Everything stopped, including One-Eye stacking his winnings.

"What?" Otto asked.

There have always been questions about Otto.

The rest of us occasionally invest a coin in a tumble with a professional comfort lady. The subject never came up before but I knew I had yet to see a single whisker below the neckline.

"Do tell," Elmo said. "And I thought it was the luck of the draw that I wasn't seeing what ought to be there."

I said, "I figured it was how mine kept from getting the crabs."

"Nope. All tied into their weird religion."

Goblin muttered, "There's an oxymoron."

One-Eye's mood faltered.

Goblin's froglike face split in a vast grin. "I wasn't talking about you, shrimp. You're just a regular moron. I was talking about slapping the words 'weird' and 'religion' together."

"You guys are trying to hex my luck, aren't you?"

"Damned straight," Elmo said. "Talking about pussy works every time. Tell me about these bald snatches."

One-Eye restacked his winnings. He was turning surly despite his success. He had come up with some great stuff, on a subject guys can kill weeks exploring, and nobody seemed to care.

I shuffled, stacked, and dealt. One-Eye grew more glum as he picked up his cards.

The last one got him. "Goddamn it, Croaker! You asshole! You son of a bitch!"

Elmo and Otto kept straight faces because they did not know what was happening. Goblin tittered like a horny chickadee.

One-Eye spread his hand. He had a trey of clubs. He had a six of diamonds. He had the nine of hearts and the ace of spades. And that last card was a knave of swords.

I said, "How many times have you said you don't have no two cards of the same suit? This time you won't be lying."

Elmo and Otto got it. They laughed harder than me or Goblin. The gallery got a good chuckle, too.

The Lieutenant stuck his head in through the front door. "Anybody seen Kingpin?" He did not sound happy. He sounded like an executive officer who had to work on his day off.

"He skating again?" Elmo asked.

"He is. He's supposed to be on slops. He didn't show. The cooks want to chop him up for soup bones."

"I'll talk to him, sir." Though Kingpin was not one of his men. Kingpin belonged to Kragler's platoon.

"Thank you, Sergeant." Elmo does have a way of communicating with errant infantrymen. "Why are you people in here, in all this gloom and stench, when you could be outside sucking up fresh air and sunshine?"

I said, "This is our natural habitat, sir." But the truth was, it had not occurred to anybody to take the game outside.

We gathered our cards and beer and shambled out to the streetside tables. One-Eye dealt. Talk dwelt on the hairstyles, or lack thereof, favored by Aloen ladies.

It was a grand day, cloudless, cool, air in motion but not brisk enough to disturb the game. The gallery settled in. Some just liked to watch. Some hoped a seat would open up. They joined the increasingly crude speculation, which slipped into the domain of one-upmanship.

I interjected, "How long have we been playing with these cards?" Some were so ragged you should not need to turn them over to know what they were, but my memory kept tricking me.

Everybody looked at me funny. "Here comes something off the wall," One-Eye forecast. "Spit it out, Croaker, so we can get back to stuff that matters."

"I'm wondering if this deck hasn't been around long enough to take on a life of its own."

One-Eye opened his mouth to mock me, then his eyes glazed over. He considered the possibility. Likewise, Goblin. The pallid, ugly little man said, "Well, screw me! Croaker, you aren't half as dumb as you look. The cards have developed a mind of their own? That would explain so much."

Everybody eyeballed One-Eye, nodding like somebody was conducting. One-Eye had insisted that the cards hated him for as long as anyone could remember.

He won again.

Three wins at one sitting should have tipped me off. Hell was on the prowl. But my mouth was off on another adventure.

"You know what? It's been eighty-seven days since somebody tried to kill me."

Elmo said, "Don't give up hope."

"Really. Think about it. We're out in the street where anybody could take a crack but nobody is even eyeballing us. And none of us are looking over our shoulders and whining about our ulcers."

Play stopped. Seventeen eyes glared at me. Otto said, "Croaker, you jinx it, I'll personally hold you down while somebody whittles on your favorite toy."

Goblin said, "He's right. We've been here three months. The only trouble we've seen is guys getting drunk and starting fights."

With six hundred forty men, you know the Company has a few shitheads whose idea of a good time is to drink too much, then get in an ass-kicking contest.

One-Eye opined, "What it is is, the Lady's still got a boner for Croaker so she stashed him someplace safe. The rest of us just live in his shadow. Watch the sky. Some night there'll be a carpet up there, Herself coming out to knock boots with her special guy."

"What's *her* hairstyle like, Croaker?"

Special treatment? Sure. We spent a year following Whisper from one blistering trouble spot to the next, fighting damned near every day.

Special treatment? Yeah. The kind you get for being competent. Whatever your racket, you do a good job, the bosses pile more work on.

"You'll be the first to know when I get a look, Otto." I did not plow on into the kind of crudities the others found entertaining. They took that to confirm my unabated interest in the wickedest woman in the world. The real story was, I was afraid that she might be listening.

A kid named Corey said, "Speaking of hairstyles, there's one I wouldn't mind checking out."

Everybody turned to admire a young woman across the street. Pawnbroker congratulated Corey on his excellent taste.

She was sneaking up on twenty. She had pale red hair cut shorter than any I'd seen around Aloe. It fell only to her collar in back and not that far angling up the sides. She had bangs in front. I did not notice what she wore. Nothing unusual. She radiated such an amazingly intense sensuality that nothing else mattered.

Our sudden attention, heads wheeling like birds in a flock, startled her. She stared back briefly, trying for haughty, but failed to stick it. She took off speed-walking.

One-Eye picked up his cards. "That one is bald everywhere that matters."

Corey asked, "You know her?" Like he had found new meaning to life. He had hope. He had a mission.

"Not specifically. She's a temple girl."

The cult of Occupoa engages in holy prostitution. I hear Occupoa has some dedicated and talented daughters.

Goblin wanted to know how One-Eye could tell.

"That's the official hairstyle over there, runt." From a guy smaller than Goblin.

"And you know that because?"

"Because I've decided to treat myself to the best of everything during my last few months."

We all stared. One-Eye is a notorious skinflint. And never has any money, anyway, because he is a lousy tonk player. Not to mention that he is next to immortal, having been with the Company over a hundred years.

"What?" he demanded. "So maybe I poor-mouth more than what's the actual case. That a crime?"

No. We all do that. It is a preemptive strike against all those good buddies who are dry and want to mooch instead of dealing with Pawn.

Somebody observed, "Lots of guys were flush when we got here. We never got no chance to get rid of our spare change before."

Yes. The Black Company was good for Aloe's economy. Maybe nobody was trying to kill us because we had not yet been fully plucked.

Elmo said, "I better round up Kingpin before the Lieutenant puts me on the shit list, too. Silent? You want my seat? Shit! Where the hell did he go?"

I had not noticed our third minor wizard departing. Silent is spookier than ever, these days. He is practically a ghost.

You are with the Company long enough, you develop extra senses. You read cues unconsciously and, suddenly, you are all alert and ready. We call it smelling danger. Then, too, there is precognition having to do with things stirring at the command level. That one warns you that your ass is about to get dumped in the shit.

Seemed like it took about fourteen electric seconds for all six hundred and some men to realize that something was up. That life was about to change. That I might not make it a hundred days without somebody trying to kill me.

The cards had stopped moving already when Hagop loped up from the direction of the compound. "Elmo. Croaker. Goblin. One-Eye. The Old Man wants you."

One-Eye grumbled, "Goblin had to go open his big goddamn mouth."

Two minutes earlier Goblin had muttered, "Something's up. Something's in the wind."

I kicked in, "Yeah. This is all his fault. Let's pound his ass if it turns out we have to go flush some Rebels out somewhere again."

"Weak, Croaker." Elmo shoved back from the table. "But I second that motion. I'd almost forgotten how nice it is for garrison troops." He went on about clean clothing, ample beer, regular meals, and almost unlimited access to a soldier's favorite way of wasting time and money.

We headed down the street, leaving the cards to the others, who were already speculating. I said, "Garrison duty is all that. The hardest work I've got to do is to weasel One-Eye into using his curative on guys who come in with the clap."

One-Eye said, "I like garrison because of the financial opportunities."

He would. Put him down anywhere and give him a week, he will be deep into some black-market scam.

Hagop sidled close, whispered, "I need to talk to you, private." He slipped me a folded piece of parchment maybe three and a half inches to a side. It was dirty. It smelled awful. One face had a small triangular tear where it had hung up on something. Hagop looked like he might panic when I opened it.

I stopped walking. The others did, too, wondering what was up. I whispered, "Where did you get this?"

The Company maintained a compound outside the city, on a heath blasted barren back when Whisper arrived to negotiate the treaties by which Aloe gained the perquisites of participation in the Lady's empire, foremost amongst those being continued existence. The compound was nothing exciting. There was a curtain wall of dried mud brick. Everything inside was adobe, too, lightly plastered to resist the rain.

The compound was brown. A man with a discerning eye might identify shades, but us barbarians just saw brown. Even so, I had an eye sharp enough to spot a new brown patch before Hagop pointed it out.

A flying carpet lay tucked into the shade on the eastern side of the headquarters building. My companions had equally discerning eyes but less troubled hearts.

We were part of a stream, now. Every officer and platoon sergeant had been summoned. Sometimes the Captain gets his butt hairs in a twist and pulls everybody in for an impromptu motivational speech. But there was a critical difference this time.

There was a flying carpet in the shade beside the HQ.

At most, six of those existed, and only six entities were able to use them.

We were blessed with the presence of one of the Taken.

The happy days were over. Hell had taken a nap but now it was wide awake and raring to go.

Nobody overlooked the carpet. No shoulder failed to slump.

I said, "You guys go ahead. I'll catch up. Hagop. Show me."

He headed for the shade. For the carpet. "I saw it here. I never seen

HURON PUBLIC LIBRARY
521 DAKOTA AVE S
HURON, SD 57350-2797

a carpet up close so I decided to check it out." He walked me through his experience. One glance at the carpet reaffirmed what I already feared. This unkempt, poorly maintained mess belonged to the Limper.

"I found that folded thing right here."

"Right here" was where the Taken sat while the carpet was aloft. There the carpet was especially frayed, stretched, and loose.

Hagop's finger indicated a fold of material torn away from the wooden frame beneath. "It was mostly covered. It was hung up on that brad."

A small nail had worked loose three-sixteenths of an inch. A wisp of parchment remained stuck to it. I removed that with my knife, careful to make no personal contact.

"I picked it up. Before I could even look at it the Captain came out and told me to go get you guys."

"All right. Stay out of sight. We'll talk later." I was going to be last inside if I did not hustle.

"It's bad, isn't it?"

"It could be bad. Scoot on into town. Don't tell anybody about this."

The mess hall was the nearest thing to an assembly hall we had. The cooks had been run off. The place reeked of unhappiness. Half the guys lived in town, now, including me. Some had women. A few even had common-law stepchildren they did not mind supporting.

Those guys would pray the carpet meant that the Lady had sent somebody with the payroll. Only, in Aloe our pay came from gentle taxes on the people we protected. No need to fly it in.

The Captain did his trained-bear shuffle up onto the half-ass stage. A creepy brown bundle of rags followed. It dragged one leg. The hall filled with a hard silence.

The Limper. The most absurdly nasty of the Taken. A dedicated enemy of the Black Company. We had screwed him over good back when he tried going against the Lady.

He was back in favor now. But so were we. He could not have his revenge just yet. But he was patient.

The Captain rumbled, “The tedium is about to end, gentlemen. We now know why the Lady put us here. We’re supposed to take out a Rebel captain called Tides Elba.”

I checked the spelling later. It was not a name we knew. He pronounced it, “Teadace Elba.”

The Captain said that Tides Elba had enjoyed some successes west of us, but none of her victories had been big enough to catch our attention.

An interesting line of bullshit, some of which might be true.

The Limper climbed up with the Captain. That was a struggle. He had that bad leg and he was a runt—in stature. In wickedness and talent for sorcery he was the baddest of the bad. A reek of dread surrounded him. So did a reek of reek. On his best day he smelled like he had been in a grave for a long time. He considered us from behind a brown leather mask.

Folks with weaker stomachs jostled for space in the back.

The Limper said nothing. He just wanted us know he was around. Important to remember. And something foretelling interesting times.

The Captain told the company commanders and platoon leaders to tell their men that we might be making movement soon. Pending investigatory work here in Aloe. They should settle their debts and personal issues. Ideally, they should shut down their Aloe lives and return to the compound.

We might see some desertions.

Elmo jabbed me in the ribs. “Pay attention.”

The Old Man dismissed everybody but me and the magic users. He invoked me directly. “Croaker, stay with me.” The wizards he told to stick with the Limper.

The Captain herded me over to Admin. In theory, I owned a corner space there where I was supposed to work on these Annals. I did not often take advantage.

“Sit.” A command, not an invitation. I sat in one of two crude chairs facing the ragged table he used as a bulwark against the world. “Limper is here. He hasn't said so but we know that means we're headed into the shit. He hasn't said much, actually. Which may mean that he doesn't know anything himself. He's following orders, too."

I nodded.

"This isn't good, Croaker. This is the Limper. There'll be more going on than what we see."

There would be. I did my best to look like a bright child awaiting ineluctable wisdom from an honored elder.

"I'd tell you you're full of shit but you don't need the special memo. You know that taste in your mouth."

He was going to come down on me for something?

"You been putting on a show of being as useless as the rest of these dicks. But when you're supposedly off whoring or getting fucked up you're usually actually somewhere poking into the local history."

"A man needs more than one hobby."

"It's not a hobby if you can't help yourself."

"I'm a bad man. I need to understand the past. It illuminates the present."

The Captain nodded. He steepled fingers in front of a square, strong, dimpled chin. "I got some illuminating for you to do."

He did know something about what was up.

"You could maybe fix it so the Company don't wallow in the usual cesspit."

"You sweet talker."

"Shut the fuck up. The Lady wants Tides Elba before she turns into an eastern White Rose. Or maybe she is the Rose. I don't know. Limper wants to go balls to the wall so he can look good to the Lady, hopefully getting us killed in the process."

"You're losing me, boss."

"I doubt it. Remember, the Limper has a special hard-on for you."

He did. "All right. And?"

"Limper thinks smashing things is fun. I don't want to be remembered for wrecking Aloe on a maybe."

"Sir, you need to give me a clue. What do you want me to do? I'm not as smart as you think."

"Nor am I."

The Captain shambled out from behind his table. He paced. Then, "The Lady thinks Tides Elba was born here, has family here, and visits frequently. She wasn't born Tides Elba. Her family probably don't know what she is."

Of course this Rebel would not have been born Tides Elba. If the Lady got hold of her true name, Tides Elba would be toast before sundown.

"You've been snooping. You know where to look. Help us lay hands on her before the Limper can catch us in a cleft stick."

"I can dig. But I can tell you now, all I'll find is holes."

"Holes tell a story, too."

They do. "Instead of worrying about this woman, how about we come up with a permanen . . ."

He made a chopping motion. I needed to shut up. "Look at you. We could put you in charge of the whole eastern campaign, you're so smart. Go away. Do what you need to do. And stay away from those moronic cards."

I thought hard. My conclusion was frightening. There was no place to conspire where the Limper could not eavesdrop if he was so inclined. I scrounged up an extra deck, more venerable than the one usually in play, and headed for the Dark Horse. Along the way, Hagop fell in beside me. "Is it time?"

"It's time. If everybody is there." Everybody being a select few like Elmo and the wizards.

"What was the big meeting? We going to move out?"

"They don't know what they're going to do. They just want to be ready to do it."

"Same old shit."

"Pretty much."

The usual suspects were there, out front, on the fringe, waiting instead of playing. Only Silent was missing. I asked Goblin with a glance. He shrugged.

Several guys started to drift over, thinking an entertaining game might break out. I handed my deck to Corey. "You guys get a game going inside."

"Quick on the uptake," Elmo observed as they cleared off. He scooted sideways so Hagop had room to add a chair. We pretended to play a five-man game.

I asked, "You all sure you want to be here? We're going to lay our balls on the table and hope nobody hits them with a hammer."

Nobody volunteered to disappear.

I produced the parchment Hagop had found. Folded, it made a square. Opened, it was a third taller than it was wide. I spread it out. "Pass it around. Don't act like it's any big deal."

"Go teach Granny to suck eggs," One-Eye grumbled. "I can't tell anything from this. It's all chicken tracks."

"Those tracks are TelleKurre." The language of the Domination. Only two native speakers remained alive. "This is an imperial rescript, from the Lady to the Limper. The ideograph in the upper left corner tells us that. But this is a copy. The ideograph top middle tells us that, along with the fact that this is copy number two of two. The ideograph in the upper right corner is the chop of the copyist."

"Accountability," Elmo said.

"Exactly. She's big on that since the Battle at Charm."

"Uhm. So what does it say?"

"Not much, directly. But very formally. The Lady orders the Limper to come east to find and capture a woman named Tides Elba. No why, no suggestion how, just do it, then bring her back alive and undamaged."

"And there ain't nothing in there about her being some new phenom rookie Rebel captain?"

"Not a hint."

"The Limper lied."

"The Limper lied. And not just to us. He isn't dedicated to the success of his mission."

Elmo asked, "How can you tell?"

"Limper had to sign both copies, agreeing that he understood his assignment. On his keeper copy, here, he added, 'Up Yours, Bitch.'"

"Whoa!" Hagop barked, awed rather than surprised.

Elmo asked, "Could that be a plant?"

"You mean, did he leave it so we could find it?"

"Yeah. To let us set ourselves up."

"I've been brooding about that. I don't think so. There are a thousand ways that could go wrong. He'd have no control. We might never notice it. But, more importantly, there's what he wrote after he signed."

They thought. Twice One-Eye started to say something but thought better.

We focused on clever tricks the Limper might try. Looking for deep strategies and devilish maneuvers. It took the least among us, a simple line soldier, to point out a critical fact.

Hagop asked, "If he signed it that way won't he get nervous when he realizes that it's gone?"

We all considered him with widening eyes and galloping hearts. Elmo growled, "If the little shit goes bugfuck we'll know for sure it's real."

"Silver lining." Goblin grinned but there was sweat on his forehead.

I pushed the parchment across to One-Eye. "See if that's tagged so he can trace it. Then see if there's a way he could tell who's been handling it."

"You going to put it back?"

"Hell, no! I'm going to bury it somewhere. It could come in handy someday. The Lady wouldn't be pleased if she saw it. Speaking of forgetting. Goblin, fix it so Hagop has no recollection of the parchment. The Captain saw him hanging around the carpet. Questions might be asked."

"I'll need to work on you, too, then. You were seen there, too."

I expect lots of guys took the opportunity for a close-up look. But fear streaked down my spine, reached my toes and cramped them. "Yeah. You'd better."

Both wizards started to get out of their seats. Goblin said, "We'll need to shove those memories down so far that only the Lady's Eye could find them."

I had a thought. "Hang on a minute. Hagop, go get Zhorab."

. . .

Markeg Zhorab was something else before he became a tavern keeper. His face alone recalled several desperate fights. He was a sizable man, often mistaken for the bouncer, whose past had left his courage a bit sketchy.

He asked me, "You wanted me?"

"I have something I need done, not traceable to me. I'm willing to pay."

"Risky?"

"Possibly. But probably not if you do exactly what I tell you."

"I'm listening."

I showed him the rescript. "I need an exact copy calligraphed by a professional letter writer who doesn't know you."

"What is it?"

"A wanted poster. But the less you know, the better. Can you do that?"

He could once we finished talking money. I did not offer enough to make it seem like I was worried. With all the practical jokes that went on around us, I hoped he thought I was putting another something together. He asked, "How soon do you need this?"

"Right now would be especially good."

Zhorab brought my copy. And the original. "Good enough? He couldn't match the parchment."

"It's fine. I want it obvious that it's a copy." I paid the agreed sum. I handed back the copy. "Hold on to this. Later on Goblin will tell you when to give it back. There'll be another payment then."

Elmo grumbled, "If we can ever get the self-righteous asshole into this place." Playing to the practical-joke angle.

Puzzled, Zhorab folded the copy and went off to bite his coins.

Elmo wondered, "Think he had more than one copy made?"

I said, "I'm counting on it. The more there are, the better. Let's get to the forgetting."

I said, "I don't know. I forget. It must not have been important. Look. I need you guys to help me dig for info on Tides Elba."

Grumble, grumble. Chairs pushed back grudgingly.

I said, "It has to be done."

"Yeah. Yeah."

I asked, "Hagop, do you read the local language?"

He shook his head. Once we were a few steps away, Elmo said, "I'm not sure he can read anything."

I grunted. "One last beer."

Inside, the Dark Horse was swamped in speculation about what might be afoot. A sizable faction did not believe that Tides Elba existed. Old hands, who had been through the long retreat from Oar to Charm, thought that the Limper had made it all up.

When asked my opinion I said I never heard of Tides Elba and we had only Limper's word that she existed.

Aloe was a city-state, a republic, a formula common in its end of the world. It was prosperous. It had the time and money to maintain civil records, which are useful for levying taxes, calling men to the colors, and imposing a corvée.

Aloe kept those records in a small stone purpose-built structure. Our advent spread consternation.

Surprise did not help. Nothing jumped out. There were records aplenty, stored according to no obvious system, to keep us busy for days.

Elmo said, "I'll put out a call for men who can read this stuff." He barely managed himself, sounding out the characters.

Silent walked in. Before I could put him to work, he signed, "Wait!" and did a slow turn to make sure there were no stinky men in brown hiding in the rafters. Then he signed, "I know where to find her."

Everybody babbled questions, negating Silent's caution. He signed, "Shut up! Unless you are hungry for a taste of knuckle. Idiots."

He said the smoldering redhead from the other day was our target.

"How do you know?" I demanded in sign.

Silent tapped the side of his head, pointed to his eyes, then his nose. Shorthand sign meaning he paid attention and he used his noggin when he smelled something off.

He saw something that was not just prime split-tail so he followed her to the temple of Occupoa. He had been watching ever since.

"Predictable," I signed. Rebels everywhere hide stuff under their houses of worship. "Let's raid the place." I was unconcerned about the wrath of Occupoa. The gods seldom defend themselves. "Send her off to the Tower."

Elmo agreed. "Along with our least favorite Taken."

Elmo and I were the responsible, sensible voices. We got shouted down. Goblin jumped up and down. Every fifth sign he deployed was a raised middle finger.

One-Eye insisted aloud, "We'll play a riff on Roses."

"Why?"

"To gouge the Limper. Maybe frame him for something."

"Or we can just give him the girl and get him out of town."

Their enthusiasm faded as they recalled the truth of that bitter winter operation in Roses. Of circumstances that started the Limper on the road to now, notably unhappy with the Company.

Silent signed, "Croaker makes a good point. Wimpy, but solid."

One-Eye, though, being One-Eye, smelled opportunity. But One-Eye had a hundred-plus-year record of being One-Eye.

That considered, the level of enthusiasm plummeted.

I refused to go to the Captain or Limper with their idiot plan. It relied entirely on the near-immortal, almost demigod Limper being too stupid to see through them. I said, "To even start that going we'd need something magically useful from our target. You guys got some of her hair? Nail clippings? Dirty underwear? Didn't think so. Let's go dig her out and turn her over."

I did, as noted, remain deft enough to avoid being the man asked to sell the scheme. That honor went to Silent.

Silent is no bumbler but he did not close the deal. The Captain's response was, "Find the girl and bring her in. That's all. Nothing else."

Nobody wanted to hear what I thought after Silent came back. One-Eye insisted, "You worry too much, Croaker. You give the little shit too much credit. He ain't some genius. He's just an asshole bully whose knack for sorcery is so big he don't need to think."

"Lot of that going around."

Goblin said, "Look at all he's been through since he got out of the ground. None of it made him smarter, only more careful about the evidence he leaves behind."

Why did that make me nervous? "He can smash us like slow roaches without breaking a sweat."

One-Eye insisted, "He's as dumbass as you can be and survive. He's the kind of guy you can hit with the same con five times running and he still won't figure out what happened."

Idiot.

Limper might be dumb as a bushel of rocks but he was not up against the first string over here. And he had arrived with a plan.

I insisted that we keep on rooting through the records. I told the others to tell me about every death of a girl child.

It was past my bedtime but I restrained my resentment when summoned by the Captain and Limper. The Old Man said, "We hear you found something."

"I did. But I think it's bogus." I reported honestly.

The Captain said, "Good work. Keep digging. But you can't use Goblin or One-Eye anymore. They're going TDA somewhere else." His glance at the Limper was so bland I knew he wanted to feed the Taken to the lions.

"They're useless, anyway. They can't stay focused even when they're not feuding."

The Captain said, "One more thing before you go."

My stomach sank. "Sir?"

"You were seen messing around with the lord's carpet. Why? What were you up to?"

"Messing with it? No, sir. I was talking about it to Hagop. He was all excited. He never saw a carpet up close before. He knew I had to ride one a couple times, back when. He wanted to know what it was like. We just talked. We never touched anything." I was babbling but that was all right. The Limper was used to terrified behavior. "Why? Is it important, sir?"

The Old Man glanced at his companion, inviting questions or comments. The old spook just stared through me.

"Apparently not. Dismissed."

I tucked my tail and ran. How did the Captain keep cool around that monster?

I fled the dread for the Dark Horse, where the useless pair and Silent waited. I passed the latter, and, in sign, added, "I don't like it, guys. The Captain thinks we're up to something. If the Limper catches on . . ."

One-Eye cursed, said something about my damned defeatist attitude, but then gave up. Even he is only blind in one eye.

Goblin acquiesced, too. Both had, at last, grasped the magnitude of the overreach they yearned to indulge. Well-founded terror settled in.

Despite all, we did not go get the girl. Goblin and One-Eye disappeared with the Limper. Silent evaded that fate by being impossible to find. I assumed he was eyes on our target.

Neither Elmo, Candy, nor the Lieutenant would let us make the catch without a complement of supporting wizards.

Elmo's call for men able to read the local language produced three and a half men, the half being a lost-cause half-ass apprentice shared by Goblin and One-Eye who called himself the Third. The Third because his father and grandfather had worn the same name. I never understood how he survived in the murky weirdness between his teachers.

The Third came by my town place. He looked less a sorcerer than did One-Eye or Goblin—and was bigger than those two squished together.

He made me wish they were. "They're going to raid the temple of Occupoa tonight. One-Eye wants your help."

The terror had not taken deep enough root. A sanctioned operation was planned for the next morning.

"One-Eye needs his head examined by incompetent authority. Somebody willing to recommend decapitation therapy." But I got armed up and put together.

The Third resembled the Captain some, though he was uglier. He talked about as much as the Old Man, too. I asked, "Where were One-Eye and Goblin the last couple days?"

"Doing something with the Limper. Developing new skills for the Tides Elba hunt."

I was skeptical.

We caught up with the runts and two soldiers who could read the local writing, Cornello Crat and Ladora Ans. I started kvetching. "Where's Silent? Where's Elmo?"

"Couldn't find them," One-Eye grumbled. He pulled his floppy rag of a hat down so the brim concealed his face. "Be quiet. Let's go."

"No."

"What?"

"This isn't going to happen. You want to play tonk with the Taken because you think you can scam some money. But you're so damned blind stupid you don't see that the real stake you're shoving into the pot is the Company. All six hundred forty of us."

Goblin looked chagrined. One-Eye, though, just wanted to be pissed off. He started to give me a piece of his mind.

"For the last time, dumbfuck. Listen! With the kind of luck you have playing penny-ante tonk you want me to help you play against the Limper? I can't believe that even you are that stupid. We'll do it the way it's set. Tomorrow. And you won't hand the Limper the excuse he wants."

One-Eye said nothing. His eye did get big. Seldom had he seen me so intense or foul of mouth.

He would have dismissed me, even so, if Goblin had not shaken like a dog just in out of the rain. "I'm going to side with Croaker on this. On reflection. Get your greed and ego out of it. Consider it on its merits."

One-Eye launched a rant about a once-in-a-lifetime opportunity.

Goblin shook all over again, looked a little puzzled, then tied into One-Eye. "How the hell do you talk yourself into this shit? How the hell do you stay alive?"

Victory! I had turned Goblin. Crat and Ans came with him. The Third had made his position clear by vanishing once he delivered me.

I had a horrible acid stomach. A slight but stubborn tremor kept my hands unreliable. Crat and Ans seemed just as rocky.

One-Eye realized that if he wanted to do this he would have to do it by himself. That startled and amazed him.

There was some low cunning under that ugly old black hat. He could back off when nobody else was greedy enough or stupid enough to let him bet their hand.

"You asshole, Croaker. You win. I hope you got guts enough to put in the Annals what a huge pussy you were when we had a chance to make the biggest score ever."

"Oh, it'll be there. Count on that. Including the fact that the Company survived in spite of you." I went on to point out that the Company's mission was not to make big scores for One-Eye.

It started to get heated. Then Silent and Elmo turned up. They, in essence, took our little black brother into protective custody, to protect him from himself.

I consulted Elmo. Elmo consulted Candy. Candy consulted the Lieutenant. When even the gods were not watching, the Lieutenant may have consulted the Captain.

Word rolled down. Make the move even though Silent's girl was unlikely to be the real Tides Elba.

Elmo was in charge. Goblin and Silent would supply sorcery support. One-Eye and the Third were assigned a critically important secondary mission: a census of goats in Utbank parish. The Lady needed to know.

The Captain overlooks a lot. A good officer knows when not to see. But that blindness has limits.

Being me, I found the dark side before the action began. "We took care of One-Eye's run for the crazy prize but we didn't get out of the cleft stick."

Goblin said, "Humor him. It'll take less time. And we won't have to listen to him grumble from now till we lay him down with a stone on top to keep him from getting back up. Speak, Wise One." He went right on getting ready. So did the others. They would hear me out but did not plan to *listen*.

"The Old Man figures that this probably isn't Tides Elba. So how will the locals respond when we break into a holy place and drag off a temple girl who hasn't done anything but catch Silent's eye?"

Elmo told me, "The same word said go get her, Croaker. That's our problem. Not what comes after. We got people who get paid to worry about what comes after. You aren't one of them. Your job is to come along behind and plug up the holes in any of these dickheads who forget to duck."

He was right. "I don't know what's gotten into me lately." And, honestly, I did not.

A platoon on the move scattered the locals, but then they followed at a distance, moved by boneheaded curiosity.

I fell in beside Goblin. "Where did you and One-Eye go those two days with the Limper? What did you do?"

His broad, pallid face slowly collapsed into a deep frown. "With the Limper? We didn't go anywhere with the Limper."

"You didn't? But the Old Man told me you were going TDA with the spook, who was right there when he said it. You were gone two days. You came back all determined to do stuff that we already decided would be suicidal."

"Two days? You're sure?"

"Two. Ask Elmo."

He turned contemplative. After maybe fifty yards he asked, "What does the Captain say?"

"Nothing. He don't talk much. He has the foulest Taken of them all homesteading in his right front pocket."

A hundred yards of silence. The big ugly dome of the temple of Occupoa now loomed over the tenements surrounding it. It had some claim to minor wonder-of-the-world status because that huge beehive shape, over eighty feet high, was made entirely of concrete. For those interested in engineering, the temple must be fascinating. It had required a generation to build.

Most Aloens did not give a bat's ass.

Goblin said nothing more but managed to look like someone who had enjoyed some surprisingly unpleasant revelations recently.

There were steps up to the entrance of Occupoa's temple, in two tiers, the lower of seven steps and the upper of six. The numbers were almost certainly significant. The risers were granite, grays mixed with bits of white. The columns and walls were greenish gray limestone, easy to work but vulnerable to weathering. Scaffolding masked the temple's west face.

It was not a holy day. It was too early for traffic related to Occupoa's principal fund-raising endeavor. It was quiet.

I climbed the thirteen steps still wondering why, still worrying the Tides Elba puzzle. I had talked to every Aloen I knew. They insisted the name was unfamiliar, that there was no Rebel leader known as Tides Elba. I believed them. That many people could not all be fine enough liars to appear so universally baffled.

On the other hand, one could wonder why they were so sure that there was no Rebel named Tides Elba.

We paused at the entrance. Silent and Goblin conjured spectral entities to lead the way and trigger ambushes or booby traps.

They were not needed. Temple defense consisted of one old beadle asleep on a chair just inside. His task appeared to be to discourage unauthorized withdrawals from a nearby poor box.

Goblin did something to deepen his sleep.

One squad moved in and spread out. The rest stayed outside and surrounded the temple. We ran into a whole lot of nothing happening inside. The main place of worship was round. The altar sat on a short dais in the middle. It was black stone without bloodstains. Occupoa had a more enlightened attitude toward the disposition of virgins. The altar was surrounded by racks of votive candles, only a few of which were burning.

The whole place was a little shabby.

I had my teeth clamped so tight my jaw ached. This was no Rebel stronghold. Had we been scammed? Why did I keep recalling the Limper's evil way of laughing when things were going his way?

I had a powerful urge to turn back but I did not.

Elmo asked, "Which way, Goblin? Silent?" He sounded uneasy, which would be because we had run into no one but that beadle.

I flashed a nervous grin, certain One-Eye would have tried to plunder the poor box had he not been handling critical empire business in Utbank.

"Straight on. If you didn't have a dozen guys clanking and whispering you could hear the people up ahead."

I began to worry about One-Eye and Goblin again. What had been done to them? Maybe Limper brainwashed them. Which could only be for the better in One-Eye's case.

Was this raid part of Limper's scheme to discredit the Company?

Elmo prodded me. "Move. What's with you, anyway? You're turning into the worst daydreamer."

Sounds of surprise broke out ahead.

The excitement was not "Run for it!" It was "What the hell is this shit?" It took place in a combination kitchen and dining hall where sixteen women, of a broad range of ages, had been sharing a late breakfast. The older women asked the questions. Elmo ignored them. "Silent? Which one?"

Silent pointed.

The girl from the street shared a table with five others who might have been her sisters. An effort had been made to make them look alike but our target stood out. She had a magnetism that marked her as special.

Maybe our employer *had* taken a gander into the future and had seen what the girl could become.

Elmo said, "Silent, get her. Tuco, Reams, help him. Goblin, cover. No weapons." All stated in a language not spoken in Aloe.

There was no resistance. The old women stopped protesting and started asking why.

Silent stood the girl up, bound her wrists behind her. He wore gloves and took care to make no skin-to-skin contact. She asked what was going on, once, then succumbed to fear. That made me feel so awful I just wanted to help her. I could imagine the horrors she expected at the hands of our like, and damned the day she caught our attention outside the Dark Horse.

"Wow," Elmo said, very softly.

"Indeed," Goblin agreed. "Potent. Maybe she *is* something special."

We left the way we had come in, Goblin and I on rearguard. Elmo, in the lead and in a hurry, caught a kid robbing the poor box. He reacted harshly.

The would-be thief was unconscious when I settled down to treat his broken arm. Elmo had avoided shedding too much blood.

Goblin stuck with me. Elmo collected the platoon. With Silent valiantly negating what the girl gave off under stress, they headed for the compound. Baffled Aloens watched. Some tagged along after.

Goblin studied the locals for signs of belligerence. Preoccupied, he did not hear what I thought I heard from the shadows inside the temple. If it was not my frightened imagination running away with me.

It was a *drag-scrape,* sudden *clop!*, then another *drag-scrape.* Like somebody with a bad leg having a hard time keeping quiet while crossing a wide stone floor.

"How come you think I imagined it?" I demanded. Goblin and I were approaching the Dark Horse. We were not needed at the compound. Elmo could handle all that. And, when the temple girl proved not to be Tides Elba, he could be the man who had to get started planning out how to find the real thing.

"Because I got a great view of the southern sky." He pointed.

From out of the distance, unhurried, a flying carpet headed across town, fifty feet above the rooftops. Two riders were visible. One wore a floppy black hat.

So. Limper went to Utbank to check up on One-Eye, then brought him and the Third back, unconvinced that the Old Man had sent them away because One-Eye's greed was complicating matters.

"All right. Must've been my guilty conscience. Let's reward ourselves for work well done with Master Zhorab's fine ale."

Goblin said, "It is earlier than is my custom but in honor of our success I will join you, sir."

We entered. The interior of the Dark Horse exactly reflected its exterior. There were no Company brothers outside, drinking or playing tonk. There were none inside, either.

In fact, there was no one behind the bar.

Goblin observed, "Nobody's home. Let's get back there and . . ."

Markeg Zhorab materialized. Goblin said, "Hello, magic man. We've done a hard day's work. Beer is in order."

Zhorab drew two mugs while eying us with unnerving intensity. "Did you catch who you were after?" He was incredibly tense.

"We did. Why does that mean anything to you?"

Zhorab raised a finger in a "wait one" gesture. He dug out the cash box he thought was secret but was not to any sharp-eyed regular. He looked around furtively while fumbling it open. He produced a ragged deck.

"My cards." Last seen in the hands of Corey and his pals. "Where did you get those?"

"Goblin told me to hold on to them till you arrested the person the Taken came to collect."

Goblin and I exchanged blank looks.

"Oh. It's not really the cards." He spread the deck across the bar, hand shaking, watching the door like he expected doom to thunder through.

Goblin asked, "You haven't sold us out to somebody, have you?"

"Huh? Oh! No! Never!"

"Then how come this place is so empty? How come you're so nervous?"

I said, "It's empty because everybody is out at the compound. Hello." I plucked a piece of parchment from amongst the scattered cards.

I unfolded it.

I stared.

I started shaking. Memories buried monstrously deep gurgled to the surface. "Goblin. Check this out."

He started shaking, too.

Zhorab asked, "I did it right?"

I pushed a silver piece across. "You did it perfectly." I found the copy, too. "Just one more step. You probably had the forger make an extra copy. We want that, too."

Zhorab wanted to lie but desisted after one look into Goblin's eyes. "It'll take a little while."

I put a second coin on the bar, with an ugly black knife as a companion. The knife was not special but looked like it ought to be.

Zhorab gulped, nodded, vanished.

Goblin observed, "He gave that up pretty easy."

"Probably has more than one copy."

"You want them all?"

"I don't mind some extras floating around and maybe getting back to the Tower someday."

"Your honey would run our smelly friend through the reeducation process again."

I shuddered. I had had my own brush with the Eye. Everything inside me had been exposed had the Lady cared to look. It had been her way of getting to know me. What the Limper would endure would be a hundred times worse, but never fatal. He was too useful—when he confined himself to being an extension of the Lady's will.

Zhorab returned. He gave me another folded parchment. I sheathed my knife. "We have to go. Be ready for a big rush later."

We encountered Hagop halfway to the compound. "There you are. The Captain sent me to get you guys. He wants Goblin to connect with the Tower so the Lady will know we got the girl, in perfect condition, before the Limper takes her and heads out."

"Shit." Goblin looked back, considering making a run for it.

It had been a while since he had made direct contact. He did not want to suffer that again.

I said, "It must be important if he's willing to put you through that."

Hagop said, "He wants to make sure she knows. He don't trust the Limper."

"Who would?" And, "The temple girl really is Tides Elba?"

"She don't deny it. She claims she's no Rebel or Resurrectionist, though. She's got the girl magic, majorly."

Goblin asked, "Croaker, it ever feel like everybody knows more than you do?"

“Every damned day since I joined this chickenshit outfit. Hagop. Take this. First chance you get, plant it back where you found it.”

He took the folded parchment. “This isn’t the one I gave you.”

The Captain was behind his table. Tides Elba sat on one of his rude chairs, wrists and ankles in light fetters. She looked emotionally past the point where she could not believe that this was happening. A torc had been placed around her neck, of the sort used to manage captured sorcerers. If she used sorcery it would deliver terrible pain.

The Lady must have seen something way down the road. This child was sitting on the only magic she controlled right now.

The Captain scowled. “You’ve been drinking.”

“One mug, in celebration of a job well done,” Goblin replied.

“It’s not done yet. Contact the Lady. Let her know. Before the Limper finds out that we have her.”

Goblin told me, “Welcome to the mushroom club.”

The Captain said, “I don’t need you here, Croaker.”

“Of course you do. How else will I get it in the Annals right?”

He shrugged. “Move it, Goblin. You’re wasting time.”

Goblin could make contact on the spur of the moment because he had made the same connection before. Familiarity did not ease the pain. He shrieked. He fell down, gripped by a seizure. Concerned, the Captain came out from behind his table, dropped to a knee, back to the girl. “Will he be all right?”

“Make sure he doesn’t swallow his tongue.” I took the opportunity to cop a feel while slipping the folded parchment in amongst the sweet jubblies. The girl met my eye but said nothing. “Maybe he’s having trouble getting through.”

The Lady responded just as the Limper burst in, exploding the door.

A circle of embers two feet across appeared above Goblin, almost tangled in the Captain’s hair. The Lady’s beautiful face came into focus inside. Her gaze met mine. She smiled. My legs turned to gelatin.

Goblin’s seizure ended. So did the Limper’s charge.

A whisper from everywhere asked, “Is that her?”

The Captain said, "We believe so, ma'am. She fits every particular."

The Lady winked at me. She and I were old campaign buddies. We had hunted down and killed her sister together, once upon a time.

The whisper said, "She's striking, isn't she?"

I nodded. Goblin and the Captain nodded. The Limper, oozing closer behind his miasmic stench, dipped his masked face in agreement. Tides Elba was striking indeed, and growing more so, employing an unconscious natural sorcery her torc did not detect.

"Every bit as much as my sister was. Who was this one's remote grandmother, to whom she bears an uncanny resemblance."

Different sister, I presumed. Tides Elba bore only a passing resemblance to the one that I had helped kill. I started to ask something. Needlessly. Our employer was in an expansive mood.

"Her male ancestor was my husband. He futtered anything that moved, including all my sisters and most of the female Taken. Enough. She was about to mate with another of his descendants. Their child would have become a vessel into which the old bastard could project his soul."

The Limper might have considered all that in whatever he had planned. The rest of us gaped, except for the girl. She did not understand. The Lady spoke a language unknown to her.

She was totally focused on what hung in the air, there, though.

She voided herself. She knew where she was going.

Something passed between the Lady and the Limper. The stinky little sorcerer bowed. He moved in on the girl, took her arm, forced her to her feet, pushed her toward the door he had wrecked.

We watched, every man wishing he could stop them, every man knowing that, if the Lady had spoken truly, Tides Elba was a threat to the whole world. She could become the port through which the hideous shadow known as the Dominator could make his return. No doubt she was sought by and beloved of every Resurrectionist cultist hoping to raise the old evil from his grave. No doubt she was the prophesied messiah of darkness.

I glanced back. The Lady was gone. The end, here, was anticlimactic, but mainly because we were out on the fringes, able to see only the local surface of the story. For the Company, the central fact would be that we had survived.

We went out and watched the Limper leave.

He shoved the girl into a sack. He sewed that shut, then secured it to his carpet with cording. Tides Elba would not evade her fate by rolling off the carpet in flight. His liftoff into the late-afternoon light seemed erratic. He seemed nervous and unhappy. He wobbled as he headed west.

I found Hagop in the shadows near where the carpet had lain. He gave me a grin and a thumbs-up. "He spotted it right away. Took it out, looked at it, and jumped like somebody hit him with a shovel."

"He got the message, then."

Goblin stared westward, eyes still haunted. "What a sad waste of delicious girl flesh." Then, "Let's round up Elmo and One-Eye and go tip a few at the Dark Horse. Elmo's got the cards, don't he?"

4

Once Upon a Time: The Necromancer at Home

The coach stopped outside a gap in a short palisade of sharpened stakes with fire-hardened tips. Each tip bore smears of poison. A putrefying animal carcass lay a dozen feet east of the gap, invisible in the darkness. The coachman did not smell it. He started singing an elaborate song he accompanied with complex ritual movements using what looked like a floppy feather duster. Done, he waited fifteen seconds, then urged his team forward.

The horses did as they were instructed though plainly they would rather have not.

"Have to hurry!" the coachman muttered repeatedly. "She doesn't have much time." But rushed as he was he did not fail to restore the lethal spells that sealed the only gap in the stockade.

The heart of the clearing, which surmounted a hill, was a low, rambling, ramshackle, cobbled-together structure. Out front of the house lay a gentle slope that had boasted few trees even before the homesteader arrived.

From behind the house came sounds of animal curiosity roused by the racket of coach and team. The conversations of swine predominated.

Two mastiffs greeted the coachman, friendly but silent. Neither had a voice.

"I got her, boys. Now we'll see if I'm right. Now we'll see if I'm going to change the world."

He took the girl out of the coach carefully despite his hunger to rush. Every minute lost might mark the critical point of no return.

He took care with her but was so impatient that he left the coach and team standing, untended, a cruelty nothing like his usual self.

As he pushed through his front door he heard a remote shriek, apparently from somewhere in the sky, back toward Dusk. Something too big to be a far-off night bird ghosted across a strand of cloud turned silver by the backlighting sliver of moon.

"What in the world?"

He knew, though. One of the Ten. One of the master sorcerers enslaved by the Dominator. Why was it aloft tonight?

The body snatcher began to shiver. Shiver turned to shake as he considered the possibility that, however unlikely, the Taken was hunting him.

Why would it? He had done nothing but take a body that had been thrown away, like trash. Common law and custom were clear. Anything, once discarded, could be claimed by anyone who could use it.

Spirit lamps provided just enough light for the body snatcher to make his way safely to the back of the house, though there was little to get underfoot. He lived an austere life, focused entirely on his illegal and perilous research, outside the restraint of the lords of the Domination. He broke no law by taking a corpse but he damned himself to death every time he performed a sorcery without license from Dusk. The task he had set himself next would invite the worst that could be done to living flesh.

He stretched the girl out on a table and began.

His core craft was necromancy. He was a true master of the darker arts. He would become a true master of the darkest art of all if he succeeded here.

. . .

The girl was absurdly beautiful. The necromancer recognized that despite his indifference to it. Her only flaws were abrasions collected while descending the waste chute. He was not moved. An equally fine young male cadaver would not have moved him, either. He was not a sexual being.

He was tired. The trip to Dusk, the collecting of the body, the return home, had been physically and emotionally exhausting. But he could not rest now. Time was his enemy. If he let time go by, even his beautiful new method could not breathe fresh life into this sweet flesh.

First he must halt those processes that began immediately after death. That took only minutes. He had the equipment in place and the spells waiting.

Corruption forestalled, he spent half an hour cleansing the girl, treating her abrasions, checking her for hidden damage. He concluded that he could not have come up with a more perfect subject had he been free to pick from all the people of Dusk. This girl had taken absolutely perfect care of herself in life.

There was one troublesome matter: This girl had been exposed to serious sorcery sometime recently. Residual pollution covered her like a second skin.

Cleansing her was not part of the necromancer's plan but cleaning her up was not difficult and did not take long.

He checked the hourglass above his worktable. Yes! This was going as smoothly as he could hope. He had an hour's cushion on his estimates. He could afford to be extra careful going through the next several steps.

Everything progressed well till there was nothing else to do but wait for the spells, chemicals, drugs, and alchemy to finish their work.

The sun was rising when he could finally afford to rest.

Only then, as he prepared himself to lie down, did he recall having left his coach and team standing in front of the house.

5

Long Ago and Far Away: The Frightened Princess

The Lord Chamberlain abased himself before the child-woman who made others call her Princess Bathdek. Bathdek was not her real name. In the upper reaches of the Domination no one used true names, even, and especially, with one's lovers. The Chamberlain might have overheard one of her sisters call her Credence, but that was likely a false flag, too.

The princess asked, "What news?"

"Only bad, Sublime. Only bad. But news."

"Proceed." Bathdek refrained from venting her spite. This worm had to believe there was hope if he crawled low enough and strove hard enough. Without hope he would give up. His driven efforts might be the best hope she had for herself.

"The soldier on sentry duty above the waste chute says there was a coach standing beside the canal at about the time that . . ." He chose not to push his luck with any further mention of her sister.

"Details?"

"Next to none. The coach may have been there for some time. The sentry did not hear it arrive while making that leg of his rounds. He did hear a splash. He called down a challenge. The coach left right away. That was why he knew that there was a coach. You can't see anything from where he was when it's dark. I checked personally."

"So a coach was waiting for my sister to come down the chute."

The Lord Chamberlain had not considered the situation from that angle. "The facts would seem to fit, Your Grace." Except, her sister was dead when . . . Or was she?

"Have the fools who disposed of her been punished?"

Carefully, "They have not, Sublime." But how he wished that they had. The girl had *not* been dead when she fell into their hands, just entangled in a drugged dream. They had smothered her, in keeping with standing orders for the disposal of used-up virgins. "But only because the night executioner has the night off. I can send for him."

"No. That's good. Let them enjoy a painful reprieve. Turn out the torturers instead. See if those people were part of a kidnapping plot."

He was sure no such plot existed but did not say so. That was exactly the sort of scheme for which Dusk was famous. He would pretend that it might be real, for his own sake.

These things never went well for the small people.

Bathdek savored the Lord Chamberlain's terror without knowing exactly what drove it.

His fear might be one of the last amusements she would wring from life. This mess could end up claiming her and all her sisters.

He grew more insane by the week, in response to ever bleaker auguries and endless talk about comets. He might forget how much He owed, and depended upon, the Senjak family.

"Chamberlain."

"Yes, my princess?"

"Check with the guards at the various gates. Night traffic cannot be that heavy."

"Of course." A step already taken. No need to irk her by telling her that, however.

Bathdek dismissed the Lord Chamberlain with a gesture. As he scooted backward she wondered if she ought not to consult her sisters.

This would involve them, too. But the situation was only two hours old, still in the deeps of the night. Best not disturb their rest just yet.

Something positive might happen.

She felt no compunction about disturbing her great-uncle, the Taken known as the Howler. Insofar as she knew he had not slept during her lifetime.

She enlisted the Howler's help. She was a favorite. She pretended to like him back, despite the smell and the creepy screaming.

The sun snaked fingers through the curtains on the east windows. The Lord Chamberlain shook constantly. He stumbled over his tongue when he spoke. "The idiots who sent your sister down the chute smothered her first. Standard orders, they claim, for dealing with His discards. They had no idea who she was. They were never warned that there would be girls who weren't to be thrown away. They're adamant in insisting that they weren't involved in any scheme to kidnap one of your sisters."

"Do you believe them?"

"I do, Shining One—though they have come to the point in their questioning where they will shape their stories to show whatever they think we might want to hear."

"Continue the treatment. I am curious to know what names they will give up once they spin their new tales."

"As you command, Your Grace." The Lord Chamberlain began his uncomfortable backward crab crawl.

"Do not be too long, Lord Chamberlain. Eventually someone will inform Him."

The Lord Chamberlain wet himself. "Oh, mad fool, I! I almost forgot. The guards at the Jade Gate had a coach pass through at the right time. There was a girl in the coach, passed out drunk according to the coachman, who said he was her father. The guards were not suspicious."

"Have they been arrested?"

"They have not. They were honest and forthcoming. Arresting them would be counterproductive. They did nothing to earn that."

Someone had to suffer. Better them than she, though she had no more responsibility in this than did they.

The Domination was as absolute an autocracy as ever existed, yet that autocracy, in a sense never recognized by the Dominator, rested on a foundation of soldiers. Soldiers enforced the will of the Dominator. If the soldiers stepped aside the empire would decay swiftly, however mighty the sorceries commanded by its deranged master and the Ten. In less than a lifetime the Domination would shrink to what could be seen from the Dominator's own Grateful Tower.

"I understand." She did, better than did her insane master, who saw nothing but Himself as truly real. He believed that He was a living god. This world and all within it were His to do with as He pleased.

His very unchallengeable power would play a key role in His downfall. Bathdek was sure that fall was not far away. History festered with recollections of empires and civilizations whose time ran out.

Any beginning foretold an ending, though it be an age in coming.

Rumors whispered about a developing resistance centered on something called the White Rose. Those always spoke of the Old Forest, the Great Forest.

Thoughts of futures grim haunted Bathdek. She had begun preparing, ever so carefully, to survive the future. She suspected that her sisters were doing the same.

But to survive the darkness rising she would have to survive this crisis first.

6

In Modern Times: Smelling Danger

The Captain was suffering one of his random infatuations with training and order. The Dark Horse was almost empty. Long days left men too tired to come relax. Markeg Zhorab met me, scowling. I showed him a coin. I had an edge on the troops. They were healthy, lately, except for an odd fungus.

Goblin and Otto were playing tonk three-handed with a kid called Sharps. Sharps was one of the recruits whose need for training had set the Captain off. Sharps being in the tavern instead of learning his trade suggested that he would not last.

Zhorab brought my beer. He took my money. I settled into a chair. "I'm in."

Goblin asked, "You slither out on your belly?" He dealt. And buried me in a pathetic mess of a hand.

"I got nothing to do."

"You would if you bothered to turn up at the free clinic."

Otto observed, "There's always something you can improve." Making mock of the Captain.

"I see you skating yourself."

"I'm teaching young Sharps the nuances of urban intelligence work."

"And your excuse?" I asked Goblin, kissing a fresh hand hopefully.

"I'm like you. I've got nothing to do."

"The standard state of affairs with him," I told Sharps. "To hear him tell. Goblin. I thought you had an apprentice to train."

"The Third? The Old Man sent him and One-Eye out for another livestock census."

Otto said, "The Captain has had a double-hard boner for One-Eye ever since the Limper was here. How'd the little shit piss the Old Man off?"

I said, "You remember. You was there. He pulled a One-Eye. He tried to use the op to scam some cash. If we'd gone along we'd all be taking a dirt nap now, the Captain, too. That's what he did."

Goblin said, "Don't get all hot, Croaker. It came out all right. We ended up looking sweet to your honey."

I deflected talk from the Lady. "That isn't the problem. The problem is what it always was. One-Eye won't learn."

Goblin used his soothing voice. "Your deal, Croaker."

I dealt. "This is more like it. I need to be permanent dealer."

"Croaker." Gently over my right shoulder, from a man who fell out of a way-tall ugly tree and hit every branch on the way down.

"Candy?" How come the number-three man of the Company was in a dive like the Dark Horse?

"The Captain requests the grace of a bit of your precious time."

I exchanged looks with Goblin. Otto and Sharps had turned away in hopes that they would not be recognized.

For Candy to catch up this quick meant he had started out from the compound before I'd gotten halfway to the Dark Horse myself.

I gathered my winnings, passed the deck to Goblin. Headed for the street, I asked, "What's up?"

"You'll find out." Candy did not speak again.

Native building materials were limited, not counting a plentiful supply of clay-rich dirt that made an excellent mud brick. The compound wall that the Captain wanted heightened and thickened, and every building wall inside, was adobe and beautiful to those who favored brown.

A hot breeze blew strong enough to toss leaves and dust around and kick up spin devils. One baby whirlwind danced in front of the Admin building. I asked Candy, "Does that look natural?"

"Not to me. It was there when I left to get you. But Silent claims it's harmless."

The spin devil chose that instant to race off across the parade ground. It fell apart before it got a hundred feet.

The Old Man waited behind the massive, crude table he used for a desk. He gestured at a chair facing him.

I sat. We were alone except for Candy. Candy did a fast fade.

The Captain was a bear of a man, none of him gone to fat. Nobody recalls why he was elected. He was a good captain. He kept most of us alive.

He leaned back in a chair as crude as his table, made a steeple with his fingers in front of his mouth. He stared. All part of the routine.

I asked, "What's up?"

"Have Goblin and One-Eye seemed odd, lately?"

"How could anyone tell?"

"An excellent point. But the question stands. Think."

I did. And my answer stood, too. "Unless you count One-Eye developing an honest streak." The little black wizard had not gotten caught cheating at cards, or indulging in black-market schemes, for weeks.

"I count it. An honest One-Eye is a One-Eye up to something. He doesn't want to attract attention."

"Sir?" He had me nervous. Once he takes official notice of something, that means he sees a real problem that needs addressing.

"I'm thinking back to the Limper's visit. Recall that?"

"I could forget? I'm still trying to get the stains out of my underclothes."

"You men were clever. You managed that slickly. But the truth found its way back to me. Think it might get back to the Limper, too?"

"Who would tell him?"

"He has no friends here. That's true. But that's not the point. He wouldn't need to be told. The information was inherent in your plan."

"Oh." I knew who had ratted us out. Me. I put everything in these Annals. The Old Man does look in occasionally.

"Focus. Goblin and One-Eye. Limper took them away. They were gone two days. We forget that."

Not me. Not Goblin, once I proved that part of his life was missing. He had no recollections of those two days, though.

"Watch them, Croaker. Though with the Limper involved it could all be a diversion. Pass the word. I want somebody watching them every second."

"They'll figure it out. It'll piss them off."

"I don't care. Maybe they'll behave. Go on. Get out."

I got, lost in wonder. That was an epic conversation for the Captain.

What was he up to? Was he really worried about those fools? Or was he trying to ramp up their paranoia, hoping that they would keep their idiotic tendencies reined in?

We had been in Aloe a long time. One-Eye was the sort who might stir shit just because he was bored.

Then I got it. The Old Man had made the point but it had gotten past me then. One-Eye was not behaving like One-Eye, and that started right after the Limper's flying carpet vanished over the western horizon.

Hagop fell in beside me as I headed back to town. I asked, "You skating out of work?"

"I noticed you never stopped at the infirmary."

The notion had not occurred to me.

"You might have fifteen guys lined up."

"To get out of work, maybe."

"Guys have been complaining about feeling dizzy."

"Not to me. All I see is purple fungus, crabs, and clap. Only no crabs or clap nowadays. Those temple girls are clean. Anybody does come up with the clap, I'll just let them squeal when they need to piss."

"That's what sets you apart, Croaker. Your boundless empathy."

. . .

Something was wrong.

Hagop felt it, too. "Is this Aloe? Where is everybody?"

There were few people in the street. The wind was rising, hot, dry, and dirty. A dead weed, uprooted, rolled with it.

I slowed, hand on my knife, thinking wishful thoughts about weapons with a bigger bite. Hagop drifted out to my right, denying the cluster target. He drew his knife, too.

Another weed bounded in from my left, flying up to chest level. I stabbed it twice, then felt stupid. But I did not relax.

The wind died down. The weeds stopped rolling. Spin devils formed, then collapsed.

"I don't care what Silent says, that's spooky."

Hagop grunted. He was fight-ready, not thinking.

I grumbled, "There's something off. I'm worried."

"Your problem is, you don't believe in Aloe."

Right. Aloe was too damned nice. The people were not out to kill me first chance they got. They were genuinely grateful when I fixed their kids. They appreciated the peace we brought and the justice we enforced. They reported villainy when they discovered it.

The Captain had men helping with agriculture and civil engineering, not to win people over but because busy soldiers get into less mischief.

I confessed, "You're right. The longer this goes on, and the longer the Lady holds off dropping us in the shit, the more I'm sure the big ugly is crawling up behind me. I'm seeing things out of the corners of my eyes." I watched a spin devil cross ahead of us, then fall apart.

Hagop paid it no heed. "Fifty yards and you'll be safe."

There it was. The Dark Horse. Almost close enough to touch. And us alone outside—though not really. I did see people when I relaxed.

We hit the door to the tavern. Doom would gnaw my bones some other day.

"I need a hobby, Hagop."

Neither Goblin nor One-Eye was inside. Our third wizard, Silent, was. He was in the tonk game in my customary spot. Hagop's buddy

Otto had his usual seat. So did Elmo. Several soldiers watched. "Shirking, Sergeant?" I asked Elmo.

"Damned straight. The Old Man is out of his fucking mind lately."

"Could be this town is getting to him, too."

"Too?"

Hagop said, "Croaker's got the heebie-jeebies because Aloe is peaceful and friendly."

"He *is* a gift horse mouth–looking kind of guy," Elmo said.

Corey had the cheat seat usually occupied by One-Eye. "I'm tired of losing. Take my place, Croaker."

I must have looked troubled. Silent signed his willingness to move.

I confessed, "I'm going nuts thinking something bad has to happen. It's getting where I'm almost wishing it would."

Elmo said, "He's lost it. He's speaking in tongues."

Otto said, "You think too fucking much, Croaker."

Elmo agreed. "It's all that education. So. What did the Old Man want?"

"He's worried about Goblin and One-Eye. He thinks the Limper did something to them."

Elmo asked, "He mention any messages from out west?"

"No." The Tower would communicate through Goblin in an emergency or by airborne courier if it was routine. We had not seen a flying carpet since the Limper left.

"How about from army headquarters?"

That was closer. Messages came by mounted courier.

"No. No messages. Don't call something down on us. Let them forget we're out here."

Silent gave that sentiment a thumbs-up, then dealt me a hand that would not qualify as a foot.

The deck moved around the table. Pots came and went. There was little table talk.

Elmo said, "If I was the Lady and wanted to get a secret message to the Captain, I wouldn't send it through Whisper's camp."

"You know something?"

"Just brainstorming."

We all turned to Silent. Not pleased to be on the spot, he signed, "Smelling danger."

I grumbled, "Why didn't I figure that?"

"Calm down," Elmo said. "Sit. It's your deal." He tipped a finger toward the door.

Goblin had arrived.

The little wizard looked more like a toad than ever, crouched between Otto and Elmo. He said, "Big storm coming in from the north."

Otto said, "Weather coming in might explain why everything feels weird today."

"North?" Elmo asked. "That don't sound right. Storms come down from the north, this time of year?"

"About every five years. They're bad when they do."

Goblin repeated himself. "Big storm coming. Croaker, I got a sore I need you to check out."

"Now?" I was trying to drink beer, eat fried chicken, and not mark the cards with greasy fingers.

"I'll bring it to sick call. I'm letting you know so you'll show up."

Elmo and Otto thought that was hilarious.

"I'm the hardest-working man in this outfit."

"Definitely in the top six hundred and fifty," Elmo admitted. "How about you stop whining, quit eating, and play?"

The cards goddess spurned me again. "You want my seat, Goblin?"

He made a noncommittal noise. He looked troubled. Was he in pain?

This might not be good.

Goblin was older than stone. He might have something really ugly.

I asked, "You all right?"

"I am now. But there's a storm coming in from the north."

Otto told me, "Pick up them cards, Croaker. Let us skin you while the skinning is good."

. . .

I opened the infirmary after breakfast. The air was heavy, humid, and still. It would be a day when nobody felt good, tempers would be short, and it would be hard to get anything done. In time, though, a hard wind came down from the north.

Three men showed for sick call, all legit. Two sported patches of purplish velvet on their legs. I saw new cases every day. The men did not know how they got it, it itched, and most reported dizzy spells before the purple developed. A fifty-fifty paste of salt and borax, common locally, cleared the stuff in three treatments.

It was not just a Company problem. The fungus was new to Aloe's physicians, too. It was not dangerous. There were no reinfections.

Goblin showed when I was about to give up on him. He was not comfortable, which was odd. I had been treating him for years. He had no reason to go maidenly.

"You do something you know better than to do?"

"I don't know . . . I think something might've been done to me."

"You said you have a sore."

He started muttering, in two voices talking about him in the third person. I interrupted. "Runt. Can the silly shit. Get undressed."

He shut up. He stripped. The pasty, doughy result would bring no maidens running.

The sore was on his paunch to the right of his belly button. It was an inch and a half across, round, suppurating, and stinky, though it did not smell of gangrene. It made a tricolor target. The outer ring was the hot scarlet of blood poisoning. That faded to black. A three-eighths-inch dot in the center was a puddle of pus.

"How long you been letting this slide?"

"A while. It started out like a pimple. I popped it. It came back. Now it's like this."

"Might be a spider bite." There were some nasty fiddlebacks out in the bush. "I'll clean it out and run a test. You try any sorcery?"

"Slowed it down. Made it stop itching. That's all."

"Climb up here." I stretched him out on a table and got busy with a scalpel. I cleared the pus and dead flesh. I treated the hole with distilled spirits. One ounce for the outside of the man, two for his soul. Goblin yelled a lot. I gave him another two ounces for the inner man, then put sulfur and sulfur acid into the wound. I followed that with a water flush. I was about to stuff the hole with fresh lichen when I spotted a black grain down deep in the meat.

"Hang on. I found something." I went after it with scalpel and tweezers, sure it was the cause of his trouble.

I finished him up, bandages and all, and added two more ounces of medicinal spirits. "Sit up. Look at this. It was in the sore."

He scowled. "Don't look like much."

"You been somewhere where you could get stuck with a thorn or a splinter?"

"I never had a splinter fester like that. Give me one of them little bottles to put it in."

"I want you back in the morning. Meantime, find out what that is. Think about did it start when you were off with the Limper."

He gave me the hard eye. "What's going on?"

"The Captain's got you and One-Eye on the suspect list."

"The Limper thing."

"Yes. Mainly One-Eye, though. He's the one acting weird."

"He is?"

"He's stopped cheating."

"Shee-it! You're right. He hasn't tried to . . . His last dumbfuck idea was that freelance raid on the temple of Occupoa. Damn! I'm starting to feel the medicine. We need to tie the little shit down and hypnotize him."

"That's an idea." I considered taking Goblin to the Dark Horse so Silent could work on him but the weather demurred.

The north wind was fierce. The sky grumbled in the distance. The air had an electric feel.

Goblin said, "I'll go sleep the storm off." He swiped a long pull of medicine.

"I might prescribe some spirits and a nap for myself."

The sky lords engaged in a savage brawl. The door and shutters rattled furiously. Rain slammed the infirmary. Water came in under the door. Major repairs would be needed. Mud-brick walls weather fast once the stucco comes off. And the roof developed leaks.

Still, encouraged by self-medication, I considered visiting the Dark Horse.

The Captain flew inside behind a wild swing of the door. He grabbed hold and strained to force it shut. I went to help.

Hailstones bounded in, some an inch in diameter. They stung.

The Old Man treated himself to an uncharacteristic oath. Then, "What the hell? This isn't summer weather."

"Locals say it happens every five years. Goblin started predicting it yesterday."

"And how did he know?"

"I don't know, boss. I do think that this isn't as bad as it can get."

A jaundiced eye. "It'll take a month to fix what's ruined already."

"You wanted something?"

"Two somethings. A report on Goblin. And treatment for the purple stuff." He hoisted his right trouser leg. "It came on fast. I had an itch last night. I got this now."

"Take the pants off."

He complied. "About Goblin. What was it?"

"I thought a spider bite. When I cleaned it out I found a little black something. Maybe a splinter. Maybe a thorn. He's going to examine it. Up on the table. Don't move while the paste is drying. You suffer any dizzy spells lately?"

"Yes. Why?"

"People with the purple all say they did."

"They get it in town, too?"

"They do. They use this same treatment."

"That feels good. The itching is gone."

A savage thunder battle broke out. The building shook. Hailstones pounded the roof. New leaks developed.

The Captain grumbled, "All this, and flash floods to come. Not good. I'll call One-Eye in. Give him a complete physical. Understood?"

"Am I looking for something?"

"You'll know it when you see it. If it's there."

The air was saturated. The poultice on the Captain's leg was not drying. He sat up, pressed a finger into the paste. "We're being inundated with distractions."

More thunder. Blinding shards of light got in around the shutters. A downpour of legendary violence followed.

Mud was everywhere. Water concealed the horizontal kind, rippling in the wind. Every structure in the compound had a melted look. Those not included in the recent improvement campaign were no longer habitable.

The wind remained strong but had turned dry. That helped some.

Nobody had been killed, Company or in town. Injuries were few. Property damage was terrible. People worked feverishly to save what they could.

The folk of Aloe insisted that their gods had protected them. They claimed past storms had been much less benign.

One-Eye came back looking like death warmed over. He had left the Third with a pig farmer, unable to travel. He said the Third had been caught in the open during a hailstorm. He had been hammered badly.

The ugly little black man with the filthy black hat got dragged to the infirmary, struggling. He screamed and swore that he did not need to see me.

My shop got rehabilitated right after the mess hall. Priorities.

"Get naked, One-Eye."

"Croaker? What the hell? No fucking way!"

"Gentlemen, help our brother shed his apparel. Be sure to wash your hands afterward." One-Eye was not fastidious. He wore clothes till they rotted off, or till he stole something he considered fetching. What he wore now would be dangerously infested.

Candy took that beaten old hat. One-Eye tried to groin-kick him. Candy drove a fist into his gut.

One-Eye screamed like a little girl thrown into a fire. Everything stopped. One-Eye collapsed.

Damn! "Gentlemen, please continue."

They finished. They took care not to hurt One-Eye any more. He was careful not to provoke anyone else.

Goblin turned up. He might be useful. "Stand by, runt. Candy, I need him on the table."

The men hoisted One-Eye and stretched him out.

"Gods," somebody muttered.

Because of One-Eye's purple legs? Or the smell? Candy's punch had knocked a crusty bandage off a nasty wound.

"We have to knock him out before I can do anything. Goblin?"

"I got nothing better than you."

I told him what to bring me, mixed in a sweet fig wine. Meantime, One-Eye got his breath and attitude back. We had to make him drink.

Eventually, Goblin declared, "He's under."

"The rest of you guys can go. He'll be out for hours. He won't feel like scrapping when he wakes up."

Candy and crew departed. Somebody wondered why we did not burn One-Eye's hat and clothes. Entire tribes of creepy-crawlies would be living in there. "Too much," I said. "Just wash them."

The Captain turned up. He had mud all over. He had been out working like everybody else. "What have you got, Croaker?"

"The worst case of purple yet. Both legs, ankles to midthigh, all the way around. It's turning green and gray where it's been there the longest. He wanted to keep it secret."

"The original case?"

"That's my guess. I'm tempted to let him be so I can see the disease's full course." I scraped graying mold to see what lay beneath.

"And the belly wound?"

"Like Goblin's but farther inboard and farther gone. It looks and smells the same. He'll be a while healing."

"He didn't treat himself."

That was actually a question. One-Eye was my backup as physician. He should have taken better care of himself.

"We'll ask when he comes around."

"Deal with him, Croaker. Goblin and I will be in the corner having a word."

Ouch! Poor Goblin.

I got out more little bottles. I put pus in one and mold scrapings in others. I cleaned One-Eye's wound. I found another something that looked like a bit of thorn. "Here we go. Same thing."

The meeting of the minds took a sabbatical. Goblin was grateful.

He looked like an eight-year-old saved from having to go cut a switch. The Captain studied One-Eye's wound. "Can you keep that from going bad?"

"I can. If One-Eye takes care of himself."

The Captain told Goblin, "If he croaks you go in the same hole he does." He stalked out.

I looked at Goblin. "Wow."

"Got pretty intense."

"Yes?"

"That man needs to get a sense of humor."

"He needs a life without hassles like you and One-Eye. He did have a sense of humor, once upon a time." That won me no love. "You get anything from what I took out of you?"

"It was a spider fang. Venomous. Not a fiddleback. The festering is a diversion. The fang was carrying a spell into my guts. You messed that up when you convinced me that I had gone missing for two days. It went on poisoning me till you took it out, though."

"That adds up, sort of. Was the spell supposed to make you do something?"

"I don't know. We can ask One-Eye. He's had the full effect for a lot longer."

That was a dim hope. I felt like we were caught in a puppet show.

"Goblin, if you was looking with a neutral eye would you say this was Limper's style?" Limper was usually a find-a-bigger-hammer kind of problem solver. This seemed too complex.

"How much do we really know about him? Not a lot. But who else stands to profit? Nobody since the Battle at Charm. Unless Whisper . . ."

Uh-oh.

I harkened back to two people in a forest clearing years ago, where Raven and I ambushed and captured the great Rebel commander of the day, Whisper. Now Taken. Now the Lady's proconsul in the east.

The other person in that clearing, then, had been a Taken making a turncoat deal. The Limper. Who had suffered terribly for his treason.

Goblin said, "He might be that clever. We don't know what he hasn't shown us. We only know that he doesn't want to do anything the Lady will notice since we got hold of that rescript."

I grunted. One-Eye was set to go.

Goblin stuck with his theme. "We've never proven that the Limper is stupid, only that he's so powerful he doesn't need to be smart."

"Maybe." But I wondered.

Goblin growled, "Damn it, Croaker! There you go thinking too much again."

Days passed. Work proceeded. The Old Man kept just two hundred men in to refurbish the compound. He seemed unusually edgy. He did not get enough sleep. Some men, me included, went to work in town part-time. The rest helped salvage livestock and crops and put fast-growing stuff into the driest ground quickly so that the Company and Aloe alike could avoid a hungry winter.

Goblin kept One-Eye in a healing coma for five days.

In normal times those two squabble like deadly enemies but neither can get by without the other.

I had an epiphany. A teensy one, but an epiphany nonetheless.

One-Eye always started those squabbles. They had not had a serious dustup since the Limper left. That had been overlooked by everyone but the Captain.

Being a rare Company intellectual resource, I indulge in manual labor only when I must. I do not operate shovels or mattocks. I felt for the blacksmiths, armorers, carpenters, and Silent. Silent was draining himself trying to make fields dry faster.

The purple loved the damp. I saw dozens of new cases. We had to hustle to find enough borax.

I staggered into the Dark Horse after the sixth day of cleanup. I was beyond exhaustion. I might never go back to the compound.

"Croaker?" Zhorab was surprised to see me. He had only one customer, himself. He sat at the bar in the light of one feeble lamp.

"Damn. I didn't think it would be this dead."

"Me neither. I thought people would come drown their sorrows. But they're all being civic-minded. Even me. I finish the day too wore out to come back and pretend. What'll you have?" He oozed off his stool, eased behind the bar. "Beer, of course. With you guys it's always beer."

He drew a flagon. I put a coin down. He pushed it back. "No point." He topped up his own drink, returned to the customer side of the bar. "I blame you."

"Me? For what?"

"Not you personally. The Company. For all your energy and determination to make things right. Instead of busting their asses most folks here would rather drown their sorrows while shaking their fists at the gods."

"The gods help most those who help themselves."

"Right. I'm telling you, you guys set a bad example."

"Sorry about that, Markeg. I got to head out before I pass out."

"Hang on."

I hung, leaning on the bar, while a man struggled with his conscience.

Markeg Zhorab, barkeep, had been something else, once upon a time. He was a big man with a lot of scars. His yesterday and today were conflicted.

He had something to tell me. He would give it up, gently, voluntarily, now, or later to men who would not be polite when they asked.

"You people have been good to me, Croaker. You've been good to Aloe. You've been good *for* Aloe."

"That's what we do. We're peacemakers. Bringers of order. Prosperity follows us." Sarcasm? From me?

"Some don't see that. Some don't want to see that."

"Uhm?"

"They're stirring trouble because you arrested that temple girl."

"Really?" I had been surprised at the lack of outrage then. The girl had had no family. Indignation focused on our intrusion into a temple.

Zhorab said, "They want me to spy on you guys."

"Go ahead. If that helps keep you safe."

"Damn! You won't force me to be a double agent?"

Yes, Zhorab would be a double agent. But he would not know it. Every word he heard from now on would be designed for Rebel ears.

"We aren't worried. Anyone who looks can see what we're doing and why. The system goes back forever. It works."

Did I believe that? Some. Mostly I do not worry about that stuff.

Zhorag decided. "There's something else."

"Bring me some sticks to hold my eyes open," I told Silent. "I'm surprised I stayed awake long enough to make it back." I exaggerated. Operating without sleep is a necessary skill for a soldier.

One-Eye was awake, more or less, shading toward less. I was standing by in case the little shit got overexcited.

I had told the Captain about my visit with Zhorab.

His one comment was, "We're on our own." Then he told me to watch One-Eye. I got the feeling that he considered my news good.

Silent and Goblin wanted to put One-Eye to sleep, but hypnotized. Silent had tried with Goblin before, with unsatisfactory results. They had better hopes for One-Eye.

Goblin whispered, "What was that with the Captain?"

"I came up with confirmation that the weird shit going on is all aimed at us. And we'll be on our own, dealing with it."

He pricked One-Eye with a pin. One-Eye did not respond. "Meaning?"

"Whisper could be involved. Limper, too. A Rebel called Cannon Shear has orders to wipe us out. He's actually been on the job since last fall. And he's Whisper's cousin, which might interest them back at the Tower."

"You came up with all that where?"

"In town. Some folks hear all the scuttlebutt."

"Grain of salt?"

"A bucket of salt. But think about this. Where did you go for two days? What did you bring back? Limper was multitasking when he was here. He was following the Lady's orders, yeah, but he was working on us, too. He fixed you and One-Eye so we can't report through you. He'd know if we tried. Right?"

Goblin tested One-Eye's. "Maybe."

"Suppose his main reason for taking you off somewhere was so the rest of us wouldn't trust you anymore. We'd have to honor the threat. But, considering One-Eye, there'd have to be more." If Company hygiene matched the Limper's abysmal standards the purple would have crippled us all.

"I see. I can't yell for Mommy, we can't go through Whisper's headquarters, and we can't get a courier through to the Tower. You set, Silent?"

Silent nodded.

I said, "I think Whisper and Limper meant Cannon Shear to be their revenge. They wouldn't need to do anything but claim ignorance because we never asked for help. After they eliminate Shear."

"That would mean Whisper is it in deep. One fly in your ointment, Croaker. That rescript. Limper will want it back, bad. It could take him down. One-Eye. Sweetheart. Wake up. You've just enjoyed a wonderful night's sleep."

I had tucked one copy of that damning rescript into the shirt of Tides Elba before Limper took her back to the Tower. The Lady might be watching him already. But I dared not mention that while Goblin and One-Eye were suspect.

I said, "Cannon Shear is headed our way. Originally, he was supposed to hit us while we were scattered and confused by the storm."

The Rebel had expected the bad weather but that had crippled them, too. They were more than a week behind schedule.

Goblin and Silent signed for silence. Who knew what ears might be listening?

Shear's force had not assembled where and when it should have. Zhorab did not know why. He said there was confusion in the underground.

Unexpected shit will screw the bad guys, too.

One-Eye's eye was open. He appeared rested, relaxed, amused, and ready to talk. His answers, though, were no more useful than Goblin's.

Goblin kept after him from various angles. It did no good.

Goblin said, "More effort went into him than into me."

"Might have to do with perceived character. Maybe we should keep him under."

Silent signed something about the Third.

Goblin nodded, started whispering about spiders. One-Eye had no use for eight-leggers except to deploy them as an affliction upon someone else. Goblin signed to Silent, told me, "Let's go outside."

It was dark, the sky was clear, moonless, stars in a flood beyond calculation. Goblin whispered, "One-Eye will sense that I'm not there to protect him."

So. Silent would do something with imaginary spiders, going for a backside breakthrough.

"We're past where we might need you, Croaker. Go make love to your cot."

The Captain said, "Not so fast." Great. He was back and determined that I should never sleep again.

"Sir?"

"Any headway with One-Eye?"

Goblin said, "No. We were about to . . ."

"Finish what you're doing, then shut it down. There's something more pressing. Croaker. You said this Cannon Shear is going to come at us from the north."

"Yes, sir. He's late."

"Goblin. Which one of you manages wildlife?"

"We all do, sir."

"Who does it best? I want a bird to find Croaker's fabulous Rebel army. I want to know where it is and is it late because it was smashed by the storm, too."

"You'll want Silent."

"Get him."

"Right." Goblin ducked inside.

The Captain said, "It occurs to me that your witness, though telling you what he thought was true, may have fed you disinformation."

Goblin let out a howl. The Captain and I charged inside.

One-Eye had gotten a hand free. He had smacked Goblin. Now he was trying to work some kind of sorcery.

The Old Man punched him in the temple, stepped round so the

little wizard could see who was taming him. He pressed a hand down on One-Eye's face so he could not breathe.

One-Eye faded. The Captain said, "Stuff him in a pickle barrel with some brine still in it. Croaker, help Goblin take care of that, then get some sleep. Silent, come with me." And he was gone.

I wondered, "What got into him? He don't usually get involved."

Goblin opined that a pickle barrel might be good therapy.

We outfitted One-Eye with said barrel, hammered its top into place, then went off in search of our cots.

It was midmorning before I wakened with what felt like a hangover. I had thirty-some clients waiting at the infirmary. Fourteen brought early purple. Word about One-Eye's legs was out. Rumor said we had stuffed him into a pickle barrel to preserve him until we found a cure for his advanced form of the purple.

There were malingerers, men with bruises and scrapes, and two who had bad colds. There was trench foot because of all the wet.

Orders came to assemble, to inspect weapons and commence combat drills. Scuttlebutt said the Old Man would seek a straight-up, force-to-force engagement once he located Cannon Shear.

Not good. We had not seen one of those since the Battle at Charm. Fewer than half of today's Company had seen that epic bloodletting.

Elmo was my last patient. He had a broken pinkie on his left hand. Something to do with a miscreant hammer. I asked what the Old Man was up to. "You got questions, Croaker, take them to him. All I know is, we got today to get our shit together, then we're headed for a badass brawl with a million crazed Rebels."

Master of understatement, the good sergeant. That should motivate the men to hone their blades extra sharp. They would need to cut down thirty or forty Rebels apiece.

There was a more subtle message for me. Need to know.

Sick call concluded, I went out to see what I could contribute. I should have stuck to the infirmary. I needed to get my show ready to hit the road. I had to have everything aboard the hospital wagons and secured before the order to make movement came.

Lots of things were happening at once, all in the open where any keen-eyed spy could see. Men drilled. Archers practiced, testing bows and strings. Wagons loaded. Farriers checked horseshoes. Teamsters checked harnesses, trees, brakes, and traces. Wheelwrights and wainwrights made sure the wagons were fit to roll. And a hundred men went on repairing the compound. They demolished wrecked buildings and used the salvage to strengthen the outer wall.

There were a lot of extra wagons. The Old Man had hired forty from town, with two teamsters to handle each, and he counted on some of them to be spies.

He materialized behind me. "You ready to go, Croaker?"

"Just about, sir."

"Good. First thing, roll that pickle barrel into Admin. Park it beside your worktable."

That would be the table where I was supposed to record these chronicles. I used it maybe a quarter of the time, preferring the privacy of the infirmary. "Shit! I forgot the Annals over there! The storm . . ."

"They're fine. All sealed up, waterproof. Thank the clerks when you take the barrel in. You want to fuss, worry about what you got here."

We had not gagged One-Eye before we kegged him. He had unkind things to say as I rolled him over to Admin, stood the barrel up to walk it through the doorway, then tipped it and rolled it on into my corner. The little ingrate kept forgetting that it was me who saved him from having to slosh around in another ten gallons of pickle juice. He might have drowned when I was rolling him.

One of the clerks asked, "How about you shove that under the table, out of the way, sir?"

"It won't fit."

"Leave it laying down. Here. I'll help you."

He did. I stepped back. I hoped the Old Man knew what he was doing. Predecessors had tried everything to tame One-Eye, with no success.

I did not feel bad for the little shit. He brought these things on himself.

"About my papers . . ."

"Taken care of."

"But . . ." My worktable was the usual mess.

"Sir, you need to prepare your wagons. The mounted vedettes are leaving now."

True. I did not have forever to get ready. "But . . ."

They practically gave me the bum's rush, moving me out of there.

A soldier shoved inside the infirmary. He held the door. Two more followed with a litter. "Damn!" If I had to saw a leg off, or anything major, I would have to unpack again. "What's this?"

Silent and Goblin followed the stretcher bearers. The human toad explained, "The Third. We need him awake so we can ask questions."

The soldiers made themselves scarce. They wanted nothing to do with what happened next. Wizardry would be involved. The stretcher was on the floor. I needed the patient on my examining table. "All right, boys. Time for heavy lifting. What's his problem?"

Goblin said, "Bad case of attempted suicide complicated by advanced stupidity and a wanton disregard for personal hygiene."

I saw the slash marks on his wrists. They ran crosswise and were not deep. The blade had not been sharp. He had not been committed.

"Let's get him restrained."

While they handled that and I prepared smelling salts the Captain invited himself to the show. "Why didn't you strip him?"

I frowned.

"You stripped One-Eye and Goblin."

I had had help in one case and cooperation in the other. "You're the boss. Untie him, guys." I pulled clothing off, had the Third tied down again.

I checked his outside. Other than a bad case of purple and complementary fungi, plus prime herds of livestock, I found nothing unusual. He smelled as bad as One-Eye had but lacked a similar wound.

The Captain asked, "Why did he cut himself?"

I handed over the smelling salts. "Ask him yourself." I cleaned and treated.

"Make sure he gets a bath."

The Third responded to the salts. Sluggishly. The Old Man slapped his cheeks. "How many fingers, kid?"

"Free?"

"Close enough. Ask questions, gentlemen. Let me know what you get. I need to make sure the Lieutenant has the vanguard moving."

I muttered, "They're really doing it."

Goblin told me, "There's a rumor that Cannon Shear is a hoax. That this is all just an exercise."

"Yeah? I heard one about the Lady being on her way to help."

Goblin grinned at Silent. "Our little boy is maybe gonna get him some nooky."

"You're here to question the kid, runt."

"He's all touchy about it, too."

They make me so mad sometimes. I missed half the questions. The thrust, though, had to do with what One-Eye was up to out in the country.

I was not surprised to hear that he kept ditching the Third and skating out on the livestock census. The man was bone lazy. He just did what he had to do to get by.

The Third thought he was up to something but had no idea what. He did say that One-Eye never stopped bitching about having to be away from the compound.

"And that wasn't the usual stuff," the Third said, still groggy. "He didn't whine about missing out on women or beer or tonk. He just thought he should be at the compound and always looked puzzled if I asked why."

"What about spin devils?" I asked. And harvested baffled looks all round. "You know, wind witches. Little baby whirlwinds."

"They wasn't any that I saw. Been too wet."

Silent shook his head, signed something. Goblin told me, "You don't get those in pasture country."

Maybe Silent was right about them being harmless. I do get distracted by side issues.

"Do your worst."

Those rascals worried the boy from nine different angles—and came up with nothing useful. In the end he gave us only what everybody always knows about One-Eye. He was up to something. Probably.

I got the Third cleaned, treated, and bandaged. He would get to skate out of the coming campaign. A racket outside told me the main body was moving out. I had only minutes left. "So why did you try to kill yourself?"

The Third's face went blank, then pruned into a frown. "I didn't."

I lifted a wrist to show the ugly cut.

Goblin told him, "The pig farmer said you did that. He didn't actually see you do it, though."

A grim speculation impregnated the ensuing silence.

One-Eye?

The muleteers on my wagons yelled at me to get my lard ass moving or I was going to walk.

We made a scant nine miles. Evening sick call produced a dozen customers, most with blisters. The Captain strolled through the camp, looking smug as he took reports. Once he visited my station everyone feared new physical-training requirements would be coming.

The men were less worried about the coming fight than about possible harsh training later.

I blame the Old Man. He had them convinced that they were invincible. Of course, what was gospel to them did leak into the broader environment. The locals believed it, too.

All the blisters treated and my body fed I figured I would go see if Goblin had gotten anything else from the Third. I could not find him. The Old Man had him and Silent looking for Cannon Shear, using owls. Then I had to get back to work.

A pioneer squad needed help. Five were injured. Two came in on litters. "What happened?"

"We got into it with some wasps." The squad leader had a thick Hanfelder brogue.

I knelt beside a litter. The man there groaned. His face and hands were covered with sting welts. He could not open his eyes. I worried that he might have been blinded.

The man on the other litter was just as bad.

"Did you beat the nest with sticks?"

The squad leader grumbled, "That idiot Marker dropped it." He said no more. He had received a warning look. They had been up to something.

I asked, "Paper wasps or bald-face hornets? Do you know?" Both made nests that hung from branches. Both were common. Both had nasty stings and a hair-trigger temper. Bald-face hornets, sometimes mistaken for bumblebees, were the worst. They were vindictive. They would hunt you down.

Unlike bees, both nasty bugs could sting over and over and over.

"Paper wasps."

"You were lucky. Bald-faces probably would have killed you."

The Captain stood a few yards away, considering the casualties, glowering. He disapproved of people getting hurt in the field. Not only would a sword drop out of the line, another man might have to stand down to care for him.

I treated the fools. The poultice was a cousin of that used on the purple.

One decision left. Keep these men here or send them back to the compound. I looked up, meaning to ask the Captain. He was gone. And still no sign of Goblin or Silent. Elmo was hard at it being an infantry platoon sergeant. There was no recreation going on. Men not on duty or asleep were fixing gear or sharpening weapons.

I returned to my wagons. The genius waspnappers had disappeared.

I finished my chores, wrapped up in my blanket, fell asleep to the joyful singing of feasting mosquitoes. I needed to recruit some apprentices. I needed somebody to bark at when I was in a foul mood.

Morning comes early in the field. Everyone was afoot, fed, packed, hitched, harnessed, and ready to roll by the time there was light enough to travel. I dealt with bruises and scrapes during the day. Nobody complained about dizziness or itching. Nobody fumbled a wasps' nest. We climbed a long hill covered by scruffy hardwoods. We descended the far slope, piled up at a rickety bridge while the engineers reinforced it. No point looking for a ford. The water was still high and in a hurry. The countryside, normally mostly brown this time of year, had turned exuberant green.

We climbed a longer, less steep hill populated by small, scraggly groves and singleton oaks. This was grazing country. Several flocks were visible, with other livestock. At first I supposed their herders were taking advantage of the new grass, then realized that they were all headed toward the thicker woods, taking their wealth into hiding. And they were headed our direction, away from their supposed liberators.

So. Cannon Shear was real, and was ten days late for his appointment with destiny.

I had not been convinced before.

We make things up all the time so our enemies will worry.

The long far slope dropped down to a stream wider and deeper than the one we had crossed before. The countryside boasted numerous limestone outcrops, brush-choked gullies and ravines, and small stands of scrub oak not connected with the denser woods off to left and right. Someone had tried to establish vineyards downslope but had given up. The view across the river was of a green plain featuring villages, satellite farming communes, and a lot more undulating pasture. In the extreme distance a dust cloud partially masked remote hills. It would take a big gang to cause that.

Our officers knew what was expected. Men began digging in before I was done gawking. Clearly, need to know did not include the medical staff.

Candy came by with a map. He showed me where he wanted me to set up, behind a screen of trees to our left, just behind the ridgeline, near the road we would use if we had to run for it.

That map was finely detailed. It was not new. More proof that the medical staff was out of the loop.

Once my hospital was good to go I went snooping.

The Captain had been ready for this. His chosen ground, with the trenches, pitfalls, tanglefoot, sharpened stakes, and whatnot added, could not have been more favorable. The Rebel would have to start by coming at us across two bridges, one stone, the other rickety wood a half mile upstream.

The Old Man did not expect Cannon Shear to come straight at us, whatever his numerical advantage, did he?

I think well of my brain. I *am* smarter than most. It is embarrassing to have to admit that I charged into the wrong story at the beginning. While I obsessed about common summer phenomena like spin devils, and the purple, so easily treated, and about One-Eye, that clumsy bear the Captain lumbered along his own path, outthinking everybody.

The Company prides itself on using deception, distraction, trickery, and occasional assassination, to avoid combat or make an enemy think wrong when we do have to fight. Mostly the wizards handle that, making people see things that are not there. They conjure specters that make the Company look bigger and badder.

Specters do not contribute much once the action begins.

Though given hints and told outright I never realized that similar tools might be used against me. Nudges delivered at the outset fixed my thinking. I saw what was *not* there and what *was* there in a wrong light.

I was still in that wrong space, trying to separate the imaginary from the real, as Cannon Shear's force moved toward the two bridges. I saw few obvious specters and fewer living, breathing men than ought to be there on our side.

I refused to believe that the Rebels, less numerous than predicted, intended to force those bridges under concentrated missile fires. Something was messed up on both sides.

The oddness irked me. I am the Annalist. I ought to know.

We splattered Cannon Shear, nearly damming that river with Rebel flesh, but he kept us fixed, twenty-one miles out, while a second column hooked in on Aloe from farther east.

The key events happened elsewhere. I witnessed nothing myself. There was a reason. Somebody smarter than me worked it out.

If you were the Limper, the most badass of the Taken, had a hard-on for the Company, and wanted to keep tabs from afar, what individual would you target? What fool always has his nose in everywhere because he thinks he has to know so he can record it in his precious Annals? You are correct, sir! Right in one. Croaker. Involuntary traitor gifted with induced paranoia and ensorcelled pens that let our little persecutor know every character he scribbled, wherever he happened to be.

The Old Man distracted, misled, and mislaid me all the way.

From now on I go into every encounter with him mumbling: "Don't judge this guy by what he lets you see."

For events at the compound I have to trust the questionable testimony of a few frightened operators who observed by the light of a sliver of moon, complemented by my own matchless imagination.

A black rectangle drifted in over the compound's west wall, settled noiselessly into the deep shadow beside the Admin building. A short blob of darkness entered the wan moonlight and scuttled to the building door. It dragged one leg. It paused, listened, but only briefly. It knew it was not expected and it had sent a sleep spell to neutralize any stay-behinds.

Inside, a word and gesture created a ball of ivory glow. It floated a foot above the Limper's head, shedding just enough light to let him avoid furniture moved since his previous visit.

He felt something. A pool of the power of sorcery, quiescent. One of the Company sorcerers, asleep, tempting him to murder. Why not? The Annalist would discover the loss of the critical evidence anyway, unless the Rebels killed him.

He did not count on those idiots to do their part, on any front. The current clatch were less than amateur.

He could not treat himself to the pleasure of a kill. The sorcerers were necessary to the execution of the plan—and would not live long afterward, anyway.

These wicked Company men were clever. They would have copies of the rescript cached somewhere. The suborned wizards would deal with those, once the original was safe. He would spell them orders through the spider fangs, which would kill them later. But he *had* to have the original document. No way could it be brushed off as a forgery. That damning insult to the Lady was in his own hand.

The spark ahead stirred as though sensing his presence. There it was. Under the Annalist's table. A barrel, on its side, rocking. Two more barrels stood close by, upright.

One-Eye, then. The key to everything. Why was he not at the battle?

They had put their best wizard into a barrel? That was insane. Maybe the answer was in the Annalist's notes. Or would be soon. Meantime, this had to be done fast. It was a long flight back to his station. He had to get there before he was missed.

He shifted the nearest upright barrel. It was not empty but its contents did not weigh much. He would dump them, replace them with the Annalist's papers, and sort everything out later. He could be headed west in moments.

Otto and Hagop, shielded against sleep spells by the Third, slipped up to the Limper's flying carpet. Otto lifted a corner. The frame was almost weightless. Hagop slipped under. By the light of a glow weaker than the moonlight he attached a round wooden container four inches in diameter and two feet long. He pulled a string on one end, then got out of there. Both men headed for town, trotting to catch up with the Third and others who had not gone out to meet Cannon Shear.

The barrel under the table rocked. The man inside wanted to make it roll. It would go nowhere because two other barrels blocked it. Limper whispered, "I'll have you out in a minute." Not meaning a word. Tools for seating and unseating a barrelhead lay on the Annalist's table. "But first . . ."

Limper popped the head out of the nearest upright barrel. It was filled with gray papier-mâché globs. Those should dump easily.

A thud. A flash. A bang. The barrel hopped a foot off the floor, came down hard and fell over. Limper caught the slightest whiff of the initiating spell.

There was another one! There, in the dark! Overlooked because of the smell of the man in the barrel! Ambush!

The wasps and hornets came awake, freed from the sleep spell.

"They tore him a new asshole," Silent signed. "Tore him a whole new set. Even bundled up the way he always is. But he kept on stuffing that barrel, screaming worse than the Howler ever did. The hornets stayed with him till he was a hundred feet up."

There was a lot of laughter. The Captain had pulled a good one. He began laying the groundwork right after the Limper's last visit, when he caught the little shit messing with my pens and inks and guessed right what that was all about.

Still, some things had not gone the way he hoped.

"He opened the barrel! I cannot believe he did that. I thought the bugs would have to get after him through the fill hole, fighting each other all the way."

I looked over at One-Eye. He was not happy, not least because somebody had washed his clothes while he was confined, but also because he now stank like pickle instead of like a moron a year overdue for a bath.

I went to get the Captain's story. "Why so glum, sir?"

"I miscalculated. Understating it big-time. Whisper didn't do what I expected. I know she must have been in on it. I thought the Lieutenant would herd his Rebels into the force she meant to sneak in behind us."

No such force ever materialized. Ambushing the second Rebel column only scattered panicky amateurs.

"She isn't stupid, Captain. She went down with the Limper once. She'll never let that happen again."

He shrugged. "Whatever, it was a good few days' work."

"Consider the bright side. I haven't seen a new case of the purple in three days."

To get back to his duty station the Limper had to overfly the deadly strangeness called the Plain of Fear. As always, giant flying things came up to contest the passage of an outsider. He ducked, darted, and maneuvered. Safe passage was no problem for one of the Taken. They had their sorcery when maneuver was not enough.

All that jerky motion caused the contents of the tube under Limper's carpet to slosh and mix. An especially violent jig finally shook a jammed trigger loose.

The explosion shredded the fore half of the carpet. The Limper was in a shrieking steep climb at the time, twenty-three hundred feet high. He arced one way. A barrel followed. Bits of carpet and frame, aflame and otherwise, scattered and began to flutter down.

The Taken called on his sorcery, then cursed all the way to the ground.

The damned Black Company had done him wrong again. They had smelled him coming, somehow. Maybe Whisper had betrayed him. Whatever, they most certainly still owned the damning rescript that, till the explosion, he had thought that he had recovered.

He was not going to be able to cover this up. He had a long walk ahead, through the worst the Plain of Fear had to offer. He was going to be late for work.

7

Once Upon a Time: All Objectivity Fled

The girl was again as gloriously beautiful as she must have been before she died, but something was missing. All had not gone according to plan. She remembered nothing. She did retain rudimentary language skills but spoke seldom and then only slowly. She showed no curiosity and little inclination to learn. She recalled only the most rudimentary elements of self-care.

The necromancer did not have to handle her as though she was an infant but, in essence, she was a blank slate personality-wise.

He told her that her name was Laissa. She was his daughter. He chose that name because he had loved a Laissa when he was younger and if they had had a child that child would be about the age of this girl. He told her that her mother had died of childbed fever, which was nearly true in his askew mind. The Laissa that he had loved had died about the time that this one would have been born. He had tried to save her once the rage subsided but by then it had been too late.

This Laissa, according to the necromancer's report, had suffered a prolonged and severe fever. She was just now beginning to recover. She should regain her memories eventually.

Laissa was not disturbed by her loss. She knew nothing so missed nothing. She was not even lonely. She just was.

She and the necromancer settled into a life together. She did small things to help around the house. He spent most all of his time in his workroom trying to discover the miscalculation that had cost the girl her mind.

He did not like to use superstitious terms but it could just be that her soul had gotten away before she could be reanimated.

He began slowly planning a second reanimation. It would not take long or require much new effort, but . . . Well, he would have to visit Dusk repeatedly before he could make a final action plan. The great evil in the Grateful Tower would not have stopped discarding corpses. It might be instructive to see if there was any change in the state of alert, too.

He could not shake a feeling that things had not gone quite perfectly when he collected Laissa.

He had no congress with the world. He spoke only with Laissa, who was not interested in conversation. Last time he spoke with anyone else was at the Jade Gate.

He needed to retrain himself to function in society.

But he dared not leave Laissa alone while he went to Dusk. She was not careful. She would harm herself somehow, although she was becoming more self-sufficient, slowly. Nor dared he take her with him. Her strangeness would flaunt itself. And some sorcerer surely would smell the necromancy animating her.

That would be the end of them both.

Six weeks after Laissa's resurrection the necromancer made a cruel discovery: She was getting slower and weaker. He saw tiny signs that a less practiced eye would not recognize for months more.

Death was stealing her back, ever so slowly retaking that of which it had been cheated.

Death's relentless bite would become ever more obvious, until even the blind would know it.

The necromancer immediately created a course of treatments, applied monthly, that would keep Laissa from sloughing off into oblivion. But those treatments were painful.

His project, his triumph, his girl, his daughter, would remain forever young, forever beautiful, but, sadly, would be forever dying, too.

Sorrow unmanned him. He had developed an affection for the girl, too strong for experimenter and experiment. He had conflated her emotionally with the Laissa who was no more. All objectivity had fled.

He knew. He saw himself caught in a cleft stick. He could sustain this Laissa while he tried to discover how to save her permanently. Or he could let her go and move on to a fresh, less flawed resurrection.

Emotion triumphed. He chose the beautiful girl.

8

Long Ago and Far Away: Sisters

Bathdek spent six days in a state nearly as awful as the Lord Chamberlain's. The Dominator could call for her or Dorotea at any moment . . .

But, no, He was distracted thoroughly, in a continuous rage because of events in the Old Forest, where three veteran brigades had been exterminated to the last animal and camp follower by White Rose savages who remained stubbornly defiant in the face of assured destruction. The disappointment there was not a first. Fires burned on every frontier. The Dominator and the Ten could not be everywhere.

In His mad rage at this latest affront, the Dominator had ordered the Old Forest cleared to the last sapling, never mind that forest's vastness. A clearing project of such magnitude would devour the full financial resources of the Domination for decades. The Dominator did not understand capital limitations. Nor any other limitations. He must crush, must destroy, must eradicate anyone who defied Him.

The self-anointed god of the Domination had lost all purchase upon reality.

The seventh morning after Dorotea vanished Bathdek received a response to her plea for an audience with her sister Sylith. The Senjak sisters were wary and jealous of one another, in the extreme.

Sylith's quarters were opulent. The lord was generous. The Senjak family had helped make Him lord of the world. Their constancy guaranteed that He would remain the world's master. One of the sisters was His virgin bride. Bathdek knew that she was not the one. She was sure that all of her sisters fulfilled the virginity requirement despite the gross usages to which He sometimes put them.

But wait! Might she be the wife without knowing it? She would not put the forging of such a secret union past her mother.

There had been no ceremony. No formal wedding. Everything had happened in secret, with quiet parental collusion. So, yes, the actual wife might not know that she was married.

Bathdek believed the wife must be Sylith or her eldest sister, Ardath. The wife could not be Dorotea. He would not refrain from using Dorotea to the fullest had He the legal right. Dorotea was the incarnation of His every physical fantasy. She might have been bred for the role. . . . But . . .

Hell would throw its gates wide were Dorotea the secret wife, murdered by ignorant lackeys.

Ardath. Scary Ardath. The eldest sister waited with Sylith. A painful surprise. Bathdek did not get along with Ardath.

Her sisters were so stunningly beautiful, she thought, although so wicked. Ardath was still only in the final season of her teens. She might even once have had a twin. Or Sylith might have. There were whispers. But Bathdek's early memories were clear. She recalled no such older twin sister. True, there had been a brother born between her and Sylith but a fever had carried him off while she was still in diapers. She did not recall him at all.

They were ferociously powerful, the Senjak girls. Each owned a talent for sorcery outmatching that of most of the Ten Who Were Taken—many of whom also sprang from the Senjak clan.

Bathdek was not sufficiently self-aware to realize that she was as stunning as her sisters, in identical fashion. A glance might suggest that the three girls were identical triplets. Only Dorotea had been different, and that only in the color of her hair. Her body had been the same, less improvements yet to be wrought by time.

There was a hint of scandal surrounding Dorotea's conception. Cautious whispers suggested that her mother might have shared an intimate moment with the Dominator, which could make a marriage to Dorotea *really* interesting.

The Senjak sisters were youthful versions of their mother. She, were she present, might have been taken for another sister, so skilled was she at defying the cruelties of time and childbearing.

Sylith asked, "This is about Dorotea, isn't it?"

"It is." That her sisters knew was no surprise. The Lord Chamberlain spied for everybody. She could only hope that terror would keep the man from reporting to Him.

Bathdek related everything she knew but not everything she guessed, then asked, "What should we do?"

Because Dorotea was their sister they were involved, up to their pretty ears, like it or not. The Dominator was especially paranoid lately, and not without reason. Chances were, He had more enemies than He imagined. He might think that the Senjaks had put together a scheme for slipping away. Any that escaped would take away a splinter of the power that made Him what He was. He would see them stealing what was His by divine right.

Sylith said, "Go on trying to trace Dorotea. We'll make sure that you're not summoned. His rage makes him easy to manipulate. The news from the frontiers will keep him angry. It's never good."

Bathdek envied the older girls their ability to remain calm and confident. She was not yet ready to try managing the madman.

Sylith added, "We'll have to tell Him someday, but that should wait till He's ferociously distracted by the latest far-off disaster. We should have every conceivably useful detail available when that day does come. We will have to build a special reality inside his mind."

Bathdek nodded, jealous of her sisters again. They were often the real forces moving the Domination.

Sylith said, "Go now."

Bathdek went, wondering why Ardath had not spoken. For Ardath life was a competition with Sylith: almost a mortal competition. She should have been second-guessing at least.

Did that mean that the situation was grimmer than she feared? That was hard to imagine. She was convinced already that she was sprinting down the road to Hell.

9

In Modern Times: Bone Candy

The campaign season was over. The weather stank. The Dark Horse was packed up elbow-to-asshole. There was not enough make-work to keep the troops busy. Markeg Zhorab's wife and sister had to help serve. The wicked of mind hoped he would bring out his delectable daughter, Sora.

Otto checked his last card, cursed. A turn as dealer had not helped. His luck was still dreadful. "You're damned grim for a guy that keeps winning, Croaker."

"Bad nightmare last night. Still feeling it."

Silent signed, "Same one?"

"Same flashback." To when I was a prisoner in the Tower. Details fled when I woke up but the creepy dread stuck. "Third night in a row."

Otto grinned. "Your honey must be missing you." The old canard.

Silent signed, "Stop that."

My turn. I pounced, down with eleven. Otto cursed. Silent shook his head, resigned. Corey, in One-Eye's usual seat, pretended to wipe away tears. He asked, "When is the battlefield not a battlefield?"

"Huh?" Otto grunted. "That some dumbass riddle?" Surprise. Otto is bad with riddles. He solves puzzles with hammers and swords.

"One-Eye asked me that last time we talked."

I looked around. Silent was the only wizard in the place. I asked, "Where *are* Goblin and One-Eye?"

Their apprentice, the Third, was missing too. He did not usually stray far from the beer. Those two can drive anyone to drink.

Otto collected Silent's deal like he feared the cards would bite. "Them two are gone together, that could be bad."

Those two are always up to no good but not always together. The table fell into a deep disquiet. Corey muttered, "Definitely not good." Silent nodded grimly.

Zhorab delivered an untimely pitcher, muttered, "Flies." He hustled off, loath to leave his bar undefended.

I discarded a seven of spades. Corey snagged it, spread the five-six-seven-eight and dumped a red five. He would be down to an ace or deuce. Otto and Silent had spread threes and fours already. He would have played on those if he could. Nobody groused. Everybody suddenly had a whole lot of nothing to discuss. Cards and drinks had become totally fascinating.

Two Dead stepped into the big taproom. Long, lean, skeletal, he needed more legs and eyes to complete himself. He opened his coat. Flies came out to circle him.

Corey repeated, "When is the battlefield not a battlefield?"

It occurred to me that that could be more than one question depending on how you heard it.

Two Dead. Real name, Shoré Chodroze, wizard colonel from Eastern Army HQ with plenipotentiary powers. A blessing upon the Black Company bestowed by the Taken Whisper. He never volunteered anything about his real mission. He was said to be an unpredictably nasty sociopath. Our main wizards disappeared right after he turned up. He was Two Dead because when he rolled in with one oversize bodyguard, all bluster and self-regard, the Lieutenant had declared, "That man ain't worth two dead flies."

So Two Dead, in vile humor, arranged for flies to follow him around. Way more than two, and very much bitey alive.

Otto dealt. The rest of us shrank. Somebody was about to get unhappy.

I met Two Dead's gaze, as always amazed that he owned two good eyes. The left side of his face featured a lightning bolt of bruise-colored scar tissue, forehead to chin, but his eye had survived. I suspected a glancing upward thrust from an infantry pole arm.

He headed our way. And . . . Oh. Not good. Something had him spooked. Never a good thing, a sorcerer with the heebie-jeebies.

We were not the cause. He held us in abiding contempt. Still, he kept his bodyguard close. He knew his Company history.

Where was Buzzard Neck now?

Two Dead pointed at me, then Silent. "You two. Come with me." Shit. We were about to take a dip in the ugly soup. "Bring your gear."

I always lug a bag. You never know when some idiot will need sewing up.

Two Dead headed for the exit, unable to imagine that we would not follow.

Silent took two steps out into the street, stopped dead. I banged into his back. "Hey! None of your mime stuff!" He had picked up the hobby recently.

This was not that. This was a response to the weather.

A wind hummed in from the north, flinging snow pellets into our faces.

The chill did not bother Two Dead. Nor had he been drinking. The cold shock had me hungry to piss but Two Dead barked, "Come!"

I came.

Buzz awaited us in full battle gear, including a goofy old-time kite shield. His expression was pinched. He looked like he had serious stomach trouble.

He was a building in boots. Guys like him usually end up being called Tiny or Little Whoever, and are dim, but this walking house was supernaturally quick, monster strong, and was twice as smarter than the creep who employed him.

He was Buzzard Neck because his neck was long and crooked and included an Adam's apple like an Adam's melon. The name quickly shrank to Buzz.

He never said much. He was as well-liked as Two Dead was well-loathed. He claimed to have survived some of the shit the Company had, including the Battle at Charm.

Two Dead headed out. We followed, me hoping I would not have to hold it long.

Technically, we could have told Two Dead to go pound sand. He was not in our chain of command. But he was tight with Whisper and Whisper was hungry for excuses to pound on the Company. Also, he might be like a cat underfoot for a long time. Not to mention, I was really curious about what could give the spider wizard the jimjams.

Aloe sprawls without being big though it is the grandest metropolis for a hundred miles around. Two Dead led us a third of a mile, to the lee of a redbrick box on whitewashed limestone foundations.

"There." He indicated a mound of brown fur in a dried-out flower patch between the foundation and street edger blocks. Wind stirred the fur and dead plants.

I opined, "It don't look healthy."

Silent said nothing. Buzz clutched his gut.

I asked, "What is it?" Not a badger. It was too big and the color was wrong. Not a bear. It was too small and I had yet to hear of native bears.

"I don't know," Two Dead said. "It smells of sorcery."

Silent nodded. Buzz looked desperate to take a squat.

I stepped left, relieved myself at last. Steam rose to meet randomly falling snowflakes. Fat flakes. It must be getting warmer.

I eased closer. The beast was curled up like a pill bug.

Two Dead said, "There were two more. They scooted when we showed up."

Buzz said, "I didn't see them."

Two Dead said, "They ran a few steps and just faded out." He was nervous all over again. How come?

I asked, "What did they look like?"

"Giant beavers or woodchucks? They were gone too quick to tell."

Well. Beavers and groundhogs are some less fierce than bears.

This one was not the right shade for a woodchuck. I did not know about giant beavers, though.

I noted a stir not caused by the wind.

Silent offered a sorcery alert.

Two Dead said, "Something magical is about to happen." He did not mean magical in any wondrous-surprise-for-the-kiddies sort of way.

The moment disappointed. It expired without calamity.

I took a knee, faked veterinary skills.

The animal breathed slow and shallow and had a faint heartbeat. Hibernating? Some bears just drop in place when the sleepy season comes.

It did not waken and shred me. Two Dead took that as license to revert to his normal obnoxious self.

Silent and I hauled the beast on Buzz's shield. Buzz was too damned big to help. The downhill end had to carry most of the weight. Plus he was having trouble keeping his trousers clean.

The beast sprawled on a table in my clinic. Two Dead perched like a spider on a stool close by, manfully keeping his yap shut. The Captain and Candy were there, too. Like Two Dead, they kept quiet while the professional worked. Buzz was off haunting a latrine.

"This is one ugly gob of snot," the professional said. Stretched out, it looked more like a baboon than a beaver. Its face was a fright mask of scarlet skin. It had teeth fit for a crocodile. Its eyes were snakelike. Each foot included semi-retractable claws and a stubby but opposed thumb.

It was nothing anyone had seen before.

"It's starting to smell like a vulture's breath," Candy observed.

Its heart rate was rising, too. “The cold must have laid it down.” Our vile weather might not be all bad.

The Captain jiggered the flue on my heating stove.

“Then these things shouldn’t be dangerous till the weather changes.” It would, local boy Corey had promised. We would see one more springlike week before winter came to stay.

Candy, our Company number three, prodded, “Croaker?” There was work to do. Critical work. He and the Old Man were here their own selves.

Did they know something? Two Dead certainly wondered.

The Old Man seldom says much. He was all fired up curious, now, and almost chatty. “It’s supernatural, right? What kind? Where from? Was it summoned? Is it invasive? Somebody talk to me.” He was sure that Two Dead was to blame.

Two Dead shook his head. “I promise, it’s new to me, too.”

“Where are Goblin and One-Eye? Anybody know?”

Candy said, “They haven’t been seen for days.”

I reminded, “The Colonel says there were more of these things. Better find the others while it’s still cold.” I was sure the critters were not our friends.

Candy mused, “Warfare by elliptical means?”

“When is the battlefield not a battlefield?”

Two Dead frowned, at a loss.

We had decimated the Rebel in the region, a success that troubled some “friends.” Vast incompetence and corruption had been turned up, which the guilty resented. Whisper’s own discomfort was probably why we had Two Dead as our guest.

I had hoped the Rebel survivors would slink away to recruit, to train, to collect weapons and supplies, and to wait for us to be transferred. With no external threats, hatreds endemic to the Lady’s forces fester quickly.

Informants told us the quiet season would never come. Senior Rebels wanted Aloe back. The Port of Shadows might be hidden here.

Most Aloens did not understand that echo out of deep time. Rebel insiders did. The honest ones sometimes got so scared they came over to our side.

. . .

I read a lot. I root around in folklore, legend, and local history. Port of Shadows references a plot to resurrect the Dominator, lord of the old Domination, who remains a demigod to some. The Port of Shadows is a gateway he can use to escape his tomb.

Some Rebel chieftains are closet Resurrectionists. The Lady has been plagued by their efforts practically from the moment she escaped her own grave, leaving her husband behind.

The Company's Aloen interlude, supposedly taking us out of the line to decompress, has been anything but relaxing. We are playing a role in some obscure maneuver by our empress. And the Port of Shadows thing smells more unsettled by the day.

The Old Man and his cronies are worried but they do not confide in the Annalist. The Annalist writes things down. What has been recorded gets damnably hard to deny.

Could this monster be a Resurrectionist tool? Our enemies had not yet gone supernaturally asymmetric. Sneaking lethal paranormal uglies into an enemy camp is more like something we would do.

The Captain leaned in, tempting the beast. He asked Silent, "Have Croaker cut it up to look at its insides? Or cage it and wait?"

Silent shrugged. He was out of his element.

The Captain asked Two Dead, "Suggestions, Colonel?" while looking for some subtle tell.

The beast had been the sorcerer's discovery.

Two Dead remained unperturbed. He had come to us suspect. That would never change. "Let it live but keep it cold. Find the others. Examine a healthy one." He eyed Silent.

Silent shrugged again, stubbornly frugal with his opinions.

I bent close, combed fur, hunting vermin. Fleas, ticks, lice all tell tales. "This thing is getting warmer . . ." I reeled back, shoved by Silent. He pointed. Flakes of obsidian ash had puffed out of a nostril. "Hand me a sample bottle." Then, "Make that a bunch."

A black beetle stomped into the light, as shiny as the flakes. It glared around, measuring the world for conquest.

The Old Man asked, "That some kind of scarab?"

A second bug marched out, bumped into the first. Number one was in a bad mood. Bam! No threat display. No ritual dance. The bugs started trying to murder one another with ridiculous bear-trap jaws.

I whined, "Anybody got any idea what the hell?"

Nope. Two Dead, though, did snag my biggest glass jar, which he shoved over the beast's head. He packed the gaps with handy rags.

Candy took off in a big hurry, leaving the door halfway open. Snow blew in before Silent shut it.

Black flakes presaged the emergence of more beetles. These were not immediate bugacidal maniacs. They just wanted to leave. The jar frustrated their ambitions.

Then they went berserk. "What a racket." The Captain was rattled, something you seldom see.

The host animal began to deflate. Two Dead stuffed more bandages. A few beetles, struck brilliant, snipped cloth chunks with those nasty jaws.

They did get distracted when they banged into one another.

"We need a container big enough for the whole thing," Two Dead said. "Maybe a pickle barrel."

Bam! Candy came back lugging a big tin box with a latch-down top that hailed from the commissary, where it kept grain and flour free of vermin.

"Perfect," Two Dead declared, nonplussed. This was too-quick thinking by people he wanted to be too dull to notice him nudging them onto a hangman's trap.

Candy said, "Push it in, glass and all." He positioned the tin so Two Dead could shove the beast inside.

Two Dead held his paws up like a dog begging. He should soil his delicate fingies?

"Really?" the Old Man barked. "Push the damned thing!"

A particularly formidable beetle chose the moment to make his getaway via the beast's nether orifice. A Two Dead finger was nearby. It took a bite. Two Dead howled, "Oh, shit! Gods damn, that hurts!"

An even studlier bug tromped forth as the beast flopped forward. It had even more ridiculous jaws and a back end like a long, thin funnel. It flew at Two Dead, literally, wing cases flung high, ladybug style. It landed on the back of his left hand, grabbed hold, took a hearty bite. Then it stood on its nose, curled its tail down, dipped its tip in the wound.

All that took only an eyeblink to happen. Two Dead shrieked again.

Silent crunched the bug.

Candy pounded the lid onto the can. The monster left several wriggling grubs on the table. The Old Man chased escaped beetles. Silent and I wrestled Two Dead into a chair. He began to shake. Shock? The bites did not look that bad. Could they be poison?

Silent signed, "It laid eggs."

The sealed tin sang like a metal roof in a hailstorm.

The Old Man killed one last fugitive bug, turned on the grubs. "Candy, take the can to the trash pit. Then get every swinging dick out there looking for the other two animals. Hire tracking dogs." He moved over to watch me dig almost invisibly small cream-colored beads out of Two Dead's hand.

Sergeant Elmo busted in out of the cold. "Look what I found sneaking around with a sack full of stolen bread and bacon." He had our apprentice sorcerer, the Third, by the scruff of the neck.

Candy left with the singing biscuit tin. Silent had to close the door behind him again.

The Third was not a happy kid. Truth be, he had had few shots at happiness since he got tangled up with Goblin and One-Eye. Falling into hot water was nothing new.

The Old Man settled into a chair, leaned back, considered the Third. He put on his "I'm eager to hear how you'll try to bullshit me on this" face.

Silent passed me a jar of carbolic. I put bug eggs in, then dribbled liquid onto Two Dead's wounds. He squealed.

The Third volunteered, "One-Eye sent me to fetch food."

Really? That little shit is not big on bacon. On the other hand, the Third would devour it by the hog side.

I worked on Two Dead. Silent watched grubs in a jar. They behaved no better than adults. The Old Man glared at the Third. The level of noise outside rose. Candy had relayed the Captain's orders.

Buzz stumbled in looking like death warmed over. His sojourn in the latrine had not helped much.

The Third said, "I was getting stuff for me. Sergeant Elmo spotted me before I started on One-Eye's stuff."

I observed, "The kid has his priorities straight."

Two Dead managed a ghost smile. His shakes continued.

The Old Man grumped, "Watch the Colonel till you're sure he'll be all right. We don't hand Whisper any fresh excuses. You." He poked the Third. "Come with me."

Buzz wanted to fuss over his boss. Two Dead growled, "You look like a man with the drizzling shits, Tesch. Smell like one, too." He poked me with his unbitten hand. "I'll live. Help him."

I thought Buzz must have drunk some bad water. He ought to know better. I loaded him with liquids and orders not to stray far from the latrine. He was unhappy about not being able to stick close to Two Dead.

"Yet here you are alive and recuperating," I observed after Two Dead suggested that the Company might have rigged all this for his personal inconvenience. "You probably conjured those animals yourself and just accidentally got the bad end."

That was plain chin music, ridiculousness in exchange for absurdity, but Two Dead found something worrisome there. Like was he maybe supposed to get it with the rest of us?

I was tempted to pin a target on Whisper's back. The more discord at HQ the less time those people would have to harass us favorites of the Lady.

I reiterated the common remark: "When is the battlefield not a battlefield?"

Two Dead eyed me. "An intriguing question, physician. Worth considering here, in these troubled times." He cocked his head, listened. I caught a vague hint of distant wind chimes. That rattled me. It tied into my recurrent nightmare somehow. "I'm going to lie down and brood on it." Two Dead indicated a cot.

I was snuggled into a cot and blankets myself, and had been for a while. The Captain poked me. "What's wrong with him?" Head jerk toward Two Dead, on his back, on his cot. Drool glistened on his ugly cheek. Snot hung from the nostril on that side. Dead sexy.

"What time is it?"

"Nighttime. We got the other beasts. What about Chodroze?"

"He was his old ugly self when I laid down." I set feet on the cold dirt floor, rose with a groan, toddled over. Our chatter had not awakened Two Dead.

I felt the heat before I touched him.

The Captain said, "The dogs found them, unconscious from the cold. The men tinned them up and threw them in the fire pit. No beetles got away."

"We need to pack Two Dead with snow. He's burning up."

"Whatever. Just keep him healthy."

Two Dead had a weak, fast, irregular pulse and a dangerous fever. "I'll need help cooling him down." I started stripping him. That did not waken him, either. "What did the Third have to say?"

The Old Man looked like he had bitten into a chunk of alum candy.

Goblin and One-Eye *were* up to something. And he might not entirely disapprove.

Dead fierce, he snagged a bucket and headed outside, where the weather had turned enthusiastically blizzardy.

He returned with a pail of muddy snow.

I indicated Two Dead's wounded arm. Scarlet threads ran up it from the uglier wound.

"Blood poisoning?"

"Some kind of poisoning. Blood poisoning isn't usually this aggressive."

Skin flexed near Two Dead's worst wound. I had not gotten every egg.

"Help me get him on the table. I'll clear the wound. You pack him with snow. Start with his head and throat. We need to cool his brain."

Move made. Snow packed and melting onto the floor to make mud. I dug with a scalpel. The Old Man hauled more snow.

"How about we just dump him in a snowdrift?"

"I need light to work. And you told me to save his blessed ass." I had excised two thin grubs. They writhed in an alcohol bath. I was after what I hoped was the last.

"Those bitty things caused the blood poisoning?"

"Their shit is probably toxic."

"Ugly."

"Life is." In some forms, ugly for lots of us.

I fit puzzle pieces while I worked, hoping I was fooling myself but afraid I was looking chaos in the crimson, googly eye.

"How come the tourniquet?"

"Keeping the poison contained. To avoid amputation if I can."

"That wouldn't be good."

No. "I should ask what he wants, worst case, but he won't wake up."

"We need more hands. Maybe Silent can get to him."

"I can't go. Where the hell is Buzz?"

"Buzz is in his rack, down and out and soaked in shit. He'd be dead if you hadn't given him that tea. Poor Corey and Minkus are babysitting." Minkus Scudd would be my current apprentice, mostly a waste of air. "I'll get another bucket, then head out on a recruiting tour."

So. Old Buzz came down with the drizzling shits right when his principal started dying from an infestation of supernatural parasites. That wanted a closer look. The timeline might tell us when Buzz picked up what was trying to kill him. Also, maybe who was there when it happened.

I winkled the last worm out. The Old Man brought more snow. I mused, "When is the battlefield not a battlefield?"

The Captain eyed me oddly, shrugged, took off with his trained-bear shuffle.

The day's puzzle might have an explanation hidden inside the recurring question. That might put me eyeball-to-eyeball with a repellent cousin question that could have multiple readings as well. "When is my enemy not an enemy?"

Otto and his pal Hagop turned up. The Captain had caught them trying to sneak off to town to help Markeg Zhorab get a little richer. They hauled snow instead.

We did not see the Captain again right away. He went off and stole a short nap. When he did turn up he had the Third in tow, all decorated with light shackles. "He's all we got left. Silent has gone missing now, too."

The Third shook his wild shock of curls, lost in the insanities.

Answers had to wait. Two Dead was not improving. Snow packs were not enough. I told the Third, "I need the Colonel awake. We need to talk. Amputation may be his only salvation. I can't decide that for him."

"Why bother? We could get shot of him."

"I save whoever I can." Not that I have not made exceptions. Not that Two Dead was insufficiently despicable to make the "he needs killing" list. "And he's Whisper's pet."

"Don't smell like that special a relationship to me." The Third eyed Two Dead. "It'll be tough. Feels like Silent put him in a coma for the pain."

"You can't bring him out?"

"Didn't say that. Said it's gonna be tough. Get ready for some serious screaming. His arm is gonna feel like it's on fire."

"Hang on, then." I slathered Two Dead's forearm with topical painkiller. "All right. Go."

Two Dead surprised us. He did not let the pain unhinge him. He was creepy normal, disinclined to shed any limbs unnecessarily.

He was short four already, you asked me.

"I won't do it casually," I promised.

He was caught in a cleft stick. I had no reason to wish him well but he did realize that I would not just maim him when death by inattention would be so much easier.

He played through the pain. "If it's the best choice, do it." His speech was slurred. I kept loading him up with painkiller tea.

The Captain talked to him steadily, gently, casually, like he was Two Dead's cousin. He wanted to slide inside the sorcerer's head while the man was addled.

I set up to cut, ever more sure that it could not be avoided. I listened. Two Dead made no sense. He was old, hard-core, and stubborn. The Old Man was unlikely to get much.

Then he did get something that I missed. He buttoned up and hit the weather and was gone for fifteen minutes.

I got Two Dead strapped down. The Third whined, "Can I go? I don't want to see this."

"You're going to be Company, you'd better get used to blood." Which sparked memories I would rather not have recalled. I have eaten a lot of bone candy with the Company.

There was no choice. Two Dead's body could not resist the poison. "Sorry, Colonel." Our senior sorcerers might have helped but they were unavailable. Best not to mention that. Two Dead supposedly had a fecund bent for paranoid violence.

He glared at the Third. The Third said, "I am sorry, sir. I'll do my best but medical sorcery isn't among my skills."

Pain kept Two Dead from helping himself.

I asked the Captain, "How goes the search for our favorite duo?"

"Still missing." He eyed Two Dead like he suspected a connection.

I asked, "Go ahead, Colonel? Final decision time."

Two Dead nodded grimly, probably rehearsing the cruelties he would visit on those who had brought him to this, deliberately or otherwise.

"Would you like to remain awake during the procedure?"

"Put me out. Tesch won't shit himself forever. Anything goes wrong, he'll see that I don't walk the road to Hell alone."

I smelled bluster and some graveyard sneaking-past, whistling.

"As you wish, sir." I soaked a bandage with pale green fluid. "Third, hold this over his face. Lightly! He has to breathe it."

The patient went under in seconds. "Third, Captain, watch me close in case there are questions later."

The Third narrowly avoided messing himself. He got the subtext.

I started. I talked while I worked. "Do Goblin and One-Eye being missing have anything to do with our beetle-infested weasels?"

No reply.

"There is something going on. I'm not blind."

"They could be up to something illegal," the Captain said, carefully. "More likely, though, you're seeing something because you want to."

The Third protested, "They were just trying to get the straight skinny on Two Dead and Buzzard Neck. Those two aren't what you think. Goblin remembers Buzz from the Battle at Charm."

I suffered a half-ass flashback to my nightmare. It did not affect my work. That was old, familiar labor. I can hack off a limb while dead drunk or ready to collapse from exhaustion.

The Captain shrugged. He knew something but he was playing it close.

When is the battlefield not a battlefield? The enemy of my enemy is what and who?

When did those two wizards turn invisible? Right after Two Dead showed up. Because of Buzz? Was Buzz something more than just Two Dead's lifeguard?

All this family drama and our empire still controls half the world.

The Lady loves the chaos. While her underlings are backstabbing and undercutting one another they are too busy to move on her. She can focus on keeping her husband underground.

The Old Man wakened me again. "Going to sleep your life away?" He did not roll out the old saw about sleeping all I wanted after I was dead. He made a hand sign. Four men shifted an unconscious Buzz from a litter to a table.

I asked, "What was that?"

"What was what?"

"Thought I heard wind chimes. Really faint."

"Maybe you're still dreaming."

Crap! I had been. The nightmare. The Lady was in there with somebody who moved in wind-chime tinkle . . . *Was* it a dream? Or something from the Tower? The Lady does touch me strangely, at the oddest of times.

No matter. I was awake now. It was gone, and what was happening in the waking world seemed less rational than any dream. I had cooked up a fresh stew of weird ideas while I was off in slumberville.

I had a client. "Couldn't you clean him up before you brought him in? I'll need a month to air the place out."

Buzz might have been belly-up now if I had not worked on him earlier. His situation was that grim.

Otto, Hagop, Corey, and Minkus Scudd had carried Buzz in. The kids were dead on their feet. Minkus told me, "I tried to keep him hydrated but anything that I put in the top end came out the bottom like there was a pipe straight through."

"Let me check some stuff."

Buzz's pulse was fast and feeble. His temperature was fierce. I peeled back an eyelid. His pupil was a pinpoint. That did not add up. I smelled his breath, risky even when a patient is healthy considering the general disdain for hygiene. I said, "Poke." Surprised.

I harvested a crop of blank looks.

"It's everywhere in the fall. A big, waxy-leafed plant that has shiny purple berries in bunches like grapes. They're poisonous. But they taste so bad that you shouldn't be able to choke down enough to do this."

Minkus Scudd asked, "So how did he get past the first mouthful, boss?"

That would be the question. "I've never actually seen poke poisoning but I'm sure this is it. Maybe it started out as something else. He didn't smell like poke before. There are stains on his lips that weren't there before. Somebody forced the juice down him." He must have been dead unconscious. Even a groggy Buzzard Neck would be hard to force.

I saw nobody looking so innocent that he must be guilty but the question was less who done it than why did he do it. Nobody hated Buzz.

Was the point to eliminate Two Dead's guardian?

I set Buzz up so we could dump fluids in as fast as they left. I ran the extra bodies out. I turned sleepy again. The Captain observed. The Third assisted me, sort of. Minkus Scudd snored his lungs out on a cot I wanted for me. Two Dead barely breathed on, awash in painkillers.

The Old Man asked, "You had a good dream? That why you want to get back to sleep?"

All I had left was a lingering nostalgia. "It was something about the Lady and the Tower."

"You don't usually dream about her, do you?"

When I was the Lady's prisoner I spent a lot of time around her, and that has cost me years of merciless teasing.

"I don't. No. Why?"

"Maybe she was trying to tell you something."

"Maybe," I admitted, reluctantly. The Lady randomly and wickedly flings fuel into the fire by contacting me.

"Remember what you can while there's something to recall."

"Too late, boss. It's gone. Only . . . Buzz was in it somewhere. He had on a smiley mask."

"Really? And us without a wizard to hypnotize you."

He *wanted* the Lady to have sent me a dream. "If Goblin was here we could make him channel the message." Rough on Goblin but I do not mind. That makes for less strain on me. And *he* does not get accused of inappropriate fraternization when she uses him.

Two Dead groaned. The knockout painkillers were wearing off. I checked the seepage through his dressing. "I've had the same nightmare every night since the wizards disappeared."

"But you didn't say anything even though *she* was in them."

"*Because* she was in them."

"Yes. Let us not deliver live ammunition into the hands of anyone who might tease us. Is there a connection?"

"Maybe." I had had no such suspicion before. We all dream. Sometimes we have nightmares. Those seldom make sense, what little we recall. I never thought that mine meant anything special. Now I got it. She had wanted to tell me something but I would not listen.

It had been a busy double dozen hours since Zhorab whispered, "Flies," the hours fat with events boasting an almost dreamlike lack of dynamic structure.

Two Dead lapsed into a deeper sleep after I applied another pad soaked green.

. . .

The door opened. Cold and snow and Elmo burst in to bellow, "Look what I caught me this time."

He had a groggy Goblin by the scruff. The little toad sagged there, cross-eyed, his pupils not right. "What's wrong with him?"

"I thumped him some to make him cooperate. He maybe has a little concussion." Thumping recalcitrants was in Elmo's job description.

Some folks find Goblin or One-Eye getting thumped a blessed notion.

The wizard rasped, "He didn't have no call to attack me. I was on my way here anyways."

Nobody swallowed that.

The Captain demanded, "Where you been? And why? Take into consideration my current lack of tolerance for your customary bullshit."

I checked Buzz again, then moved in on Goblin.

His eyes uncrossed. His little turd brain began to function, sort of. "The Lady touched me." He gave me an ugly look. "I was happy out there in my cave. But here she came because her honey bear was always asleep or drunk when she tried to get with him. I run off because when Chodroze turned up I remembered his sidekick from Charm. Him and me went eye-to-eye and claw-to-claw back then."

Buzz was on the other side, then? Not a window-rattling reveal. Others had shifted allegiance in preference to getting dead, Whisper herself included. I had helped set her up. She has nurtured an unreasonable animosity ever since.

Goblin said, "I needed privacy. I had to dip into the demon realms to winkle out the truth."

The Old Man made an impatient "Come on!" gesture.

"I also wanted out of sight so Tesch wouldn't remember me." He would not have forgotten having gone head-to-head with a wizard who was still with the Company. "Back then he was called Essentially Capable Shiiraki, the Spellsmith."

I remembered that odd name. "I thought he went into the mass grave with all the other Rebel wizards."

"His family thought so, too. But I found a surviving familiar who knew the real story. Adequately motivated, it barfed up the details."

"Adequately motivated?" the Old Man asked.

"I told it I wouldn't report it to the Lady. Seeing as how it had gone to the Tower once before, after the fighting, it was not inclined to go again."

I understood that sentiment.

"So what *is* going on?" the Old Man demanded. "You having had a heart-to-heart with this friendly devil."

"It's complicated and insane. Chodroze thinks he was sent here to see if we've already found the Port of Shadows. He's supposed to destroy it if he can. Messing with us would be a bonus. But Tesch had a darker mission. He was supposed to kill Chodroze and frame the Company for it, then get hold of the Port of Shadows. *Not* to destroy it. And he had orders to take out the Company leadership if he got the chance."

I blurted, "Buzz was supposed to murder Two Dead?"

"Chodroze must've made Whisper really unhappy."

Two Dead was a longtime favorite of Whisper. "She is one vindictive bitch."

She had loathed the world with smoldering fury from the moment she had become Taken. That made her one of the most powerful beings on earth—but it made her a slave of the Lady at the same time.

My drowsiness fled. "Two Dead could be the good guy? Buzz might be the villain?" Everything I had worked out had to be wrong. "Where does One-Eye fit?"

The Captain leaned in, daring Goblin to be less than completely forthright.

"I don't know anymore. He stuck with me at the start, but he grabbed his poison sack and vanished after Tesch called up the infested *chinkami*. He knew what they were. Don't ask me how. The little turd knows way too much shit that nobody ought to. He said we would be in the shit really deep after the cold weather broke. That's the last we saw of him."

The Captain asked, "You got that from the Lady?"

"Mostly I figured it out. She only touched me because her honey wouldn't listen. Going to suck to be you, Croaker. Your woman ain't happy with you." He grinned, showing teeth in desperate need of cleaning.

Why worry? She was weather. I would suffer through. "Instructive, though, eh? Her knowing what's going on out here when she's denned up a thousand miles away?" Some of us have trouble remembering what she can do.

The Old Man observed, "What is instructive is that while she sees every sparrow fall she mainly just lets them go *plop!* People like Whisper keep digging deeper holes by going right on pulling stupid tricks. They'll cry hard when she finally brings the hammer down."

That was long-winded for him. Remarkable things must be going on inside his head.

He fixed Goblin with his hard stare. "Tell me again, magic munchkin. Where is One-Eye? What is he up to?" He gestured. Elmo moved over to wrangle the Third when the questioning turned to him. "What's the blowback likely to be once HQ hears that Buzz and Two Dead screwed the pooch?"

Goblin shuffled. "Some major ass-covering. Tesch will turn out to be some deep-cover Rebel mole. Chodroze was always a loose ballista who let personal grudges color his judgment. It will be all our fault, somehow."

I observed, "Same old same old. How about if they both survive? Will that shift the battlefield under everybody's feet?"

"You pull them through, we could see some wicked real excitement down the road. *She* might even show an interest."

The Captain said, "I don't doubt that. We're the cow flop she uses to distract the flies out here."

Yes. Our big boss was running a long con. This was another knot in the cord. I said, "I *will* save them."

"Standing around with your thumb in your ass?" The Old Man turned to Elmo. "Have him show you where he was supposed to take that food." He indicated the Third. "One-Eye will be there. Hurt him if you have to but don't break him. I want him helping Croaker. Goblin. You're Croaker's boy till Buzz and Two Dead are healthy enough to dance at his wedding."

. . .

Elmo and crew found One-Eye snoozing in a derelict shack on the edge of town. They got his head in a sack and his hands tied behind him before he could bark. Nobody came out of it needing splints or stitches.

The Old Man was in a foul humor. He stood back, iron gaze fixed while One-Eye received the Word. The little black man wasted no time getting his shit together. "Focus on Shiiraki. We can't do anything more for Chodroze except maybe add a slider spell to fight infection."

"Goblin did that. Laid on a sleeper, too. Minkus can handle him. You fed Buzz poke juice?"

"After the *firenz* he got in some wine that he thought would help with the shits. You can't taste *firenz* in sweet wine. It just gives you a stronger buzz. Blackberry is the best."

And it was the same color as poke juice. "The juice disguised the real poison?"

"Yep. He got drunk and then did a major stupid. He was already messed up with the shits." Not exactly confessing. He ransacked my medicine stocks while he talked. "Here it is." He held up a phial of dirty brown powder. "This will neutralize the *firenz*. The poke will take care of itself, you put enough liquid through."

I did not know what *firenz* was. A poison, clearly. As Goblin did note, One-Eye knew a lot that nobody should. Came of being older than dirt, mostly.

The Old Man reminded One-Eye, "They need to pull through. The Tower is watching. The Tower wants it to happen."

Wind chimes sang on cue, louder than ever. Everyone heard, not just the poor crazy Annalist. A lightning-bug flash in a corner turned into an expanding O ring of sparkle that reached a foot and a half in diameter. A dark-haired, to-die-for beautiful brunette teen looked out at us. She smiled a smile that lighted up the universe. She winked at me and pursed her lips in an air kiss that I would hear about forever. Then she faded without having said a word, leaving a tinkle, a hint of lilac, an impression that someone had watched from behind her, and a message clearly delivered to her favorite band of bad boys.

"Oh, my!" One-Eye blurted because the Lady had considered him directly and deliberately before flirting with me.

He had to improve his sense of discipline. And he would. For a while. But he was, is, and always will be, One-Eye. He cannot be anything else.

He bustled around Buzz with Goblin and the Third helping. I decided to step outside. I had been too long safe from clean air.

It was daytime out there, still not thirty hours since Zhorab whispered "Flies." Snow no longer fell but the wind remained busy. It was warmer. The ground had begun to turn to mud. The world felt changed. Definitely not new but forever changed.

The Captain joined me. "I don't know what's happened but we have stumbled into a fresh new future."

"It's that line. When is the battlefield not a battlefield? We'll win one big-time without lifting a blade if those two survive."

"When."

"Yes sir. When."

"A handy friend, Two Dead. He's almost Taken caliber but less subject to outside control. Buzzard Neck could be a useful badass, too."

"We should seduce them."

"We keep them alive, they're ours. *She* is counting on us, Croaker. Stuff like this is going to keep happening. When is the enemy not an enemy? When it's your friend patting your back with one hand while sticking a dagger between your ribs with the other."

"I'd best get back in there and supervise." It would not be impossible for One-Eye to precipitate a lethal mishap if there was something he thought needed hiding.

"Yes. No doubt One-Eye already thinks he sees some clever way to turn himself a profit." The Old Man clasped my left shoulder, touching me directly for only the third or fourth time in all the years we have known one another. "You played your part well. Go win us a brace of new magicians."

Yes. So. No direct confession, but . . . He had been part of a scheme with roots in the Tower. Somehow. Maybe *he* was the one romancing the crone.

"I'm on it, boss."

10

Once Upon a Time: Stormy Night

The necromancer worked every day till he collapsed. Then he would sleep for a few hours, often in his workroom, after which he would get back to work, inevitably to be disappointed again.

Nothing he tried took him over the final hurdle. Death had its talons into Laissa and would not to turn loose. It could only be held at bay, but not permanently. And, every time he beat it back, he became more attached to the girl, and more determined to become her salvation.

The man who dragged a corpse out of a canal would have been appalled by the entanglement of the man who had lived with her for two months. She was now family. She was close to becoming a lover, not in a carnal sense. Though maybe someday . . .

The mission he had set himself, conquest of the ultimate, had become much more than an experiment.

He did not understand. But he had no idea who his Laissa had been.

It was part of what she was, bred in the bone. Anyone exposed for any extended time could not help but love her.

. . .

A stormy night. The thunder frightened Laissa. Each furious crash wrung another whimper from the child. She needed comforting. The necromancer sealed his workroom, settled into his one comfortable stuffed chair, held her in his lap while the gods contended for dominion of the night. Out back the horses and hogs raised their voices in protest. Laissa clung closer, shaking. For the first time since she had come to his house the necromancer became aware of her as a woman. So she, in her position, should not help but be aware that he was aroused—though she seemed not to recognize what that meant.

He wrestled ferocious temptation, knowing full well that he could get away with whatever he chose to do. She knew no better.

The mastiffs howled in counterpoint to the hogs and horses. The necromancer started. The dogs never howled. They never barked. He had thought that they could not. No other storm ever inspired them to complain. Then, in midsong, they did go silent.

Distracted, the girl never reacted to the necromancer's arousal in any fashion.

The necromancer paid the mastiffs no heed. Neither did he note a whiff of sorcery that tainted the rowdy night for an instant after the howling stopped. He did not, however, overlook the monstrous blast of light and thunder without any lag that rocked his house to its foundations. Something crashed in his workroom. Laissa clutched him so tight that it hurt. The wicked thoughts deserted him. This was his child. This was his daughter. He rocked her and crooned a poorly recalled fragment of childhood lullaby.

The storm moved on. Laissa did not. The necromancer thought he ought to go to his workroom to check for damage. He ought to check on the livestock, too. But this moment was so pleasant . . . He realized that Laissa was warm. Not full life warm but more warm than ever he had felt her before.

They fell asleep there, snuggled together, as the great storm ambled on.

11

Long Ago and Far Away: Oblivion Fall

The Howler's carpet rocked and staggered in the gust front of a truly savage storm. He raced the wind, dropped lower. A scraggly stick of an arm extended to point out the clearing where, now months ago, he had spotted a coach standing unattended on the night that Dorotea had vanished.

Tonight's adventure was based on evidence no better than that and some wishful thinking.

This was the only lead developed since that night—and, probably, was not any lead at all. The Senjak girls were grasping at straws.

Howler orbited the clearing a hundred yards outside its bounds, saw nothing of obvious interest, though two massive dogs did come from somewhere to stand watching the carpet, their teeth bared. Howler had to use second sight to see them. They did the same right back. Howler said, "There might be sorcery here, Bathdek."

"No might be about it. I smell it. It's a dark, dark magic."

The gust front caught up. Thunder and lightning galloped in close behind. Howler grounded his carpet under the canopy of a massive oak. From there he and Bathdek studied the setting, in particular the gap in the palisade surrounding the ramshackle house. Bathdek whined because the second sight became so damned painful when lightning flashed.

The mastiffs stood two yards behind the gap, teeth bared, focused on the carpet riders, indifferent to the rain, which brought a few hailstones along.

At ground level the sorceries saturating the hilltop were more obvious than they were from above. The warding spells were so finely wrought, so well woven together, that even an adept of the Ten failed to sense them until too late to deal with them without becoming catastrophically unsubtle.

Somebody was determined to be well protected while attracting no attention from casual passersby.

That somebody would be a rogue sorcerer of remarkable skill and talent, of that sort that the Dominator was determined to enslave or exterminate because they might someday challenge his mastery. This would be a bold one, too, to have remained so near Dusk.

Howler dragged his carpet into better shelter under an immense chestnut tree. The ground there would stay dry a long while. He sort of folded himself into a small package, like a spider wrapping itself in its legs, sleepily announced, "I will wait here." Balled up like that he could not get much breath behind his screams.

Bathdek approached the palisade. The air raged around her, hurling leaves and twigs, yanking at her clothes like an impatient lover. Continued study showed her that any attempt to breach the barrier spells would trigger alarms.

The silent mastiffs watched her from behind the gap, daring her to mount an invasion.

The rain arrived, one drop, two drops, deliver me a hundred and a deluge. Bathdek hated the sudden cold wet but it did present an opportunity.

She carried a potent suite of ready spells impressed on what looked like fortune-telling cards. She selected one, caressed it, kissed it, whispered secrets to it. When the moment seemed ripe she flicked it through the palisade.

Lightning and thunder arrived together, violently. Bathdek staggered backward twenty feet, fell on her bottom in the wet, finding herself almost entirely deaf. She must be all right, though. Uncle Howler never uncurled. He would have if she was in any real danger.

She was a Senjak sister, just sixteen but already able to manipulate anything with a penis with no deliberate thought.

She got her feet under her and stumbled forward. The protective spells were gone. A dozen feet of palisade to either hand had vanished as well. A few shattered stakes still smoldered.

The mastiffs sprawled in blasted death, one broken open and spilled, the other burned to the bone and steaming. Newly sprouted vegetable and herb patches to either hand had suffered badly, too.

The rain recovered its earlier vigor.

Bathdek figured she looked a disaster herself. She would make use of that. She stumbled to the house, tried the latch. The door opened. She stepped inside. A savage gust slammed her in the back, drove her forward while throwing sheets of water in behind her. "Help me," she whimpered as she went down.

The place was dimly lighted by two spirit lamps. It smelled of putrefaction and chemicals. Bathdek gagged as she tried to push herself off the filthy floor. She added to the filth as feet in tattered slippers approached.

She let herself collapse. She moaned, "Help . . ." She rolled onto her left side.

The man was nondescript, not worth a second glance in public. He wore a plain, threadbare brown robe. His expression betrayed both confusion and fear. His mouth moved but either no sound came out or her hearing had not yet begun to recover.

The man gave up trying to communicate. He went to the open door, leaned into the weather. A volley of hail bounced in past him. Gripping the doorframes with either hand he leaned out farther, peered around, still mightily confused. Apparently he saw nothing that troubled him more than he already was.

Bathdek made another effort to prize herself off the floor. She discovered that she truly did not have the strength.

She thought about just sliding into sleep, to buy sympathy, but that would leave her at the mercy of a complete unknown. She could not withstand a physical search. But for those cards she could be some stupid girl who had gotten lost in the woods just in time to get beaten up by a furious storm.

The man must be a master sorcerer. He could not help but recognize the nature of her deck, though the level of sorcery required for their creation and manipulation would be well beyond him.

The sorcerer closed the door thoughtfully, latched and barred it. There would be no more surprise intrusions. Bathdek felt some leakage as he deployed previously prepared spells to reinforce his privacy. Those were robust but Uncle Howler would be able to break past them—if he was able to see past them and recognize that she needed rescuing.

The sorcerer stood with his back to the door, shoulders slumped. He frowned unhappily. He was looking her way but did not appear to be looking at her.

He was trying to decide what to do.

Bathdek whimpered. That was not all drama.

She became aware of dirty bare feet a yard away. A girl's feet. A girl who dropped down onto her hams and stared at Bathdek as though she had seen nothing of the like before. She was dirty all over. She wore rags that might have been the sorcerer's castoffs. She was quite pretty, for all that. A bath and a smile would leave her striking.

Bathdek croaked, "Dor . . . Dor." She tried to reach out.

She had found her missing sister. Or maybe her missing sister's ghost. Or fetch. Something that was Dorotea's body in peasant filth and rags that might not have Dorotea inside.

She should hide the fact that she knew Dorotea.

Dorotea seemed entirely astounded by the discovery that there were people in this world other than herself and the man with whom she lived.

Bathdek had lost every ounce of the confident drive that had brought her out here. Partly that was because she realized that there was something badly wrong happening now. She should not be this weak. She should be able to jump up and deal with the renegade sorcerer, then hustle Dorotea off to Howler and the carpet. Worse, she ought to be able, in the ugliest circumstances, to touch her great-uncle with a plea for help.

She could do none of those things.

The sorcerer reached a decision. He came toward her, saying something. Dorotea, with hair longer than before and tangled, looked slightly disappointed. She rose and shuffled away.

The sorcerer pulled a rickety stool over, settled, stared at Bathdek, clearly troubled but more composed than he had been just minutes earlier. He spoke, probably asking a question. Bathdek had just enough strength to brush her ear and shake her head.

She was beginning to be afraid. She had jumped without knowing where she was going to land, which was in an epic tangle of subtle sorcery, spells camouflaged by or as other spells, spells that were only there to misdirect . . . The totality had to be the creation of a mad genius driven by paranoia, an artist who had had countless lonely years to perfect his treacheous protections.

She could not summon her uncle. She could not warn him. . . .

The sorcerer considered her for a moment more, then nodded. He set his right palm on her forehead. His hand was hot. Oblivion claimed Bathdek. It fell so suddenly and gently that she was gone before she understood that there might be something to resist.

12

In Modern Times: Mischievous Rain

Gurdlief Speak wrapped up a folktale about the revenge of a village orphan sacrificed during hard times. He made her sympathetic, a victim instead of the usual evil revenant.

The kid could put a unique spin on any story.

Gurdlief was an orphan himself, though unacquainted with hardship. All Aloe served as his parents. His destined sacrifice was to become a celibate priest of Occupoa. At ten he found that fate unappealing already.

Orphans featured in many of the stories Gurdlief traded for access to the Company compound. The Captain reckoned him to be a spy. I figured he wanted to weasel his way in so nobody would squawk if he tagged along when the Company moved on. Which did not matter, really. Our secrets were few and inconsequential. And he did not eat much.

As we entered the compound, Gurdlief told me, "Once there was a girl called Lilac Shade. She was the prettiest girl in her village and really popular after she got old enough for boys to notice."

I gave him a look askance. He was not that old himself, though boy-girl stuff was no mystery to Aloens. Local attitudes were quite relaxed.

Gurdlief skipped to keep up. I was in a hurry. I was running late. The crowd at my town clinic had held me up. Every kid within five leagues had a dripping nose. Gurdlief was no exception. The pestilence did not bother native adults. It made children and outsiders miserable but did not kill them. It just made you *want* to die. I had enjoyed my dose already.

A baker's dozen of surly clients awaited me at the compound clinic. It included all of the usual malingerers.

It was a chilly, blustery day. Cotton wads scooted westward overhead. We had passed winter's nadir but the locals insisted that the gods were only teasing us with empty promises of spring. I had mixed feelings. Better weather meant less shivering but also heralded the campaign season. I prefer sitting on my ass, doing garrison duty.

I was not alone in figuring that our Aloen holiday was nearing its end. Unease lurked everywhere. Ages had passed since last the Lady used us. The more she held us back the deeper and stinkier the next pool of shit was likely to be.

Men drilled and exercised on the parade ground, hardly grumbling, inspired by self-interest. The Company might be on the move again, soon. There might be hazards to survive.

Gurdlief and I were approaching headquarters when we heard wind chimes, clear and sweet, from everywhere and nowhere, just barely this side of audibility. Rat-footed dread tramped my spine. I turned slowly but saw only pale-faced comrades also looking for the source of the sound.

The Lady?

Who else?

Damn, Croaker! How come you have to think about her? Thought alone might summon the attention of that horror.

Wind chimes tinkled again, louder.

A flying carpet drifted down, into the shade beside Admin. A woman stood atop that carpet, which was wildly colored and iridescent, like peacock feathers. The multihued fabric had been stretched onto a boxy wooden frame twelve feet long, eight feet wide, and one foot high. Bags, boxes, and trunks cluttered the carpet. The woman tinkled in the breeze. She tinkled when she moved. She tinkled when she breathed.

Gurdlief murmured, "One of the Taken." Awed.

One of them. Yes. Absolutely. Had to be. Beyond any doubt. But which? I did not know this one, though I thought that I had seen them all.

"A new one."

New. Of course. Astonishingly pretty, too, though I could hardly tear my attention away from her yukata, which was blacker than any worldly black, black with no surface, like the zenith on a cloudless night. It contained a million remote lights shining in a thousand pastel colors.

The chimes turned orchestral as she stepped down from the carpet. A gust tossed her hair in streamers as black as her clothing, but shining. Her hair included several intensely scarlet streaks. A silver and lapis lazuli butterfly clip sat at the root of the boldest red stripe. She was as slim as a maiden but her face suggested past strains beyond those of any maiden's years.

So, truth absolute. She was Taken. She had gone to the Tower. She had come out of the Tower a bespoke servant of shadow.

Nobody moved to greet her. Nobody doubted what she was, either, though no Taken had visited us in months. The Limper had been the last.

She turned my way, frowned slightly, then smiled just as the sun sneaked out from behind a cloud. Its light kissed her. Her face suddenly seemed coated with white makeup on which thin blue lines had been sketched. The light faded before I got a good look. Then I got distracted by the cat that ambled out of her shadow.

It was a three-eyed cat. You do not see many of those. It was as black as her hair. The rationally placed eyes were yellow—except when they looked straight at you. Then they became a pale lilac rose, and glowed. The third eye, above and between, was a slit visible only from straight ahead. It shone crimson for a moment, then purple.

Alley kitty, not. It was longer and skinnier, in an adolescent female sort of way, than any normal cat, but it would prove to be all male.

Its gaze was almost hypnotic.

I focused on the girl. The woman. She seemed familiar. She floated my way. Gurdlief gurgled his admiration. Thirty additional witnesses rendered worshipful agreement and thunderous lust.

The cat did cat stuff, trying to get between the Taken's ankles.

She stopped in front of me, inclined her head slightly, met my eye. "Thank you, Annalist."

Another cloud unmasked the sun. The Taken cast her own hard shadow again. From behind her, to either hand, came children, twins, her miniatures, a boy to her right, a girl to her left. They might be six years old. The boy looked as crabby as an old veteran whose wounds tormented him in winter. The girl had devilment in her eyes. She flashed me a grin and a wink while her mother's face whitened. The tattoos I saw now were not the ones that I had seen just moments ago.

I was too distracted to care.

"My children." The Taken laid a palm atop the boy's head. "Beloved Shin." Then the girl. "Blessed Baku. But we call her Firefly."

The boy sneered. "Baka is more like it."

The Taken snapped, "Ankou! Friend!" at the cat, which had begun to stalk me, tail lashing, teeth exposed, those more numerous and sharper than any installed in your standard mouser. It backed away, resumed trying to trip the Taken.

"Mischievous Rain," she said, as though reading my mind. I flashed back to another Taken who had had the mind-reading knack, the demon Soulcatcher. "I was once Tides Elba."

Not possible. That was only half a year ago. That Tides Elba had had no children.

The crowd expanded fast. The Captain and Candy, along with Elmo and some other noncoms, clustered outside the headquarters entrance, uniformly grim. For unfathomed dour, though, nobody exceeded the renegade wizards Two Dead and Buzzard Neck.

Gurdlief observed, "The wicked flee where no man pursues."

Two Dead and Buzz had plenty on their consciences and not half a sense of humor between them. The Taken's appearance might mean trouble over them having deserted Whisper and the Eastern Army—notwithstanding the fact that they had been expected to get themselves killed while trying to sabotage the Company.

Mischievous Rain ignored them, as she did the arrivals of our other sorcerers. She just glided closer to me, settling a gloved right hand an inch above my left elbow, gently. Wind chimes sang all round.

Gurdlief wanted to stick with me. He was for sure an Annalist-in-waiting, determined to be the witnessing eye. But he went to his knees, suddenly. I failed to notice that. It happened behind me. He told me later that it felt like his feet got nailed to the ground, after which several tons of weight pressed down on his shoulders.

Plenty of other feet got nailed, as well. Minds went too numb to move bodies. I stumbled toward Admin while the gallery gawked, Mischievous Rain beside me. Candy and the Old Man stepped aside, then followed us in. Working staff began leaving immediately. They claimed that the chimes told them to go. It did not occur to them to refuse.

The Taken knew her way around. Nothing had changed since she was Tides Elba. She headed for the Old Man's cluster of crude furniture, where she eschewed the seat of honor, the Old Man's big plank armchair. She gestured at the seats normally occupied by him and Candy and the Lieutenant, who missed the moment because he was off leading a recon-in-force.

The Old Man and Candy settled. Candy fidgeted. The Captain betrayed no special interest. He had a knack. He could make the Lady herself unsure that she was of any actual consequence.

The Taken squeezed my arm, then rose on her toes to kiss my cheek. "Thanking you for before. But not the part with the hand." Then she kissed me again, nearer my mouth, warmer, holding it a bit longer. I wondered why I had skipped shaving. "That is from the One Who Binds Us All."

Chimes sang. Mischievous? You bet. Two witnesses only, both infernally laconic, but word would get out. I could expect a major ration of shit.

Why did the Lady torment me so?

Though nearly lost in my inner wilderness I managed a moment of curiosity. "What happened to the kids?" They were nowhere to be seen. And the devil Ankou had gone missing, too.

"They are with me." She clung to my arm almost possessively.

The Captain asked, "You have come back because?" A sudden raging show of impatience for him.

"I am here to seal the Port of Shadows. Someone will try to open the way. You will help me stop them."

I blurted, "But weren't you . . . ?"

The Old Man gave me a hearty scowl. "You are here to witness and record." Not to comment. Not to participate. Naturally. That should not need saying. I bobbed my head and sealed my lips.

One more blurt and I would be outside witnessing the weather in progress.

Mischievous Rain said, "Perhaps then. Not now. That nightmare destiny has passed. We must find out where it has gone."

So. Our immediate future featured a hunt for some other wretched witchy girl unwillingly conscripted by the supernatural. Oh joy, for us. And, oh, so much sorrow for her.

There would be fighting. Those invested in the Port of Shadows and the Dominator's resurrection would struggle with all their hearts to find him a way to return to the living world.

The Old Man nailed me with a piercing look as my traitorous mouth watered with questions that would have to go unasked.

I received a gentle, reassuring squeeze to my right arm.

I confess to having developed a bad attitude as I become ever more certain that my importance as Company Annalist exceeds that of my role as Company physician. Gifted with free time most days, I have immersed myself in local history and folklore, a passion understood by no one else. A passion that, I admit, borders on addiction.

The hobby pays occasional dividends. The Captain indulges me because my research leaves me less time to spend at the Dark Horse, where too often I become too wasted to function as a physician.

Nobody likes sorcery. Most of us, especially those in charge, believe literacy equals sorcery. Things written down are less than ideally mutable. It is hard to weasel out from under recorded facts. What is written on the wind can be revised or denied at one's leisure.

The Taken released me. I oozed away, putting myself beyond easy reach. She was amused.

Candy said, "The Company will, of course, assist you in whatever fashion you require." Like a condemned man offering final thoughts.

"Of course you will. That is why I am here. You are her most dutiful and faithful sons." Wind chimes tinkled. Laughing? Mocking? Cynical old fart me, I assumed the latter.

Most dutiful and faithful could be right. The Taken are no more faithful than they need to be to survive. They plot and conspire, collude and cautiously rebel, every one a fallen angel who has not fallen far. We, the Company, have shown ourselves to be a tool less likely to turn in the Lady's hand.

Our continued fortune depends entirely on her constant favor. We have made ourselves some powerful and abiding enemies amongst the stumbled angels.

Candy and the Old Man, each with hands folded on the table before him, still as death, eyed the new Taken, and waited. I waited, too, wishing I could manage their calm.

This was only a meet and greet but already I was all fidgets and pounding heart.

Mischievous Rain could have played their game and waited them out. She was having fun in a quiet, internalized way. I had not known her well when she was Tides Elba so was not convinced that this Mischievous Rain was anything like a new personality.

Still, she had been inside the Tower long enough to have been rebuilt.

"We will begin the hunt once the weather turns. Meantime, I will get to know you here in order to understand whose skills can be used in what fashion, given the demands of the moment. And I will develop a more efficient intelligence program. For now, though, I need to be assigned quarters. Fancy isn't necessary. Spacious is. I must have room for my work and room for my family." Slight pause. "I'll need a place to lie down soon. I'm exhausted. A long carpet trip with children takes it out of a girl."

We had no place that suited her, and no space lying fallow. Even the Old Man did not live in a luxury grander than having a private room—which was just large enough to house a bed and two chests.

Mischievous Rain mentioned that she had brought money.

The Old Man promptly announced, "We can build you whatever you need. Shouldn't take long if we can pull the materials together."

Candy got him a sorry, snarky look that he aimed my way. "Croaker has a place in town. He won't mind if you use that until we get something thrown up. He can bunk in at his clinic here, which is what he's supposed to be doing anyway."

I dared not respond but, boy, did I want to. My hole-in-the-wall in town had caused contention from the start. Candy was obsessed with the risks of me spending nights outside the safety of the compound. I considered Aloe completely tamed. Plus the place was close to my free clinic and even closer to the Dark Horse.

The Captain blessed me with a brilliant smile. "An elegant, combined arms solution to multiple problems, First Officer."

Mischievous Rain did not cooperate. "I would prefer to avoid town, gentlemen."

They did not argue. It takes a special sort of insanity to squabble with the Taken. The Old Man said, "Look around, then. See what will do for temporary. Then do tell me what you're going to need. We'll throw you up a place purpose-built."

Just free and easy and the soul of cooperation, our Captain. He lived to serve his masters.

Something was perking in the shadowed deeps of his mind.

"Croaker, give the lady the tour. Make her feel at home."

I glanced at Mischievous Rain. She winked. She knew a game when she smelled one.

Or maybe she was just flirting, the old perv within dreamed.

The woman *was* a tasty morsel.

. . .

The Taken and I were a dozen steps into daylight when the weird cat Ankou blew past us, headed for the pigeons working the verges of the drill ground. Her children were right behind the cat.

"Where the hell were they?" I blurted.

"Hidden in the shadows." Her smile felt less genuine than its predecessors had been.

Blessed Baku ran with her eyes shut. She crashed into Gurdlief Speak at full speed. Gurdlief had just turned to watch the streaking cat. He toppled onto his belly in some mud, then suffered the further indignity of having a small girl crash down on top of him, cooties and all.

Beloved Shin neither slowed nor looked back.

"Firefly, you need to watch where you're going." Mischievous Rain sounded like every mother of every small child ever. Smirking, she asked, "Isn't that odd? One of the Taken being domestic instead of all thunder and pestilence."

"It is disconcerting."

Her smile had no strain in it now.

A breeze wandered by. Mischievous Rain tinkled as she brushed her daughter off. I expected the kid to put on a big pout and produce a double ration of tears. My expectations were disappointed.

The girl did eye Gurdlief like she was wondering whether to murder him or marry him.

I thought it was cute. Gurdlief thought it was creepy. Mischievous Rain pretended not to notice.

The Taken completed her ministrations. "Be more careful, dear. There are a lot more people here than there were back home."

Firefly had her right hand up behind her head, her body turning back and forth, kind of chagrined, not meeting her mother's eye, bashful. She nodded.

Mischievous Rain considered Gurdlief. "Gurdlief Speak?"

"Yes, ma'am?" How did she know his name? From back when? He was officially a temple orphan.

He had not yet recognized today's Mischievous Rain as yesterday's temple girl, Tides Elba, transformed.

"Gurdlief, I apologize for my daughter."

"It's all right, ma'am. She's just a kid."

"True enough. And with that being true, and with this being an alien environment for her, might I ask a major favor of you?"

"Uh . . ." Reluctantly. Gurdlief Speak believed that adults invariably wanted more than he ought to have to give. "I guess." Stated with totally underwhelming enthusiasm.

"Just keep an eye on them. Make sure they don't fall down a well or jump off a roof to see if they can fly. They aren't used to all this much outdoors."

"Uh . . . All right?" He looked to me.

I said, "Sounds like a good idea. Keep them inside the compound."

Sigh. Thumbs tucked into his waistband, Gurdlief went after Blessed Baku, who had gone a short distance, then had stopped to wait.

Beloved Shin was nowhere to be seen.

With Gurdlief and Firefly out of earshot Mischievous Rain said, "It will be good for them to be around someone nearer their own age."

"You may have picked the wrong kid, though. Gurdlief thinks he's twenty-five."

"Then they will be good for him, too. So show me around, Annalist. Just the essentials. And catch me if I drop."

She did sound as tired as she made out earlier.

We threw some cots into the armory, which Mischievous Rain insisted would be adequate. The armorers were seriously put out. She would try to stay out of the way during working hours but those boys had mountains of stuff that needed frequent shifting. They were prepping for a campaign season headed our way all too fast.

I did not get included in construction planning. I learned more about that at the Dark Horse than I did during working hours at the compound. Our procurement people had no trouble acquiring materials. And the Taken's war chest apparently had no bottom, though the Old Man seemed determined to find one.

The project kept growing. Mischievous Rain would have herself a rustic palace and the compound would feature its first not mainly adobe structure.

. . .

Goblin brought warning. "One-Eye is looking to score the Taken's war chest, soon as he figures a way to frame Whisper or Two Dead for it."

I asked, "Is he really stupid enough to try that?"

Little old toad-looking Goblin shrugged. "There are no bounds to One-Eye's stupidity. Aloe is driving him crazy. It's too clean and too straight. Relatively speaking."

"Relatively speaking." One-Eye had become self-destructive, generating one lunatic scheme after another, each more mad than the last.

Goblin could, occasionally, be that bad but he did have sense enough not to yank the tiger's tail—which was an order of magnitude less dangerous than would be trying to rob one of the Taken.

Goblin explained, "He figures she's got to be naive because she's so young. He says look how we got one over on the Limper, one of the heavyweight old-time Taken."

"The Limper makes One-Eye look like a genius. He isn't anything but poorly contained urges and emotions unfortunately bound up inside the same package as a raw talent for sorcery of a city-flattening scale. Plus, the Lady covered our asses on the last one." I did not mention my confidence that the Limper would keep coming back until he had satisfied his hunger for revenge. "Mischievous Rain isn't stupid and she isn't on the Lady's shit list. Explain that with a cane if you have to." I tilted a little finger in a field sign. When Goblin could do so casually he took a peek.

Ankou was curled up in a handy shadow, pretending to be napping. But his ears kept twitching.

Our conversation began outside my clinic. It continued as we strolled toward the drill field. Goblin eventually muttered, "That's the weirdest cat that I've ever seen. Hunts down shadows the way most cats go after sunbeams."

"You do know that he's not really a cat, don't you?"

"I am aware. I didn't realize that you got it."

We had not talked much lately. In fact, I had had few conversations with anybody since Mischievous Rain's arrival. She monopolized my time, often to the point of auditing my work during sick call. She did not tag along when I went to town, though. That left me curious about who or what she wanted to avoid.

Her presence was no secret. No way that it could be. Our guys were in and out of town by the hundreds, every day. Some had formed relationships. Others were local recruits who visited their families regularly. If Mischievous Rain's reluctance to go to town *was* about avoiding someone . . . That someone wanted to avoid her, too. No one came looking for her.

When the Taken was not in my pocket herself, Ankou was sure to haunt a shadow nearby. Or the kids would be underfoot.

Goblin observed, "Your girlfriend must really be worried about you cheating on her."

"Makes as much sense as any notion that I've been able to conjure." Killjoy Croaker stealing the wind from the runt's sails, agreeing instead of protesting.

We arrived at the drill field. The pigeons taunted Ankou. There were no shadows into which he could vanish. I made like I was checking to see that there was water enough in the water buckets, a point that I did have to make again and again.

Ankou decided that suffering so much sunshine was not worth the agony if he did not get to kill something. He left. Kids gravitated toward me immediately.

"Warn One-Eye. Make him understand. She's already on to him."

One-Eye is the most valuable man amongst us when the Company stumbles into the deep shit. The rest of the time you want to drown his ass because you know how good it will feel once the pain goes away.

We separated, Goblin going off to confer with his occasional partner in crime, me to check construction progress.

I hoped my situation would become less familial once the Taken had a place of her own. That hope proved vain.

The boss carpenter was grumbling. "More changes. It never ends. It's always more 'Make it bigger!'" The Old Man, not compelled to invest Company funds, refused to be niggardly. Mischievous Rain's new shack would be a major permanent structure that could be handed over to the locals when the Company moved along.

That won us some new friends, as did our profligate spending for materials and craftsmen.

He being him, the Captain doubtless had a reason for letting outsiders roam freely inside the compound. Maybe he wanted Rebel spies thinking that they had eyeballed all of our secrets, although we did not have any, really. Or maybe he just wanted to watch outsiders react to Mischievous Rain and her kids.

She could not avoid notice while determinedly maintaining a death watch over me. I was out and about all the time.

I confess, there were times when I was flattered that people thought this homely old fart was worth the attention.

The day's last would-be malingerer shuffled off, muttering because I had prescribed vigorous exercise. Mischievous Rain tinkled. I had come near forgetting that she was watching. She could be as still and quiet as death. She asked, "How did the in-town clinic go this morning?"

"The cold epidemic has broken." Her kids had not suffered despite regular exposure to Gurdlief Speak. "A few scrapes. A cut that didn't need suturing but that I stitched up anyway to make a point. Boys shouldn't play stupid games with knives."

"So now you're a plague-smashing hero."

"Clever me. I didn't tell them that they'd get over it just as fast without seeing me."

"The essence of the trade, yes? Taking credit for Nature's handiwork."

"Thou art a cynic, woman. A cynic thou art." Then my heart did a flip. I was bantering with one of the Taken.

She showed me her mind reader's smile but said only, "Gurdlief Speak hasn't been around much lately. I had hoped to see more of him."

"Don't be upset. But he thinks your kids are creepy."

She tinkled, not happily. "Why is that?"

"They're supposed to be six years old," though she had yet to define their ages exactly. "But they act older and colder and do weird things."

"They're curious. Children are naturally curious. You must have been a child, once, who wanted to know about things."

"Children are curious. Yes. But normal kids don't squat in one place and watch people do nothing for hours on end. Real kids have no attention span. They go on to the next thing almost as soon as they start whatever they're doing now. Firefly and Shin creep out even old hands like Two Dead and Silent." I held back on Ankou. The demon cat had made himself universally loathed, with no one able to say exactly why.

"The more reason to get them socialized, yes? Before Gurdlief they never met another child."

"How protective will you be?"

Tinkle tinkle. Less angry but definitely still not merry.

I suggested, "Send them into town. The kids there will whip the weird out of them." Actually, they would teach Baku and Shin to keep their weirdness hidden.

"Not a good idea. Another thing they don't know well is self-restraint."

I got that in one. They might be children but they were deadly dangerous junior Taken, too.

"On a separate matter, why are you determined to know every little thing that I do?" There. The question finally asked.

"Excuse me?"

"You, the kids, the cat, one of you is always within a few feet. Always watching."

A quick smile and merry tinkle. "No one was there when you told Goblin to warn One-Eye not to do anything stupid. And you have your trips to town to yourself."

I did not believe that. I had gotten more than one earful about a weird Company cat that would not let anyone approach it.

Mischievous Rain shrugged. That generated an extended rattle of chimes. I wondered how the sound happened, what it meant, and why someone who arrived with luggage enough to stash clothes for a female regiment never wore anything but the one midnight yukata.

She did not explain when I asked. She just looked sad.

I did not understand but I had spent time in the Tower, too. No one comes away unchanged. Mischievous Rain's big problem, I was sure after ten days, was a too-human concern for children there was no reasonable way that she could have borne and brought to their current age.

The hovel the Old Man tossed up for the Taken was a mansion by any standard. It had room for offices she could never use and an absurd acreage of private space as well. There was purpose-provided office space for the Company Annalist even though he was fully satisfied with his cramped little corner in Admin. His space included an apartment where he could nap or overnight if he lacked the ambition to stroll on back to his clinic. And then there was still another two thousand square feet of floored ground-level space that the Company could use any way it wanted.

Mischievous Rain would take up residence on the second floor. The third floor would allow servants to be quartered and junk to be stored.

Two thousand square feet on the ground. The Old Man, that crafty bastard, had made us a shitload of prime indoor space at zero cost to the Company.

Which explained his smugly cooperative attitude.

Even Gurdlief was thrilled. Mischievous Rain had asked for a children's playroom. Gurdlief Speak was welcome to visit whenever he wanted.

On reviewing my recent scribbling I see that I have become more of a historian than a participating observer, more bland, more neutral, less focused on personalities and less concerned about the who, how, and why instead of the what. I am sure that that is a function of the Annalist being compelled to live a sedentary life in a safe environment.

"All right," the Old Man said. "You have five minutes to whine. Begin by explaining why I should give a rat's ass."

"This thing with the Taken. What is it?"

"What thing?"

"You have pushed us together from the moment her feet hit the ground."

"You think so? I don't agree. Availabilities have been provided for convenience's sake. There is no need for you to have . . ."

His remarks went on to make even less sense.

"Some guys are accusing us of living together."

"Ah. Now the real whining begins. Could it be that you are?"

In a strictly literal sense, maybe, since we resided in the same building, but . . . "If that was what I wanted . . . To me it looks like somebody wants to make it happen." I gave him the hard-eye.

A minute passed. The Old Man offered no response. Finally, he did say, "We are all of us obliged to execute the orders that we receive. That's how the soldiering business works." Meaning, maybe, that my discomfiture was being engineered from the Tower.

Maybe. The Old Man was exactly the kind of son of a bitch who would use the Lady as a tool with which to manipulate me. But . . . Why the hell would he? Where was the upside for him?

I was not emotionally prepared to accept the obvious, that he might be thinking the other way round.

Weird shit began happening. Weirder than the usual weird shit.

I began to hear more than normally superstitious muttering. People kept seeing spooks or monsters or spirits. Local folks believed that divinities and spirits inhabited every rock, pond, and tree, and most of those spirits loved nothing so much as messing with their human neighbors. Which could be frustrating when you wanted to do something but the locals held you up for an age while they placated the appropriate spooks.

Aloens could be cold-blooded pragmatic one minute and foaming-at-the-mouth superstitious the next. Even after a year I did not get how it all worked.

Gurdlief Speak, and Markeg Zhorab of the Dark Horse, were my resources for Aloen myth and legend. They were not much help with this.

Paper strips began to appear on doors in town and inside the Company compound. Thirty strips turned up the first night. Each stood sixteen inches tall and was three inches wide. Each boasted thirteen unfamiliar black characters that had been inscribed with a slim brush and special ink. Locals called the strips "talismans," which apparently made them monstrously important.

There was no pattern to where they appeared. One defaced the door of my own town clinic. I grumbled obscenities as I stripped it off.

Bam! Which was no more a true bang than Mischievous Rain's tinkling was a true wind-chimes song. A flash and smoke did accompany that not quite sound, though.

Characters previously brushed on the paper were now burned into the face of my door.

That happened whenever and wherever anyone removed a strip.

The Old Man turned out the Company wizards. One and all professed ignorance and bewilderment. He then conjured the Taken.

"No, I can't read the characters," she told us. "They're foreign to me, too. They might be meant to create a barrier to keep someone or something in, or someone or something out. Because there's not always anyone or anything inside the places where the talismans turn up, it follows that they must be meant to keep something out."

"Something?" I asked.

"Pressed, I would guess that someone is creating spirit barriers."

Yeah. Sure. But who? And why slap the strips up so randomly, all inscribed in an unknown alphabet?

There was an answer.

There was a reason.

Mischievous Rain was, likely, both. Somebody wanted her distracted while they searched for the Port of Shadows.

Still, even stipulating that, the talismans were an odd angle of attack. They did nothing obvious. Ankou and the twins were not affected. No one ever suffered any real inconvenience, in town or in camp.

But the talismans definitely gnawed at the composure of the superstitious.

So. Stuff happening in town was easily understood, but how did a Resurrectionist get into the compound to slap paper strips all over without getting caught? Security was sloppy, sure, we so seldom had trouble. But security was not that lax.

Sorcery had to be involved, of a sort that made witnesses fail to take note of a vandal in action.

Mischievous Rain led me to the hog pen, a noisy and noisome acre west of the compound, on the side away from town. Two talismans sealed the pen gate. That made less sense than any other talisman I had seen the past two mornings.

She told me, "You're almost there, aren't you?"

"Ma'am?"

Gust front tinkle. Hard-eyed look. It got sudden cold out. Really cold. What did you do now, Croaker?

Somewhere, Ankou unlimbered a mighty yowl.

"'Ma'am'? What's that? You're twenty years my senior, Annalist."

It was closer to ten but I was not going to argue.

Candy, Elmo, Two Dead, and several other sets of curious eyes trailed us. Some foul beast snickered. A second beast choked on his attempt to suppress his laughter. Mischievous Rain turned. "Go away." Her tone was conversational but the chimed accompaniment was ferocious. The stars on her yukata danced.

I said, "Wow. I've never seen . . ."

"Be silent."

I took the suggestion to heart. She was in a sudden foul mood and I could not help suspecting that it might be my fault. My advanced age would not protect me. If I did anything more I might get a chance to make my third mistake from six feet under the clover.

She snatched the talismans off the gate. They burst into flames. She used her free hand to draw the smoke to her nose. "Yes. I thought so."

I ached, so desperately did I want to ask. My training in the Tower left me just barely able to restrain my curiosity.

"You may speak, now."

A bit of grovel might be in order. "What did I do? So that I never offend again."

"I can't explain in words that you will understand. You are you. You are what you are: the sum of your lifetime experiences. The only women you ever knew were family or whores. And her, in the Tower, who might know less of men than you know of women."

Well, maybe. But that did seem pretty cryptic.

She cursed and shook her fingers, having held a burning talisman a moment too long. "Let's go." And so ended Mischievous Rain's first incursion into the world outside the Company compound, her purpose apparently forgotten.

A pigpen to remember, though.

Despite having permission to speak I kept Croaker confined to the interior of the obsessively inquisitive physician-Annalist-historian.

I sat in the background while Mischievous Rain interviewed potential servants. She wanted four girls. Her requirements remained mysterious except that she wanted no males nor any girl who had served in the temple. Maybe she wanted to avoid anyone who had known Tides Elba.

Only six girls asked for the work. None of them really wanted it. Their elders probably figured it was time they started supplementing the family income—unless, of course, they were meant to become spies. They were all very young, the oldest being thirteen. It might be hard to find many girls older who had not done time in the temple.

Mischievous Rain sent them home with a promise to decide quickly. She asked me, "Which four would you add to your personal collection?"

"That question is both unfair and based on the absurd assumption that I lust after children."

Big grin. Merry tinkle. My sin at the pigpen gate had been forgiven.

"Remember, I know only my sisters and comfort women."

"And me, now, sort of."

"You are unusual."

"Oh yes, I am indeed. Let's have supper."

"Huh?" Was she messing with me?

I followed her upstairs. Her quarters were in showplace order. Just what a single young mother's establishment ought to look like—assuming she was incredibly powerful and owned inexhaustible resources.

Each minute I spent with her left me wondering more what the Lady was thinking.

Mischievous Rain had two young soldiers serve supper. She and I and the kids sat at a small square table with her across from me. Beloved Shin sat to my left, Firefly to my right. Demon cat Ankou feasted on raw fish in the least trafficked corner of the room.

Yet again I find myself recording details outside the customary. Why must I chronicle my slow descent into domesticity?

The soldiers were locals, borrowed with the Captain's connivance. What the hell? Was the Taken working a game on me?

On Croaker the man? Or on Croaker the Company physician? Or possibly on Croaker the Company Annalist?

Sometimes people do try to influence how I remember them. But why would Mischievous Rain give a rat's ass how she looked in the Annals?

Made no sense that I could see.

How about a game on the imagined consort of the monster of the Tower? That had a certain absurd plausibility given a gargantuan dose of suspension of disbelief.

Or, plunging headfirst into thoroughly imaginative conspiracy theory, was Croaker being leveraged into the minds of the Lady's enemies, who might be the sort of whack jobs who went around slapping combustible talismans onto the gates of pigpens?

"You think too much," she told me after the dessert course, and after the soldiers had taken their leave, probably to retail vastly inventive eyewitness reports in exchange for drinks at the Dark Horse. "And you worry way too much. Almost nothing really means much. Most everything is exactly what it appears to be."

I had no clue.

"Lean back. Relax. Let it happen. Take it for what it is."

No clue at all.

Mischievous Rain told the children to get ready for bed. Neither kid took that with good grace. I reminded them to brush their teeth. All that handled, the Taken told me, "It's well after dark. Let's you and me go find out what the talisman business is all about."

Determined to cooperate and thereby stay healthy, I joined her for a moonlight stroll. She left the compound for only the second time. This time she made it all the way into town.

The stroll proper lasted a single turn around the side of the new building. It ended at a tall, narrow white door not yet tagged with a talisman. In fact, no talisman had appeared within the compound after the first night. That was suggestive, but I was not sure of what, other than that somebody did not want to get noticed during a heightened state of alert.

A half-moon lurked thirty degrees above the western horizon, behind scattered stripes of cloud. It looked particularly silvery and cold.

"Give me a hand, here, Annalist."

Mischievous Rain had the skinny door open, revealing her carpet standing on edge. She wanted to bring it out without dragging it. She made it float until we could tip it down.

She stepped aboard the carpet. It settled. She said, "I know you've done this before. Let's go."

"Um." A grunt, not thrilled. "It's been a while."

She tinkled. "Hang on tight, then. I'm still learning myself."

I said nothing about her having managed to make it to Aloe without losing Ankou, her kids, or her plunder—which triumph buoyed my own confidence. Just a little.

The carpet stirred, rose, leaned, turned. I ground my teeth. She told me, "I'm going to stay low. You'll only have time for one good scream before you hit the ground."

Sure. Right. Truth be told, I was more troubled by her friendly attitude than by the prospect of a sudden desperate need to learn to walk on moonshine.

Up we rose, then scooted southwest, leaving startled shouts behind. Somebody was alert. We headed away from town first. There was moonlight enough to show me swiftly changing ground features that were way too far down below. Mischievous Rain's low flight was still high enough to avoid treetops and, later, man-made obstacles when we got to town.

We stole into Aloe from the east, with the moon out in front, and took station in the shadow of the dome of the temple of Occupoa. From my belly I peered over the edge, every finger squeezing the juice out of the frame beneath the fabric. I did not see much. Initially I thought that was because there was too much down underneath us but soon I realized that it was because Mischievous Rain had positioned us where we were least likely to be seen ourselves. But that meant that *we* could not see much. It was the classic problem for the intelligence gatherer. The better the look you want the more you need to expose yourself to get it.

The carpet rocked and tilted. I squeezed harder. The frame whimpered. Or maybe that was me. Mischievous Rain sat down beside me. "Have you worked it out yet?"

"I can't see anything from here."

"There isn't anything to see."

"You know what's going on?"

"I think I do. Because I haven't let preconceptions cloud my thinking. You have the facts that I do. You have more experience than I do. Your tardiness to judgment concerns me. Are you willfully refusing to see the truth? Or are you just too dim to gather the facts into the obvious solution?"

I reflected briefly. "I lean toward the latter option."

"So you'll disregard facts that, at first glance, don't appear pertinent?"

"Possibly. What am I missing?"

"Take this to bed with you tonight. *Every* possibility has to be examined before you deny its place in the equation."

Sorcerers, sorceresses, and the Taken in particular, love to mess with you that way, by being vague, opaque, completely ambiguous. Always for your own good, of course, so you will commence to begin to think about considering engaging in critical thinking yourself.

I was alone. The world around me wobbled. The temple dome drifted up to mask the starscape. My companion told me, "Watch for a lone skulker."

Right. Easy peasy.

She slid the carpet around the south side of the temple, which seemed unnaturally quiet. Then we cruised along six feet above the surface of a secondary street, heading into a familiar quarter. Light shone ahead, accompanied by noise and what pretended to be music.

That would be the Dark Horse and its environs, home away from home for most of the Company. You could not get laid there but Markeg Zhorab would, otherwise, make you supremely comfortable while he relieved you of those pesky coins threatening to drag your trousers down.

The earth fell away suddenly. I squeaked and grabbed me a more solid grip on the carpet frame.

The carpet bucked, lurched, stopped. "High enough, I think." Mischievous Rain jumped up and tromped over to me. The carpet sagged and slid sideways sickeningly. "Stand up."

"I would love to do that but my hands seem to be locked on, here."

"Did you ever fall when you were flying with the Lady or her sister?"

"Never. Not once. But the times that I didn't fall aren't the ones that bother me. I'm fussed about the time when I will fall."

"Just flap your arms real fast."

I could not respond.

"All right. Yes. I do find your terror amusing. But I promise, I'll catch you if you go over the side. Now, I need you to at least get up onto your knees so that I can tie this sheen across your eyes."

Something almost invisible stretched between her hands. It glistened silvery when the moonlight struck it right. "Hurry up! We can be seen silhouetted against a cloud if somebody looks up."

I did manage to get up onto my knees. She told me, "Keep your eyes open. This will be a waste of time if you don't."

More scary stuff. I am sensitive about my vision. But I felt only a gossamer touch before my view of the world shifted dramatically.

Stars became black pricks in a sooty gray curtain. The moon went black, except that the dark part turned a misty red. The world below shone in reddish shades, as well, varying from almost orange to a cardinal verging on old dried blood. Aloe, except where lights burned, was as plain as if it were daytime once I adjusted.

"What do you see?"

I told her.

"Live animals should appear in shades of brown, though smaller creatures may fade toward the red. People and other large beasts will stand out. Watch for a human shape skulking around alone."

I was inclined to argue but figured she would not trust me to handle the flying while she did the looking down.

Using the Dark Horse as an origin, she circled, lengthening the radius gradually. I spotted a clump of brown things wobbling in the direction of the Company compound.

The Taken repeated, "The one we want will be alone and sneaking."

I spotted him soon afterward, making a grand pretense of being drunk and lost, but occasionally he darted aside. When we dropped down to check out what he had done we found a freshly installed talisman.

Mischievous Rain said, "We've got him. Now we'll see if my hypothesis holds water. Keep the sheen on. And come here. I need you to direct me. I want to drop down right on top of him."

The Third was just a kid, younger than Mischievous Rain, talented in the extreme but unfortunately apprenticed to Goblin and One-Eye. He needed to find the balls to tell them to fuck off when they tried to drag him into something corrupt. Otherwise, sure as shit, someday he would eat the blame for some crime that he had nothing to do with.

He led us to a rented sleeping room just two hundred yards from the Dark Horse and one block off the direct route between the tavern and the Company compound.

I observed, "The little asshole sure crammed a lot of crap in here."

This room was where the talismans were produced using homemade paper, homemade ink, and some nicely crafted calligrapher's brushes. There was magic in the air, thick enough for a no-talent like me to taste.

"Look at this," the Taken told me, having unrolled a scroll found

storage his natural born villainy wouldn't bleed off. The pressure would build and build. When we did bring him out . . ."

He made a two-hands explosion gesture with sound added and let the rest hang. Everyone chuckled. But that, likely, was just how it would go.

One-Eye failed to appreciate the humor. He was inclined to squabble about it, too, but did exercise unusual self-control. He did recognize the depth of the hole that he had dug himself.

"Way deeper than usual," I said, thinking out loud.

"Croaker?"

"Sir. I just realized something. Our colleague's behavioral problems escalated substantially only this past year, while growing a great deal less subtle."

"Uhm?"

Many pairs of eyes, and one singleton, turned my way.

"The One-Eye we had underfoot this time last year was a serious pain in the ass part of the time . . ."

"All of the time." Goblin pretended a cough into the crook of his arm.

". . . but he never tried anything this boneheaded. That One-Eye had a well-tuned sense of self-preservation. He would've stuck to things less likely to get him killed."

An enduring feature of One-Eye's schemes is that they blow up or burn down. Only . . . I suspect that that is because we only find out about the ones that do fail.

The Old Man saw where I was headed. "The Limper."

"Yes. That evil little turd. One more time." We knew that the Limper had done wicked things to One-Eye's and Goblin's minds. One-Eye's recent heightened dumbassedness could all be Limper-designed.

Mischievous Rain said, "Let me straighten him out."

One-Eye went from slumped, passive, and resigned to bugfuck berserker in a wink. But Buzzard Neck, three times his size, was behind him and primed. Eye wild, wide, and white, One-Eye froze. Buzz pushed down on his shoulders. Mischievous Rain slapped him before he could complete a spell. His eye rolled up. He toppled onto his ugly old face.

The Captain told Mischievous Rain, "There you go. He's all yours. Don't break him. He's not precious but he can be useful."

"My sole purpose will be to make him whole. Assuming he hasn't just gone totally old-man batshit crazy."

I was not privy to what happened with One-Eye once the Taken took over. Neither did I get to witness her follow-up work with Goblin. The Third took a turn following those two. Two Dead and Buzz presumably endured less aggressive interviews, but they were not pleased when they emerged, either.

Silent, though, never had a one-on-one with the Taken.

Silent had no agenda. He had no interest in much but his service with the Company. Our supreme mistress and her Taken had no need to be concerned.

It took Mischievous Rain weeks to wring out and tame the demons and afflictions that the Limper had installed in days. Even then she managed only an approximation. One-Eye would always be One-Eye.

Poor, whining the Third suffered the least. The Limper had seen that he was not wicked enough to be used for anything freaky. The kid was, therefore, humiliated because he was considered a lightweight.

Buzzard Neck and Two Dead were another issue. Their loyalty was assured by the refuge the Company provided. They would not survive on their own. Not in this part of the world.

Winter packed it in and slunk off for an eight-month holiday. Light snows became regular rains. The rains in time relaxed into random light drizzles. Then the mud dried up and agriculture set in.

I treated a lot of foot fungus. I got our cisterns cleaned and refilled with captured rainwater, which was healthier than the water from the creek at the bottom of the hill or from our open on-site well. I agitated for recruiting a veterinarian. The Old Man had convinced himself that us owning big herds would increase our range and mobility. I was skeptical. Having lots of animals meant needing lots of people to take care of the animals. We had accumulated riding and dray horses, donkeys, mules, cattle, oxen, sheep, hogs, goats, and several camels. I do what I can but I am an amateur, just skilled enough to know which end of the critter the chow goes in.

Gurdlief Speak got over his discomfort with Mischievous Rain's kids and started taking advantage of her hospitality. He would visit me briefly, bringing some supposed new folktale or fresh gob of gossip, then would announce that he had to get going. He would just pop round to say hello to Firefly and Shin before he headed back to town.

The boy had changed. He was no longer eager to latch onto the Company. He thought Mischievous Rain's presence guaranteed that we were headed into some serious shit. He was disinclined to join the communal swim.

He based his assessment on snatches of conversation overheard while playing with Firefly and Shin.

I heard nothing that interesting, ever, in the time that I spent with the twins and their mother.

So, who was playing what with whom? Was the Taken feeding select disinformation to the Aloen community?

The ribbing about me being the Lady's snuggle bunny gained nostalgic appeal considering the crap I suffered now, because I lived in the same building as a real live pretty woman—the most beautiful woman that most of these guys had ever seen. They could not believe that there was nothing going on. Too often I overheard something like, "She's got to be fucking somebody, yeah, but how come it's got to be Croaker?" Meaning, "Why couldn't it be me?"

The Old Man had to know. He was the dick who set it up, undoubtedly on instructions. Candy and the Lieutenant probably knew something, too. And so might any sorcerer perverted enough to join in. None of them were likely to ease my burden.

Croaker's personal discomfort never signifies.

The children had been put down in beds that looked like they got used only when witnesses were around. Ankou had gone out to terrorize the night. He might be no real cat but he enjoyed doing tomcat stuff. He had turned up missing half of his right ear a few days gone. Mischievous Rain got rattled, which did not seem appropriate. Tomcats get into fights.

I said, "You're not wearing the midnight yukata today."

"It has to get washed sometime." Wistful smile.

"The lamb was good."

"Sana is a superb cook. For a child. What's bothering you? Why not just get to it?"

I did like that. Whether she was Tides Elba or Mischievous Rain she did not waste time dancing around things.

"It's the living arrangements."

Big smile. "You don't want people to think we're knocking boots?"

"Uh . . . sort of."

"Take that into town. Half the women there will want to find out what makes you special enough to service one of the Taken."

I had run into a touch of that already.

Mischievous Rain laughed but did not tinkle, not being in her usual outfit. "You're blushing. At your age." Then, "I shouldn't be cruel. There is a reason for our arrangement."

"I assumed that. But I don't get it."

"It's so that people do believe we're attached at the groin. That saves me having to deal with six hundred other horny studs. Somewhat. Because of the stories about you and the Lady . . . Which have become believable because she checks up on you sometimes. Right?"

I nodded.

"Usually when it's inconvenient? With witnesses around?"

"Yes." I recalled several contacts that had come with wind chimes singing in the background.

"So the man who went inside the Tower for a while seems to have become especially favored by the entity that dwells there. Who would risk her wrath by messing with him?"

"But I don't want . . ." Oh, why bother? I had caught wind of the bear in the woods.

Croaker's imaginary special relationship would be used to shield Mischievous Rain from unproductive distractions. The woman had a mission. The Annalist's steadfast support had been crafted by the playwright in the Tower.

I considered asking who would protect her from me but that seemed both a little lame and a lot sour grapes.

"Want to go flying in the moonlight?" She had that look that made me think she was peeking at the inside of my head. "The moon is almost full. It would be romantic."

"Don't. This is tough enough without you taunting me."

An instant of venomous darkness uglified her. Deep anger followed. Then a forced smile surfaced. "Of course. Of course. Only family and whores."

That mantra had to be the default response to a question not yet asked. Or to one that I had not recognized as a question if it was asked.

I had stepped into something. Again. But what?

How come getting along with folks has to be so complicated?

Lest I get something thoroughly wrong and sink into my error up to my chin, Mischievous Rain told me, "Contrary to common prejudice it *is* possible for a woman and man to be friends."

"Bet you it's a shitload harder for the man. He'll always be thinking with his other head."

She went way out somewhere else but did not lose me entirely. "This quiet time won't last much longer."

"No. Probably not." Spring planting had begun. Admin had developed rotations whereby the men would "volunteer" to help work the Aloen fields. One of the Old Man's hearts-and-minds exercises.

That worked, some, because imperial taxes are delivered mostly in kind, which fed us and added to the Company herds.

13

Once Upon a Time: Gone Without an Echo

The necromancer surprised himself with his ability to remain calm under pressure. Relatively, considered. Considering that this was the first time he had had to deal with anything like this.

But he had been preparing for it, physically and mentally, from the day he and a wagon loaded with tools had come to this remote hilltop.

The woman who blew into his home was not half as clever as she thought. She was a youngster, hasty, but incredibly strong, able to call down the lightning. From an old and ranking family, certainly. The quality of her clothing gave that away.

She really thought he would believe that lightning would shatter his palisade and destroy his mastiffs just at the moment when a little girl lost in the woods happened to wander by?

He would have placed no faith in her innocence even had she not reeked of Dusk. He did not credit coincidence or random connection where sorcery was concerned. Skepticism was his earliest self-taught lesson.

Blessed was the paranoia that had compelled him to saturate his environment with thousands of gentle, almost undetectable gossamer spells that would cluster anyone who was not himself or Laissa.

He tried to question the invader. She was unresponsive except to indicate that she could not hear. The sorcery used to blast through the stockade had deafened her, possibly only temporarily.

So, naught to be gained from conversation, he put the outsider to sleep. He was troubled by the fact that she was so young. He was missing something, he was sure—though youth could be an illusion meant to disarm. Those who dwelt in Grendirft . . .

She was from Dusk but there was no cause for anyone from Dusk to be interested in him, outside the usual contrived legal finagles. Unless . . . Could it be the waste girl? But that made no sense. She had been thrown away.

They were all crazy in Dusk. The full madness of those people could not be encompassed. He knew that he was not quite sane himself but he did believe that he was nearer the norm than any of those people.

Which was more an ideological vision than a clear view of reality.

The two did come close to meshing, though, this once.

The invader was little older than Laissa. But she had called down the lightning. He must remember that, and must forget that she reminded him so much of his daughter. She was not slow. She was not harmless. And she would wake up eventually, probably before he realized it. One incautious moment, then, and . . .

He did a quick search. "Almost forgot . . . What's this? Oh, my!" He took his time thumbing through the fortune-telling deck. "You clever girl. But you were much too sure of yourself, dear. You didn't lock these so no one but you could use them."

Further search only turned up a couple of haunted rings that he could not use. Those he just tossed across the room.

So. Neutralized for now. Time to grab a peek into the face of tomorrow.

"Laissa, I have to go see about the animals. I need you to watch this girl while I'm out back. Can you do that?"

He did not expect a verbal response and he did not get one. Laissa spoke seldom, though she was never uncooperative.

The urge to take physical advantage touched him again, for a moment. He shoved it down, angry and disgusted. What kind of man lusts after his own daughter?

The necromancer had not told his daughter the whole truth, nor even much of the truth. But she really needed only one truth, the truth that he had shown her when he took her and held her during the most awful moments of thunder and storm.

What else did she need to know?

The necromancer considered his girls briefly, then went out into the wet and wind, being careful with the door so the girls would not be at risk for colds.

Laissa squatted in front of the girl for a while, just watching her breathe. She touched the girl's cheek. She was so warm. Almost as warm as Papa.

After another minute of vacant wonder Laissa collected the jewelry that Papa had removed from the girl. The two heavy rings were warm, too. And they had a comfortable, relaxing, almost familiar feel. After staring at them for a while she pocketed them and went back to staring at the girl.

The necromancer shed tears for his mastiffs. They had been with him his whole time here, so long that they were no longer any real threat. But they had remained impressively intimidating right to the end.

The sorcerer resumed walking, passed through the remains of his stockade. He headed for the woods, sure that he would find something interesting there, all the while being hammered by heavy rain. By a vast and furious rain that was not singling him out. Already dry washes were roaring with galloping runoff.

The necromancer had come here, to punish himself, after he lost his Laissa, thirteen years ago. Fourteen? Whichever, they were years of continuously inventive, obsessively precise spell creation. His handiwork now tangled every bush and tree for a quarter mile around. His guilt and his paranoia, and his growing obsessions, had ruled him completely. And he did not sleep much.

Trip lines for his defenses extended well beyond the quarter-mile mark in directions that felt like a likely approach—except that not once had it occurred to him that the invasion might come from above. Those who would come against him—he was certain that someone would—would become entangled and steadily more enmeshed in cobwebs of spells long before they stumbled into his more obvious protections.

He believed that his creation might be subtle enough and in-depth enough to entangle and capture the Dominator himself.

On this one night, in the deluge delivered by what had to be the most ferocious storm in modern history, he received confirmation that his craft was fine enough and clever enough to have captured one of the Ten Who Were Taken.

Following hints and cues passed on by his web, he found the flying carpet under the giant chestnut tree. That tree was a favorite. From descriptions he had heard he recognized the sleeping Taken. So. The invader had been delivered by the Howler. Disturbing.

The necromancer had little intercourse with the world but he had been under the impression that the Taken were all out on the frontiers desperately trying to salvage the Domination. Could it be that the political situation was less dire than rumor suggested?

Domination politics meant nothing to him. He was an empire unto himself, with an isolationist foreign policy. A nation of one . . . No. No longer. Now he was head of a nation of three.

He rested a palm on the forehead of the Taken. Howler would not awaken for at least a day.

He rested that same hand over the cards now securely settled into an interior pocket. A blessed windfall, those. Blessed.

The Howler had become a blob of live flesh of no special value. He carried nothing of any special value, either. Done with a search, the necromancer rolled his victim off of his carpet, dragged him into some brush, tossed on a few sticks and leaves, then forgot him. No need to be troubled by him except that he was what he was and had come here to inject himself where he was not welcome.

The necromancer was not middle-of-the-lane sane. He was off the road most of the time. But he was not suicidal insane. He understood clearly that what had happened here tonight had written the end of the latest cycle of his life. One of the Taken had come after him. That meant that he had come to the attention of the Domination. His sole option now was to get himself and his girls well lost before another wave of snoopers and punishers arrived.

14

Long Ago and Far Away: A Far Piece

Bathdek awakened in blistering sunshine, with a cool, dry wind ripping past her. She was not inclined to wake up, though. She had a savage headache and a stomach a half inch short of another unwanted puke. Confused, she tried to remember what had happened.

A storm. An amazing sorcerer. Her sister.

Those were the ingredients that would not come together and make any sense.

Her cheek rested on something rough. Something that smelled of her uncle Howler. So. He must have rescued her after all.

She did not open her eyes. The sun was in her face. It was too bright to confront.

She had to be aboard the Howler's carpet, traveling at high speed, somewhere where there was no overcast.

"Oh, my," she murmured. Something was not right.

Someone moved close by her. The carpet shifted and swayed. A small hand touched her cheek. A voice said, "She's waking up, Papa."

Dorotea's voice. Absolutely. But who was Papa?

Small hands spread a cool wet cloth across Bathdek's face.

Bathdek opened her eyes. They worked the way they should. She knew already that her hearing had returned. But had her strength returned as well?

No.

Not quite. Only a little, leaving her not much stronger than pudding.

She tried to sit up. The carpet rocked. Hands helped her . . . Her sister's hands. Her *dead* sister's hands.

"Thank you." She bit down before she used Dorotea's name.

Taking care, she removed the cloth protecting her eyes. They soon adjusted to the bright.

Yes, she was aboard the Howler's carpet, miles above the earth, headed eastward at high speed. She did not recognize the land below but possibly only because she could gain no clear look at it. Clouds mostly obscured the view.

Howler was not flying the carpet. The sorcerer from the woods was. But that was impossible! Not even one of the Ten could take control of another Taken's carpet. Unless . . .

Of course. The cards. She had no need to check to know that they were gone. One card would have let her control Howler's carpet in an emergency. His idea.

The rogue sorcerer must have worked everything out from first principles, in practically no time.

What kind of mad genius was she faced with, here?

She would have to be very, very careful, starting right now, never to underestimate him. He ought to be one of the Taken. Why was he not one of the Taken? How clever he must be, to have avoided being noticed by the Dominator, there just a dozen miles outside Dusk.

Clearly, he did not have the "got to show off" flaw that betrayed most clever sorcerers.

While Bathdek looked round with panicked eye her sister poured her a cup of steaming tea from a flask charmed to keep its contents hot. "Thank you."

No response. Dorotea sealed the flask and returned it to a wicker hamper. She took out a hard sausage, a block of cheese, and one slightly shriveled apple.

Bathdek continued examining her surroundings.

The Howler's carpet was six feet by ten, measured generously. It was piled with random miscellany, little of which Bathdek recognized.

The sorcerer said, "Don't make any sudden moves. We didn't have time to balance the load. Too big a hurry to get away. We'll reshuffle it next time we stop for a rest. We're far enough out that we can afford the time. Laissa, dear, be a treasure and dig me out some rye crackers. Three should be enough."

The girl opened the wicker hamper, retrieved the requested crackers. Those in hand, she tapped the sorcerer's shoulder. He took them. "Thank you, dear." His lower legs were dangling off the front of the carpet. He seemed to be enjoying himself.

Bathdek eyed the girl. "So you're Laissa? I'm Melondi."

The girl just looked at her.

The sorcerer said, "Laissa doesn't talk much. No point trying to force a conversation."

"But she can talk?"

"As you know from when she told me that you were awake. Melondi? Sounds made-up." He chuckled. "What's your family name?"

"Kloester. My father is Brinker Kloester." A real person, a senior official in imperial finance, but no actual relation.

"Brinker Kloester. A powerful man, I believe. Crooked. And not the sort that I would expect to have a daughter who would roam the night with the Howler, let alone be able to call down the lightning."

He was teasing. Maybe he knew who she was. Maybe Dorotea told him. Only . . . Only Dorotea did not know who *she* was.

Bathdek did not know what to say. She did realize that what she wanted to say would be wasted breath if she said it. She was a captive. Maybe a hostage. She was miles above the ground and an unknown distance east of Dusk. And there was no way anyone could find her, help her, or rescue her.

Dorotea would be no help. She was uninterested in helping herself. She was content. Which was ironic. Dorotea before had been content with nothing. Her whining and complaining had never stopped.

Bathdek resisted an urge to say, "Mother should see you now." Instead, she asked, "Where are we?"

"East of Dusk. Heading east. We may be over the Great Forest."

"What I guess I should have asked is, where are we going?"

"Somewhere outside the Domination. Somewhere where I can attend my research safely and you girls can have a hope of a normal life."

That sounded totally, parentally reasonable, and it highlighted the madness of the man.

He existed in multiple realities. She wondered if she would have to deal with multiple personalities. And, if so, if the ugly personality would dominate, as was the case with Him.

Bathdek wanted to say, "I would rather go back to my life of power and privilege," but suspected that it would be unwise to challenge his delusions just now. He would be unstable after the recent stress.

Clearly, he did believe that Dorotea was his daughter. So when he was craziest who did he think that she was? Or was he just messing with her on that?

In a tiny voice Dorotea piped, "Papa, I have to pee. I don't think I can hold it very long."

The carpet plunged so fast that Bathdek feared she might lose her snack. Near as she could tell the sorcerer was thrilled. He turned to Laissa. "I'll find you a place as fast as I can, baby." He was grinning.

He turned to look at Bathdek. "Isn't that marvelous, Kitten? That's the most that she's said at one time since the fever broke."

Kitten? Name or nickname? Why? She could not imagine what these people were thinking. For certain nothing that could be framed as conventional sanity. And she was at their mercy.

The sorcerer set down in a clearing in a forest that rolled away to every horizon. Bathdek had studied the woods all through the descent. Not once did she glimpse anything suggesting a human presence.

Laissa jumped off the carpet and ran toward the closest trees. She still had some pale sense of modesty. The sorcerer said, "We should all do our business while we have the chance." Some seconds later, as Bathdek was getting her land legs, he added, "We're far enough east now that we're not likely to run into anyone conversant in TelleKurre." Basically daring her to make a run for it while he had his trousers down.

She did not need the warning. The lack of human sign promised that staying with him was the better survival option. She was a spoiled city girl. How would she manage in the Old Forest, where anyone she met was likely a bitter enemy?

The sorcerer entered the woods twenty yards from where Laissa had. He did not look back.

His arrogant certainty regarding her intelligence irritated Bathdek as much as condescension or disparagement would have.

She stalked into the woods and took care of her own functions. Then she helped redistribute the carpet's cargo. Once that was all balanced up, Papa could manage the carpet more easily.

Bathdek said, "I hope we can get a bath wherever we're going. I'm nasty. I wet myself while I was out."

"We could all use some cleaning up. I'm glad you decided to come with us." He had his back to her, tying off a length of cord, so he missed her reaction when he said, "Your sister hasn't had a decent bath since the fever took her."

Did he know? No. That could not be possible. This was just more of his crazy.

Had to be the crazy.

Papa did not push as hard after the break. He felt safe, now. His girls were at peace. The passage over the Plain of Fear went without incident. Journey's end came two unhurried days later. He landed in the rugged wilderness locals called the Ghost Country, in a supposedly haunted quarter that the natives shunned.

15

In Modern Times: Honnoh

Something changed. I sensed it while treating whooping cough, spring colds, and the first rash of agricultural injuries. Last patient bandaged, I headed for the Dark Horse.

Markeg Zhorab was surprised. "Croaker! We don't see you much these days."

He was a good man. Whatever he had heard, however absurd, he would not task me with it.

"You may have heard that I've stumbled into new personal circumstances. And you won't starve because I don't come around as much anymore."

The Dark Horse had no customers just then. Even the Company's worst slackers were otherwise engaged.

"A fair point. And I do blame my good fortune on your circle." His expression clouded. "I hope I get enough put by before the good times end."

The Company presence, once so resented, was today the linchpin of the Aloen economy. The hearts and minds were mostly ours.

"I can't imagine you not already being set for a generation."

"When you go your absence will leave a vacuum."

Oh. Yes. Our enemies would come out of hiding. Any friend of the Company, anyone who had profited from our presence, might suffer reprisals. "I will relay your concern to the Taken." No evil would befall a friend if we left no enemy alive.

Mention of Mischievous Rain brought a shadow to Zhorab's face again, darker than before.

There was a problem there, not yet obvious to me. The Taken would not come into town. The townsfolk would not talk about her. I figured it must have to do with religion.

Religious stuff confuses me.

I applied myself to a bottomless mug while Zhorab chattered. I told him, "I miss this beer more than the games. It's good stuff. You're really getting the knack."

"And you're complimenting the wrong guy. My vats can't keep up with the demand, these days."

"Hope I didn't bruise your feelings, then."

"You didn't. So why don't you get to it? What brought you here?"

"You are too perceptive. Here it is. Something's going on. Aloens apparently see it. My people don't. But nobody will fill us in."

Zhorab pottered with barkeep busywork. I waited some, then asked, "That the way it has to be?"

"I do like you, Croaker. You're maybe the best man in your gang. But you're also the man who took the woman away and you're the man who's stuffing her now."

"Markeg, read my lips. I . . . am . . . *not!* . . . screwing Mischievous Rain! Not! But I do like her. As a person."

That just made him more uncomfortable. I asked, "This all has to do with her?"

"It has to do with her. Yes."

"How so? What can I do to fix it?"

"You can't fix it. A fix became impossible when you took her out of the temple. She was the destined one."

We were speaking Aloen, of course, and although I have a gift for languages I do not master colloquialisms easily. Something such had to be at work there because what he said made no sense taken literally. "Because she was supposed to become the Port of Shadows?"

"No. That's something else. But it is part of what bothers people. We all get that you did the world a favor by aborting that business. And you saved her, too."

"We saved the world, but! And that's the problem. Right?"

"We cannot reconcile it all. Mischievous Rain, as Tides Elba, was the destined one." That again. This time I realized that it was a non-Aloen word. It sounded like "konzertosma," although that is only a phonetic approximation. I recorded it as "destined one" after Zhorab explained its meaning. It was a unique title. Later I learned that "konzertosma" was the preascension appellation of the "konzertasa," a sort of living divinity/mother superior of the temple. In addition to her administrative duties her divine side would be expected to bestow Occupoa's special blessing on any man of Aloe in extreme need, one time only.

Again, some religious practices confuse me.

Markeg confused me a lot more once he opened up.

In these parts the consecrated play roles executed by supernatural agencies elsewhere, like the Fates, with a maiden, a wife, and a crone. Chosen at ten, the maid, the konzertosma, trains for a decade. Unlike other temple girls she remains unsullied until she takes over from her predecessor. A young man of the town would be elected to elevate her to konzertasa status, the wife role. And after ten years she would yield to the next konzertasa and join the pool of crones, the senior sisters, who oversee the everyday work of the temple.

The Occupoa cult is not unique to Aloe. Though marked by plentiful local nuances it is widespread. No pun intended.

Before the Company's intervention Tides Elba was scheduled to become konzertasa this coming Midsummer's Eve. She ruined everything when she got herself arrested. Then, worse, she came back to Aloe with children. And *then* she took herself an outlander lover.

Tides Elba, a most important religious actor, had let herself become tainted time and time again.

That was one weird way to look at it all, I thought, in a culture where chastity is of no value and a faithful spouse is reckoned to be somebody who remains a steadfast partner, not one who sleeps in only one bed. This was a culture where fathers puffed up with pride if their blooming daughters got picked to become temple prostitutes.

Yet again, religion is the strangest stuff—though the religion you grow up with yourself is, naturally, the blazing exception. That sizzling exception always makes perfect sense.

"Markeg, I promise, Mischievous Rain has more trouble with the situation than anybody else does. Not one thing that happened to her was something she chose to suffer."

"Which only makes it more troubling. The goddess let it happen."

So there it was. Tides Elba, made konzertosma without consultation, also got tagged to be the Port of Shadows, no honor that anyone wanted, and once we aborted that the Lady made her over into a shiny new Taken, never consulting the wishes of Tides Elba, either.

I suggested, "Here's a thought. Blame it all on the Dominator. He started everything."

Zhorab chuckled without humor. "Naturally. But that doesn't really help. The old konzertasa is supposed to step aside this summer but there isn't anybody to replace her."

"There wasn't an understudy? With life as chancy as it is? I'd think you'd have several. Lightning does strike."

He shrugged. "I run a tavern. I hang out with foreigners. I'm not trusted by older Aloens. I don't know what the temple leadership is thinking, except that they want to make sure the next konzertosma isn't also the next Port of Shadows. And, anyway, that's their problem, not yours."

That was nonsense. We had the power here. We represented the woman in the Tower. We were responsible.

"That's not likely, is it? The Resurrectionists wouldn't want to get into it any deeper with the temple, would they?"

"I know even less about that shit."

Maybe. Or maybe not. I do not trust myself one hundred percent when religion or politics are in play. It did seem reasonable that the enemy would not want to alienate the temple—unless, of course, the perfect konzertasa really would make a perfect Port of Shadows, too.

"Question," I said. "There have to be backups. Could they possibly have the same background as Tides Elba?"

That startled Zhorab. I had double zagged when he had expected a hefty zig. "No way I could know. Why?"

"The Port of Shadows has to come from a bloodline that reaches back to the Dominator. Same for the guy who mates her. Which sounds like incest in the twentieth generation."

"I don't know much about history, Croaker. Especially not about what happened in Domination times. But most everybody in these parts can claim the Dominator as an ancestor. He made great sport of rape when he captured a place that resisted him. He supposedly fathered ten thousand bastards."

That was the legend but the number had to be exaggerated. The man could not have had the time and stamina, however virulent his seed. After an extended silence, I said, "I see."

The replacement Port of Shadows had to be a woman of childbearing age with a strong concentration of the Dominator's blood. By examining vital-statistics records I might be able to determine her probable identity. I just needed to give up sleep and work on nothing else. If I could find unsullied and reliable records. The Resurrectionists might have their own secret genealogies. They might even be running a breeding program.

Worth some thought, that, and worth mentioning to the Taken.

Resurrectionist cells began forming even while the White Rose was creating the Barrowland to guard the graves of the Dominator, the Lady, and the original Ten Who Were Taken—none of whom were actually dead when they went into the ground.

Zhorab decided to be more forthcoming. "I did poke around, some. Just for my own curiosity. To find out why you grabbed that particular girl."

"And?"

"There wasn't much to learn. She was a foundling. She turned up at the temple before she could walk. She was always a warm, happy, beautiful child. Everybody loved her."

"Lilac Shade."

"Excuse me?"

"Nothing. She sounds like a girl from one of Gurdlief's stories."

"There is another girl a lot like Tides Elba, three years younger than her, also a foundling. She's supposedly as personable and popular as Tides Elba was. I've seen her. She looks a lot like a younger Tides Elba."

"Do the temple folks try to trace foundlings' backgrounds?"

"No. But they're hardly ever any mystery. Somebody's inexplicably fat daughter suddenly loses a lot of weight and a bundle of squall shows up on the temple steps."

"I see." So Tides Elba might have been a Resurrectionist plant, maybe specially bred, meant for harvest once she reached breeding age. Far-fetched? No doubt. But not impossible. The Resurrectionists have pursued their nightmare for centuries. Only they have any real notion why they go on and on.

The Domination was a gruesome historical passage, ugly, cruel, despotic, and humiliating to most. But, as with most regimes, it would not have been harsh for those on the inside.

If Tides Elba sprang from a breeding program meant to create a Port of Shadows her creators definitely would have created backups because of the iron law of reality: Shit happens. Redundancy would be an absolute necessity in a scheme that required decades to mature.

"Markeg. I appreciate your candor. Truly. You've given me much to ponder."

Sick call wrapped, I looked for Mischievous Rain. She was unusually scarce. Wizards of all stripes were scarce. And the tall, skinny door on the side of the house stood ajar. The space behind it was empty.

I considered going back to town but that was too much effort just to drink beer and play cards. I decided to mess with these Annals instead.

An hour passed. I brought the Annals up to date. I was considering doing the same with my medical journal when I noticed Ankou, nearly invisible, napping under a nearby chair. How did he get in? He had not been there when I arrived. I harassed him till he fled outside. Not that he had been up to anything obnoxious. It was the principle of the thing.

Shin and Firefly arrived minutes later, engaged in a ferocious row about who had started it. What "it" was never became clear.

"Hold it down to a low roar, kids. I'm trying to work."

They eyed me suspiciously. I was being nice. I was that grouch Croaker who was never nice to anybody less than five feet tall.

So. I now knew for sure that I was being watched every second. But why? Because of the company I kept?

The kids got quiet. That was spooky whenever it lasted more than a few seconds. I studied my notes while trying to think of some way to identify Mischievous Rain's forbears, which might help me find other orphans who had been planted in Occupoa's temples.

I ought to take it all up with the Taken herself rather than waste time reinventing the wheel. "You kids know where your mom went?"

"Exploring," Beloved Shin replied. He sat cross-legged in a corner, boxing with Ankou. Firefly was scattered in a chair, apparently asleep.

"Exploring what? Where?"

"Don't know. She said we had to stay behind because it would be dangerous."

Firefly was awake after all. "She told us to stick close to Dad because this might turn out to be a dangerous day." That is what she said. "And we should make sure that you don't leave the compound after you get back from town."

I wanted to call bullshit but that "Dad" snagged a trip line way out yonder in my mental hinterlands.

I said nothing for a long time. The witch! I would bet the "Dad" was a deliberate plant, an emotional booby trap. It would entangle my thinking for days.

Firefly showed me the child's version of her mother's knowing smile. She whispered to her brother. Shin snickered.

Mischievous Rain returned. I heard no tinkling but Ankou and the kids knew anyway. Ankou indulged in a kata of kitty stretches, then headed for the door. Beloved Shin let him out. Firefly pretended to wake up again.

Mischievous Rain appeared fifteen minutes later, freshly groomed. She did not look like she had spent time anywhere dangerous.

"Mom!" Firefly flew at the Taken like her appearance was a complete surprise. Shin was almost as demonstrative.

"Were they much trouble?" the Taken asked.

"None whatsoever." Carefully neutral.

She asked Shin, "Was there any trouble?"

He shook his head. Unlike normal brothers his age he did not try to lay anything off on his sister.

"I'm glad. That's good. Things have begun to move. I was afraid . . ." Of what she decided not to say.

I told her, "I had an interesting visit with Markeg Zhorab. We need to talk about it."

Her facial tattoos, all but invisible for several months, stood out prominently for a moment.

Those damned things only ever turned up when you forgot that they were there. "After supper, then."

There was almost no moon. There was just me and Mischievous Rain, two hundred feet up in a chilly nighttime sky. Neither Ankou nor the children were with us. No way could anyone eavesdrop

The air had a cold, moist feel of imminent storm. Lightning flashed off to the east.

Mischievous Rain asked, "What is it?"

I reiterated my conversation with Zhorab, leaving out nothing. "I learned more in twenty minutes of gossiping with him than I did with all my research. He gave me several ideas about where to look next. But let's don't duplicate anything that's already been done. What do you know about where you came from?"

"Nothing. The temple girls I knew mostly did know their backgrounds but they didn't care. I never worried about it. I wasn't the only one who had no real idea. I did wonder a little more after I got tagged to be the konzertosma. That must have been a surprise for whoever handed me over to the temple. Maybe a happy surprise, considering where that would put their agent." She remained quiet for a bit.

I waited. Then she said, "I may have been given to the temple to hide me. Who would look for the Port of Shadows there?"

"Silent."

"Yes. He did."

The carpet rocked, slipped sideways, and here was Firefly, rubbing sleep out of her eyes. She climbed into my lap, wiggled around some, got comfortable, and went back to sleep.

Mischievous Rain told me, "Better watch your back, now. Anything Firefly likes Shin will feel obliged to hate."

I kind of snuggled the kid but had no real idea how. Family and whores, and my sisters were all older.

"She walks in shadow," the Taken said, vaguely addressing the question nagging me, that I did not ask. It might be safer not to know.

Mischievous Rain returned to an earlier thought. "The Lady is no goddess. Not even inside her own head. But her knack for seeing, knowing, and concluding correctly based upon gossamer thin evidence—so long as she never leaves her Tower—*is* almost godlike. I can't tell you anything about her that isn't common knowledge already—except that she does have a genuine affection for you. And she doesn't understand that any better than you do. And she is far more terrified by that than you are frightened by her interest."

I ground my teeth. I could not have been more defensive. Here came the same old crap. Only . . . Only Mischievous Rain was not yanking my chain. She believed what she was saying.

"So I know how to find important information in unlikely places."

So when would she start looking? I had yet to see her do anything.

"Should we take this one back and put her to bed?"

"Not yet. If she wakes up now she'll be all wound up. Hang on till she starts talking in her sleep. Then we can shift her with no trouble."

"All right." Still not asking how the kid could have turned up aboard a flying carpet miles from home and two hundred feet in the air. Nor why she had climbed onto me instead of onto her mother. "Then let's do that. Have your unlikely sources produced anything the rest of us should know?"

"I provide your captain with regular reports."

Well. Of course. I was out of the loop again. Need to know married to freedom from potential recollection in the Annals.

The carpet sagged and slid. Beloved Shin settled beside his mother. He glared daggers at his sister and me. Maybe that was why I had been chosen. Then Ankou appeared, climbed into Mischievous Rain's lap, and pretended to sleep. I ground my teeth some more. I would not ask. I would not ask! I would *not* ask!

The surprises kept coming.

"We will move against Honnoh soon. The Lieutenant will take his reconnaissance crew in first. That won't seem unusual."

For months the Lieutenant had roamed the province more than he had stayed at home, randomly, making no pretense that he was doing anything but looking for Rebels. He found some once in a while, usually through ambushes that did not go well for the other side. He always had a sorcerer handy.

I do not know if his patrols learned much. How could I? I was on the mushroom farm, kept in the dark and fed nothing but bullshit—when I got anything at all.

"Why Honnoh?"

"There is a tunnel complex under the town. It is intended to be the logistical base for an offensive against Aloe. The Rebel doesn't know that we've found out. The Lieutenant has visited Honnoh several times, always apparently without noticing anything. If we attack when they're assembling their main force we can ruin their whole summer."

That made operational sense. And was not anything that I had to know about to do my job.

Firefly began to make soft, nonsensical noises, perhaps murmured in words in a language that I did not recognize. "Is this it?"

"It is. Yes. Time to put her away." Conveniently, we were approaching the Company compound. Mischievous Rain gently shed Shin and Ankou, came to me on hands and knees. She brushed a wisp of hair off Firefly's face. "She's grubby. I should have made her take a bath."

Firefly had little use for water polluted by soap, especially where her skin might come into contact.

She did smell, and not pleasantly, though I had not noticed it earlier. "Has she been sick?" I had yet to see either twin show any sign of ill health.

"No. We'll be down in a minute. You take her inside. I'll handle the carpet."

"Right." And, bump, the ground arrived. "Ouch!"

"What?"

"My leg is asleep."

"Shake it out. Go. Put her to bed. Cover her up." She lifted Beloved Shin off the carpet, onto a patch of grass, but ignored Ankou, who shifted himself only after she began to tilt the carpet.

I stood over Firefly, looking down while the Taken tucked Beloved Shin in. She joined me. "What do you think?"

"She's an all right kid. Scary smart. Scary well-informed for her age. And she'll be as good-looking as her mother when she grows up."

Firefly's mother did not disagree. "And Beloved Shin?"

"He's a boy. Otherwise, same story." I had not yet asked about the names. I was increasingly uncomfortable in circumstances growing ever more domestic.

"I worry about them. I really do."

"Mothers are supposed to worry."

"I hope they'll survive the coming darkness. I hope they'll make us proud."

"Huh?"

"Oh. Yes. I've been putting it off because I don't know how to tell you. Maybe I shouldn't tell you at all."

My right eyelid began to twitch. Something was about to happen that I was not going to like. I might be about to learn something that I did not want to know.

"Shin and Baku are your children, too."

I gulped a gallon of air. Then I sucked down another. And then I squeaked, "That's not possible." Those weird kids my children? I never touched her! And, no kid of mine could ever be as weird as those two.

Mischievous Rain was ready for an argument because we never . . .

I did cop a feel that one time but that just would not do it. As a trained physician I knew how babies got made. She told me, "Don't get all excited and loud and wake them up. They don't need to know." She toyed with the end of the reddest streak in her hair, which drew my attention to her blue hair clip. Despite my distress I noted the fine craftsmanship of the piece. "You were in the Tower a long time."

"I was."

"A lot longer than went by out here. And She can make time move how she wants. Like the legends of the night in elf hill, only backwards."

Elf hill stories are universal. They exist even where people never heard of elves. Always there is the tale of the handsome or beautiful stranger who takes you to dance in paradise. And then you come back. Your newborn daughter is a great-grandmother who hates you for abandoning her mother and her. And no one else remembers you at all.

"You don't remember much of what happened in there," she said. "I don't remember much, either, except that I was there a lot longer." A gesture indicated the children. "They remember everything. But they won't share."

"You don't look any older, though," I blurted. "Just prettier." Undeniably true but I managed to sound like a dirty old man saying it.

"I aged inside of me. But I *am* prettier."

A ghost of a recollection of my Tower time fluttered through my head. Me, face-to-face with the actual, living Lady, who was a ringer for Tides Elba, and every bit as young, everywhere but in the eyes.

"Despite having produced your twin children, I remain technically qualified to become konzertasa."

"I am seriously uncomfortable talking about this."

"I'm not. I'm trying to connect with the father of my children."

"Uh . . ." Real articulate.

"Exactly. That is you."

"Uh . . ."

"Tides Elba is Taken. The Lady saw something in her that was overlooked by everyone else. She wakened it. Tides Elba will become one of the great powers of the world, stronger than anyone in this province, Whisper included. She is . . ." A moment's hesitation. "She is an almost thoroughbred descendant of . . . She is a remote niece of the woman in the Tower, which she did not ask for. She did not ask to be the Port of Shadows, the mother of your children, nor even the konzertosma. But here she is, trying her best to be a good mother while she does what she came to Aloe to do, hopefully without having to waken the unfathomable terror slumbering inside her."

I said, "Uh . . ." again, uncomfortable in a whole new way. She was getting emotional.

She had been staring at her hands in her lap. She looked up now, fixed me with a ferocious stare. "They *are* your children. Your time in the Tower wasn't a one-way experience. Oh! Don't start that! I'm not one of your idiot Company friends. I know you. The Eye works both ways. Never mind. Listen. We have children. If I could manage this out here without you knowing that we do I wouldn't have mentioned it."

She never broke eye contact. I tried but failed. I could think of nothing to say that did not sound whiny, however totally true.

She turned me loose but still held my hand lightly. I managed not to jerk away. I managed not to panic and run.

"I don't expect you to be a husband. You didn't ask for this, either. But I do expect you to help while I'm out there being Mischievous Rain. This could be a harsher summer than anyone expects. The divinations show nothing concrete. They get murkier the farther ahead you look. If I try to be the Taken and our children's mother all at once I'm likely to lack focus when focus might make the difference between victory and a miserable death for all of us. So I'm spilling the truth and asking for help, just for this summer."

She sounded completely sad. Maybe Sorrows would have been a better Taken name than the flighty Mischievous Rain.

What was the Lady up to? "If that's what she set up and that's what she wants, I have no choice but to acquiesce."

Ah, hell! I did it again. Amidst all the emotion, here came that smoldering, ugly dark look that told me I had my foot in my mouth up to the kneecap. Again. "Sorry. You know me. Sisters and whores, never lovers or wives."

"I do make liberal allowances, darling, but I'm running short on allowances to make."

I struck a thin vein of nerve and mined it. "Hey, you're the one who said she knows me."

"I did?"

"I didn't imagine that. You said you know me better . . ." I stopped. Not smart. I would just dig my grave a cubit deeper. "I will do what I can. You take into account my utter lack of experience and the fact that I have professional responsibilities of my own."

I should have been a dick and just walked away. But the woman did know me. She seduced me by dangling paternity under the nose of my sense of responsibility.

"Thank you. I just hit you hard. You need time to get your mind right. I'll say good night for tonight. We'll start our life as parents tomorrow—unless you're in a mood to go flying. There's something I need to look at out Honnoh way." Her tattoos were crawling. She tinkled briskly when she moved.

I was tempted to go, just to distract myself with my fear of falling. But she was spot-on about me needing time to get my head together. "Not tonight, darling."

She shrugged. She handed me a piece of lapis lazuli likely carved by the same hand that had produced the clip in her hair. "Keep this handy, love. If anything happens with the kids you'll hear it and be able to help."

"All right." The clip looked like a cuddle puddle of serpent devils mating.

The Taken had several more similar pieces lying around.

Another something to add to the think-about pile.

I spent time better invested in sleep inscribing this in a personal journal instead of the official Annals. Annalists to come ought not to have to relive my personal traumas.

I held the carved blue stone to my ear, heard Firefly and Shin snoring. Those kids produced a vigorous racket. Then, having eavesdropped,

I speculated about the artifact forever fixed in the Taken's hair. My bit of blue was smaller and flatter but more intricately carved.

Had she sent a message with it? The children did not need much oversight, really.

Maybe nothing we shared remained private. The Lady did like to know everything that happened, especially when the Taken were involved.

Here on the frontier the problematic Taken get away with more than they do when posted closer to the Tower.

Exhaustion caught up. I had to go lie down.

Turbulent thoughts did not keep me awake for long.

Just before darkness claimed me I saw Ankou staring at me with all three eyes from so close that I could smell his fishy breath.

The Lieutenant turned up at sick call. I was surprised. He does not get sick. "I thought you were out in the country."

"I was. And so shall I be. But, meantime, I'm pretty sure I broke my right big toe. Have a look."

I did. "You're right. Look at it, all swollen and purple. How did you manage that?"

"Running in the dark, barefoot. The Taken swooped in on our camp with no warning."

"I'll talk to her about that. Not much I can do here but tie it to the next toe and have you stay off it. Check in with the quartermasters. They'll get you ice from the icehouse. Ice will help with the swelling."

He nodded. He would take my advice, some, being a more reasonable patient than most. But he did have more on his mind. "I had that talk with the woman myself while she was bringing me here."

"I'll reinforce it, then. Hang on. I need to fit you with crutches. And you need to switch off with Candy."

"Something happen between you and her? She was in a really odd mood and it seemed like you were why. Plus, you're a bit odd yourself."

"I'm just tired. I haven't been getting much sleep."

"Like that, eh?"

"Not what you're thinking. Let me scribble a note to the Old Man. We need time to get you healed. We'll want you to be in perfect shape come summer."

"You know something the Taken hasn't shared with the rest of us?"

"Only that she thinks it's going to get hairy."

The Captain surprised me by grounding the Lieutenant for as long as it would take for his toe to heal properly. I showed the Lieutenant my own gnarly right great toe as an example of what could happen otherwise. Then the Old Man stunned everybody by assigning Two Dead to replace the Lieutenant. "Time we got some use out of the man." He sent Goblin out to relieve Silent, too. That made some sense. Silent needed time to relax. Silent did not say much so most guys did not notice but he was the hardest worker in the whole damned outfit.

I just do not understand how the rumor mills gather their grist. There were no witnesses to my conversations with Mischievous Rain, saving Ankou and possibly the Lady from afar, yet word began circulating saying that we would marry to give our children a legitimate name.

The rumors did not exactly proclaim my paternity, they just had me and the Taken making our night sport official and legal.

I first heard about it when I got called in for a disciplinary review. Candy said, "The Company discourages marriage between its members and outsiders." Well . . . There are a few wives in the ranks, mostly women more fierce than their husbands. Sergeant Chiba Vinh Nwynn was the prime example.

I said, "I can't imagine how this crap gets started. It just does. And then it takes on a life of its own."

"And if you have a knack for sniffing you might catch a whiff of the truth behind it. What's going on with you two?"

"Nothing. But since you and the Tower are determined to make us a couple I know you'll see what you want. We're going to work together for the kids' sake. That's it. That's all. There ain't no more. No touchy, no feely, no push me, no pull you."

"Really? And you're both still alive?"

"Yes. I am that old. I lied about my age when I joined up."

Not true, but I do misstate my age occasionally, should being younger or older shake a little grime off my apparent stupidities and misdeeds.

Candy chose to believe me because I do not often lie. But he did find it hard to credit that a man able to get as close to Mischievous Rain as I was would keep his hands to himself.

They all kept forgetting that Mischievous Rain was Taken, not just a really desirable girl. She had yet to demonstrate that dramatically.

Supper with the family, with Croaker on the daddy job.

I did not visit the Dark Horse much anymore, nor did I miss it except in that I could no longer head on over whenever I wanted. I felt that difference right away. Mischievous Rain felt it, too. For the kids it was business as usual. They remained barely restrained demonic entities, too mature to be real—in my estimation, based on my inadequate experience.

Mischievous Rain told me, "I need you to check Firefly's bottom. Thank you, Flora." One of the servant girls had exchanged an empty platter for one bearing cubes of pickled fish. "She has a rash. Maybe she's not cleaning herself right. But maybe she squatted in some poison ivy."

I noted Flora being slow to leave. She was thirteen, short, pretty, and well blessed up top. She had inspired the Taken to put out draconian warnings about touching her girls. So. I had not considered servants when wondering how rumors got started.

Eavesdroppery and a bit of poetic license could explain everything.

"Poison ivy? They aren't supposed to leave the compound." They would have to go a good way outside to run into that insidious vine.

"They aren't. They definitely aren't. And yet they did." Mischievous Rain laid a savage glare on her offspring. "They cozened Gurdlief into taking them to the woods on the other side of the creek."

Firefly volunteered, "We saw some rabbits. I almost caught one."

I, rather than their mother, countered, "And what almost caught you?"

Kids and mother alike eyed at me with open mouths. So. Even the Taken had not considered the situation in that light.

Ankou, in a curl around his food bowl and pretending to nap, opened an eye and awarded me a wink.

Maybe the kids had not been as much at risk as I thought. As with Mischievous Rain, there was much about Ankou not yet shown. "The Rebel must have scouts watching. A chance to grab the Taken's kids would be hard to pass up."

Mischievous Rain eyed her little villains, and Ankou, but said nothing. The kids nodded, abashed, even so.

We could only hope that the message had gotten through.

The Firefly bottom problem proved trivial. A good scrub and a smear of ointment, with instructions as to better self-care, dealt with that.

The Old Man caught me as I passed headquarters. "How close to being ready to make movement are you?"

"Into the field? I could be out the gate in six hours. Maybe less. I've prepped everything that I can."

"Good. I knew I could count on you. How're you getting on with the wife?"

My expression must have turned fierce. He stepped back. "All right. But there is a reality that we're trying to project."

Yeah. Sure. Got it, boss. "We get along. We're as domestic as we can be." I told him about Firefly's cross-creek adventure and diaper rash.

"I'll caution the sentries. As for the rest, take the ribbing and just bust out the random smirk." He held his hand in front of his mouth as though hoping to frustrate lip-readers. "It won't be forever. And, on a personal note, what the hell is your problem? I'd love to have that woman beside me while every swinging dick in the province goes bugfuck with jealousy."

I was flabbergasted, that was so far out of character.

He continued, "And the town library tell me they want their scroll back."

"Oh. I forgot. She has it. I'll take it back tomorrow."

"Later, then. Things to do." I watched the Old Man go. He was so much more hands-on, lately. Tended to make a man wonder.

I told Mischievous Rain that the library wanted its scroll. She glanced at Seijou, doing maid stuff with an ear cocked. "I'll go with you." And she did, wearing midnight under a silvery robe that suggested angel wings when she raised her arms. The robe's inner face was all shimmery metallic colors that pulled at you, threatening to swallow you up. She sat by in serene silence while I handled my patients, observing, never once volunteering to help. The first few all stared, then backed away. I figured that folks with lesser afflictions would start not showing up soon. And so it went.

Our visit to the library caused considerable consternation. The Limper himself, with his unutterably foul reputation, might not have troubled those people as much as did Mischievous Rain.

Still, there were more librarians around than ever I had seen before. A Taken who was once the konzertosma was a curiosity indeed.

Several women lost their nerve early and turned scarce. Those that held their ground sweated and shook and stared. My wicked soul would not be restrained. "What did you do to these people, sweetheart?"

"Not funny, lover. This is why I stayed away."

"Let me do the talking." The staff knew me. I was a regular. Some did try to find me interesting stuff. All but one were volunteers who just worked the occasional hour. The full-time goddess of the books was a maiden lady a decade my senior. She had made a point of letting me know that she had not served in the temple, never had married, and never had let herself to be touched by a man. I thought she protested excessively, maybe trying to goad me into taking a shot at adjusting her status. I had let the opportunity pass.

I did not know her name, neither given, family, nor clan. Her associates called her Snow Woman. She had become a sort of friend because we shared an appreciation for books and history.

I arranged access to material I wanted Mischievous Rain to review.

She might spot something that I had missed because of cultural blindness while I was looking for her.

Snow Woman had stuff brought to us. Her volunteers reeked of conflicted emotions. They were terrified of the Taken but curious about the lapsed konzertosma. None seemed to have known her as Tides Elba.

We were alone with a midden of ancient paper. Mischievous Rain whispered, "Your Snow Woman is a flaming hypocrite. She loves the man-bone more than most. Your Goblin is one of a dozen men, unbeknownst to one another, who serve her lusts. She has them all thinking that they alone have succeeded where every man before them failed. Snow Woman is deeply, emotionally invested in a virginal persona she created when she was a maiden who failed to attract any male attention."

"Really? How could you know all that?"

"I read her secret journal."

"Huh?"

"Some nights I have trouble sleeping. I find ways to amuse myself."

That brought home what I overlooked because I was close to her. She could do things that only a Taken could. Not only could she discover Snow Woman's deep secret, she could root out the hidden lore of most Aloens. She might be able to sort the good folks from the bad. Well, make that sort out our friends from our secret foes.

She had warned me that she meant to create her own intelligence system. And she had, obviously, without me noticing, despite my being so close.

Seldom do I have trouble sleeping.

I asked, "Can you read any of the old languages? Like Levanev?"

"Levanev, Khansai, and Margelin, some. They beat those into you in the temple. You need them to read the sacred texts."

"All right, I'll sort out what I can handle and leave the rest to you."

"Isn't that always the way?"

"Excuse me?"

"Just bitching because I always get the hard part. Pay no attention."

I smiled, suffered it, sorted materials, then said, "I went through most of this when I was looking for you."

"And you found me, you clever man. And now we have children."

Library women, lurking close by, overheard every word.

We found nothing of interest. Mischievous Rain told me, "I don't see what you get out of this. I can't make myself care about anything that happened before I was born."

"A nice long soak in the past helps you understand why today is the way it is." I thought I was starting to get a handle on the woman behind the Mischievous Rain mask. She never meant half of what she said when she talked like that. She just wanted to see a reaction.

I reminded me that, although she was Taken and a mother, she was also a girl who had been shielded from the real world most of her life. It was surprising that she was as well-grounded as she was.

I said, "I don't see anything that we don't already know. How about we go root around in vital statistics?"

"It's late. Won't they want to close down soon?"

"They won't mind doing a little something extra for one of the Taken."

The records people got grim behind their efforts to be helpful. Then Elmo turned up. "Go home and get some rest, Croaker. Captain's orders. No questions, no discussion. Immediate execute." He bowed to Mischievous Rain. "You, ma'am, are, of course, welcome to do whatever you deem appropriate."

I headed for Admin once we reached the compound. I found the Old Man. "You wanted to see me, sir?"

"No. I wanted your ass back here so you can rest. We move out in the morning. Did Elmo screw that up?"

"No sir. That's what he said. Minus the part about movement. I just assumed . . ."

"You know the mantra about assuming. On your dumbass way to bed tell the Taken that I would like a word if she has the time."

This when there was still some light out.

Beloved Shin awaited me out front. I told him, "Tell your mother the Captain wants to see her."

"Tell her yourself. She sent me to get you. Supper is ready."

She had not prepared that herself, of course. The town girls had. They would need locking up till after we rolled out in the morning.

"Fish again?" Beloved Shin complained. "How come so much fish? Why not pork? I like pork. Where does all this fish come from, anyway? Not that puny creek down there?"

"I like fish," Firefly announced.

Of course she did. And she would love fish until Shin discovered a taste for fish himself.

Mischievous Rain said, "There is a lake northwest of here. I go fishing there when my patrols take me that way. I like fish, too, Firefly."

Beloved Shin looked to me for support. I told him, "Half a vote, kiddo. I prefer mutton. But fish will do. It's good for you."

"You just don't want to irritate Mom."

His mother told him, "He doesn't need to irritate me, Shin. You manage admirably on your own."

Firefly stuck out her tongue.

I then relayed the Captain's request.

"I'll see him once we're done. I can guess what he wants."

The compound locked down. Troopers came in but did not leave. Reliable noncoms collected men otherwise disinclined to return from town. Anyone interested had to realize that something was afoot. I was so far from inside that I was surprised completely when I was awakened before first light and told to get ready to travel. As I headed for my clinic I saw Mischievous Rain's carpet go airborne, staggering under the weight of a crowd.

A soldier called Sharps awaited me at the clinic. He had brought me two horses and three mules.

"What's this?"

"Load your stuff on the mules. One horse is for you. The other is for Edmous Black. You're to take the road to Honnoh and push hard. Captain's orders."

Said Captain himself shambled out of the darkness, demanding, "Where *is* Edmous Black?"

Black was my current apprentice, a local younger man who, at this point, had been my understudy for a scant ten days. I had recruited him only because he had veterinary experience.

"Here, sir," from behind the Old Man. Black was still arranging his clothing. He asked me, "What are we doing, sir?"

"Looks like we get to participate in a nighttime exercise. Get the field supplies aboard these mules. I'll join you in a minute." I considered the horses. Both were saddled and ready. I do not ride often but riding is a required skill. The Company does act as mounted infantry sometimes.

Speaking of, a racket arose as horsemen began moving outside the compound wall.

The Captain told me, "You're already working on getting left behind. Do you want to cross hostile ground on your own? Corey, Sharps, help Black load the mules." Then, satisfied that he had rained on my morning, he stalked off to visit misery somewhere else.

Though we wasted no time Black and I were well behind when we did move out. The mules were not eager. Time fled. We fell back farther and farther. Other slow starters kept passing us. My patience thinned. I would be irritated severely if I got to Honnoh and found out that somebody had died while waiting for me.

These things happened at Honnoh while I was en route. Two Dead and his scouts rushed in at sunrise, not unexpected. They fixed the attention of the locals. Then Mischievous Rain came out of the rising sun with the rest of our wizards, each accompanied by bodyguards. They spread out. The Taken joined the fun. Resistance collapsed. Our mounted men collected fugitives as they advanced toward Honnoh.

When I arrived the only action was in the underground, where our sorcerers were making being a Rebel an unhappy life choice. The other side had to fight without magic users of their own.

Aboveground other sorcerers sorted enemies from ordinary folks. Company brethren who had nothing better to do lugged plunder up out of the underground.

The Company suffered no fatalities and only a handful of injuries. The attack had gone off like an exercise, thank you Mischievous Rain.

That all left me with a nervous stomach. Things never go smoothly once the enemy gets involved. He has ideas of his own.

I treated my people, then waited on the triage of the locals. I would fix up injured innocents but not a Rebel unless instructed to do so. Why help somebody who was about to get dead anyway?

I had commandeered a small shop for my surgery. There was a bench out front where in normal times old guys sat and swapped lies about their glory days. I sprawled there and swatted flies while Edmous Black entertained himself by cleaning instruments.

Mischievous Rain plopped down beside me, leaned against me. She had produced no hint of a tinkle approaching. Her tattoos were dancing ugly. "I'm beat. All those men on the carpet . . . That was too much." She snuggled closer. "Don't wake me up for anything less than the end of the world."

"There's a cot inside if you want to use it."

"This is fine. I'll be good in a few minutes."

And she did sleep, right there, right then, right in front of any part of the world that wandered by. I started thinking that, all else aside, Mischievous Rain was extremely desirable. Deeply manipulative, too.

Black Company guys, Rebel soldiers, local civilians, everybody got a look. Way to sell the story, woman.

She kind of clung to my left arm and sprawled across my chest. And snored.

I endured it bravely until people asked for my help. It was not that hard to take.

Honnoh was another heartbreak for the eastern Rebel, again delivered by the Black Company, made possible by a woman I never saw do much. A woman who garnered poor Croaker untold gobs of resentment when she insisted that he return to Aloe with her, aboard her carpet, leaving her former passengers to walk or ride liberated livestock. Edmous Black had to manage our horses and mules and equipment on his own.

Six prisoners joined us aboard the carpet. Two were older men, senior Rebels. Four were girls, each one a copy of Mischievous Rain.

Mischievous Rain's nap had refreshed her. I was not so lucky. I dozed off while we were airborne despite being the only one available to wrangle captives.

I wakened to excitement in progress. The male prisoners had gone after the Taken despite the carpet being a hundred feet in the air and them having no chance of making it work if they did overpower her.

One was unconscious and leaking from a torn right cheek. Beloved Shin stood over him. The second, although nearly as big as Buzzard Neck Tesch, was on his knees, fingertips raking his throat, while Blessed Baku squeezed his left shoulder with her little right hand.

Ankou had the female captives herded into the left rear corner of the carpet, which sagged four feet lower than the right front.

Shin glared daggers. Firefly said, "Seriously, Dad, how could you go to sleep?" Ankou delivered a judgmental glare of his own.

Mischievous Rain said, "Ignore them. I was never in any danger. We're about to arrive. You jump off. I'll hover while you round up somebody to take control of these people."

In minutes I was updating the Captain, who kept interjecting questions.

Five minutes after that I watched the Rebel officers being put into irons while the captive girls were shown to the stockade. And they were just girls. The oldest might be seventeen.

Five minutes later still the Taken and I finished sliding her carpet into storage. We agreed that we needed rest badly. After supper. Interrogations could wait.

I went to my quarters. She went to hers. I did not want company. I was starving, having skipped my noonday meal. Her attitude was the same.

I snacked on hard cheese and harder bread that I washed down with nasty local wine, then for the second evening running I went to bed before the light of day expired.

Edmous Black made it back with my equipment intact and our animals still healthy. He wrapped everything up without complaining despite being totally unhappy with his boss. I was pleased with him and let him know, obliquely.

The troops who returned by traditional means, herding prisoners serving as pack animals, began to arrive late next day.

The Honnoh triumph would improve our standing with anyone who loathed the Rebel and the Resurrectionist. Those people were plentiful but carefully not outspoken. The Rebel was neither big on freedom of speech nor tolerant of other ideologies.

Mischievous Rain got to work on our captives long before the raiders began straggling in.

I found Edmous Black snoring in the clinic. Normally he spent off-duty time with family in town. This once he had been too fagged to make the walk.

Only a dozen guys showed for sick call. The most badly injured raiders went straight to the hospital now installed in the Company-claimed space in the Taken's new building. The wards lay on the other side of one wall of my new quarters.

Always thinking, our Captain. Always scheming.

In time my whole clinic would move.

Elmo turned up while I was working on the shoulder of a fool who had become distracted in the presence of a mule and had gotten herself bitten. "Avoid Admin and the Old Man if you can."

"What's up?"

"I don't know. The Taken and the Old Man were talking about you."

"And?"

"And she wanted you for something. The Captain didn't want to give you up. He don't have anybody to take your place."

"Being needed is almost as good as being loved."

"You think? He maybe got overruled. The Lady weighed in. Anyway, I figure that if they can't find you they can't fuck you over."

"The One-Eye option." One-Eye had been conspicuously invisible since his exorcism, though he had turned up for the raid.

He probably came back with his pockets sagging.

"Exactly."

"Elmo, you're a good friend. Thanks. But me trying to skate out of whatever the Taken wants, let alone what the Lady wants, would be what the philosopher meant when he said, 'This shit is hopeless.'"

"You're probably right. But I thought you might want to get a running start."

I could not imagine any situation that dire. "I'll wait and see."

He shrugged. "Your funeral." He had done what he could. Now he could get busy thinking of clever things to say as Outsweeper put me into the ground.

The powers might not be planning something to make me happy but I could not see them imposing anything too terribly awful, either.

The Captain told me, "The Lady wants the Honnoh prisoners brought to the Tower."

Oh my. Maybe I should have run. "How do I slide out of that?" Mischievous Rain could not handle that by herself. "Suicide?"

"Save that for a darker day. You're not going. You'll stay here, doctoring and daddying."

"What?" Deflation, seriously.

"Did I stutter? Did I speak a tongue that you don't understand? The Taken wanted to drag you along. The Lady wanted to see you. I reminded them that I have seven hundred soldiers and a thousand animals all in need of medical care that only you can provide."

Oh. I was disappointed. But why? I had to study on that, the way the Tower gave me the jimjams. "Look out for the kids. Got it." Having only a limited notion of what that would entail. "For how long?"

"Ask her. Did Edmous Black do all right at Honnoh?"

"He did. And he does know his animals. He's the man I've been looking for."

"Keep an eye on him. Buzz thinks he's a plant."

Crap. Just my luck. A traitorous assistant layered atop an unwanted wife and some even less wanted children.

"Four days for travel," Mischievous Rain told me when I asked how long she would be gone. "A couple more to rest and deal with business, but probably longer for me in inside-the-Tower time." She was uneasy, probably because the trip would be dangerous. Crossing the Plain of Fear was never without risk, even at high altitude. "Can you handle the children?"

"If they give me any grief I'll stuff them into pickle barrels the way we did One-Eye that time."

"Seriously." She was more worried about her kids than about what lay ahead for her.

"I'll cope. You just put the fear of the Lady in them before you go. Why does she want to see those people in person, anyway?"

Her hand strayed to the clip in her hair. Need to know, evidently. "Those girls could be my sisters. My twins, even, but younger. We all share the same birthmark." She chopped air with her right hand, a suggestion that we cut the chatter.

"Oh. So then we got luckier than we hoped at Honnoh."

She nodded, then made that chopping motion again.

"All right. But that just worries me more, you being alone with six desperate . . ."

"I won't be alone. Colonel Chodroze will accompany me."

"Two Dead? A one-handed guy that . . . You know . . ."

"I do know. But I'm a big girl, sweetheart," with a steaming helping of sarcasm. "I did want you to come with. Your Captain convinced the Lady that you're more valuable here."

Again a moment of elation morphed into brooding disappointment. How come?

"We all had to settle for second choice."

And Two Dead for last. "I'm sorry. For Two Dead."

"He'll be fine. She isn't half as bad as you think."

Really? Are you insane, woman? What She are you referencing?

Or was that just something you put out there because somebody might be listening?

"I told the kids what their responsibilities will be. They'll try to behave while I'm gone. But they are children. Children sometimes act without thinking."

So do big people. She was stalling. She did not want to go where she had to go. She said, "While I'm away I want you to visit the temple. Take Silent and the twins. Check out everyone, konzertasa to the youngest orphan, and even the outside employees. No exceptions. Find anyone who looks like me."

"That could cause problems."

"For the temple if they make difficulties. I've told them to expect you. There is a potential health crisis that only you can avert."

"But I'm really finding you a sister?" What had Markeg said?

"If one exists. Announce your findings aloud in my bedroom."

Ach! The implications had a fiercely chilling effect on a notion that had begun to creep into my imagination.

She gave me her "I'm reading your filthy mind" look and winked.

"Don't," I squeaked.

Sisters and whores.

"I'll be good, my love." On which note she went off to admonish the children about their behavior in her absence yet one more time. She was at it still when Two Dead turned up, packed, ready, and as grim of aspect as year-old death.

The kids and I watched the carpet depart. Something more than a cold mist but less than a mild drizzle made the morning especially miserable. Two Dead, Mischievous Rain, and the prisoners accompanying them were going to get soaked to the bone. And that would be the least of their troubles.

For some reason I had a feeling that the Taken's departure was a watershed moment. The thought induced an inexplicable sense of loss, a sense of opportunity squandered, of a chance gone ere ever it was recognized.

Melancholy set in.

16

Long Ago and Far Away: The Far Country

The carpet's cargo appeared to be mostly tools and the kinds of tools you used to maintain tools. The sorcerer said, "Before anything else we have to have a place where we can get in out of the rain. A place where we can keep everything dry." He took Bathdek's hands. "So soft. This might be hard for you at first, dear. But we have to work hard and hurry, for Laissa's sake."

He did not explain that.

He had a severe case of selective hearing when Bathdek asked questions. She let the remark slide.

The sorcerer was average in every direction but stamina. He worked tirelessly. First he threw up a temporary shelter that was mostly a shallow cave with lean-tos in front, facing one another. Then he started on a permanent place that would perch like an eagle's nest atop a jagged granite upthrust that was extremely hard to climb. He used sorcery to move materials and the carpet to move girls. He was as much a genius with his hands and tools as he was with sorcery, which he mixed in flawlessly. Bathdek was amazed at the quickness with which he could fell a pine, strip it of waste, then turn it into lumber for building his new stronghold.

He seemed to need no plan. At the beginning he just studied the granite outcrop from every angle, then started building.

After just a few days Bathdek could see that it would be a sizable little fortress when it was done. Maybe a small wooden castle.

At first she did her best, as part of her survival strategy, but she was a princess. Never, even as pretend, had she done anything resembling work.

She rebelled.

The sorcerer shrugged. "As you wish, Kitten. But in this family if we don't contribute we don't eat." He thrust his chin Laissa's way.

Laissa worked till her hands were raw, doing donkey's work. She did whatever Papa asked without complaining.

That astonished Bathdek. Dorotea, the Senjak baby, had been more spoiled than she.

The sorcerer was as good as his word. Bathdek's rebellion passed quickly.

She noticed that Papa seemed troubled when he watched Laissa. Her eye not trained to it, Bathdek did not understand until they had been in the Ghost Country a month. Their new home was halfway built. Her body was growing accustomed to long days of hard work. And then she did not so much see the change in Laissa as she began to smell it.

Laissa had been getting slower and less responsive but so gradually that it did not stand out. But the smell . . . Even a bath with her sister in the frigid creek at the bottom of the hill did not help for long.

Bathdek thought about warning Papa that something was wrong but kept quiet. He knew. That was why he was troubled. That was why he was driven.

It was clear, now. Dorotea had been dead when the necromancer collected her. He had wrought a miracle by bringing her back to life. But it was only life of a sort. The reanimated flesh remained dead.

At the rarest high levels of the Domination, with the Dominator, the Ten, the Senjaks, and a core couple dozen others, death had gone down to defeat. But that was only before the fact. It was life prolonged until misadventure sprang a fatal ambush, not life restored.

The closely held secret was one huge reason the Dominator was so hated.

He might be a trial from which the world would never escape.

But He would be a trial no more forever if anyone ever figured out how to kill Him. Unless this necromancer's work came into His hands. Then not even death itself could relieve the world of its pain.

Papa said, "You see it all now, don't you, Kitten?"

"You mean what's happening to Laissa?"

"Yes. I do." There was a hint of smug satisfaction there. Bathdek suspected that was because she had not tried to dissemble about her ability to observe and reason. "I'm really starting to worry."

"Can you take care of her for a few days while I go get some things we need to fix her?"

"Papa, she's always taken care of me." Bathdek used that "Papa" without calculation, mostly because it was the only name she knew to call him. She was startled after the fact. She had meant to save that for a moment when she could milk the maximum emotional advantage.

Who was manipulating whom in this insane situation?

And since when did a hostage's success so vigorously depend upon a kidnapper's success?

The leverages here were unique.

Laissa did not know that Kitten was her sister. Papa did know, but only in his insane mode, not in his real-world person. There was no way that Bathdek could get out of the Ghost Country on her own, let alone managing that while rescuing her mindless sister. Only Papa knew how to work the flying carpet even if Dorotea did dare flee. Papa had not said so in so many words but it was clear that only by his skills could Dorotea go on.

Papa said, "That's partly true, Kitten. She does. She's a good daughter and a good sister and she wants the best for you. But now she's the one who . . ."

"I understand. Maybe more than you want. I will do my best for her, forever. She is my sister."

Papa was pleased. He glowed. "Thank you, Kitten. Thank you."

Bathdek had amazed herself. Yes, Dorotea was her sister, but in Dusk she would never have delivered such a passionate and genuine statement. In that world sisters were only one's most intimate and ferocious competitors.

Everything changed that stormy night on a hill near Dusk.

Credence Senjak, who insisted on calling herself Bathdek, had become one member of a unit of three who could not survive without one another. Whatever else her ambition had sought, wherever else her dreams might have soared, this was her life now. Her own choices had brought her here. Railing against the unfairness was pointless on both the practical and the moral levels. For once she faced reality. There was no one else to blame.

And her situation now faced her with roles that she never imagined possible, as a dutiful daughter and caring sister.

And she wanted to be those things. To fading Bathdek's dismay.

The necromancer readied the Howler's carpet for flight. He was nervous. He was headed out into the world. He did not do well with people, usually. And he would have to deal with them without attracting attention. He would have to create a strong, forceful character for the mission.

A mission in a part of the world where it might be impossible to find anyone who spoke a language that he did.

Bathdek stood with her left arm around Laissa's waist, watching. "Please be careful, Papa." She did not think she or her sister would survive for long if he did not return because by the time they could be sure that he was not coming back Dorotea would be past saving and Bathdek had no hope of finding her way out of this wilderness on her own.

Being a powerful sorceress would help only a little.

She could not stop obsessing over the fact that she was an incredibly spoiled city girl who never once had had to lift a finger to care for herself, in a survival sort of way.

This business had shaped her mind for a struggle but had not delivered an education in practical, hands-on skills.

"I will be exceeding careful," the necromancer promised. "I treasure my girls too much to let myself fail. I'll be back, hopefully sooner than you expect." He climbed aboard and made the carpet elevate a foot. "Kitten, I left written instructions about things you can work on while I'm away. Also about taking care of Laissa. Don't slack off just because I'm not here. And remember that your sister has to come before anything else."

"I understand, Papa."

Bathdek rubbed oil into her sister's skin. That seemed to help. The oil was strongly scented but not to mask other odors. Whatever produced the scent also kept Laissa's skin smooth and supple.

Laissa almost purred. She liked this. But she did not say so.

The cave was crowded with all the things that Papa wanted kept safe from the weather. That did not leave much room for people.

"This is ridiculous!" A Senjak daughter, living in a cave! Two of them, in fact, though one could not truly be said to be living.

She stopped there. She was about to throw a tantrum that would do nothing but trouble Laissa. And there was no point rehearsing anything that happened before those hopeless idiots smothered her sister.

No point. No point at all. Laissa remembered none of that. No point thinking about Dorotea anymore. This girl *was* Laissa. But she was still Bathdek's sister.

And what about her? She was stuck here, a prisoner of her own intelligence. Yes, she could take out Papa if she awaited her moment. They both knew that, though he might not remember it most of the time. But that act of rebellion would not improve her situation. It would worsen things by shedding the most useful member of the family. She would still be lost at the end of the world. She would still lack the skills to save herself and Laissa. She might as well become Kitten for real.

After reclothing Laissa she quit feeling sorry for herself and got busy eliminating tasks from Papa's list. He had been quite generous. But with him away she felt free to indulge her skills as a sorceress. That let her accomplish much more than she would have by attacking it as straight physical labor.

17

Once Upon a Time: Shadow of the Moon

The sorcerer began by flitting off to the nearest large town, hoping a stranger would not be an object of too great curiosity. If his luck was in he would find someone with whom he could communicate.

Luck would not bless him this time. The natives were xenophobic. His skin was so pale they thought that he must be a ghost.

He tried another town. That one was worse. He had to use sorcery to save himself, then again to hide himself until night fell and he could get aloft without being seen in flight.

Dread filled him. There was no option. He had to return to the Domination.

Logically, that should not be a problem. The Domination was huge. He just had to stay away from Dusk and make sure he was not seen flying. Only . . . There might be questions raised about some of the things he needed for Laissa.

He cursed himself for having been so focused on tools that he had failed to load one of the boxes of stuff he needed to keep Laissa going.

Hey. He could go back to the old place. The box was still there. And he could throw together another load of useful stuff. Laissa could remain safe indefinitely.

It was all for Laissa.

Only . . . Again.

The Howler would, long ago, have extricated himself. There would be a watch on the old place. That was an iron-bound certainty. The lords of Dusk would be in a ferment. A man who could entangle and trap the Howler would remain the object of intense interest until he was caught and domesticated. The Dominator himself would be involved. He would feel threatened.

Damn! Whatever he did now, it would take time. A lot of time, relatively. And Laissa did not have a lot.

Had he done the right thing, leaving her with Kitten? Kitten was not as reliable as he would like. She cared for her sister but he remained unconvinced that her care was all that it should be. Too often, in too many ways and about too many things, he got the sense that she was just pretending.

Still, there was no way he could have brought Laissa and left Kitten. He suspected that Kitten was not a girl who did well by herself.

Odd. He understood that parents never knew their children as well as they desired but there were times when he felt like he did not know his daughters at all. That was partly because there was something wrong inside his head. He was well aware of that but had no idea how to overcome it or even how to manage it.

He could not recall a single detail of his daughters' childhoods.

He could not recall much of anything when he tried to plumb the deeps of his past. Those rare times when he did remember came only when it felt like there was another person doing the recollecting, living a parallel life inside his body. That person kept a journal that he never reread.

Safe in the dark, he took the carpet as high as he could endure, in hopes of getting lost against the backdrop of stars, then headed west at the most wicked speed that he could manage.

Morning found him racing along above cloud cover. He was pleased. He would not have to go into hiding while the sun was up. And shortly after nightfall he was able to drift down into the city called Lords. In a relatively short time a combination of generosity with coin and bloody terror visited on a couple of people who meant him ill found him happily equipped with everything he had come west to collect. He was up and away again before morning's light.

He was happy. He could fix Laissa now. He could keep her going until he found a way to beat death permanently.

But he was unhappy, too. What he had done in Lords, and the way he had done it, was going to draw attention. No help for it.

He raced eastward a hundred miles, then found himself a place to hide and sleep while the sun was aloft.

Sleep was slow coming. He hated to waste the time. It was time during which Laissa would continue to fade.

18

In Modern Times: Dark Water Rising

There are more Company brethren now than there were when first we came to Aloe, but, sadly, there are too many fewer of our old fellow travelers. Those whose clay we managed to save and honor now sleep amongst the apple trees on a hillside a half mile southwest of the Company compound. We have a deal with the owner, one of the first friends we made when we came here. We keep thieves away, help with the harvest, and lay our fallen brothers down in the cool, sweet shade. Only a cherry forest might be grander.

I went to the orchard because I was in the grip of a deep melancholy. The days stretched on and still Mischievous Rain did not return. Maybe she never would. So I decided to go honor the fallen instead of curling up in bed feeling sorry for myself.

I fought the melancholy by recording what Outsweeper, the Company's dedicated grave keeper, had inscribed on the memorial slabs among the trees:

TUDÈLE LAGLEIZE: Unblemished by too pedantic a regard for the truth
SLEEPY EYES: Overcome with ugliness
FANCY PRANCE: Even if I die in the gutter I have to fall forward
GUUST NOLET: Cross-dressing in plain sight
HIKA NOLET: Redheaded cross-dressing demon whisperer
These sisters had been seriously nasty. Hika may have fallen to friendly fire
FLEA HJALTI: Inflexible Irresolution
DROUGHT: Evil is hard work
INGRATH BAT: A cowbird's egg in a nest of lies
FADE SHULABAT: A Child of Mist and Darkness
MINKUS SCUDD: Put to death with special indignity
Executed, not slain by enemy action, for criminal stupidity
OTTERS: The proud do not endure
THREE APPLES: We are none of us infallible, not even the youngest among us
WILT: I do not think that he will have been improved by death
COPPERHEAD: He heard the stars
SERGEANT POOR: Getting on with the ass-kicking
MISTRY: Worn weak with lack of wonder
BACHIMEN: He had to blink

Silent turned up after sick call, while Edmous Black cleaned up. Apprentice Black had done the doctoring while I kibitzed. He was better with animals than with people, but he was adequate with both. Damn! I do hope that he does not turn out to be a Rebel. Or, worse, an operator for Whisper's villains.

Silent signed, "Ready when you are."

The cat Ankou, heretofore unnoticed, oozed out of an unnaturally thick shadow. He stretched.

I asked, "You in a hurry?"

Silent signed, "Best to get it done before Mischievous Rain's absence becomes common knowledge."

"Right." I glanced at Ankou. The cat was no longer there. Silent looked, too, and frowned.

Had he seen Ankou at all? Surely he knew the beast was a monster, not a pet.

I said, "The Taken wants her kids to go along. She didn't say why."

He bobbed his head. He was aware but did not know why, either.

I delayed movement till the children had had lunch, then headed for town. Ankou ran ahead, scouting, more like a hunting dog than a cat. He failed to chase baby rabbits when he kicked up a clutch. He ignored fleeing voles as well, and went so far as to disdain a challenge from a large orange tomcat.

Ankou for sure had more than murder on his mind.

He disappeared like morning mist as we neared the temple steps.

This was supposed to be the twins' first town visit but they seemed indifferent, as though they were seeing nothing new.

Had they been sneaking out at night, like the time when they turned up on a flying carpet miles from home and high in the sky?

An old man sitting watch by the poor box levered himself out of his chair and shuffled inside.

A woman emerged as we approached the old man's post. She was about fifty. The twins obviously disturbed her. As obviously she wished that they would go away. Non-orphan children were not welcome here—but Blessed Baku and Beloved Shin had to be welcomed.

Their mother would insist.

I knew this woman. She suffered from persistent back pain because her left leg was shorter than her right. I asked, "Did the special shoe help?"

"It did. And I thank you." Guardedly.

So. She was comfortable enough with the Company physician but said physician had Silent and the twins in tow. I said, "I but carry out instructions here. I wasn't told why, only what to do."

"I understand." Unhappily. "Such is life. What will that be?"

"The Taken Mischievous Rain is concerned about the health of her onetime sisters and mothers. Evidence unearthed at Honnoh convinced her that the Rebel command intended to use Occupoa's temples to spread an ugly new disease."

Temple leaderships would be appalled that anyone could even think of such a sacrilegious effort.

"The Taken gave me the tools to spot the early symptoms—*if* the Rebel has sunk so low."

The old sister was appalled. "What must we do?"

"Set me up somewhere and then run everyone past me. Everyone! Temple maidens, sisters, orphans, even the outside people who work here, voluntary or paid. Start with the konzertasa."

The old sister was not happy about that.

I said, "I do apologize. This is uncomfortable for me, too. But my orders come from the Tower. Even the Taken can't argue with that."

"Must those children be present?"

"My instructions say yes."

"What must be must be. Come."

"Thank you. One more thing. I'll need to know about anyone who tries to sneak away to avoid seeing me."

The temple's denizens cooperated sullenly. My first client was the konzertasa, as requested, setting an example. After having survived my fake screening she stood by to observe and to support the sisters who followed.

The temple hierarchy let themselves be examined, also example setting, doing what was necessary to get along with the mundane power.

Ankou prowled restlessly, sniffing, batting things invisible, interspersing kitty stretches, never loafing. Maybe he was being a distraction. Or maybe he was playing to his image. He had been around long enough to have become *that* cat.

The twins were restless, too. They turned up hither and yon, never seeming to cross the space between.

I found a Tides Elba "sister" right away. She was younger than mine and had reddish hair but with a costume change could pass as Mischievous Rain.

I kept the line moving but did not fool the older sisters completely. They noted my reaction to that younger Tides Elba and did not miss my interest when fourteen-year-old and nine-year-old versions turned up later. These younger girls had the Taken's raven hair.

How many Mischievous Rains could there be? Well, just one, really. And she was Taken. She was unique. But it now looked like we could round up imitation Tides Elbas by the dozen.

I had no specific instructions about what to do. Mischievous Rain had thought that there might be one more of her here. She had not imagined that there could be a troop. I glanced at Silent, standing guard by the doorway where the temple people came in. He could curb any mischief before it got started but was unlikely to be a source of useful advice.

Well, then, nothing to do but cull the special girls and shift them to the compound, which was sure to make me even more unpopular with the temple.

Beloved Shin blasted an expletive and dove into a shadow. Firefly did the same on her side of the room. Both just vanished, "hiding in the shadows." I expected wind chimes but was disappointed.

Ankou vanished, too. And then Silent faded away. I noted his absence only after he reappeared accompanied by three temple girls, one of whom was the red-haired Tides Elba from earlier.

Firefly materialized, startling me. "They were trying to sneak out."

Two of the girls were pint-size, one about three and the other the age of my twins. "Good work, kiddo."

The temple people were impressed.

I said, "Round up the others. Keep them together." I asked the konźertasa, "Didn't these girls ever seem odd to you?"

She did not understand. Neither did her companions. The girls were girls, better than average looking, but . . .

"Silent, is there a glamour at work here?"

He considered the girls, looked puzzled, looked irked, then looked determined. He gestured forcefully. The world went black for a blink, after which he offered me a tilt of the head.

A murmur passed amongst the older women. They now saw the sameness. The konzertasa asked, "What does this mean?"

"It means that Tides Elba was the first of a line of identical girls planted by the Resurrectionists. We found another four at Honnoh."

The konzertasa could not get her mind around that.

I asked, "Are there more people that I need to see?"

"Just toddlers, babies, and employees who haven't taken vows."

I found no more Tides Elba girls. The two youngest I left in place, thinking that they should be easy to monitor. I arrested the older girls.

"Nine girls, now?" the Old Man asked. "All exactly alike?"

"Pretty close. They're all different ages. The oldest one has red hair, the rest all black. The Honnoh girls all had black hair, even the one who looked like she was almost the same age as the redhead we caught here."

"Your wife is actually the oldest, as far as we know. Right? And didn't she have red hair, back when?" He sounded unsure.

I could not recall. Except for that moment when I planted Limper's rescript between Tides Elba's breasts I could recall almost nothing of what happened back then. That might be worth some thought in itself.

The Captain said, "So, if one new girl got popped out every year after her, there might be a bunch more floating around. Not to mention, some of the ones we already caught look like they're the same age. So what does that mean, Croaker?"

"Don't ask me, boss. I have no idea how you make identical babies. I can't imagine why you would want to. Somebody more smarterer than me might get it, though. Like maybe some spooky Tower lurker."

Candy and the Lieutenant were listening but keeping quiet. Candy was set to lead the next long patrol, hoping to conjure up another Honnoh kind of raid. Buzzard Neck Tesch would be his field sorcerer. Candy was not happy about that. Neither was Tesch. They did not get along.

The Lieutenant mused, "We have us here a case of eggs in a basket."

The Old Man grumped, "Meaning what, dickwad?"

"They're all Tides Elba, whatever their age. So any of them that are old enough to bleed ought to be old enough to be the Port of Shadows. We have no way to tell if one girl is more likely than any other. Maybe we should look for the guy who's supposed to breed them."

Grunt. "Luck with that."

I mused, "So say one new girl every year . . . Mischievous Rain will be twenty in about two months. The next-oldest ones both look like they're about seventeen."

The Captain said, "Which would suggest that there are several more totally ripe ones out there somewhere."

"At least. Like you said, some of them look like they're the same age."

"Twins in the mix?"

"Or maybe whole litters?"

A distracted Candy asked, "Is there any sure way to tell how old a gal is? They don't have rings like trees."

The Old Man said, "This might not be all bad news. We might have enough Tides Elbas to go around. A man could pick one at just the right age for his taste."

I blurted, "What the hell, boss?" That was way out of line for him. And he did wear a dreamy look when he said it.

He had a lust-crush on Mischievous Rain? I should be surprised? Every swinging dick in the Company still breathing had one. But the Old Man? I just could not believe that.

Candy said, "There's not enough for everybody but maybe enough for senior staff."

Were they serious? Or were they just screwing with me?

Probably both.

Hardly anyone who finds Black Company life condign would scruple to mass-produce pretty, pliable bed buddies.

I tried picturing us blessed with a hundred Tides Elba camp followers. How would we tell who was messing with whose woman? We would have to brand them to tell them apart . . . Though mine did come with distinctive tattoos.

"Oh!"

"What?" the Old Man asked.

"What if they really are all alike? Exactly. Not just as potential Ports of Shadow but also with the talents that Mischievous Rain has?"

"Shit. You always find a downside, don't you? Yeah. Means we need to get them rounded up before the Rebel goes to wondering about that, too."

I figured those assholes would be way ahead of us. That could have been why they created whole flocks of such pretty sheep.

The Captain continued, "Lieutenant, how cooperative were the religious folks in the towns you visited?"

"Very, considering that Rebels would be watching. Nobody likes those guys better than us anymore." One big reason being that a lot of Rebels were fugitives from farther west, foreigners who were little more than bandits now. The Company's banditry was more genteel.

I said, "I'll have Gurdlief make up some drawings of the girls we have at different ages. You can show them around." The boy was a talented sketch artist as well as a creative storyteller.

The Captain snapped, "Perfect! Do that! We'll get every damned konzertasa in every damned temple to tell us every damned thing she knows about anybody who ever showed the slightest damned interest in any of those damned girls."

Sprawled across his chair, the Lieutenant said, "I just had me a win-win inspiration. We breed these girls ourselves. Bam! We have us some fun *and* we ruin them as Ports of Shadows prospects!"

I knew about seven hundred troopers who would buy into that strategy. And the Old Man appeared inclined to adopt it, too.

Suppertime with the "family." The kids were wary but unafraid. Ankou, too, was attentive to my mood, suggesting that something was expected of me.

I ate while paying close attention. Shin should be pleased. The main dish was not fish. I considered the lapis artifacts on the mantel behind Firefly. "You kids know how I can get in touch with your mother? She needs to know what happened today."

"She knows," Firefly said, touching a blue clip in her hair. "And she told you how. I heard her tell you."

"Oh. Yeah." These kids paid better attention than I did. "She can't have gotten there yet, can she?"

Firefly shook her head. "Tomorrow morning."

Beloved Shin asked, "Did you remember to give the man the jug?"

"The man" would be Candy. "The jug" would be a half-gallon

stoneware jar full of treacle-thick shadow. Candy was supposed to set it out whenever he made camp, upright and open somewhere remote. Mischievous Rain supposedly insisted but I had yet to see the jar in any hands but those of the boy.

"I did. I told him it's critical that he carries out his instructions exactly." Candy was used to receiving unusual instructions from Goblin and One-Eye. This would be little different.

"Thank you." The boy made that sound like he was the grown-up.

Firefly asked, "You'll stay with us while Mom is gone, won't you, Dad?" She kept using that word. Her tone made it sound like my response meant everything to a six-year-old.

"Sure." But I would not feel comfortable doing it.

Firefly certainly looked pleased.

Middle of the night I wakened groggily to find Firefly wriggling in with me. When I awakened again later, in need of the chamber pot, she was gone. Gone gone, as were Ankou and Beloved Shin, though the cat went missing most nights. Despite having no idea where they were or what they were doing I felt no special distress. Their absences fell within a range of weird to which I was becoming accustomed. I went back to sleep.

Shin was in his bed when dawn came. Firefly was back in with me. Ankou lay curled around his bowl, an eye cracked in case somebody put something tasty into it.

I heard nothing from the Taken, not even a tinkle. The kids just shrugged. They did not care. Life was easier when Dad was in charge.

Candy spent eight days in the field with Buzzard Neck as his tactical sorcerer. Buzz performed well. The team captured three Tides Elbas of breeding age and another two not yet ripe, all with raven hair. And they learned that the Honnoh raid had been so perfectly well timed and executed that the Rebel had decided to give up his summer offensive entirely. The number-one Rebel had gone down, along with a dozen other senior commanders. The top leader surviving had been left paralyzed from the waist down. In one day, in just part of one day, the Black Company had handed the Lady's enemies more hurt than Whisper and the Eastern Army had inflicted in two years. And we made the populace love us for doing it. All thanks to Mischievous Rain.

She was bad beyond bad. Not once did it seem like she was doing anything, but then, suddenly, our enemies started dropping in ridiculous numbers.

Almost daily new prisoners joined the girls already collected. They were confused. They were frightened. And they were amazed that they all looked alike, except for age, minor scars, and personal style. Every girl had a little wine-stain birthmark in the small of her back.

News of the Honnoh raid and the Aloen temple visit spread. Temple hierarchies everywhere showed eagerness to distance themselves from the Rebel, the Resurrectionist cult, and the Port of Shadows. A few even tried to turn over girls they thought fit the descriptions of those that we were seeking.

I was there for Candy's report. The Old Man was in so sweet a mood that he let me ask some questions. My first was, "Has anybody, anywhere out there, shown any special interest in these girls?"

"Yes, and it started right after you snagged the ones here. People who know people say that the Honnoh raid convinced the Resurrectionists that we're on to what they're truly doing. It also convinced them that we have somebody so deep inside that he has to belong to their central committee. Only four of those guys survived the Honnoh operation, and that only because they ran away as soon as the shit started coming down. They're supposedly paralyzed by mutual distrust, now. Anyway, about the girls. Some shrines had their girls disappear. The oldest one of those was about thirteen. We also left some in place because they were so young."

The Captain asked, "And how do you know all that?"

"We got it from people who know people and are willing to talk to us. And we caught a Rebel courier that Buzz made give up everything he knew." Candy's tone betrayed a certain admiration, much as he disliked Tesch.

Candy's confidence buoyed my belief that we were forging positive connections with the locals.

The Old Man said, "Collect every girl from now on, even the ones in diapers. Find a wet nurse if you have to."

The Lieutenant said, "This all screams that there's got to be lots more girls. Which means that a crew of women must be hatching them. Or maybe there's just one weird old broad who shits babies like a queen bee."

"The girls can't help us any," I grumbled. "None of them have any more of a clue than the Taken ever did. None of them knew they had sisters till we showed them." Really.

The Old Man asked me, "When is she coming back?"

"I don't know." Truth be, I figured he would have a better idea than I did. I was still the mushroom man. "She said she'd be gone for six days but it's been nine already and there's still been no word."

Leers from Candy and the Lieutenant. The Captain asked, "Single-father routine getting to you, Croaker?"

"That started before her frigging carpet was out of sight." Still, the twins were cooperative, mostly. They did what they were asked to do with minimal kidly lawyering, except at bath time. They were like cats when it came to using water for anything but drinking.

I had no idea what they got up to when I was not looking.

The Old Man had no actual interest in my domestic situation. He asked, "About the girls that disappeared. Where did they go? Why did they go there? To get away from us? The girls we found in Honnoh. Did they come from the temple there? Or were they part of the Rebel force? Is there any chance that there are gangs of them that were never distributed to the temples?"

I shrugged. I did not know. Neither did anyone else. I said, "I was busy patching people up when I was out there. You need to ask the men who nabbed them."

Restraining a smirk that said everybody had seen what I was doing out there, snuggling up with Mischievous Rain, Candy suggested, "Check with the wizards. They were in the middle of everything."

The Old Man grunted. "See to it, Candy. Is Tesch ready to run his own patrol?"

"Sir?"

"You just had your turn."

"So did Tesch."

"Was he useful?" The Old Man tipped a hand toward the Lieutenant, whose right foot was still in a makeshift cast. "*He* isn't ready yet. And Chodroze has gone off to the Tower."

"I can go out again," Candy said.

"Sure you can. If I need you to. But we need to get a solid read on Tesch. Send Goblin and One-Eye with him."

"That could be a real test."

"Absolutely. That's why."

It sounded like a recipe for trouble but I kept my mouth shut. I was not in charge. I did say, "Whoever does go, I have some stoneware jars that they need to take along."

Candy gave me the fisheye. "Like the one you had me take?"

"Exactly like that."

"But nothing happened with it. It was a waste of time."

He was not right, not even a little. I had to stick up for my kids. Or kid. The jars were Beloved Shin's thing. "And that was because you followed the jar regime exactly as you were instructed."

"Are you shitting me?"

"Would I shit my favorite turd?"

"All right, ass-wipe . . ."

"Gentlemen!" The Old Man refused to let us divert ourselves.

"Yes, sir. I don't know how it works but the jars are full of concentrated shadows. The Taken's kids are all about shadows. They can reach out anywhere through shadows . . . They might not really be kids—even if I am their father somehow—but their jars definitely work. Candy avoided some seriously ugly shit because he followed their instructions."

Candy admitted, "I did do what I was told. What's to lose? After all these years I know that's usually best even when I don't have half a frigging clue what's actually happening. I reckoned Croaker got his inspiration from the Tower somehow."

The Lieutenant asked, "What kind of ugly? And how do you know?"

I said, "Candy was south of Emeru, headed for Rabbit Creek. He had prisoners. He mistakenly set up camp at the foot of a cliff, beside a river running fast and loud with meltwater. The Rebels tracking him launched a night attack, intending to rescue their friends."

The Captain raised a hand, stared at Candy hard. "With nowhere to run? And with ambient noise?"

Candy confessed, "I got lazy, boss. I got overconfident. It won't happen again."

The Old Man dropped his hand. I continued, "The Rebel gang included two small-time wizards who were supposed to handle our sentries. But Candy had the jar out. Something came out of the jar, something so awful that the Rebels didn't even try to defend themselves. They just ran. In the dark."

Now Candy asked, "And how do you know all that?"

"The kids told me. Like they were eyewitnesses." I produced two silver rings given me by Beloved Shin, rings of the sort that Rebel officers wore.

The Old Man would not touch them. They might be cursed. The others exchanged glances but said nothing. Shadows haunted the room. Who knew what might be lurking within them? Maybe a six-year-old who might not be human, inclined to report back to the Tower? Or a cat that was not really a cat?

Mischievous Rain insisted that the twins were real kids. She insisted that she was their mother. That might be true but that truth might be only a fraction of the whole truth.

And I was on the hook for being their father, somehow, though that could not be the whole truth, either. Those brats for sure had a healthy dose of devil in them.

The Old Man demanded, "Croaker? You still here?"

"I am. Though sometimes I wonder."

"Sometimes you wander. Get it together. I need you focused."

"Is there something you're not telling us?"

"Not *us,* no, but you, yes."

"But . . ."

"Need to know, Croaker. You write things down."

Candy said, "Someday your Annals are going to get nabbed by somebody that doesn't like us. And they'll use them against us."

It could happen. It would not be a first. A lot of eyewitness Company history has gone missing over the years, to be recalled only at second or third hand in those Annals that did survive.

But as for the Annals being used against us, that was superstitious dread on the part of the illiterate. There is little in these pages that could benefit any enemy going forward.

Superstition dons innumerable forms and faces.

We began fielding multiple patrols, each with a wizard along. Skirmishes went badly for our enemies. Encounters became less common. Our patrols ranged farther afield. The surviving Rebel hardcore retreated into the deep wilderness. Less-committed types abandoned the insurrection business altogether. A few came over to us because soldiering was the only life they knew.

Our patrols kept finding more Tides Elba girls. Those ranged from two to fifteen years old. Every religious establishment, whether a basilica or a coffin-size shrine, seemed to have been blessed with at least one.

We collected them all. The older girls cared for the younger. Those that I saw all owned personalities and attitudes little different from those of Mischievous Rain. They all coped well even when they were terrified.

The scale of the roundup forced construction of a dormitory and mess hall for the girls. Sergeant Chiba Vinh Nwynn and several other female soldiers took charge of the girl collection. But, as Goblin wondered, who would protect the girls from their guardians? Chiba Vinh Nwynn had a reputation.

Nwynn and her cohorts were sure to have adventures, riding herd on those girls while surrounded by hundreds of horny young men.

The Old Man proclaimed a schedule of draconian punishments for any idiot who broke dangle discipline and tried to get at the girls. He made certain that no one failed to understand that the Lady herself was taking an interest. And he reminded all hands that Mischievous Rain would return before long and was extremely unlikely to be sympathetic to any young soldier's erotic ambitions.

She would be back soon? The prophesied duration of her Tower visit had expired weeks ago. And I enjoyed no respite from the single-father curse. Nor did I hear anything from the Tower, though there were late-night moments when I imagined that I heard distant wind chimes.

The children were not happy anymore, either. They became ever less adventurous, ever more withdrawn, and ever more disinclined to interact with anyone but me and Gurdlief Speak. That was a major change. Right after their mother left they had gone at it hard, trying to make themselves Company mascots.

Firefly, a miniature of her mother (which caused occasional complications because we held all those look-alike internee girls), could lay on a blaze of little-girl charm when she wanted. She had claimed herself several adoptive uncles, including Elmo and Otto.

Shin was popular because he was behind the shadow pots. No casualties occurred if a patrol handled its pots correctly.

Rumor said a small boy sometimes flickered through in those moments when danger was at its most intense.

I did not hear much about that. Supposedly nobody wanted me to get the idea that they were criticizing my children. However, soldiers being what they are, their ultimate motive would be to avoid inspiring me to make Shin stop.

Understandable. You always want to stack the deck in your favor.

In situations where a severe threat did develop and where someone that might have been Shin or Firefly or Ankou had been glimpsed from the corner of an eye, mutilated corpses inevitably turned up once there was daylight enough to reveal them.

So. The twins and their cat were popular, some, but at the same time they scared the shit out of anybody unprepared to be immersed in sorcery. That included almost every Company brother who joined us after the Battle at Charm, maybe barring Two Dead and Buzzard Neck. Those two were agents of darkness themselves—although they had become extremely useful Company sorcerers.

Even One-Eye was intimidated by Two Dead. Normally, that little shit was too damned dumb to be afraid of anybody but the Limper. Anybody without the sense to be scared of the Limper was guaranteed to get himself a worm's-eye view of the daisies.

It did feel so good when the pain went away. Only . . . I lacked evidence but suspected that the Old Man had put Two Dead up to reining One-Eye in. Whatever, One-Eye was behaving. He had become, in effect, almost invisible.

But Two Dead was doing time in the Tower, now.

I worried about his absence. I worried about One-Eye's unnatural silence. That little scruffleupagus might be trying to create a new legend, a reality that would exist only within the minds of the rest of us. For sure anyone who believed anything that One-Eye wanted believed would be rewarded with abiding regrets.

There are few moments on the gods' green earth when One-Eye is not up to something. The little shit schemes in his sleep.

"What the hell are they doing here?" Markeg Zhorab demanded, having abandoned his bar long enough to visit the table where I had settled with Elmo, Goblin, Corey, and Buzz, with my kids watching.

"Checking out what it's like when Croaker gets a chance to relax," I snapped. I was about ready to crack. I needed the Dark Horse. I needed me a huge dose of the Dark Horse. My brain and my sense of responsibility had been fully engaged for too long. "You got a problem with that?"

Zhorab could not have had a problem on any grounds other than that the twins were who they were.

Using the little finger and forefinger of my left hand I indicated Goblin and Buzz while checking my cards with my right hand. "They'll keep us honest. Find the kids something to nosh."

Markeg sighed. I tried to strategize an ugly hand. Zhorab worried because the kids might be doing something more than just observing.

"Relax, Markeg," Goblin said, making it more of a command than a suggestion. "They're harmless. Maybe. You. Girl. Are you peeking at my cards?"

"Yes. I am. It's the only way I can keep my dad from getting cheated by your crooked deal."

The game stopped. Corey asked, "Are you serious, kiddo?"

"Yes. Some of the cards came from the middle of the deck. Some came off the bottom. He has very nimble fingers." A six-year-old talking.

Several silent seconds dribbled into the abyss of time. Then Elmo giggled. "Ha! Called out by a crumb-crunching ankle biter. Let's check it out. I call dead hand. Everybody show your cards."

I did not doubt Firefly's claim that Goblin had cheated. The toad would do so if he thought he could get away with it. Maybe he figured the distraction of the kids would let him manage it unnoticed. But then I had to wonder about his motives. Nobody, Goblin himself included, laid down anything even vaguely resembling a good hand. It was almost impossible to imagine five players all having been dealt such a clutch of ugly.

A sweating Goblin seemed to be more amazed than anyone else.

Firefly looked smugly pleased with herself.

She had done something, somehow. Something way more than just nailing that toad-face rat.

I cared only a little. I was determined to achieve me some serious relaxation.

The others agreed that the stakes were not grand enough for anyone to be officially offended.

"He wasn't really trying to rip anybody off," Firefly told me, sitting in my lap like she was some normal kid snuggling up with her dad. "He just wanted to mess with you all."

Blessed Baku. Firefly. My snuggly little genius. Tonk is a simple game for simple people. She figured it out in about four minutes and then did whatever she did.

"Yeah. That's Goblin. If it was One-Eye . . . One-Eye would've been cheating so he could rob everybody."

One-Eye might have launched a more complicated and nuanced scheme because he had to reassure himself repeatedly that he was the cleverest weasel around.

Thinking about One-Eye got me fussed all over again. He had gone so low-profile that he had stopped feuding with Goblin, nor had he tried to cozen Goblin into joining some idiot plan because the toad was so gullible. One-Eye even avoided obvious cheating on those uncommon occasions when he surfaced and joined the never-ending tonk tournament—about which I knew only secondhand.

I could not help wondering if One-Eye was not honking up his filthy sleeve because his uncharacteristic behavior had everyone anticipating a sudden prodigious rain of shit.

I did not let that stress me, nor did anyone else who had been with us since before the Company came over the Sea of Torments. One-Eye's asshole-iness was like foul weather. It came. It went. Only a modest effort was necessary to make ready for it. One could endure it and emerge grinning, thinking, "If this little dog turd wasn't so damned useful when there's no way for us to get out of a fight . . ."

Said dog turd was all too cognizant of his value.

We all knew, One-Eye himself excepted, that one day he would overreach. And then the Captain would just sit back while fortune filled its gullet.

Meantime, I nurtured dread. Summer was coming. The Taken was away. The long, gentle Aloen sojourn, with its infrequent challenges and relative lack of existential perils, *had* to be approaching its end, never mind that massive triumph at Honnoh.

Really?

I have been at this all too long. I have become convinced that the good days are tossed in only to raise expectations so they can be more deeply drowned in blood and sorrow. Garrison duty can be boring but boring old tonk and barrels of beer are so much preferable to potentially lethal adventures.

I am, after all, a family man these days.

Spring did desert us. Summer slithered in. Mischievous Rain, and near-Taken Colonel Shoré Chodroze, did not return. Each day a third of the Company was away on patrol. Another third was engaged in agricultural assistance or civil engineering. The remaining third worked at improving camp defenses or plain old maintenance. No patrol or work party left the compound without a shadow pot. And none of our people suffered misfortune by night.

Our enemies were not so lucky. Whatever wickedness they tried, the results were catastrophic. The survivors finally ceded the night, which belonged to the Rebel everywhere else in the east. You could almost smell the virulently angry envy from Eastern Army HQ.

I could prove nothing but was convinced that my little dears were entirely responsible for the Rebel's nightmare season.

The men thought so, too, though they did not talk about it where I might overhear. They were getting scared. More and more tried to stay away from the kids.

"This is so cool," Elmo said, on returning from a patrol during which his gang had eliminated eighteen Rebel fighters, had collected three Tides Elba sisters, and had uncovered an actual Resurrectionist assembly place. "It's like the gods themselves watched over us from dusk till dawn. We just buried those eighteen after the sun came up. They were already dead."

Elmo was not one to be intimidated by good fortune.

"Might not be gods," I said. "Might be a darker sort of divine."

Elmo shrugged. He had grown up in a different country where gods and spirits were an endemic pestilence. Those divinities had not been the sort who divvied up into good guys and bad, same as people mostly do not. He said, "So we've got some wicked fairy godmothers looking out for us. That's good enough for me. Only, how do I con them into sticking around for another hundred years?"

That sentiment definitely grew. I considered it unreasonable because the same people strained to avoid Shin and Baku. And the same folks had made a big effort to avoid Mischievous Rain's notice, back when, too.

The effect was not new. I had seen it while the Company followed Soulcatcher, and more intensely still when we had had the Taken Shifter along to help with some heavy lifting. Friends can be more terrifying than enemies when they are that awful and are operating at your hip.

The old Taken, of times now gone, had been unpredictable and almost always in a foul humor. They sometimes bit whoever was nearest—and then would not forgive you if you somehow survived.

So my urchins lived in the eye of a baby cyclone of love and fear. Both emotions waxed stronger any time a jar of shadows saved a patrol.

Beneath the tension was the growing conviction that, however clever we were at neutralizing the Lady's enemies, this would be the summer when the Company faced its next great existential challenge. Success only fed the common dread. The Old Man, the Lieutenant, and Candy never said a word. They just kept on getting jumpier. They shied from shadows despite shadows having become our most intimate friends. They did not sleep well. I had trouble sleeping myself. The Captain and several others approached me looking for some philter that would get them through the night.

The twins prospered while everyone else frayed. They showed more color in their cheeks, though that could be just because they spent more time outside.

I was confident that they were not the cause of the growing malaise. But there were whispers, according to Gurdlief, that claimed they were feeding off the life forces and happiness around them. That was so bone stupid that I could not imagine how it got started without being an enemy plant.

The Rebel can make up clever lies, too.

We had plenty of prisoners and Tides Elba girls. We did not need to feed ourselves to any hungry vampires. Pointing that out, though, only generated the "Yeah, but . . ." response of a dope with a mind already made up.

Damn it, I needed Mischievous Rain to come home! Before somebody, maybe even me, lost it and did something that could not be taken back.

I slid in to see the Old Man. He gave definition to the adjective "haggard." "What do you need, Croaker? Got a staff meeting in a couple." His tone was testy.

Everybody was testy. Several disagreements had gotten physical.

"We had any news from the west? Any at all? The situation is getting serious. We've got guys volunteering to go on patrol just so they can relax."

"We all have our trials, some more onerous than having to babysit six-year-olds." He raised a beefy hand, showed me a palm. No more whining allowed. "There have been no communications concerning you or of concern to you. But they have not forgotten you." I may have imagined the most remote merry wind-chimes tinkle. "Suck it up, Croaker. We need to be examples. This will pass. Meantime, we have seven hundred men suffering from anxiety and malaise. Time for my meeting. Go somewhere. Do something useful." Then, as though thinking out loud rather than addressing me, he added, "We need us a good old-fashioned heads-up fight. That would blow off the tension. As long as we came out on top."

Yes. As long as that.

He was not taking the emotional climate seriously enough. I had begun to wonder if we were not experiencing something artificially induced.

I started to ask what Whisper was up to these days. The Captain cut me off. "Shoo!"

I stepped aside for the Lieutenant and Buzz. Neither spoke. Both looked stressed. I went outside, took a look at a low gray sky that seemed awfully busy changing shades. But the air that was all excited up there was not moving at all down here on the ground.

It was late afternoon. It would rain after sundown. Meantime, the town girls should have supper ready. The kids would be waiting impatiently. They were in a growth spurt. They ate like lumberjacks for that and to support whatever they did in the deep of the night, in the shadow of the world, while their father snored.

Sana would be serving lamb kabobs. My mouth watered. I lost interest in the Old Man's scheming. Me knowing would change nothing.

I bumped into Candy headed for the meeting, then Silent a moment later. Neither shared anything with the Company Annalist.

They did not trust me not to record something because I remember the truth too clearly? Or might they not trust me not to talk things over with somebody that they wanted kept in the dark?

That better not be the Lady or Mischievous Rain. There was a weird-looking cat doing stretches in the shade on the east side of HQ.

I bumped into Gurdlief Speak next. Surprised, I said, "Haven't seen you lately, kid. What's up?"

"Got you a great new story. Plus, Firefly asked me to find you. Says if you don't come home right now she's going to die from hunger. And then she'll haunt you for the rest of your life."

"She's been threatening that since she got here. But she lives on. I don't get where a kid her size puts it. I assume you're staying."

"Shin asked me. Sana and El said it would be all right."

Clever lad. He had not gone hungry much since he met me.

Shin ate less than Firefly but he still scoffed down ridiculous amounts.

I continued to wonder but without much ambition.

The general down mood touched me as much as anyone.

People did cope, some with less success than others.

Sana's kabobs were remarkable. And, oddly, even with Gurdlief's extra mouth and the twins' bottomless stomachs there were kabobs enough left over for the town girls to enjoy some, too.

They made the best of their situation, those girls. I did not mind. It was not my money. But I would get to barking if they started trying to take something home.

Gurdlief's new story was about a vixen who fell in love with a man so fiercely that she appealed to the gods to turn her into a woman. The gods granted her prayer—then caused her death two weeks later. The mood of the moment left me indifferent to what, once I became aware of the weight of fox spirits in local lore, was a culturally significant myth.

Gurdlief said, "Honestly, I don't tell it so well. Not to mention, I had to leave out the stuff you don't want little kids to hear. A pro storyteller would have you bawling by the time he got done."

Mention of storytelling reminded me that, before we all almost died at Charm, I had done regular readings from the Annals so my brothers could understand that they were part of something centuries deep, not just a gang come together last year that might evaporate before the winter solstice. I had not done many readings since Charm. I am not sure why. Mental trauma must be in there somewhere.

The Company had seven hundred effectives, now, and way too many camp followers. I really ought to make the new people understand that they were part of something timeless and bigger than individuals.

"I ought to take that up with the Captain."

Several pairs of eyes considered me, puzzled.

One of the girls, Flora of the ridiculous knockers, whispered, "Sir, there is a smelly old man with an eye patch here who insists that he has to see you." Her cheeks were red. She faced away from Gurdlief, who was old enough to appreciate her assets but not old enough to understand that he ought not to stare.

No pederast I, even I found that difficult sometimes.

Having met Flora's mother in the course of my town practice I was sure the girl would grow into those monsters. Twenty years from now they would not draw a second glance.

So. One-Eye wanted to talk? To me specifically? "Gurdlief, do me the honor of hanging out with these savages. Don't let them destroy the furniture or set the house on fire. I'll see what the wizard wants."

The twins awarded me exaggerated sour looks. Neither reminded me that they went unsupervised most of the time and an apocalypse had yet to occur. They knew I was teasing. I hoped.

Gurdlief nodded. Of course. That would give him time to further admire Flora's outstanding cantileverage. Flora was a responsible girl. She would feel obliged to stay with the children while their father handled business.

I thought it odd that an Aloen girl could be so self-conscious, but then got that that was it. Self-consciousness is personal. What I considered to be a culture of excessively relaxed morality was not personal at all.

I found not only One-Eye but Goblin seated in the western-style chairs in the Taken's antechamber. Both seemed fiercely uncomfortable. What the hell?

I chose my words carefully. I had no idea what was going on. I did not want to set One-Eye off.

I had no reason to trust him. His behavior lately was a dramatic improvement over what it had been before his sessions with Mischievous Rain but his temper had grown more volatile. We had not yet been able to identify his triggers. The popular wisdom was, do not provoke. Do not joke.

I looked from one untrustworthy wizard to the next. "What is it?"

Goblin seemed slightly embarrassed. "This is kind of on the down low right now. Have you noticed how everybody is kind of edgy lately?"

"Yes. Though 'edgy' is putting it mildly."

Goblin grew more embarrassed. My expression may have projected my skeptical estimation of his probable innocence of anything that might be going wrong.

"We maybe figured something out." One-Eye nodded in rare agreement. "He figured it out." Goblin jerked an accusing thumb at One-Eye. One-Eye nodded again, maybe mildly chagrined.

Curious. One-Eye showed none of the tells that always appear when he is working a scheme.

"All right. What have you got? And why bring it to me instead of to the Old Man?"

Goblin confessed, "The Old Man ain't so happy with us. If we could even get in to see him he would just figure that we was finagling."

One-Eye nodded again. A real talent show, the little man. And keeping his damned mouth shut while he demonstrated it. Amazing.

"So you figure old Croaker is more gullible, eh?"

"You're more likely to listen until we get it all told."

"Could be. Do some talking."

One-Eye cleared his throat. "All of us feeling like shit all the time. It's on account of them girls."

"The captives?"

"Only girls around, aren't they?"

"They are. And?"

"Yeah. See, they're all exactly like the Taken. Only they don't know that they are. They don't know that they probably got hidden powers. But when they rub up against each other they feed off each other emotionally. And the more of them you toss into the pot the more those emotions are gonna tangle and build up until some kind of out-of-control power explosion happens."

"Like spontaneous combustion," Goblin said. "If you add many more of them girls that are like over about twelve you're gonna get you a serious blowup of totally uncontrolled sorcery."

I studied One-Eye. Still I saw no tells. He just looked completely worried. I asked Goblin, "Is something like that possible?"

"It is. It's as rare as frog fur pelts but it happens."

One-Eye said, "Look up the Wasting of Habenev next time you hit your library. That happened about ninety years ago."

Habenev was a trivial kingdom the Company had visited ages ago, long before the Wasting that One-Eye referenced. It was not likely that anyone in Aloe had ever heard of it. It got only a passing mention in the Annals. The Company had spent a winter there. A five-month holiday.

I would see what my predecessors had to report.

I asked, "How many girls do we have?"

One-Eye shrugged. Goblin shook his head. "Ain't you been checking them in?"

"No. I only get to see them if they get sick. Sergeant Nwynn is taking her job seriously serious. No men within rock-throwing distance unless it's an emergency. And she gets to call the 'emergency.'"

I paid a brief visit to the Captain. He did not ask how I had come up with the notion that we were tottering on the brink of sorcerous disaster. He said, "You could be right." He scrawled a note on a scrap of confiscated talisman paper. "Show this to Nwynn."

The note instructed Sergeant Nwynn to cooperate with me one hundred percent, however I chose to investigate.

Sergeant Chiba Vinh Nwynn was the foremost and most ferocious of the Company's few female soldiers. We had lost her husband at Charm. She was stronger and scarier than most of the men.

Nwynn ruled the Tides Elba dorm. And no man was going to taint her kittens.

I presented myself to the sergeant, with my note from the Captain. She considered me with deep suspicion. "So, you been doing without your regular pussy so long that you come here shopping for a new one?"

In the normal course Nwynn and I seldom interact. She did not get sick. She was no malingerer. But when we did collide we sparked ugly. I stifled my temper. "I don't need to see or trouble any of the girls, I just need you to talk to me."

Nwynn studied the Captain's note. She consulted her professional side, then her cumulative experience with the Company medical staff. "All right. What do you want?"

"Those girls are all copies of Mischievous Rain. You know that. So. Here's the problem. It looks like they might all be sorceresses, too, only they don't know it yet, and, despite their ignorance, they're starting to feed off each other. The rest of us are feeling the effects. That's why we've been going through the awfuls lately."

"They are weirdly alike," Nwynn admitted, still eying me coldly.

"How many do we have?"

"Twenty-nine. There are nine more in the wind that we know about."

"Damn! That would mean that there are a shitload more. Give me a rundown."

"Not sure what you're asking for, physician."

"You do have a girl inventory, don't you?"

That irked her. But everything irks Chiba Vinh Nwynn, at least where a guy called Croaker is involved. I did not understand it, did not like it, and it was why I had as little to do with her as possible.

She asked, "An inventory? What are they, ammunition?"

"Call it a roster, then."

"Oh." She nodded. "Yes. I do." Hearty scowl of disapproval.

In fact Nwynn was making an uncharacteristic effort to get along. She did understand that I was not girl toy shopping. Maybe mention of the awful emotional weather won her over.

Nwynn had strong opinions and strange prejudices but she was an effective and useful member of the Company.

I waited. She failed to understand that I expected her to show me the aforementioned roster. I told her, "We're trying to figure out if the universal foul mood happened because we packed your twenty-nine girls in together."

Nwynn got it, then. A smart woman, she. Who right away suffered a thought that left her wide-eyed and snarling, "Shit!"

"What?"

"The ones that have been here the longest. The ones that are old enough to breed. Their monthlies have begun to synch up." She drew a deep breath, exhaled dramatically. "I should of figured that, the way them pretty little bitches been making each other miserable."

Could it be? Them falling into a natural rhythm? The whole damned clowder?

Nwynn said, "They was just eight or nine matching up in their courses this time. But if they keep synching up it's gonna get dog-shit uglier every month from now on, I guarantee."

My turn. "I hope that isn't it." While almost certain that I was whistling in the dark. "That would be ridiculous."

"It *could* be just because we been clumping them all together."

Now Nwynn sounded like *she* might be whistling in the dark. She said, "Let me get my cat log."

She left me there, watched by two grim armed and ugly women. She disappeared into territories a man could only dream about penetrating. I heard a cacophony of chattering girl voices for the moment that the door was open. What was going on with that platoon of lovely young Tides Elbas back there?

I did not ask. The sentry women looked to be in a mood to honor any excuse to give me a thump. They had not yet shaken the foul-humor season. I considered blowing them kisses but refrained. Edmous Black was not yet fully qualified to deal with severe blunt-force trauma cases.

Just when I began to suspect that Nwynn had ditched me, she and a helper turned up. The latter carried a big register bound in frayed wine-colored cloth. She was Aloen. I could not recall her name. She was as wide as she was tall, all muscle, and she looked resentful, like she had been awakened untimely from a nap and her misery was all my fault.

Sergeant Nwynn said, "Here is the roster you want, sir. The entries were made chronologically. That might make finding what you're looking for a little more difficult."

The Aloen troll offered me the log, properly oriented.

"Thank you." Did I have any hope of finding something useful?

To my surprise the log began with information about Mischievous Rain, including everything known about her when she was just another pretty girl in Occupoa's temple.

So. A quick scan of some later entries. Same thing, down to an estimate to the month of the age of every captive. Each girl had been assigned a serial number according to her order of capture. Each went by the name that she had given when captured. I said, "This is excellent work, Sergeant. Please allow me to borrow it long enough to make a copy."

Sergeant Nwynn showed me a skeptical expression but swallowed her protest.

We all have to take orders that we do not like.

"Next month is going to be a lot worse," I told the Old Man, the Lieutenant, Candy, the wizards, and a number of other people, including Sergeant Nwynn. "By then we might have caught more girls and more girls should have their courses synched up. Plus, according to Sergeant Nwynn, some of them may be starting to realize that they aren't your regular orphan temple girls. They all look alike *and* they all favor the newest Taken. Which is something they know only by hearsay." Slight frown in Nwynn's direction, though she and hers would have seen no need to keep that a secret. "Because the only girls who ever actually saw Mischievous Rain herself went off to the Tower with her."

"Your point being?"

"They'll all be as smart as Mischievous Rain so it shouldn't be a leap for them to figure out that they might have a talent for sorcery, too."

Nwynn nodded vigorously. I made a beckoning gesture, deferring.

She said, "Sirs, I do think that some of the older girls are experimenting. Just with little stuff. They don't got no one to teach them and they are smart enough to understand that they're playing with deadly fire."

Buzzard Neck said, "There is nothing more dangerous than a self-taught sorceress, to herself more than anyone else. This could get really ugly if they're experimenting and feeding one another emotionally at the same time."

I said, "I made up some charts . . ."

Even the Old Man groaned.

I said, "I know. It can get tedious. That's the sad harsh truth about facts. They're never as exciting as speculations." Then, to let them know that they were in the finest company, I said, "I presented all this to the Taken this morning. I think." I had visited her bedroom to make my report according to instructions given me back when. I did not know if the information got through. The only evidence that anyone might have been listening had been a faraway, painfully faint bar of wind-chimes music.

"What's all that?" the Old Man asked, indicating my lovingly created master chart, sounding like he hoped that I would not actually explain.

We all have to suffer our disappointments. Even commanding officers. "It's an age chart of Tides Elba girls based on Sergeant Nwynn's information."

All twenty-nine captives, and the Taken, were there. Mischievous Rain was example zero based on a complete absence of older versions anywhere. "These gaps mean that there might be a girl who fits there. Red dashes in the gaps indicate hearsay girls, generally those who disappeared before our patrols got there. There is a pattern. From late seventeen years old downward a new girl seems to have been born every three months. We have yet to identify any twins."

The Captain said, "Then if your chart is right, we've only rounded up a third of them."

"I'm figuring closer to half, after adjusting for disease and misadventure." Which could be conservative. Life was hard for kids and young people, and more so for orphans. Though the Occupoan temples did take good care of their motherless children.

"But those numbers would make our current strategy pointless, wouldn't they? There are still a shitload that we don't control. And do we know if they're still turning them out?"

"I am sure that they are. In their place I'd keep on, if I could, especially now that they know we know they're up to no good. I'd keep making them so that I could always have a few more hidden, no matter what the Lady's people did."

Candy stirred. I had thought that he was asleep, so quiet had he been. "What about the ones that ought to come between the Taken and the seventeeners there? That would be a good ten more all perfectly aged."

I thought he would melt under Nwynn's ferocious gaze. But he was indifferent to her disapproval.

"Good question. But I can't even speculate." None of the girls knew anything about their provenance. Neither could any of the temples tell us anything useful. "Hey. Who found that Resurrectionist place that Elmo told me about? Did we get anything useful out of that?"

The Lieutenant said, "Elmo found it. He came up with some kind of records that are in UchiTelle or TelleKurre, one of those old-time Domination languages, only on modern paper. We don't have anybody who reads that stuff anymore, unless you remember how."

"Me? TelleKurre, a little. I managed Limper's rescript. But it's been years since I tried anything really technical. If Raven was still with us . . ."

"There's a name that ain't come up for a while."

I grunted. "I'll look at the stuff, maybe dig out some sense. I won't guarantee anything, though. I have real trouble with the grammar."

I am pretty good with languages. A fast learner. On the spoken side. There are only a handful of TelleKurre speakers still living.

I continued, "Or we could find some way to pass everything on to the Tower. The Lady could read it, easy." TelleKurre would be her milk tongue.

The Lieutenant eyeballed me momentarily, like he wondered if he ought to accuse me of shirking, then said, "They don't look like something that would have anything to do with a project like this."

I sighed.

Sergeant Nwynn asked, "Might I make a suggestion, sirs?"

The Old Man said, "Certainly. Go right ahead."

"The big thing bothering you is that the girls have an unconscious connection that might cause trouble later. But I'm wondering if somebody who knows what she's doing, like the Taken, couldn't winkle out all the girls that we don't already have by tracing the connections between them."

I said, "That's good thinking. I think." And immediately began to worry about how Mischievous Rain would handle falling into the mind field here when she finally came back.

The Lieutenant asked, "If she could do that wouldn't she have done it before?"

Candy said, "She left before we knew that there were any more like her but the girls from Honnoh."

I gave Nwynn a thumbs-up. "That's right. She only suspected that there might be another one at the temple here. Somebody she remembered from her own time there."

Candy glared at my chart. "There could be a hundred of them. And maybe that ain't only because the Resurrectionists wanted to make sure they got them a Port of Shadows. Like a frog laying a million eggs. One of them is bound to work out. Uh . . . Sorry. Got off track. What I'm wondering is, was there some plan for them to get clustered up together sometime so they would start feeding off each other and get totally insane scary?"

That notion did nothing to cheer anyone up.

Were we seeding our own destruction by being too damned successful? It could happen. But I could not believe that to be a deliberate ploy. The Rebel was tough and stubborn and patient but he was never that chess-master clever. A scheme like that would require a foundation of too many improbable events.

One thing that we had not yet managed was the capture of someone from far enough inside the Resurrectionist cult to reveal their true strategy. Our informants, although becoming more numerous, still had nothing to report on that score, either.

I said, "I'll pass all this along as soon as we're done here." Which remark gained me narrow looks from guys who were sick of me whining about getting no news from the Tower.

The meeting ended when the Old Man had heard enough. "You

stay," he told me. "And leave your charts after I turn you loose. I want to study them."

Had he seen something that had eluded me?

The room cleared. The Captain asked, "Are we getting too focused on the girls, Croaker?"

"Sir?"

"They're all we talk about lately."

"The patrols haven't found anything else interesting, have they?"

"No. Nothing. Right now it looks like any Rebel who hasn't quit has fled into the deep woods, mainly the primal forest north of Rhymes."

Rebels who tried to disappear into the populace had no luck staying hidden. Said populace's sympathies had gone face-about since last summer. The Company's good behavior (relatively speaking), its signal battlefield successes, and the unusual fairness it imposed along with order and stability, contrasted fiercely with the situation that obtained where the Rebel sat atop the food chain—so we took pains to proclaim. Order was what regular people wanted. Order and security were necessary before prosperity could take hold. The political crap, the who is going to be in charge, did not matter to most folks.

The Company might be the bad guys in theory but daily life for regular people was way safer than it had been before we arrived.

Markeg Zhorab was an excellent example of a local caught in a perilous bight. His situation had become far sweeter with us in control. But every Aloen faced an iron truth: The Black Company would not remain here forever.

Maybe we could train the Zhorabs to look out for themselves. Markeg himself had scars to show that once upon a time he had worked in a trade less gentle than barkeeping. If we gave the Rebel holdouts a few more good thumps, honest folks might be able to . . . Only . . .

"Do we have any idea what Whisper is up to?" I had heard no news, not even any meaty rumors. The marshal of all the empire's eastern forces appeared to have no plans at all for the summer—nor, for that matter, did she seem to have a plan for pursuing her grudge against the Company.

"None. I think she'll be as careful as she can now that Colonel Chodroze is our guy and has gone to the Tower."

And Mischievous Rain would have taken to the Tower knowledge about everything going on out here in the wild, wild east.

That did not worry me. We were in high favor.

What did concern me was the pernicious absence of communications from the Tower. We were getting no instructions. And Mischievous Rain should want to know how her kids were doing. And the Lady should want to know more about the how and why and potential of the pool of Tides Elba girls . . . Unless she was just laying back, doing the trapdoor-spider thing, awaiting her moment.

Might be. Could be. The woman has a patient streak, and while she does lose a battle here and there she never loses a war. Never in all the years since she had clawed her way out of the Barrowland.

Once more I received no feedback after I spent an hour trying to make sure that Mischievous Rain and the Lady were fully informed of the latest.

Feeling like a flea on an insignificant mongrel of a frontier outpost, I gave up hope of having any meaning in anything that happened after my speculative reports about the Tides Elba girls. And when my attitude turned hopeless Beloved Shin, Blessed Baku, and Ankou were all inclined to agree.

The kids seemed immersed in a funk of their own. Shin would not discuss it. Firefly wanted to ignore it, too, but was not as stubborn. She was afraid that her mother had abandoned her. I am sure that Shin felt the same way. And there Dad was, ignorant but inclined to make excuses for a woman who was not present for her children.

The situation was getting insane.

Firefly snuggled in with me every night, now. And once when I wakened in the middle of the night I heard Shin whimpering.

What the hell? I could not imagine even the Lady's will overwhelming Mischievous Rain's concern for her children.

I was a man whose mundane life left him with an imagination entirely inadequate to his present circumstances.

19

Once Upon a Time: A Deeper Shade of Horror

The sisters Ardath and Sylith lived in constant terror. The Senjaks all did. The Dominator knew about Dorotea. The men responsible had paid. Gods, had they paid. None dared accuse the Dominator of lacking imagination when it came to discovering new ways to inflict pain. Others had paid as well, many of them innocent, all to assuage His rage. But that rage stormed on unabated. He wanted to know what had become of Credence. Although the Howler had been entirely forthcoming the Dominator was not convinced that the Senjaks were not up to something underhanded. Despite the evidence out there, where remnants of what had entangled the Howler had come close to doing the same to Him.

The physical evidence suggested the long-term residence of a true master sorcerer, a necromancer, whose sole interest in the rest of the world had been that it should leave him alone. But the Dominator judged the world by His own lights. A man with such skills, with such talent, with such power, must surely mean to use it to subdue the world and bend it to his will. Any such man *must* have been plotting against Him.

Nothing to suggest anything like that had been found. There were a couple of dead mastiffs, some unhappy livestock behind on their feed, and a coach that might have been the one the guards on the Jade Gate had seen the night that Dorotea disappeared. Inside the house there was only ragged furniture and, in a sizable room in back, a workshop that boasted most everything that a necromancer would need to pursue his craft.

The Dominator Himself had examined the place thoroughly. He had found nothing to alarm Him further. But still He had declared the site off-limits to everyone else, reasoning that He might have missed something that could be turned against Him.

The Senjaks were disappointed. Ardath and Sylith alike were convinced that, if Credence was still alive, she would have left some sign. And then there was the question of what the necromancer had done with Dorotea's remains.

There was no longer any doubt that Dorotea had been dead when those morons had sent her down the waste chute.

A burial ground had been discovered in the woods behind the necromancer's house. The remains of a dozen girls had been exhumed, suggesting that Dorotea was not the first discard fished from the waste canal—unless the necromancer had been using live girls in his experiments.

What the graves suggested about the mind of the necromancer appalled even the denizens of Grendirft.

None of the exhumed corpses belonged to Dorotea. None were fresh enough to have been her or Credence, so the necromancer must have taken them with him when he fled.

The fact that some mysterious nonentity had stolen a Taken's carpet rattled the Dominator Himself and terrified nine of the Ten. A man would have to be insanely powerful if he could unattach and then control something as personal as a flying carpet.

The Howler told no one about the card deck that Credence had carried. Anyone with the ability to create one of those would inflame the Dominator's paranoia more than the inferno that it was already.

The Senjak clan stayed within calling distance of one another. If He turned they might have a fighting chance, working together.

The summoning home of the Taken from the frontier hot points offered the enemies of the Domination an invitation that they could not refuse. Conflagrations blazed up everywhere, out there and in the towns and cities. For the towns and cities the price of rebellion was absolute. The mad god was in no mood for fine distinctions. He knew that however thorough He was there would be survivors who could breed up a fresh crop of subjects. He had time to wait. Centuries, if need be.

He had slight grasp of the economic consequences of widespread destruction. But He did not care. He would see only that His will was being defied.

But not every city revolted. Not even a majority did. In most the urge faded quickly. Lords, in the east, was among those cities where the insurrection was barely a feeble poot that dispersed almost instantly.

Well after there was any chance that the information might be timely enough to be useful Domination agents in Lords reported that someone had been there purchasing unusual items and materials. He had been willing to pay generously, without haggling, for what he wanted. He had not tolerated normal human mischief. Several would-be villains had suffered grievously. Then he had disappeared without a trace, leaving behind only the most vague of descriptions.

That all could mean something, or it could mean nothing. Odds were, the latter was the case. But it might mean that the necromancer had gone east, far to the east, intent on reestablishing himself outside the Domination.

Nothing else surfacing, the Dominator ordered the Ten to march their armies eastward, and damned be the Plain of Fear if it became defiant. The campaign was to begin immediately after they exterminated the lands and cities and peoples now in revolt.

The clearing of the Old Forest could wait a generation.

This mysterious necromancer would not remain outside the Domination forever. The Domination would find him.

20

Once Upon a Time: An Absence of Pain

The necromancer stared. "How did you manage all that?" Kitten had run through the entire list he had left her.

She did not answer that. "Laissa is really sick, Papa. Did you get the stuff to fix her?"

"I did. Yes. Everything we'll need. I just had to go farther to find it than I thought I would have to go."

"Is that why you were gone so long?"

"That's why." Once again he eyed the structure atop the granite outcrop. There was no doubt. The girl had done the work and had done it right. "Kitten, I'm going to need your help fixing her. She doesn't like these treatments. They hurt. I don't like hurting her but they're the only way that we can keep her going."

Bathdek nodded. She heard the almost sane sorcerer talking, though still heavily tainted by Papa. It would seem that, rather than being more than a distinct personality unaware of others sharing the same mind, this man drifted back and forth across a spectrum. Only the nethermost ends were unaware of the opposite extremes. The man with whom she was speaking now would be the determined research necromancer with a touch of the devoted Papa of Laissa, willing to burn down the world to save his girl.

An aching small piece of Bathdek wished that she could stimulate Papa's emotions to equal devotion.

She said, "Just tell me what to do, Papa."

He smiled a cynical smile that betrayed the fact that he was almost completely the pragmatic necromancer now, fully engaged with the quotidian world. He replied, "I hope so, child. I hope so. Because I'm pretty sure that you hold the key to . . ."

Something happened. Something dramatic. He changed. He grabbed his head with both hands, fell to one knee, made whimpering sounds, began shaking like he was naked in the snow.

No! "Papa?" She remembered an uncle doing something similar when she was six. A massive stroke. He was gone within the hour despite everything that everyone tried.

Seconds of dread passed, then he said, "I'm sorry, Kitten. I have these attacks. Forget it for now. We need to work on your sister. It will be hard to bring her all the way back."

He stopped talking. He froze, looked like a statue briefly, then resumed, "We *have* to bring her back. I don't think I could go on if I lost another daughter."

Bathdek had no idea what that meant. "So why are we standing around talking? Tell me what to do."

The following hour was hectic.

Laissa was lethargic in the extreme but even so she whimpered and struggled and even mouthed a few words of protest once she understood what Kitten and Papa were going to do. She did not understand that they were trying to help her.

Laissa, Papa, and Kitten spent a long time just lazing. Relaxing. They had been stretched almost to the breaking point. Two of the three vowed never to let Laissa slide so far again.

One of the two told the other, "You know the secret of the Dominator's conquest of death." A declaration from the worldly necromancer.

Bathdek immediately found herself being Bathdek Senjak instead of Kitten. That frightened her. Could she actually forget who she was, the way that Dorotea had?

Maybe. But, more likely, she was just tired. Dragging Laissa back from the precipice, guaranteeing her months more life, had drained her. The challenge of the sorcerer might force her to reclaim her mental footing. "Papa?"

"The Dominator and the Ten, and their intimate circle, share the secret of eternal life."

"Eternal? I really don't think anything is eternal."

"All right. Stipulated. Then call it life that will go on forever until fatal misfortune intervenes."

"Oh." True. No way could you protect yourself from bad luck forever, nor from determined enemies, nor from disease. Nor even from seditious betrayal by your own body if it decided it was heart-attack, kidney-failure, or cancer time. "The Blessing, I have heard that called. Supposedly He uses the Blessing to keep His henchmen in line."

"How old are you really, girl?" The necromancer's smirk was nasty.

"Sixteen. My birthday came while you were away finding the stuff to fix Laissa."

"Truly?" He seemed surprised. "You aren't one of the Dominator's toys, been around for a hundred years?" His tone grated.

"Really! He doesn't have favorites. He uses them once and throws them away. And I'm too old to interest Him, anyway."

That irked the sorcerer right back. It touched him in the tickle spot that remembered whence his favorite daughter had come.

Laissa chose that moment to whimper and mumble what sounded like, "No, Papa! Please!"

The necromancer surged to his feet, made a barking noise, then collapsed in a twitching tumble.

"Not again!"

But, yes, again, and this time more dramatically. Papa had his hands to his temples, trying to crush his skull. Was this something mental? Or was it the stroke that she had feared before?

"No! No! No!" Him dying or becoming permanently dysfunctional would be a death sentence for her and Laissa. "Papa?"

She fell to her knees beside him, felt his forehead, checked his pulse. His heart was fluttering, racing hard. Instead of the fever heat she expected, his forehead was damp and cool. "Clammy," she thought the word was. "Papa! Talk to me, Papa! Tell me what's wrong! Tell me what to do!"

There may have been a minor physical component but she decided that the event was psychosomatic. The necromancer remained unresponsive for less than ten minutes. Then he opened wild eyes briefly, saw her there, shedding genuine tears. He smiled hugely and husked, "You are a good girl, Kitten." Then he lapsed into a normal sleep. His heartbeat settled into a healthy rhythm. He stopped shivering. His color improved. His temperature leveled off to where it ought to be.

Bathdek covered Papa with a ragged light blanket, then checked on Laissa. Laissa was sleeping normally, too. Satisfied, Bathdek went out into the cool of the night in hopes of getting herself calmed down. She settled on a boulder from which she could study an incredible swath of silvered sky.

It was time for some serious thought.

She could not keep on living from moment to moment. She had to plan what she was going to do and then execute her plan, not just be content to wait for something to happen. Something almost had happened tonight and it would have done nothing good for her or Laissa if it had.

She needed to have a serious talk with Papa about long-term planning. And once she had done that she would have to make sure the plans got carried out.

There were lots of shooting stars, two of them spectacular and one whose death lit up the entire world for one blinding instant.

A large animal came snuffling around, curious because of all the strange smells. Bathdek chased it off with a shower of sparks.

A while later, now calm and determined, she went back inside and lay down with Laissa. Laissa was cool but not nearly as cold as she had been before Papa treated her.

Bathdek whispered, "We'll find a way, Sis. I promise. We'll find a way." Or maybe that was Kitten whispering.

21

In Modern Times: Shadow Soup

We had us some serious weather. For days the rain came down in sheets, seldom letting up. Watercourses ran ridiculously high, washing away banks, brush, and nearby trees. Fields became waterlogged to the point where farmers feared they would lose their crops. The Old Man pledged the Company's assistance wherever stoop labor might make a difference. He began trying to recruit volunteer helpers from town.

Our enemies offered nothing.

The Rebel even gave up nuisance terror attacks on those who cooperated with us. The silence seemed ominous. Those devils, however badly hurt, must be up to something. When it happened it would be a something that I would not like even a little.

High water and impassable roads put an end to patrols for a while.

Ten days had passed since the malaise epidemic peaked. It had touched people as far off as downtown Aloe. Locked into worry mode, I wrestled a dread that I could not master. If Sergeant Nwynn was right the malaise would begin to build again in a few weeks. It would get worse. And it might be killer the month after that, especially if we caught us any more girls.

I asked Nwynn, "How do we keep that from happening?"

"Scatter the herd."

That did seem logical. "But then how do we keep them controlled?"

"That's the trade-off, isn't it?"

"I wish the Taken was here. She'd know what to do."

"That might not be good. If she was here then, being pulled at by them all."

Our chat was taking place at my desk in my new hospital. Even my clinic had moved there, now. I had just two inpatients at the moment, neither injured in action. Edmous Black tended them, muttering something about how could you find a cure for stupid?

"It might be too personal to ask but it might matter. Did the synch-up affect your squad?"

"It did. It was bad. It will get worse." She got red-hot angry suddenly, either at me for asking or at the universe for its cruelty toward women. "Bottom line, we'll probably get synched up, too."

"Not good?"

"Very much not good. Every woman in sight could get sucked in. This shit goes on for six months, the whole damned province could become part of whatever happens."

There were a thousand sexist jokes that could have been born right then. I was not tempted, not even a little. I was able to feel, fully, just how distressed Nwynn was. Hers was the soul-deep kind of dread I had felt while watching wave after wave of Rebel killers smash against our weak lines in the Battle at Charm. It was one trigger moment short of a surrender of all hope.

"So what . . . ?"

Gurdlief blasted in. I had not seen the kid since the night One-Eye came to warn me about the girls. "Carpet!" He puffed violently. "Slapback saw a flying carpet sliding along east right on the other side of the trees across the crick."

I exchanged puzzled looks with Nwynn. That sounded like a Taken on the sneak. Mischievous Rain had no reason to sneak. "Could Slapback tell who it was?"

"No. They was too far away."

Firefly materialized, I am unsure how. I did not hear a door. She looked troubled. She crowded up against me on my right, fingers in her mouth. That was little-kid behavior I had not seen from her before.

She had only just moved in when Ankou and Shin appeared, also with no door noise. They emerged from a shadow that drew no notice until it birthed something unexpected. Shin looked as troubled as Baku was.

"What's going on, guys?" O ugly thought. That might have been the Limper out there, scouting chances for executing some wicked monkey business. And he was unlikely to harbor any affection for a fellow Taken's offspring. Neither kid responded to my question. After a long silence, though, Shin did say, "Things are going to change." He moved in close on my left, not quite touching, as though to enter the safety of my shadow.

Sergeant Nwynn grumbled, "If it's gonna start raining shit I better put myself where I can do some good." She took a couple steps, stopped. "Maybe we'll get some answers, now."

"Let us hope."

She left. Edmous Black appeared, spied the family moment, decided that something needed doing somewhere else. Gurdlief did a nervous sort of pee-pee dance. Like me he had no idea why the twins were distressed. I did note, however, that he was hiding a considerable state of distress himself. I could not imagine what was tormenting any of them.

I said, "We won't accomplish anything hanging around here. Let's take it out into the sunshine."

I thought that might bother the twins, what with their affinity for shadows, but the suggestion seemed to brighten them up. Firefly, especially, showed an improvement in mood.

I was never going to understand Tower people, young or old. Hell, I was still too young to understand me.

. . .

Word was out. A carpet had been spotted. I seemed to be alone in fearing that that might mean trouble.

A lot of people found excuses to be outside, doing nothing productive. As the kids and I hit the street, the Captain and the Lieutenant emerged from Admin. The Old Man looked my way, did a double take. I suppose I did look strange there with my right arm around Firefly and my left hand on Shin's shoulder while Ankou sat on his haunches a foot in front of my toes. How much more of a familial picture could I present?

A shadow rippled along what, because of recent construction, had become the central street of the compound. If we put up any more structures the drill ground would be gone. The shadow was that of a carpet that streaked over, banked through a full turn, and came back slowly, wobbling as it shed altitude. There were two people aboard, and more plunder than Mischievous Rain had brought out last time.

The carpet settled right where it would be easiest to tilt it and slide it into storage. That was not, unfortunately, the best place to unload cargo meant to go into the Taken's quarters.

A bit of dust puffed out from under when the carpet touched down. I had not yet planted the grass that she had asked me to plant before she left. In truth, there was no chance that I would ever get around to doing that.

The passenger person rose and stepped down. That was Two Dead, paler and more tired than he had been when he left us. He was wobbly, which was not unreasonable after a stressful thousand-mile flight that included a passage over the Plain of Fear.

There was more there, though. Without talking to him or even getting close I knew this Two Dead was not the Two Dead who had gone to the Tower with Mischievous Rain. This Two Dead had spent months inside the Tower. Years, maybe, the way time gets corrupted there.

So how had my woman, the mother of my children, weathered her visit?

Neither twin rushed to greet her. Devil cat Ankou remained motionless, too. For a half minute the Taken did not move, either. On her knees, bent forward, her head almost in her lap, she let tension drain away. Then, at last, she rose and stepped down carefully, feeling with her right foot as though she could not see all the way to the ground. She was so wobbly that Colonel Chodroze took her right arm to help her maintain her balance.

The passage over the Plain of Fear must have been more terrible than usual.

Coming east the Company crossed the Plain by following a dedicated caravan route the Plain's denizens generally respect. We lost only two idiots who just had to go explore. The rest of us came to our new post safely, though Plain things continually tried to lure us off the hallowed path.

The Taken took a bit longer to collect herself, then straightened, lifted her gaze, surveyed her surroundings. She zeroed in on the girls' dorm right away. She looked like she had developed a sudden severe case of gastric distress.

Meantime, I surprised myself with the pleasure I felt at her return. I had missed the midnight yukata and its swirling stars, and I had missed the woman who wore it.

Her attention shifted to me and the children. Or maybe just the twins. She headed our way, expression shifting from hangover discomfort to a smile that looked like it would have been real if she were not constipated.

From behind me, Gurdlief whispered, "Slapback says that's not the carpet he saw before. He told me to say."

Oh, joy! But there was no time to pursue that. The Taken was upon us. The kids responded without excitement.

It might be stomach pain or hangover but the Taken did not act like this was a long-anticipated reunion. She bent down to scratch Ankou's ears. Remarkable. I never saw her touch the cat before. She then rested a gentle hand atop Firefly's head, caressed Shin lightly on the right shoulder, and said, "Let's go inside. After we put the carpet away."

The Captain had a work party unloading the carpet already.

The Taken's soft words sounded mechanical.

The twins' absence of emotion puzzled me. They had been devoted to their mother before.

Had she been changed that much?

We did what the Taken suggested. The Old Man and everyone else tried not to interact at all, not out of respect for a family reunion but out of fear. The Taken did not appear to be in a forgiving mood.

The children remained withdrawn, and Ankou downright depressed.

Something was wrong. Seriously wrong. Could it be connected with that other carpet and Taken out there?

We shared a meal during which no one spoke. The main course was fish but Shin never whined. Sana made her first trip in from the kitchen bearing a platter of slices of early local melon. She stared at the Taken with a puzzled, goofy expression.

"Ma'am? Why did you change your hair? It was so much more striking when it was that black with red stripes."

She was right! Mischievous Rain's hair had gone back to the shade that it had been when we sent her off to the Tower.

There must have been a glamour meant to keep the change from being noticed. It failed with Sana. Her saying so broke the spell.

The twins studied me guardedly.

I studied Mischievous Rain. The hair was the only change I could see, other than her subdued attitude. "How long was it for you, this time, inside?"

Shin sniffled. Firefly rolled her eyes. They knew something that I did not. They were exasperated because, even with the spell broken, I still did not see it. But, of course, they were not going to make it easy and tell me what it was.

"I don't know." Husky, little more than a whisper, dreamy-eyed, as though only a fraction of her was with us now. "I don't remember. It must have been a long time, though." Her journey back from wherever she was went slowly. She did everything, including basic eating, like she was having trouble reacquainting herself with me, the children, the cat, the place, and with how things were done in daily life. "I need to sleep. I have done without for more than two days."

Flora stepped into the room. "Doctor Croaker sir, that Gurdlief boy was just here. He said to tell you that you're needed in the hospital."

"Tell him I'm on my way."

"He already left, sir."

"I want to go, too, Dad," Firefly said. She had something on her mind. I glanced at Mischievous Rain. She did not object.

"Let's go, then." The kid was unlikely to see anything too gruesome for her.

Firefly halted the moment we stepped outside. (The hospital entrance was around on the far side of the building.) She said, "You do know that that isn't our mother, don't you?"

"What?" I jerked a thumb in the direction of the second floor.

"Yes. Her. That isn't Mom. She might not know that she isn't Mom, but she isn't. Shin and Ankou and I saw it right away but you didn't. You should probably keep pretending that you think she's who she wants you to think she is."

"I'm confused."

"I have noticed that about you, Dad. You only ever see surface things, what you expect to see. Mom says surfaces are really only mirrors."

Six years old, spouting philosophy. And, scary stuff, she understood what she was saying.

"I'll take your word. You know your mother better than I do. But if that isn't her, who is she? And why is she here in your mother's place?" I thought about Slapback's mysterious carpet, not seen by anyone since his lone glimpse.

Firefly shrugged. "Grown-up stuff. There are lots of copies around. Right?" The brat had a smile on like she knew she was smarter than, and knew more than, the nearest grown-up.

"A good point." Things going as weird as they do inside the Tower, this Mischievous Rain could be one of the Honnoh girls all grown up. "Do you know what's going on?"

She referenced her previous answer. "Nope. I'm just a kid. Nobody tells me nothing."

There was a load of guano.

She added, "We better go see what's happening. Some soldier might get mad if he dies while you're out here worrying about family stuff that won't change any because you're fussing."

No way this little beast was only six. She was a devil wearing a kid disguise. As cute a disguise as they came, though.

The emergency patient was Colonel Chodroze. I got called because Edmous Black had gone home. Two Dead was unconscious but making noises like a man trying to speak in tongues.

Sergeant Nwynn and her trollish Aloen henchwoman had brought him in. Gurdlief watched them like he thought they were about to break pieces off the Colonel. I told him that he needed to leave, then I asked Nwynn, "What's the trouble?"

She was in a foul humor. She made a huge effort not to let that interfere with business. A calming breath taken, she explained, "This dickhead tried to bust into the girls' dorm. He ain't back three hours and he's drunk and acting like a raving asshole."

There was a character conflict here. Colonel Shoré Chodroze was, absolutely, an asshole, but not that kind of asshole. "Got my kid with me, Sergeant."

Firefly's presence did not impact Nwynn's future word choices. But . . . Well . . . Firefly had heard it all before. She did live among seven hundred soldiers.

"So he wanted in and you didn't let him get there. And that's how he got hurt." I could see that Two Dead had taken a royal beating.

"Basically."

"Basically? So? Is there more? Did say why he wanted in?"

"He claimed it was business and we should get the . . . uh, out of his way. He was such an arrogant prick that . . ."

"It was me that lost my temper and hit him," the Aloen woman said. "All my fault. Not Sarge's. He really asked for it."

Nwynn said, "He was drunk or hopped up. You couldn't understand half what he said, but it boiled down to he wanted to get at the girls and he didn't care what our orders were, we weren't going to stop him."

It did sound like Two Dead had been begging for it. I looked forward to hearing his side. "But you did stop him."

"That we did."

"*I* did," the Aloen woman said.

"Uhm? Two female troopers took down a sorcerer of near-Taken caliber?"

Nwynn said, "He was wasted. And he's only got one hand."

The other woman insisted, "One trooper. Me. He had his back to me. I probably overdid it. But I was scared because he's a big-time sorcerer."

I extracted a reluctant and creative description of the pounding that Two Dead had taken, then said, "You two should get back to your posts. I'll handle it from here."

Nwynn looked like she wanted to argue. I said, "Out. I'll deal with it."

"Then I owe you one."

"Keep that in mind when I do decide to come shopping."

"Dad!"

Not the best idea to tease in front of your kid and in those circumstances. Nwynn might have blown up had Firefly not been there expressing her own disapproval. Blessed Baku's eyes were harder than chrome when she looked at the sergeant. Nwynn took a moment. That was all she needed to get that I was yanking her chain.

"Bad taste, sir, considering."

"I need to pick my moments better."

Nwynn indicated Two Dead. "Especially around short-tempered women. Cato! Let's go!"

Firefly clambered onto a tabletop to watch while I looked Two Dead over. I asked her, "What do you think the story is on the woman who is pretending to be your mom?"

The kid was not wrong. Up close the differences were obvious. No way could the woman pass for the Mischievous Rain that I had shared a house and family with before. But from a distance . . . Yet even then, only for a while.

The kid shrugged. "I don't know. Grown-up stuff. Politics."

No doubt. "So where is your real mom?"

"Back there, I guess. Watching."

"Watching? What?"

"You. Us. Everyone. To see what happens."

"Know something, kiddo? I don't like this. I wish it was her that came back so we could go back to the way . . ."

Firefly grinned from ear to ear. "Ha-ha-ha!" Not a laugh but a statement. "Me, too, Dad! And Shin three, Dad. And, wow, that man has got some really wicked bruises."

He did, and they were still developing.

I had Two Dead mostly stripped. He had bruises on his bruises. He had bruises enough to start up a medical museum dedicated to contusions. At first I figured that he must have had a whole load before he tried the girls' dorm, but now I could see that every one was fresh.

Either Nwynn and Cato were dedicated workers or they had had help. Two Dead had been stomped as thoroughly as I have ever seen. I would guess, after closer examination, that he had been well trampled by lots of smaller feet in widely varying sizes.

Cato had lied. No way could she have done this. She would need legs like a centipede, every foot with a different-size boot on.

So, dumbass Two Dead had made it all the way into the dorm. Maybe then Cato whacked him from behind. And then the Tides Elba girls took turns. Maybe the good sergeant rescued him but then blessed him with a vigorous stomping of her own before lugging him over here.

I might ought to remember not to irritate Sergeant Nwynn unnecessarily.

Two Dead would not be happy when he wakened. The question would be, had he been thumped well enough to discourage him permanently?

Firefly went on watching me work, grinning like some happy little nightmare.

Two Dead started awake, in a panic. He recognized me, relaxed slightly. He rolled his head, saw what sort of place he was in. He began to shake. He would be hurting bad.

Before he spoke he checked his missing hand—still missing—then inventoried his other extremities.

I had opiate tea ready. He should have a killer hangover to go with everything else. "Painkiller?" I showed him the mug. He reflected, concluded that I was not trying to kill him. I had had him at a total disadvantage already. He extended his good hand.

"Let me sit you up, first." I had him laid out on a cleverly designed table that Edmous Black had brought out from town. Parts of it could drop down or raise up, to turn it into an uncomfortable chair. I sat Two Dead up, then gave him the tea, with a bamboo tube in so he did not need to do any fine motor work with his shaky hand.

That done, I pulled up a tall stool and waited to hear his version of what had happened.

However, he demanded, "What happened?" He took a long draw from the mug. "I feel like I've been beaten."

"Because you *were* beaten. Vigorously, and then some more. Which you very clearly asked for. You don't remember?"

Chodroze frowned, which made his facial scar stand out more than usual. "My last clear memory is of me helping the Taken keep her balance when she stepped off the carpet. After that there is a vague recollection of an exchange with the Captain and the Lieutenant. From then on, nothing."

"No drinks? No drugs, just to loosen up after that awful trip?"

"I don't drink. I don't use drugs. I don't like not being in complete control. What happened to me?"

"I would love to say that you fell down some steps but the truth is a whole lot uglier."

He laid a calculating look on me, decided that I was not lying, probably. There should be witnesses to corroborate or disagree.

"While you were gone we collected twenty-nine more girls like the four that you took to the Tower."

"I know. That was a key topic before we left." He frowned ferociously, trying to understand what had led him to say that.

I nodded. "Last night, just a couple of hours after you arrived, you tried to force your way into the dormitory where those girls are kept. You acted like you were falling-down drunk. Most of what you said was incoherent or in a language nobody understood. The soldiers guarding the girls tried to stop you. You kept trying to break in. The guards eventually used force, in accordance with their standing orders."

Two Dead stared like I had to be spinning the grandest lie ever spun. He grumbled, more to himself than to me, "That doesn't sound like Shoré Chodroze. I don't even like women."

"Even so."

He shook his head and kept trying to remember.

I said, "One trooper admitted to the violence when they brought you in, but your bruises say that you did get into the dormitory, where the girls banged on you till the guards dragged you out. You have bruise marks from shoes in many sizes, from little to big. You really set them off."

He looked blank.

I have been drunk often. It helps, sometimes. But never have I been so drunk that I lost a chunk of time. All good sense, yes, but I suspect that most claimed memory loss is fabricated to avoid having to take full responsibility for bad behavior.

"There'll be an inquiry. It won't mean much if none of the girls got hurt. I haven't heard that any were."

Two Dead's eyes narrowed. The infusion worked fast. When the pain receded it distracted him less. He understood that he would be the accused rather than the plaintiff, a situation someone of his stature seldom faced.

"I stayed here last night so I haven't talked with the Captain or the Taken. I hope the rumor mill hasn't gone crazy. And I'm hoping the Taken can figure out what happened."

I had a suspicion. If those girls were synched up mentally more than anyone thought, they might have read Two Dead's nature from the Taken, have decided that he was a threat, and so have drawn him in for disposal.

"You knew about the girls before you came back. Did you get any special instructions concerning them?"

His reply might have been instructive. "Not that I am aware of. She didn't seem concerned. My brief was to resume my role as lead sorcerer of the Black Company."

It is not bragging if you can back it up. Two Dead could, though in this case he was embellishing.

"Ah. Edmous. Good morning. When you collect breakfasts for the patients pick up a double for the Colonel." A thought. I peeled back Two Dead's lips. "Open wide. Feel any damage in there? Any teeth loose? Any pain in the teeth or jaw?" No. His attackers had kept their feet away from his head, possibly a message that he was unlikely to get.

No sheltered temple girl would think of something like that but Chiba Vinh Nwynn might.

Much to think about. "Edmous?"

Black stared at Firefly like he was nose-to-nose with a nightmare. Baku wore a tiny devil smile, pleased with herself about something.

"Uh . . . Yes sir. Get the Colonel double rations. Should I bring something for you and . . . her?"

"Absolutely."

Black asked Two Dead, "Will you be able to manage solid food, sir?"

"I'll want oatmeal, scrambled eggs, and tea. If they're available. Use your own judgment if not. But lots of tea."

"Yes sir." Black took one more look at Firefly, then lit out. He did not consult our other patients about their breakfast preferences.

I talked with Two Dead till Black returned. Chodroze was abnormally civil and chatty but just did not have anything to add. He was not being cagey, either, except in that he wanted to hide the fact that he was extremely upset.

He had been proven vulnerable. He did not like that even a little.

Black brought mush and eggs for everybody. I gobbled mine, said, "Edmous, I was up all night with the Colonel. I'm wasted. I'm going to nap, now. I'll be next door if you need me."

"Yes, sir. I won't disturb you unless it's an emergency."

Firefly stuck with me, began her bed preps beside me. I asked, "Why don't you go back upstairs?"

"No."

"I'm too tired to argue."

"Good."

"But you have to go back eventually. I need a spy on the inside."

"Then talk to Shin and Ankou. I want to stay with you."

I was climbing into bed then, sleep starved and even less inclined to argue. She climbed in behind me. I asked, "What did you do to Edmous?"

"I just haunted him."

"Why?"

"It's all settled. It won't happen again if he doesn't do something else that he shouldn't if he's going to be my dad's good helper." Then she fell asleep, or pretended to fall asleep so stubbornly that I could not get another question answered.

Gurdlief's prodding and Firefly's mumbled threat to rip off his arm and brain him with it awakened me. I felt miserably unrested, yet got a spark of warmth out of the moment. When I was little my mother used that same threat in multiple name situations. Those befell my sisters more often than they did me, but I did have my moments of glory.

"What?" I snarled it. I was in a foul mood despite the spark of nostalgia. The warmth only briefly preceded a cold hollow where I wondered what had become of my kin. Bitterness followed. None of those people gave a damn about what had become of me.

This time Gurdlief poked me.

"I'm up. I'm awake. And I'm about to . . ."

"Sana said to tell you it's suppertime. And she says that there's something wrong with the Taken. Maybe she's sick. I didn't think they could get sick. The Taken, I mean. So maybe she's pregnant. She's been that kind of moody all day. Maybe you're going to be a father again."

Firefly looked like she wanted to chop Gurdlief into Ankou chow. But she said, "That ain't possible, Gurd. Dad never touched her. He never even touched . . ."

Six years old but she knew about that stuff. Definitely a devil, not a child.

I told the devil, "This is something we need to deal with."

. . .

The town girls laid on an outstanding supper: bread still steaming from the oven, early harvest turnips and peas, baby onions, and ridiculously tasty pork sausages. There was fresh butter and honey for the bread. Most kings did not have it so good.

Those girls were determined to show the new Mischievous Rain that her predecessor had hired the best, most talented young women to be had.

They had not wanted the work back when their families pushed them to apply for it. Now they were willing to fight to keep their positions. They could not wish for anything better.

The new Taken did not care. To her the girls were furniture.

Beloved Shin awarded each girl a grand smile when she delivered a fresh course. Blessed Baku offered verbal thanks. Both were breaking character, all for the Taken's benefit.

She did not notice. She was indifferent to everything. She had gone missing inside herself and was straying ever farther from the quotidian. I might have to move her to the hospital and start force-feeding her.

How had a stump like her flown a carpet all the way out here? Or had this state come about because of the stress of that passage?

Had to be more than that. Physical and emotional exhaustion must have left her vulnerable to something else.

So. Two Dead went rogue, fresh off the carpet. Now Mischievous Rain had gone lost, too.

Those girls. This one's sisters. I figured them for the common denominator.

We might have us a boiled-frog situation. The Taken and Two Dead would be frogs tossed into the pot once it was already boiling. The rest of us had been in the water since before the fire was lighted so we never noticed the water getting hotter.

The Captain glared past me but said nothing about Firefly tagging along. That would betray the possibility that sometimes he got up to stuff that he preferred the Taken not know about, and even less wanted to abuse the Tower's blissful ignorance. "A sit-down with all of the sorcerers? We spend too much time talking instead of doing already."

"Yes. We're into something unlike anything we've ever seen. We don't know what it is. That's why we keep talking and talking. I can't even express it. It's something that we can't handle the way we usually do. We can't trick it. We can't crush it by being the nastiest killers on the field. It's all inside. Insidious."

A grin for wordplay that went right by him. I was making a mash of this. But it was nothing concrete. The words might not exist to define it.

I soldiered on. "The problem with the girls being concentrated is worse than we thought." I vented my full theory.

"That'll put a smile back on Two Dead if you're right. He's making himself crazy trying to figure out how he could have done what he did and not be able to remember it."

"Is he all right otherwise?" Two Dead had fled the hospital while I napped.

"No. He can hardly move. Even blinking has got to hurt. But he's a stubborn asshole. He'll do things his own way even if it kills him." He took a moment. "All right. Let's do it now. Before anything gets any crazier. Silent can't be here, though. Him and Elmo, with eighty men and four shadow pots, went to give that Resurrectionist place another look."

"I was going to suggest that we do that."

"You looked at those papers yet?"

"I did. But they're in UchiTelle, not TelleKurre. The only one I got any sense from was a kind of tax roll."

"We need to get them to the Tower somehow. Messenger! Front! I have work for you." To me, "Get the Taken. She should be here, too."

"She's practically a vegetable right now."

"Then carry her. But get her here."

Everywhere I went, there Blessed Baku was. She seldom said anything so it was not always easy to remember that she was close by, big eyes watching and cute ears listening. As I was on my way to collect the Taken she said, "You should tell Mom what's happening."

"I did that already."

"Do it again. I'll do it with you. She hasn't taken this stuff seriously enough."

Six years old.

The faux Mischievous Rain remained at the dinner table, eyes open but empty. Ankou watched from nearby. He had his third eye open for the first time in an age.

Beloved Shin was nowhere to be seen.

Firefly shrugged, took my right hand, and led me into her mother's bedroom, which had become the repository for all the clutter that had come east with the Taken. I had to move two chests so we could position ourselves. I said, "You hide in the shadows. You walk through the shadows. Could you run all the way to the Tower?" Maybe I had a way to get those papers to the Lady.

"No."

"Too far?"

"Way too far."

"Too bad. I'm ready." I ran through the formula, Firefly prompting, my hand on my bit of carved lapis. Merry wind chimes filled the room.

Baku started jabbering before I could open my mouth. Her delivery was rapid, forceful, and smooth. I did not understand a word. The language was alien. It seemed to include no accented or stressed syllables. I did get that Baku was unhappy. She thought it was time somebody got off the pot.

She finished, sudden as a sword stroke.

The wind chimes sang, chagrined.

My bold little girl, giving them hell in the Tower.

"What is going on in here?"

"So you finally woke up."

"I asked a question." Red-eyed angry.

I might have grumbled something stupid but Blessed Baku stepped in front of me. "We were consulting Mother about how to proceed with you."

Wind chimes let us know that we were being watched. The chimes were neither merry nor melodic. The Taken felt their anger.

"Very well. Proceed." She turned away.

"Hang on," I said. "We have a meeting with the command staff when Baku and I finish here."

The kid was talking softly at the same time, the other direction, and, apparently, was getting answers that I could not hear.

The Taken started to vent something. Chimes forestalled her. The stars on her yukata, that had gone lifeless the moment she stepped off of her carpet, began to stir. Had the light been brighter would I have seen tattoos move on her face? "Very well. I shall need a few minutes to prepare myself."

She did look like death on a stick. "Please be quick. The discussion is time-sensitive."

She gave me a poisonous look but nodded. "This is where I will need to take care of myself. Not so?"

"It is. We won't . . ."

Baku said, "We're done. For now." She gave the Taken a steely look. She did not speak the formula for breaking contact with the Tower.

I saw Ankou at his bowl as I shut the bedroom door. He winked.

Firefly and I settled at the table to wait. Formerly missing Beloved Shin was there, playing solitaire with a shiny new deck. Where had he come from? When? While we consulted the wind chimes, obviously. He laid out his cards. He noticed Firefly staring at those. "They came out with her," pointing toward the bedroom. "Mom sent them."

Firefly grinned wickedly.

I asked, "Did you tell her about the carpet that Slapback saw?"

"I did. We will hear more about that soon. Things have not gone according to plan out here. Some changes might be coming."

I did not ask. I would not get a straight answer. "Yonder woman sure recovered fast once we started talking to the Tower."

"She did." Baku considered Shin. "Where have you been, bonehead? And doing what?"

"Observing." He slapped at some cards that had not come up the way he wanted, like that would change their spots. He had the patience of stone with things that mattered but could be volatile with things that did not.

I asked, "So who is she?" not actually expecting an answer.

Baku said, "Mischievous Rain."

Shin said, "Tides Elba," at the same time.

"But she's not your mother."

"No."

"So then who . . ." The Taken stepped out of the bedroom. She had accomplished wonders in a scant few minutes, having fully restored her glory of a year ago. Her mood seemed elevated, too.

Had she gotten a pep talk from the Tower during her reconstruction?

She said, "If this thing is that important, we should get to it now."

Shin began laying out a new game. When the Taken was out of sight he produced a miniature beer stein of the sort that has the pewter flip lid, which he handed to Firefly. Firefly made it disappear inside her jacket.

The Taken was not pleased by the crowd in Admin. But she was not pleased with anything, anyway. Every sorcerer but Silent was there. They all looked like they had bitten into something foul. Goblin, One-Eye, the Third, and Buzz were scattered around the room, as were Candy, the Lieutenant, and Sergeant Nwynn. Two Dead looked like death warmed over, like he had added the drizzling shits to his hangover and his aching thousand bruises plus one. He had him a fixed ugly vengeance look on. He aimed it more at the Taken than at Sergeant Nwynn.

The Captain practically glowed at the center of his the-father-of-all-around-him body language. He told the Taken, "Explain yourself."

"Excuse me?"

"You girls are bright, every one. You were the first one, Tides Elba, before you went to the Tower. Now we have twenty-nine more of you, all different ages, caught since a version called Mischievous Rain took our first four captive girls off to the Tower. Explain yourself."

This Tides Elba was not Mischievous Rain, though she claimed the title and believed that it belonged to her. A puzzle hidden inside an enigma surrounded by mysteries. The other Tides Elba, so different in personality, so much warmer, had known every smallest thing that Tides Elba ought to know . . .

The Old Man believed this to be the real Tides Elba. He might be right, but I did still doubt. The Tides Elba we sent to the Tower was more self-confident.

Of course, during a real-world year in the Tower her whole soul could have been reconstructed.

Whoever she was, and whatever else she might be, the woman was Taken. Only the Taken, never more than ten of the most powerful sorcerers in existence, received the knowledge and power needed to manage a flying carpet.

She said, "In truth, right now, I can't answer with certainty. I have no exact idea of my place, here. I was sent to help end the menace of the Port of Shadows. The hard work was supposedly done already. The mop-up would be my first mission. I would spend a few months here, where I know my way around, doing make-work." She choked. Literally.

Every wizard there blurted an expletive, though I was convinced that they had expected something. They did wizard stuff. Blessed Baku squealed and clapped beside me.

The Taken froze. The stars on her yukata scampered wildly, then froze too. Then they unfroze, scampered, and froze again. The cycle repeated several times. There was not light enough to show what any tattoos might be doing.

Beloved Shin, sprung from nowhere, served the Taken's left cheek a savage slap, spun round, then was no longer with us. The sole evidence that he had appeared was a knave of swords card stuck to the Taken's cheek.

From the corner of my eye I saw Blessed Baku slip that stein back inside her jacket.

The Taken moaned. She cried, "They are too strong for me, Mistress! They are too many! They devour me."

Sergeant Nwynn observed, "In about thirteen days it gets worse for the rest of us."

Seldom have I seen so many men so much at a loss for what to do about a flock of pretty girls—though I am sure they all expected the Tower to be cruel. Outsweeper should ought to start digging now. We might need a lot of holes.

This was getting ridiculous. The Company has encountered numerous existential threats across the centuries but never any this uncomfortable, nor as much a product of our own good intentions.

The Captain asked, "Is this what it looks like, gentlemen?" He got only shrugs in response.

Sergeant Nwynn said, "It is. And it might be worse than we imagine."

The Taken, hand pressed to her slapped cheek and the knave of swords, shed a flow of tears while saying, "She is correct. The girls are developing one mind—with no direction or plan. They're all little girls lost, crying themselves to sleep at night, terrified of what might happen next." Then her eyes glazed over. Her face went slack. She began to sink back into the overmind that had seized control as she left her carpet. Shin's card may not have kicked her completely free.

Two Dead, of all hard cases going, growled, "This sucks! This bites totally and completely. And the Tower will see only one possible solution."

The Lieutenant raised a hand. He looked embarrassed.

I took it. "Captain, do you recall the bad joke the Lieutenant made a while back? About the girls?"

"I do."

I said, "That might be an alternative to killing them."

"Hell of a choice, rape or murder."

"Sergeant Nwynn once suggested that we scatter the herd so the girls couldn't feed off one another. That'd solve the problem that we have now but there'd always be the threat of them coming back together later."

The Taken said, "They would try to find one another. The ones here are trying to find their sisters now that they know those sisters exist."

I said, "Sergeant Nwynn has been obsessively attentive. She gave every girl a detailed physical exam." Nwynn had concealed nothing done to create her roster. "Only two aren't virgin. Assuming that matters."

Nwynn was not embarrassed. "The oldest is sixteen. She mothered a child who became an orphan at the same temple. The other is fourteen. She made a poor choice only hours before we snagged her. It will be a while yet before we can be sure how poor a choice she actually made. The others haven't been touched. I can't report anything about girls that we don't have in custody. Somewhere out there a Port of Shadows girl might be having herself a great fun time with the man destined to father the child who will become the Dominator reincarnated."

This all seemed especially absurd because the girls belonged to the temples of Occupoa. I said again, "The Lieutenant suggested that we neutralize them by making sure that none of them are virgins."

Every guy leaned in, prurience piqued.

The Taken was regaining control of herself. After several deep breaths, she said, "A mass rape? No good. To close the Port of Shadows you'd have to make sure that every girl got pregnant by one of you. Which still probably wouldn't help with the mind thing."

Two Dead grumbled, "Folks, we're going to have a lot of dead little girls on our consciences."

That was a stopper. Nobody would have bet a corroded copper on Two Dead knowing what conscience was.

No human who ever lived was without a hidden surprise.

Two Dead had gotten his mind clear.

The Taken had recovered and regrouped as well. She said, "Although I am one of them I must admit that there may be no alternative to decimation, from the imperial perspective."

Hard as stone, every one, we had spent vast tracts of our lives in a brutal profession. Physician Croaker was the softhearted candy-ass of the crew. But no one else said, "Screw it! Put the pretty little bitches in the ground."

Buzzard Neck opined, "There must be a way to save the children."

The Old Man said, "Saving them isn't a problem. But saving them while stopping them from doing what they've been doing, and from becoming what they are becoming, that is a problem. They could destroy us and the empire both if they get there."

I added, "Plus we have to make sure that none of them get together with the man who will make one of them the Port of Shadows."

The Taken had her legs under her again. She told Sergeant Nwynn, "If you cut out the five strongest girls, the potentially most dangerous ones, Colonel Chodroze and I will take them to the Tower. We should be able to remove two sets before the next lunar cycle."

Nwynn said, "That would for sure kill a synch-up more serious than the last one."

I said, "But . . ."

The Taken pointed a finger like it was a weapon. "They will not be murdered."

I surrendered. She was one of them herself. "Then do that. Take them all, if you have to."

"If we have to. If that is what She wants."

One cannot forget where the final authority lies.

Two Dead went gray when he was conscripted to help make deliveries to the Tower. Like anyone who had gone inside and had returned, he recalled nothing but was convinced that he had suffered a passage through Hell. He said, "Much as going back to that place horrifies me, that may be the answer. The girls we delivered before were not mistreated." But how did he know that?

The Captain looked to me for an opinion. All I could do was shrug. "I wasn't, either. Other than having my mind wrung out. Far as I recall."

The Lieutenant said, "I smell some interesting math. We have twenty-nine girls, fifteen under age. We would be out of the woods if we got rid of ten." Then, "Crap! You had that figured out."

I said, "But we'll find more of them. Maybe lots more. That's some stinky interesting math, too."

Goblin spoke for the first time. "True, that. I got a pigeon from Silent just before I got told to come over here. Him and Elmo caught nine more girls yesterday. They killed some Rebels, too. And they think they might be on to some more Resurrectionist stuff."

The Old Man grumbled, "And you're just getting around to telling me now?"

"Shit's been happening, boss. We're all busy dealing with it. This's the first chance I've had to tell you. You're all worried about girls having periods instead of . . . Now you know."

The Old Man scowled fiercely. "I wish we had more carpets . . . What, Croaker?"

"The carpet that Slapback spotted. That's something else we need to worry about." I faced the Taken. "Do you know anything about that?"

She did not. Her arrival was a unique event. No one outside the Tower should know about it. Which meant that there could be no connection.

I had to be content with the knowledge that the mystery carpet had been made known to the Tower. It should be a mystery to Her for no time at all. Jumping subject, I told the Taken, "I have some captured Resurrectionist documents, in UchiTelle, that need to go to the Tower, too."

"Weight?" she asked. "There's only so much I can haul."

I recalled all the luxuries that she had brought out with her. "The stack isn't that big."

My bold response got me some looks. Half these people did not yet realize that this was not Mischievous Rain with her hair color changed.

The Captain said, "Everybody shut it. Goblin. Tell me what you got from Silent."

Five minutes later Two Dead and the Taken had orders to go find Elmo and see what he had stumbled into. Then Buzz got told to take a ranger platoon out to reinforce Elmo. It sounded like he and Silent might be in trouble.

Clever me, I hitched a ride to the country. I carried Firefly's little stein, that she had pushed up under my shirt, and some cards that Shin had planted on me as we hauled the Taken's carpet out of storage. The stein was cold against my ribs. The only card I saw during the planting was the Hanged Man, which brought to mind one of the old-time Taken, nearly as foul as the Limper: the Hanged Man.

The flight was too intimate for me to check the other cards. I wasted mental energy trying to figure out what the point of carrying them was, and why Shin had been careful to transfer them unseen by anyone but me.

We flew eastward at a speed that threatened to pull my curly locks out by the roots. Then, "Holy shit! You guys feel the change?"

Twenty miles into a thirty-five-mile run we crossed a boundary. Once beyond it we sensed nothing from the captive girls. I felt like bellowing an aria in praise of the moon.

Meantime, at least for the moment, Two Dead reverted to the sour-face tight-ass of unfond memory. But then he broke into a toothy grin while the Taken morphed into the Tides Elba I recalled from last year, although uncertainly.

I said, "We're out of range."

She replied, "We are. And you two would have been free much sooner if I weren't with you. So. Colonel. While we're free we should ready ourselves for what we'll suffer when we have to go back to collect our cargo."

Two Dead growled, "I'm not going through that again."

I do not know what he meant. It did not matter. The point was, we were beyond the clowder's influence. Being aware of that influence, now, they should be better able to resist it.

The change in the Taken was striking. She had become a woman much like Mischievous Rain before. She had been overwhelmed by all those younger sisters.

The moon would be full in two more nights. It was high and bright tonight. I could see reasonably well even down in the woods.

"So what happened?" I asked Elmo. Two Dead and the Taken were content to let me do the talking, which I did while attending men wounded during an attack that our arrival had scattered.

"I hadn't opened the shadow pots yet. They're open now, and I'll never make that mistake again."

"Let's hope those dickheads try it again, then. Not what I meant, though. I was being more general." I swept an arm around. "Is this the Resurrectionist place?" All I saw was trees.

"You look that way, straight west, you can maybe make out a hump something like a barrow."

I could not make it out.

"Come on. I'll show you."

I asked the Taken, "Could you make a fast flight back with these guys?" I indicated the wounded.

"I am not going back into that."

Two Dead showed us that he had had a change of heart since his own proclamation of a similar sentiment not long ago. "Of course you are. We all are. It's our job."

The Taken scowled, then said, "You're right. But I will need you with me. Otherwise I'll get swallowed by the mind field."

"Of course. But first let's look around here. Resurrectionists are masters at hiding things inside sophisticated glamours."

Once again we saw a fresh side of Two Dead. He was completely diplomatic while saying that Elmo might have missed something. Had time in the Tower hammered him into a facsimile of a decent human being?

Silent, as yet unseen, would not be pleased to see his work double-checked, even so.

Elmo's "barrow" was a hump six feet tall at the low end and fourteen feet on the high, hard to make out even with the moon so bright. The surrounding "clearing" lacked old-growth timber but did boast saplings and young oaks. The ground cover was grass. There was no brush close in. The grass had been trampled down. There were bodies scattered around. This was where the fight had drifted after our arrival. An injured enemy fighter was trying to drag himself toward cover.

I asked, "Do we need this one?"

The Taken said, "If he'll talk I'll take him to be treated with our own injured."

I would hear it from the Old Man tomorrow. Why was I away snooping when we had wounded coming in?

I would have to go back with the ambulance flight.

Elmo said, "Over here." He led me to a tangle of blackberry canes.

"What's this?"

"The entrance to elf hill."

Two Dead said, "This is mostly illusion, but effective in this light."

Elmo said, "If you look hard you can just make out a strand of red string. Put your right hand on it. It will lead you through the real brambles."

I got in line behind Two Dead. Elmo came behind me. The Taken stayed with the wounded enemy, trying to determine whether salvaging him would be worthwhile.

The string led down a steep stone stairway. The blackberries probably ought not to be navigated at night. Too many were not illusions. I gathered an unpleasant collection of thorn bites.

"The thorns aren't poisoned," Two Dead assured me.

"That's good." Inanely.

Eight steps on I noticed that there was a flow of air going down with me. You would want good circulation if you gathered people underground.

"There must be other ways in and out."

Elmo puffed, "Still looking for those."

The bottom of the stair was six more steps below. We pushed ahead through curtains of swirling cloth strips that, by feel, were almost new, then we were in the Resurrectionist hall. It was obvious immediately why a brisk breeze came with us.

There had to be a hundred candles and lanterns burning there.

Everything sloped uphill from where we entered. The floor was hard gray stone set in steps eight feet wide. The ceiling was metal concealed by lampblack. "This feels more like a place of worship than a secret meeting hall." The high end boasted a stage raised something over two feet above the floor there. On it was what, out west, might be called a pulpit. But maybe the whole just served as a speaker's rostrum.

The hall being tilted, heated air flowed uphill. If Elmo really wanted to know where the exits were he could make some heavy smoke, then go outside and watch.

I would have put the rostrum on the low end so my top people could enjoy the sweetest air.

I now knew what Silent was up to. He and two soldiers were dismantling the rostrum, one short board at a time. He paid us scant attention but did make a small, quick field sign urging caution.

I observed, "This is fine for a hole in the ground." Expensive materials had been used to build the place. Fortunes had been spent to decorate it.

Elmo said, "It ain't that old according to Silent. Built since the Lady's resurrection."

I tried to calculate how long that might be but could not put it together. "This is really far from the Barrowland." An ugly historical mosaic covered the eastern wall. "This was about the last country that the Dominator conquered before the White Rose yanked it all out from under him."

The west wall had been set up for storage. Cabinets of varying sizes ran from floor to ceiling along the entire wall. Every drawer or door had been painted a color different from any contiguous neighbor. That wall must have been a sight before Elmo's men took it apart. No doubt the captured documents had come from there. And, no doubt either, anything of any imaginable value found there had vanished into the ether.

Two Dead said, "That stage is booby-trapped, Silent."

Silent waved, held up two fingers. Elmo translated, "He knows. There are two traps, one behind the other. They weren't there when we were here before. He's trying to figure them out."

"All right. Good to know that he isn't just all talk."

Again with a surprise. That was an amazingly clever remark for Shoré Chodroze.

"Here we go," said one of the men with Silent, carefully lifting a strip of flooring eight inches wide and three feet long. Then he blurted, "Holy shit!" He tossed the board and tried to dive into the widened gap. Silent and the other soldier stopped him. Silent turned him till they were eye-to-eye. Silent did not actually need to remind the fool that they were trying to disarm a booby trap.

Two Dead said, "Must be gold where the cheese usually goes."

He was right. There were fifteen gold coins under the stage, all fractional pieces, but even that was more than most men would earn in several years. Yes, most anyone would find it difficult to rein in his acquisitive instinct.

Two Dead said, "The second-layer trap will be behind the gold rat bait. And it's almost undetectable." He indicated Silent. "This is one talented man, to sniff it out without knowing it was there beforehand."

I said, "He is talented. But he works hard to hide it." Kidding on the square.

The Taken joined us and helped us stare at the gold. She said, "Sergeant. Elmo. Word was, you caught nine of my sisters here." She made gestures over the gold that awed both Silent and Two Dead. Silent's mouth hung open for several seconds.

Two Dead told the soldiers, "You can remove the coins safely, now. But do it slowly and stop instantly if someone tells you to." He mused, "The man who engineered this may have been cruel enough to lay in a third-level trap."

Greed and terror tormented the soldiers, and the rest of us, too.

There were coins enough for everybody to get a couple.

Two Dead addressed that obliquely by saying, "We all know exactly how many coins there are."

The Taken did not get distracted by things that were shiny and round. "Sergeant. The girls. Where are they? I don't feel them. And how did you come up with them?"

I dragged my attention away from the shiny while Elmo stumbled through his story. Like the coins, the girls had been bait for an ambush. But the shadow jars had been deployed in time to break that one.

Talk about shadow pots baffled Two Dead and the Taken.

My right hand strayed to the little stein that Firefly had given me.

A lot of weird was going around these days. Dark water rising, higher and higher.

I asked, "Nine girls? How old?"

"Thirteen, now. We caught four more that were with the guys who attacked us tonight."

"Thirteen?"

"Yeah. From about five to maybe sixteen, mostly postpubescent. One of them is pregnant."

"Look at you, using big words." I turned to the Taken, stifling the fear that Elmo's remark had sparked. "How about we keep this bunch out here, away from the ones at Aloe?" Except for the pregnant one. She *had* to go to the Tower, first cull. Only . . . Resurrectionists would not have put her at risk if she was the Port of Shadows, would they? They were desperate, now. They would hide her. They would bury her deep if she was carrying the reincarnation of their lord. Would they not?

Maybe. But they had fallen so far that they might start doing stupid stuff. Or, they could have been so sure that they would succeed that they had not bothered to consider the risk.

Guaranteed, we would see a shitload of excitement if the pregnant girl actually was the Port of Shadows. The suicidal behavior of our enemies would escalate way beyond insane, although there might not be many of them left to act.

"We have no choice. If we want the most dangerous girls gone before the next synchronicity crisis we really can't add more girls to the mix." She turned on Elmo, to press him about the pregnant girl.

Though she was a problem girl herself she was not complimentary to her newfound sisters. That said plenty about where she stood when she was free of the mind field.

Silent, helped by Two Dead, carefully studied a second-level trap created by crazy people.

I told the Taken, "Buzz is headed here with thirty more men. Him and Silent can keep the girls here till after the synch. The most dangerous ones will be gone, then. And we'll know Her plans for the rest."

"What was that? You shivered."

"Oh, just . . ." No. Not just. Something. Without thought, I barked, "Silent! Two Dead! Don't move!" Three quick steps and I was there with them, Shin's cards in hand. I plucked one and flicked it into the hole in the stage. It flew like a thrown dagger and stuck just inches from two gold coins not yet retrieved.

Everyone gaped. If I had had a mirror I would have seen myself gaping, too. What did I just do?

The air seemed to go out of the hall. I felt like I was about to pop. My ears hurt. My eyeballs felt like needles were pushing them out from behind. Then came the rebound. I felt like I was being compressed to the size of an acorn.

The Taken said, "That was rough but it got stretched out so it wasn't fatal. Colonel Chodroze and you, sir," indicating Silent, "you need to join me outside. There will be a follow-up attack launched on the assumption that we in here were killed."

Everybody gawked. Elmo asked, "How could you know?"

She snapped, "Move it! Soldiers will die if we don't help."

Elmo said, "But the jars are open."

Silent poked him. This Taken did not know about Shin's jars, nor did she need to know. But the enemy did know and his ultimate booby trap included a secondary spell that shattered all nearby crockery, whereupon a bloodbath was supposed to ensue. Our guys were expected to provide the blood.

But I had aborted some of that with the card. The Taken and Two Dead remained healthy and able to assist an equally healthy and thoroughly pissed-off Silent.

One of the soldiers cried, "But what about . . . ?"

Elmo snapped, "You're in charge. Keep in mind that these people know exactly how many coins there were."

I said, "You two come up with any fairy-gold nonsense, your names will go in the Annals as having been delivered to Outsweeper."

The Taken seized my arm, yanked, and barked, "Let's go!"

"I liked the Mischievous Rain version better. She was nice."

"I *am* Mischievous Rain. And I'm nice when I'm allowed to be—unless I have to deal with a man who gropes me uninvited."

"I could apologize but I wouldn't mean it. That was a once-in-a-lifetime moment that I'll treasure forever because you are such a remarkable woman."

Gods defend me! I must have been expecting to die, real soon. There was no way that the Croaker I had known all my life would have said that to any woman, let alone one who could turn him into a eunuch frog. Metaphorically speaking.

She smacked me upside the head. "Move your ass. And I'm thinking that maybe we should take one girl less, first trip west, so you can go snuggle the Mischievous Rain that you like best."

I hit the steps to the real world boggled by the conversation. Tonight's Taken was not the sad pancake that she had been before we left the compound.

I stepped out of the blackberry bushes into the seventh level of Hell.

The forest was afire. All kinds of visually weird stuff was afoot. Nothing I saw inspired any confidence in my side's ability to prevail. Someone attacking had the support of numerous minor but competent and motivated sorcerers.

I panicked. It looked like the end of my world.

I opened the stein that Firefly had given me.

I saw nothing that happened after that.

I was aboard the Taken's carpet with the wounded, headed for Aloe. I had a serious hangover. Tides Elba had a case of self-confidence that would intimidate a mountain. After what happened out there in those woods, once I opened that stein, it was unlikely that Rebel or Resurrectionist would be a challenge in our province ever again.

They had designed a huge, clever trap meant to drain our strength by driblets but unforeseen circumstances turned the tables so darkly that they now must be almost extinct.

When Buzz arrived he would learn that his main job, besides keeping twelve girls away from the insanity at the compound, would be to dig big, deep holes so the stench of decomposition would not make that part of the woods unlivable.

Some men were not happy despite our professional success. Somebody had shot his mouth off about the gold bait in that booby trap.

I told Elmo to channel the corporate anger into tearing the meeting hall apart. He could claim that the enemy kept coming back because there was still something valuable hidden here.

There was, but it was hidden in plain sight: thirteen girls less the one with us aboard the staggering carpet.

Most of the twelve were past puberty. Silent, Elmo, and Buzz might have some trouble keeping them safe.

The youngest among us lack any concept of consequences.

I did not get dragged off to the Tower. The question never came up. The Taken's carpet was burdened enough without me, with the Resurrectionist documents, the pregnant girl, four other girls selected by Sergeant Nwynn, and one grim Two Dead to wrangle them all while Tides Elba did the flying. He and she were almost seasick green.

Once she was back inside the mind field the Taken was no longer as fierce as she had been outside. She began to suffer a strong empathy for her younger sisters. At the same time, though, she nurtured a burning rage against those who had created her, and all these copies of her, as nothing more than tools, never people at all.

Nobody wants to be a thing. I might know only sisters and whores but even I understood that no woman wants to be seen as nothing more than a convenient pussy.

Supper with the kids, without Gurdlief Speak. Beloved Shin asked, "Can I have my cards back?"

I grunted, handed the survivors over.

"You only needed one? Excellent!"

I asked, "Are you all right?" He was pale and looked ragged, though his appetite had not suffered. He was shaming Firefly. There might be no leftovers for the town girls.

"Had a rough night last night. I didn't get much sleep."

I figured broken crockery might have been involved.

"Luckily, I found a way back." Shin eyed Baku with what might have been real gratitude.

So I was right, though I had heard nothing about any savage children rampaging amongst our enemies out there.

Apparently our luck did improve dramatically after I opened Baku's stein. Even without, I believed that Silent, Two Dead, and the Taken would have proven adequate to the challenge eventually.

I did not ask for details. I might not like the answers on the improbable chance that either kid actually responded.

I caught Firefly smirking at her brother repeatedly.

I could guess what had happened—if I put the hints together in a conspiracy theory sort of way. Beloved Shin—the Shin behind the illusion that presented itself as a boy—walked the shadows hither and yon using the shadow pots, wherever those pots happened to be. Blessed Baku and Ankou did the same, sometimes. The shattering of the pots had stranded Shin with no hope of escape until I opened the stein. The stein had not shattered because it was not pottery. It had been carved from soapstone, probably by the artist who had produced the lapis communication pieces.

Beloved Shin answered a question that I had not yet thought to ask. "Buzzard Neck Tesch's platoon has two shadow pots. They will get there before nightfall. The sorcerers who broke the pots did not survive. I'm hoping that they didn't share their plans before they perished."

There the boy put his finger onto an iron law of warfare. No matter how clever you are at finding a new tool, your opponent will come up with a counter long before that can possibly be convenient for you.

There was some serious perishing happening before I opened that stein. Elmo's band suffered a lot of casualties, some of them fatal. I will record the names in the books of the fallen once Outsweeper has had his way and say.

I worried that the pot-cracker spell had outlived its inventors. There are always survivors. That is just a fact. An enemy survivor of the biggest battle ever was out there leading a ranger platoon right now although nobody from the other side was supposed to have gotten away.

Still, I did say that the Rebel was almost extinct. The intelligence all agreed. That seemed to please the locals as much as us.

I suspect that they were less thrilled at Eastern Army headquarters.

Or was that baseless paranoia? These people had not done anything... Crap! Wait! They might be rooting for the Company right now, but we had Two Dead and Buzzard Neck among us as living, breathing evidence that Whisper meant to do us harm.

Which was a fact that would not be unknown at Charm, now, Two Dead having been there and almost certainly having had an opportunity to engage with the Eye.

So the night was now our friend. But the night surely yet held a harvest of surprises.

22

Once Upon a Time: Papa's Girls

Papa was evasive and unforthcoming but Bathdek remained persistent. She let some Senjak arrogance leak through.

"You suffered two seizures in one day, Papa!" Never mind that it had not happened before, nor had since. As yet. "What if you never recovered? Where would Laissa and I be then?"

His response suggested that he had not considered the possibility.

The longer she spent with Papa the odder a mix he seemed, not just two men in one body but each of those two both an idiot and a genius.

For all that Papa was determined to conquer death his determination seemed more an intellectual quest than a hunt for a rabbit hole down which he could duck to escape it himself. The only real-world application he had in mind was to salvage Laissa. And maybe Kitten a little. But Laissa was the obsession. Invocation of Laissa's name could keep Papa focused.

"All right, honey. I surrender! Tell me why you're upset."

"I told you. I told you five times. We're a hundred miles from the nearest human being—which is probably a good thing for Laissa's sake—and we're two thousand from anybody who could understand what we said if we had to ask for help." She blasted that out in one long breath, drew a couple deep ones before she continued, "That maybe makes us safe from Old Ugly but if we have any kind of a real emergency we'll all be dead."

She saw the saner necromancer oozing toward the surface. Papa developed a sly look when that happened. The necromancer never realized that he gave himself away. He had no experience dealing with people on a prolonged basis.

She told him, "Don't fool around. You don't have to play games. The situation is what it is. We're here. There is no cure for that even if Laissa and I wanted one. There is no need for you to play coy and keep hiding from us. And you definitely need to make arrangements."

The sly fox withdrew.

"I said I surrender."

"All right. Good. Making progress. So, other than hide from the Dominator, what to you mean to accomplish out here? And why this particular here?" She suspected that he had known about this place before they came to it, despite its distance from Dusk.

"Here because here is so remote that it will take the Domination generations to expand this far. That will be time enough to resolve Laissa's problem."

Generations? Was he overlooking the fact that he was mortal? "Not the best answer, Papa." But he did think it was true, right now.

What had he been doing all those years before he found Laissa and brought her back to life?

Bathdek thought she knew. And the thought turned her stomach.

Laissa was not the first. He had hinted as much once, saying that he did not want to lose another daughter. But Laissa was as close as he had yet come to success. And there was no doubt that, when he was fully Papa, he did love Laissa.

Sometimes too much. Bathdek had witnessed moments when clearly he wanted to be something more than Laissa's Papa.

He directed nothing like that her way. Why not? Because Laissa would be more pliable? If that was what Papa wanted that was likely what Laissa would do. On his side of the transaction he would not be putting himself in the way of potential emotional injury.

Bathdek did not like that. She was not sure why. She would have had no objection, nor even much interest, had Laissa been fully alive. Dorotea Senjak alive had been Bathdek's closest enemy. But now . . . How could Papa taking advantage do Laissa any actual harm? She was an animated corpse with almost no mind. Why care?

Bathdek wasted hours brooding about that.

In her own way she was becoming crazy protective, too.

Their new home, the castle perched on that upthrust, remained under construction indefinitely, after first being completed quickly in timber, in slightly more than two months. Bathdek stopped pretending to have no skills as a sorceress. Using sorcery was easier and faster than direct physical labor. After they moved in, the necromancer concentrated on research but he did make time each day for work on home improvements, which mainly meant a gradual upgrade from timber to stone.

Clearly, he planned to stay awhile.

Credence Senjak, who called herself Bathdek, sank into the role of Kitten so deeply that, most of the time, she did not recall having been anyone else before she became Papa's daughter. Mostly she spent long hours creating stone blocks for improving their castle. When her assistance was needed she did what Papa wanted in order to help Laissa. And she helped with research where she could, but that was depressing. She could imagine no way to conquer the monster that meant to devour her sister. And she managed everything when Papa made his forays into the world to acquire what they could not make for themselves.

She became adept with tools. She studied necromancy and the related sciences. She acquired agricultural skills, both gardening and animal husbandry. Papa brought in chickens, geese, hogs, sheep, goats, and several dogs to look out for them. Having animals meant having to learn to slaughter and dress, to butcher and preserve meat and cure hides, most of which was bloody, smelly, exhausting work, and all of which Papa knew well, suggesting a rural boyhood.

Papa never talked about his past. He never gave up a name. Well, no sorcerer would volunteer a real one, but Papa was content to go by Papa alone.

Kitten looked forward to Papa's trips. She could relax her vigilance, then. She could poke around in his laboratory. And, most of all, she could look forward to the gifts and treats he always brought home. The best of those were fresh fruits.

Life stayed busy. It seemed only a few eyeblinks and they were performing Laissa's sixth rejuvenation since their arrival. Kitten realized that she was eighteen, now. Had she remained in Dusk she would likely be married to some creepy old man who would lend even more influence to the Senjak clan. Unless, like her older sisters, she just flat refused, daring her parents to do their worst.

Their worst could be pretty fierce. But Sylith and Ardath were fierce themselves and willing to fight their parents if they considered the fight worthwhile.

But one of them was married already, even so.

Two years. These days she hardly thought about getting away, back to the world that was her own, the world of the old darkness.

That world might have no room for her anymore. That world might have moved on. But now she had skills that would help if she chose to run.

She did not have the skills to save her sister, though, and likely never would.

"Papa, we've been here more than two years."

"We're well into our third, yes." He sounded a little sad, a little despondent, and a lot resigned. "And I just can't crack the secret." A tear trailed down his cheek. He was Papa at the very end of the personality spectrum. The almost sane necromancer had not surfaced for almost two years. Kitten hoped that he was gone forever.

Wishful thinking, that, she knew.

The right emotional cues would resurrect him just as the wrong emotional cues could bring on one of Papa's seizures.

. . .

During those increasingly infrequent times when Bathdek did recall that she was not Papa's daughter she prepared herself to flee.

She had worked that out before the wooden castle was finished. What she never could get set was how to take Laissa along with any hope of her sister lasting more than a few months.

At the moment Bathdek refused to abandon a sister for whom she had had no love at all before her plunge down the garbage chute.

"I keep hearing you say you almost have it but I don't believe that you do, Papa. I think you just want to do it so bad that you make yourself think that you're getting closer."

"I'm open to suggestions, Kitten. If you see something that I've overlooked, tell me."

"I'm not saying that you overlooked anything, just that there's something that you don't know."

"Which would be what?" Said with a faint hint of sly.

This was hard. She had to give up her most precious secret. If she did they might get Laissa past the final roadblock. And, before long, she might be in good enough shape to run away.

"Papa, I was one of the people who received the Blessing."

He stared. This was going to be harsh. This was going to blast him out of his comfortable end of the personality spectrum.

Before anything else she had to make him remember that he was not actually her father. She was an uninvited visitor to his old home and he had kidnapped her for her trouble.

He shuddered. He went on staring, without seeing, his internal population beginning to stir. Bathdek feared that he would lapse into a seizure rather than recognize reality, though he had not suffered an episode for more than a year.

Then the serious necromancer broached. "And that explains why you never get any older, and why you looked younger than the age you claimed from the start."

A silent minute passed. Then Papa came back. "That could be useful, Kitten. If you can recall the process."

"I remained aware throughout it." Neither version of Papa showed any interest in who she might have been, to have gained so rare a gift. Nor did either ask why she had hidden this news until now. There was nothing but iron-hard interest in rehearsing exactly what had happened that afternoon, when the Dominator, under the eyes of, and with the assistance of, Bathdek's mother and father, had spent six hours gifting her with life that would end only when she stumbled into catastrophic misfortune.

Sustained youth went with the Blessing. Physically, she would age less than a year each century.

The hard necromancer kept surfacing, throwing sly looks around.

His agenda might not exactly match Papa's own.

Kitten spent a lot of time with Papa the next several days, talking about her Blessing while she let her chores slide. She recalled every detail of the procedure that she could. Her memory was not eidetic but it was quite good. Papa betrayed frequent moments of excitement. He was certain that they were onto something.

He said, "I'm pretty sure I understand what they did and it should be repeatable. I think that we can help Laissa a lot if we copy that and get it right. We can fix it so she won't need the treatments anymore."

"That would be good. I'm glad."

"But there are still some critical details missing. What I want to do, if you will permit me, is . . ." Papa spent twenty minutes detailing a scheme for putting her under hypnosis to regress her to those formidable hours during which she had become an immortal.

Kitten said nothing about a girl named Dorotea Senjak having received the Blessing that same afternoon, only to run into her catastrophic misadventure just slightly more than a year later.

Not once did it occur to Bathdek to wonder what impact the Blessing might have had on Laissa's accession to her present condition.

Even after long exposure Bathdek had to overcome considerable stress in order to trust Papa enough to let him put her under.

23

Long Ago and Far Away: New Hope for the Dead

Kitten wakened thirsty and starving and deeply confused. She must have been out a lot longer than the few hours Papa had promised that the regression would take. She felt like it had been days.

She was on her back on a table in Papa's research hall. She felt hands touching bare skin where no one else should be touching her. Before she could protest Papa moved into view. He carried a big metal bowl and some wet cloths.

So. He had been cleaning her. She had been unconscious long enough to have soiled herself.

She had no sense of having been violated.

She tried to speak.

Papa went from glum to radiant. "Oh, excellent! You've finally come around. I was afraid that we had . . ." He stopped, pulled a sheet over her, faced away. He began humming.

Kitten turned her head. That was hard work.

Papa was cleaning Laissa now. Laissa was on a table four feet away.

She was asleep or unconscious. Kitten said, "Papa, I have a really bad headache."

"I'll get you something as soon as I'm done with your sister."

Kitten did not like the way Papa eyed naked Laissa, nor the way he touched her, though he was doing nothing unlawful or immoral. He was just being creepy.

"I'm almost sure that we were successful, Kitten! We are over the hump! Laissa won't wake up for a day or two, but I think she will be as good as new."

Kitten was up and around, now, slowly doing catch-up chores. She had been unconscious for four days. Papa said he had tried to feed her soup and water but had had only limited luck. The same with Laissa. Kitten did better getting water and broth into her sister.

Kitten had awakened with aches and pains all over, and several small wounds on her stomach, none of which Papa explained. Laissa had wounds in the same places. Kitten wanted to be suspicious but, near as she could tell, nothing perverted had been done to either of them. She should be safe, anyway. Laissa was the one who inspired Papa's imagination.

Kitten asked, "If she's going to get better do you think she might start remembering things?" That should not be a worry, she realized. Papa could only learn about them if he paid attention during one of his forays back to the Domination. He would hear chatter about the missing Senjak daughters.

"I doubt it. Definitely nothing from before the fever. I don't recall most of my life, either, but I still get along, out here with my girls."

"You're getting creepy again, Papa."

Laissa was slow recovering. She did not reclaim any Dorotea memories. She did retain memories of her life as Laissa. Gradually she became more animated, more personable, more responsive. Best of all, she talked. Not a lot, and always with some difficulty, but she did form full sentences and did demonstrate interest in her world.

She and Kitten became closer, working shoulder-to-shoulder. She followed Kitten around when Papa would not let her stick close to him. She was in the laboratory with Papa for hours every day but sometimes, he said, he could get more done if she was not there, distracting him.

The improvements in Laissa accumulated. Her intelligence increased slowly. By winter's end she could not only follow simple conversations but could participate. Best of all, she did not need her treatments anymore.

She might not yet be wholly cured of death but she was, increasingly, filled with life.

Papa was thrilled.

Bathdek was thrilled. Summer would see the end of this.

Just a few months to go. Their getaway kits were ready. They could grab them and be gone in half an hour, sometime when Papa went back west. They would get at least a four-day head start. Maybe as much as seven days.

Then Bathdek's plan came crashing down.

"Kitten, I need to talk to you."

Papa was all cool and stern on the surface but she saw real fear behind that. Something bad had happened.

"Of course, Papa. What's wrong?" It could not be anything that she had done, nor something from outside. He had not been away for more than a month. It could not be Laissa. Laissa was the best that she had been since she stopped being Dorotea. Laissa had made a feeble joke at breakfast, something she had not managed even as Dorotea Senjak.

But it *was* Laissa. And it was the last thing that Bathdek expected.

Papa said, "Laissa is pregnant."

"Huh?" A long silence. "What?" More silence, another dumbstruck grunt, then, "No. No way! It isn't possible!" Still more silence, then, "What did you do, Papa? When did you do it?" Then back to, "It's impossible! She isn't even . . ."

Laissa was dead. Dead girls did not have periods or anything. Dead girls did not have babies.

"Until last week I would've agreed, Kitten. But I've checked and checked. There just isn't any doubt."

Nor any doubt who the father might be. When had he managed? When Laissa was in the lab with him? *How* had he managed, for the gods' sakes? What did it take to get a dead girl pregnant?

In a gallows humor moment she told herself she had better make sure she stayed on the far side of the room from him—which might not be far enough if he was potent enough to impregnate a dead girl.

"I need to sit down, Papa. This is a shock." Beyond the immediate impact loomed the long-term certainty that Laissa would be unable to run away this summer. "How far along is she?"

"About three months."

It must have happened right after Laissa recovered. But full term would still steal most of the summer. And then they would have an infant to care for. Maybe.

"Papa, I'm really, really mad at you right now."

"I'm not exactly happy with myself, Kitten. One day I just couldn't fight it anymore. After that there was no stopping. But . . . It was stupid, sure, but we can't undo it. We have to deal with the situation that exists right now."

Kitten took several careful breaths. Papa was really stressed. If she upbraided him as ferociously as she wanted, now, he might suffer a seizure. The last one had been savage. He had been laid up for days after it ended. The next one might be fatal. Then where would she and Laissa be? "So what do you mean to do about it?"

"I don't know. That's why I'm talking to you. This could have more impact on you than on me or Laissa."

What? What did he suspect? Wait. He probably just meant that there would be lots more housework. Laissa, however much improved she was, would still be lacking as a mother.

Would this baby even be a living thing? Or human? Or something undead that suckled the teat of the night?

How *would* it feed? No way would Laissa be making breast milk. But, then, there was no way she should be making a baby, either.

"Papa, I know nothing about babies except that I have to have been one, once upon a time. I've never even seen one up close. This is . . . I don't know." This had rattled her more than had the loss of Dorotea or her own capture. "What were you thinking? Never mind. I know what you were thinking. You never hid it very well. But I did think that you had it under control. And I'm babbling. Papa, I can't help you with the decisions you have to make. I don't know anything about that kind of stuff."

She could learn, though, she supposed. She had learned a lot that she never expected to have to before the night her unbeloved sister got dumped down a garbage chute.

In her own world she could have expected to bear a child or two out of duty, but she would have had little to do with the beast after it was delivered, until such time as it stopped smelling bad and was domesticated enough to be presented publicly.

"I don't know what else to say. I can't help you. I don't know how."

"Thank you for listening. That was kind. It was unfair of me to put any of this onto you."

"And I just keep on wondering, how could you, Papa?"

Kitten could not control her thinking. She was becoming obsessed. When had the thing happened? And, how? Why would Laissa . . . ? On reflection, she recalled progressive changes in her sister since her recovery. Changes in addition to the obvious physical and intellectual improvements. Little sister was almost always in a good mood now, was eager to help, and sometimes actually initiated a conversation. That might be at a child's level but it was markedly better than the Laissa of a year ago.

Might what had happened between Laissa and Papa have contributed to the changes?

Repugnant though Kitten found that idea, she did know that there were schools of sorcery centered on tantric principles. There was power there, power enough to shatter reason in the most reasonable people.

Lately Laissa stuck to Papa like a worshipful puppy. But Kitten had her chances to talk when they were busy with some routine chore.

Laissa had become more useful than she had been before, and was more cheerful in her work.

"Because Papa wanted to," she said when Kitten asked her why she had let the sorcerer have his way. "And it was warm. I like it when Papa makes me warm."

The exchange that followed was the longest that Kitten ever had with her sister, and it horrified her. Laissa insisted that she really liked it when Papa made her warm. She chased after Papa all the time because she wanted to get warm again and again.

"Papa said don't tell Kitten. Kitten might get mad. Laissa was careful so Kitten wouldn't know. But it was hard sometimes, when Kitten was being nosy and Laissa wanted to get warm so bad . . ."

Kitten wanted to make a crack about she should sit closer to the fireplace, then. But that was almost petty.

Still, this was awful. This was unbelievable.

A dead girl ought not to have any interest in physical things. A *live* Senjak daughter ought not to, either, except as a political ploy.

She bowed out of the conversation. Laissa was too willing to describe everything directly and graphically. She owned no shame.

Kitten wondered if Laissa had any idea what it meant to be pregnant.

One thing became clear. Laissa no longer felt like she had to hide her interest in getting warm.

Papa began barring the door to his laboratory so he could get some work done.

Kitten went on, eyes cast down, unable to believe life's latest repulsive twist.

Laissa was in her seventh month. She was carrying a baby, there was no doubt, and it was getting active. Laissa even looked more pregnant than she was. And she was happy.

She was now more bright and cheerful than Dorotea ever was before she died, though she did mope frequently because Papa did not want to get warm as often as she did.

Kitten remained appalled. And did not know exactly why. In Dusk girls much younger than Laissa were given as gifts to men older than Papa all the time.

She and Laissa were outside, feeding the animals. Those numbered in the dozens, now. Papa brought some back every time he went traveling. Laissa said, "You're thinking about running away, aren't you?"

Kitten did not deny it.

Laissa said, "Go ahead and go if you want. I won't warn Papa. But I'm not going to go with you."

Kitten was not surprised. "We can take care of the baby."

"I don't *want* to go, Kitten! I don't. I won't! I want to be with Papa!"

What could you do?

You heard about these situations almost before you were old enough to understand them. Bizarre relationships, not uncommon in the Domination, often flaunted by those involved in them. But Senjaks did not . . .

Bathdek sucked it up, crushed it, and put it in its grave. She reminded herself that this was not actual incest, the most common Domination perversion. This was necrophilia, and that was not common at all.

For half a second she managed to make a joke out of it. It was *consensual* necrophilia, and the deceased participant was more enthusiastic about it than the live participant was.

24

In Modern Times: Lost Treasure Rediscovered

Two Dead and Tides Elba completed their first round trip in six days. The two oldest Honnoh girls came back with them. Both had been reeducated as huntresses meant to winkle out their feral sisters. Though the strongest captives had left the compound, the mind field remained potent. The Taken still turned pale and got shaky inside it. I wondered how folks out west would manage once the girls began to clutter up the Tower.

The Taken promised, "This will become tolerable once the next group goes west. The ones that are still here won't be able to sustain the field."

Most of those would be prepubescent.

We did still have that mob of twelve out there in the woods. And now that we had the returned girls to hunt them down, it would not be long before we harvested a whole new crop.

Once the second shipment headed west the Honnoh girls began pinpointing sisters not yet collected. Which turned out to be somewhat less amazing than we had anticipated. Our huntresses had to be within five miles of a free-range Tides Elba before they could tell that she was around. Neither girl liked riding but riding was, for the moment, the only way to move them hither and yon.

The Taken had not brought much out but the girls and a quarter ton of clerical plunder that went straight into Admin's clutches. There were no messages for me nor any for the children. Whatever else they might be, Baku and Shin were kids enough to be disappointed.

I was disappointed, too. Mischievous Rain was an orphan herself. She ought to understand what it was like to feel abandoned.

Weird. My head. The course of my thoughts. I was no longer the Croaker so favored at the Taken's initial appearance, so long ago. I had to concentrate ferociously to remember Mischievous Rain despite my yearning for her return. Was her hair black, then? And something about tattoos . . .

I was not sure about anything. But I wanted to see the real her again.

Despite the workload brought on by having to examine potential recruits—thirty-four since the Honnoh success—I found time to get back into the Annals, the books so hated because they remembered so resolutely. What I had written down was impossible to unremember. My latest scribbling was more detailed than what I used to do, probably because I had extra time available, being in garrison. I found nothing remarkable but I *was* amazed at how thoroughly I had forgotten so much.

What that meant I could not guess but I did find it irksome. I was not yet old enough to be forgetting details of my own history.

Still, it seemed we were all getting senile where this one story was concerned. I asked around. Only Sana remembered as much as I did. Her recollections were perfect. She did not understand why nobody else remembered everything. Everybody else had been there, too.

"Does it matter that Sana remembers stuff that none of the other town girls do?" the Old Man asked. For him hardly anything mattered unless it related to the Company's welfare, prosperity, or safety.

"I don't know, do I? We might be losing information that could be invaluable down the road."

The Captain, Candy, and the Lieutenant all gave me the fisheye.

They thought I was stretching things so I could get some help feeding a case of the curiosities. They could be a little bit right, but . . .

I was more right, I was sure. My premonitions of that sort usually turn out to have some reliable intuition behind them.

So I got the benefit of the doubt despite a general air of skepticism.

I said, "I don't know why it's important but the effect is real. The Tower wants us to forget the first Mischievous Rain, even to the point of piling heartaches onto the twins."

From the corner of my eye I caught a flicker of cat's tail protruding from a shadow for an instant. Deliberate or accidental, it did offer a valuable reminder.

It told me to get as much written down and hidden as I could because ink and paper never forget.

The Honnoh girls did not contribute a great deal at first. Riding with the regular patrols took a lot of time for not much in the way of returns. Once the flying carpet was back and available their mission should take off.

What information the girls did discover often made no sense. They operated entirely on emotion and empathy.

Tides Elba did not come back after delivering her second squad of sisters to the Tower.

The Old Man grumbled, "Here we go with the gamesmanship again." He decided to send out lots of smaller patrols, some with a sorcerer and all with shadow pots through which the twins could duck back and forth, providing swift, sophisticated communications as well as close terror support.

The man never seemed like he was paying attention but he figured stuff like that out, then insisted that my kids earn their keep.

Everyone got used to the system fast. It became part of regular operations. Fast long-distance communication and quick insertion of reactive horror gave us a huge edge over what was left of a decimated and demoralized enemy.

Meantime, Buzz and Elmo dismantled the Resurrectionist site stick by stick and brick by brick.

And the lucky boys did find real treasures, including something more valuable than the Tides Elba girls that I had been convinced were what the fighting was all about.

Two Dead once did say that the Resurrectionists had elevated magical camouflage to an art form. Buzzard Neck Tesch, in a foul humor because he had to protect a delectable collection of split-tail not only from his troopers but from himself, proved Two Dead's assertion when he vented his frustration by way of a huge indulgence in magical vandalism. So there he was, muttering and flinging minor destructive spells left and right, making a racket, further irritating all those men he was keeping away from the poontang, when some random spell triggered a chain of secondary magical reactions.

Elmo would later declare, "And then something magical happened!" whenever he told the story.

A host of camouflage spells collapsed. Elmo discovered that wrecking the meeting hall had been a waste of time. The precious things that the Resurrectionists had wanted to hide were scattered around the woods, mostly under illusory brush. Our guys came within inches of some back when they were burying the enemy dead.

Gold revealed itself in small quantities, in fractional coinage.

Silver revealed itself in only slightly larger quantities.

Copper was there but it was less big a deal than was the iron and steel in a weapons cache vast enough to arm thousands.

Most intriguing, though, from the perspective of somebody who was me, were two Domination-era teakwood caskets, suitably grotesque and showing no decay, that turned up. Each contained documents in the local language, as it had been written and spoken one or two centuries ago. I could sound out the text and understand some of the words, but making sense of it all was very slow going.

I sat at the dinner table, eating with one hand. Sana and El came and went and peeked over my shoulders, to no avail. My other hand stayed busy shuffling papers.

The evening's main course was something rich and beefy and if I had had a hand to spare I could have rubbed a tummy beginning to show proof that Sana really was a tremendous cook.

Those documents were seriously important. They had something to do with the creation of the Tides Elba girls. I got most of the nouns. There is a saying amongst those who decipher ancient documents: The worms ate the verbs. Here the verbs had survived but they had been imaginatively conjugated while the nouns had been imaginatively spelled. You could find the same word in two or three different spellings in the same paragraph—where there were recognizable paragraph breaks. Even the concept of sentences must have been sketchy, back then.

There were fewer agreed-on rules in the old days. Or this particular writer had had no respect for the rules that did exist. And his or her penmanship fell far short of qualifying as calligraphy, as well.

The documents were mostly in one hand but had marginal notes in another ink and hand.

I found something older in the bottom of the second casket. That was in TelleKurre, in a hand that was calligrapher fine. But I could not figure out what the sheets said. I could only sound out the alien words.

Firefly asked, "What's your problem, Dad? You look like you swallowed a bug."

"These papers are more important than the ones we sent to the Tower before. They all have something to do with the girls that look like your mother."

"Dad, I love you, but you're hopeless. I'm not sure what Mom ever saw in you. Go in the bedroom and read the stuff out loud. How hard is that?"

"Pretty hard if you don't know what you're trying to read. Do you read Levanev from a hundred years ago? Or TelleKurre?"

"I'm a little kid. I can't read yet."

An outright lie, though she did lack adult proficiency.

She said, "Shin, do something with this idiot."

Then Sana distracted us all with delectable desserts.

Shin shuffled his cards. "There isn't anything here for that. Oh. This might help, looked at from the corner of his eye, held bottom up. Seems like a waste, though. Be like killing a tick with a sledgehammer."

Six years old? Or a ten-thousand-year terror?

Maybe. One or the other. Or both.

Firefly asked, "You can read them, can't you? Even if you don't know what the words mean? Those look like modern letters."

"Yeah. That's true. I could."

"So go in the bedroom and read them out loud. Somebody at Charm will know what the words mean."

The kid made me feel like a drooling retard. How come I never thought of that? It should have been bone obvious. Assuming anyone at the Tower end bothered to listen.

Firefly said, "You're worried about what's in those papers, let's find out if you need to be."

I sighed. Children were beginning to consume my life. Especially this child. "All right." I swept the documents into a pile. "El, please light the lamps in the mistress's bedroom."

Except for the occasional remote chirrup of wind chimes I had little sense of anyone listening to my reading—except for Firefly, who kept popping in to correct my pronunciation. I asked her, "Why don't we save time by having you read this stuff?"

Again she fibbed. "'Cause I'm a little kid and I can't read."

I did not buy that, though it might only be a half fib. I read for another hour. Kindly Sana brought tea laced with lemon juice and honey but even so my throat began to protest. The pile of documents was not dwindling as fast as I would like.

Despite no blatant reaction from the Tower I had a sense that excitement had begun to build out west. Something that I had read had proven interesting.

There was an explosion of wind chimes.

A smoldering circle formed in the air. Either the Lady or my Mischievous Rain looked out of it. I figured Mischievous Rain because of the streaks in her hair. And because Firefly asked, "Mom, when are you coming home?"

Mom replied in a language that Dad did not understand. Baku said something petulant. Her mother responded with a prolonged speech. I did not have to speak the language to understand that Firefly was getting a list of instructions.

Baku's attitude did not improve. When her mother finished Firefly responded with a speech of her own. It sounded fierce. And it did have impact. Her mother looked a little embarrassed, a little defensive, maybe even a little shamed.

The Taken responded. Firefly seemed placated, sort of, but not a whole lot.

The Taken caught my eye, winked, pursed her lips, then followed on with a kiss blown my way. Then she snapped at Blessed Baku and went away. The circle of fire shrank to a spark in a second.

Although distracted I wondered, "Why didn't she wait to hear it all?"

"Maybe she'd heard enough?"

Yeah. That made sense. But she had not told me what to do about anything, either.

Sometimes Croaker has a hard time remembering his place on the mushroom farm.

25

Once Upon a Time: Baby Time

Laissa got spooky as her time approached. She no longer slept. She was aggressive with Papa, and shameless. Kitten seldom had a chance for a private word.

Papa gave up on privacy entirely. "Kitten, it's going to be two more weeks." In theory Laissa was at term now. From the little Kitten knew about this stuff she thought that was unusual in a first pregnancy.

"Two more? Isn't that . . . ? Is it dangerous?"

"She'll be fine. It doesn't look like she'll have much trouble."

Papa was leading up to something. "What's going on?"

"I've never delivered a human baby. Animals, yes." Kitten had assisted with a few animal birthings. "It shouldn't be much different. But I'd feel more comfortable if we had a midwife to help."

Kitten stifled a flash of irrational irritation because it was always all about Laissa. "Are you considering rounding one up?"

"I am."

"Leaving me to handle everything if the baby comes early."

"The divinations are clear. The timing is exact. The baby will arrive during the afternoon thirteen days from now. It will be male." He hesitated, then. "But it gets cloudy after that. There could be something special about the infant." Something might be not right with a baby whose mother was a dead girl? Imagine that.

Divinations were often inaccurate, especially if you had enemies who knew you were trying to spy on the future. They could slip a finger in and make the future tell you lies.

That did not seem likely out here.

"If you're absolutely sure."

"Nothing in all creation is one hundred percent sure, Kitten. Not even death itself anymore. But I am close to sure on this."

"Well, then, go. Do it. Don't waste time. And be careful. Don't get noticed. Because this midwife is going to be missed."

Had he thought about what they would do with a midwife once they had their use of her? Not likely. That was not his way. But they could not have someone running around raving about flying carpets and stone-cold dead girls having babies inside impossible castles in the Ghost Country.

Laissa tried to drape herself on Papa. She ended up hanging on sideways because her belly got in the way. Kitten was amused. Laissa whined, "Papa, I'm really, really cold."

The baby took a lot of warmth from its mother.

Kitten had needed several months to realize that when Laissa talked about Papa making her warm she was actually talking about warmth. Life-energy warmth, not animal pleasure, though Laissa had confided that sometimes when Papa made her really warm she felt really, really good inside, too.

Kitten's envious, petty side made her want to tell Papa to bring in three or four strapping farm boys to keep his precious Laissa near live-girl temperature.

As Credence Senjak, who insisted on being called Bathdek, Kitten had been the pivot of her own young universe. She had been as selfish as she could be in her circumstances. That girl would have had no trouble stating the facts then, however much Papa and Laissa might have been stung. Now, though, she could not be that small. Some insidious influence had seduced her into taking an empathetic outlook.

Her Senjak side was appalled.

Papa's girls watched his carpet race out of sight. Laissa said, "You should go now. I know you're ready."

"Are you crazy? I'm not going anywhere."

"This could be the last chance you'll ever get."

"No. It won't be. And I won't leave you here with nobody to look out for you when you're ready to pop."

Laissa sighed. "You're a good sister, Kitten. I love you for that. But if you don't go now you *really* might never get another chance."

"If that's how it goes then that's how it goes. I'll live with it. You're my sister . . . I was never a good sister before . . . I found you. Before I found my way . . ." It was hard to express what she felt. "Just understand that I'm not going anywhere until we get through this and I know that you're going to be all right. And now I need you to sit down and put your feet up while I go feed the animals."

She could use that time to reflect. Because Laissa might be right about there not being many more chances. They were almost entirely self-sufficient now.

Feeding the animals included work that could be critical to her escape if she really had to leave without Laissa.

Damn that girl. She refused to even think about leaving Papa. So. Kitten finally worked out what Laissa and Papa had not yet. Their physical intimacy gave Laissa the energy she needed to go on mimicking a living human being.

The woman Papa brought in was about thirty, short, wide, brown, and really unhappy about her new circumstances. Kitten thought she was young for a midwife but she had a big reputation where Papa found her. Papa promised her that she would be taken back home with a huge reward once Laissa's baby had been delivered. She did not believe him, though Papa probably meant it. How could she know exactly where she had been? Kitten and Laissa tried to reassure her, too. She refused to be reassured.

She did do as she was told. She might not believe that she had any hope but she refused to do anything that would call down the darkness upon herself. She said almost nothing at all, ever.

Within hours of her arrival she worked out who the girls in this wild place were. Papa still had not done that. But Papa did not care.

Bathdek whispered, "I promise, I'll get you out of here if the birthing goes well." She placed a long-odds bet. "I have been making preparations to go for years. I've only stayed to help my sister."

The midwife grasped that straw and held it to her heart.

Bathdek could not believe that the thing her sister birthed could so thoroughly mimick a human being. Well, a human infant, as she imagined they probably looked.

The midwife did not act like the little beast was a monster.

Laissa produced no breast milk. Of course.

How could it be otherwise? Bathdek and the midwife prepared goats' and sheep's milk. The midwife demonstrated how best to get that into the infant. She told Papa, "This is only a stopgap, sir. Your son won't prosper without mother's milk."

"He will grow, though? Right?"

"He will, but he'll be weak and he'll take sick easily."

Papa decided that goats and sheep were not the solution to Laissa's limitation.

It took him just hours to pull the baby into the heart of his Laissa obsession. Nothing would do but that the boy get human breast milk. He would find a woman who could provide that.

Papa mounted his carpet and went in search of a lactating woman.

He was barely out of sight when Laissa said, "Time for you to go, Kitten."

"But . . ."

"Kitten, you're ready. And this *is* the last chance you'll ever get. Go. I can milk the goats."

She had not yet named her baby. Neither had Papa made any suggestions. Despite the infant's quiet presence Kitten had trouble believing that he could actually exist. Or that he should be allowed to exist.

The midwife said, "I'm ready to go." And, "I want to live. I want to get back to my people. I don't believe that I'll have that option if I stay here. But I do know that I can't get away from here on my own."

Laissa said, "Kitten, please! Go! I can manage. Honest. And I'll still have Papa forever."

Although she felt like a traitor Kitten did recall that she was Bathdek Senjak. "All right. Right after you prove to me that you can handle the milking and feeding. The animals have to be . . ."

"Kitten! Stop. I know how. I helped you do it a hundred times. Just stop fussing and go!"

Bathdek looked at the baby, held so close by his cold mother. He was quieter than babies were supposed to be. Maybe she should smother it before . . .

Papa had not locked his laboratory before he left, though normally he did that only when he was inside and did not want Laissa to disturb him. Bathdek made a quick sweep through, collected some deadly toys and recovered the special cards that Papa had taken from her back when.

Laissa had been saved. Papa was working on something else, now. He would not talk about it even though he did have Kitten help when he could not manage alone.

Bathdek was tempted to vandalize the lab, for the hell of it, but instead just walked away, for Laissa's sake.

The midwife carried the escape pack that Bathdek had put together for Laissa. It was heavy. Bathdek's was equally massive. Even the three dogs, that Bathdek had worked to make her own from the day that Papa brought them home, carried little packs.

Kitten now fully recalled that she was Bathdek Senjak, born Credence Senjak, third daughter of the most powerful family in the Domination. This tempered Credence Senjak headed west. She had years of practical training to help her survive. She had a companion who owned extremely useful commoner skills. She had hounds to sense trouble coming before she could smell the danger herself. And she had an aura as fierce as that of any member of her clan who had become Taken.

Things and beasts did not mess with her in the wilderness. But people tried, later. People were never as sensible as the wild things.

She got a full seven-day lead on Papa, although she would never know that. Not once while in flight did she have to make an effort to remain unnoticed from the air. Papa apparently made no effort to find her.

She had expected that he would because he would want her back to help with Laissa and the baby.

No doubt he was too busy fussing over his lover. The poor girl had been on her own for days and days, without a soul to wait upon her. And he would want to ride herd on the wet nurse.

If he ever did come hunting he had no luck. Bathdek never sensed his presence. Her feelings were bruised. Never was it more clear that he only cared about Laissa.

Sad Kitten sank into the quagmire of history.

Bathdek did the same when she and her hounds emerged from the Plain of Fear months later, after a long grim passage. The Plain of Fear and the woman who was no longer Bathdek Senjak would remember one another for an age.

The Taken called Stormbringer, who was Credence Senjak's second cousin, came to collect her once her family heard that she had returned to the realm of the living. Then anyone who mattered amongst the people of the imperial capital insisted on hearing every detail of the Credence Senjak story from the girl who had lived it. Even the Dominator had her in for an evening visit during which He was more sane, self-controlled, and solicitous than ever she had seen before.

That was, almost certainly, a function of his paranoia.

Papa's existence truly worried him.

He provided a feast that was too rich after her years with Papa. She nibbled and told her tale again, telling it true except for a handful of details. She left out the fact that she and Papa had rescued Dorotea from death. And although she never said so directly she let her listeners think that she had slaughtered Papa before she ran away.

She said she had no idea where Papa's hidden fortress lay except that it was in some mountains on the other side of the Plain of Fear. She had needed months to find her way out of there. And that was inarguably true, though there were those who believed that she was holding out because there was something back there that she wanted to collect as soon as she obtained her own flying carpet. She never mentioned the name of the mountains, if she had heard it right herself, because greedy or crazy Domination folk might go haring after something they thought they could use to make themselves more powerful.

Credence Senjak felt good about herself.

Credence Senjak was far away from all that insanity. And now Papa and Laissa, who were not bad people, could live out their years together, free from the madness of the Domination.

Credence told everyone that her great mission now would be to manage the campaign to clear the Old Forest away.

That did earn her a certain amount of attention.

The Senjak girls were famous for not doing much but squabble amongst themselves. This one suddenly wanted to do something useful? Her long trial sure had changed her.

Credence believed that such a vain project might keep the Domination focused on not doing any real harm elsewhere for several generations.

The morning after Credence's audience with Him she received a luncheon invitation from her mother, Banat. Dread clawed at Credence immediately. However the invitation was phrased, it was a summons.

Banat Senjak was not a sorceress. She had wormed her way into, had married into, the clan by means of several fierce small talents. Getting her own way was the greatest of those. She was a strong personality. She made everyone but the Dominator and her most stubborn, ingrate daughters eager to do her bidding.

“That is what I suspected,” Mother said, halfway through the meal, although the conversation had been inconsequential. “You haven’t been completely honest.”

Credence faked a befuddled look. She was determined to be as stubbornly uncooperative as Ardath and Sylith when facing parental ambition.

“You left them to their bizarre love. You’re too sentimental, dear.”

Mother was a genius at discovering truth while armed with almost no solid information. Her daughters inherited the knack, though none of them would realize that for years.

“Whatever you choose to believe, Mother. I have no idea how to find those people now.”

That was true. And Mother believed her. “And I have no interest in finding them, dear.”

And she did not press. Thereafter, Credence took care not to betray anything she knew that might help someone who wanted to lay hands on Laissa and Papa.

Almost anyone who haunted Dusk, knowing what Mother had guessed, would have become determined to find Papa and Laissa—even without knowing what had happened out there.

Mother chose to let the matter slide.

Mother said, “Tell me again about the time that man hypnotized you.”

Oh! And just when she was starting to think she might get through this unscathed.

She told it again. Nothing that happened then could possibly matter now.

“Did he discover the secret of the Blessing?”

Ah. So. Mother was unable to hide her excitement. That must be what this lunch was all about: the chance of penetrating that secret, of breaking His hold over dozens of dreadfully powerful women and men.

“I know what you’re after, Mother. But, too bad. I’ve been thinking about it ever since. The only reason Papa got it to work was because Dorotea had received the Blessing already. He just woke it up again.”

"Uhn." Disappointed.

"I never told Him that part."

"I see. That's good, then. Show me your stomach."

"Mother?"

"Show me where you were wounded when you wakened from his hypnotic spell."

Could she get out of this? She had nothing to hide. It was just a matter of modesty.

"Come, girl! You have nothing that I haven't seen before."

Credence bared her midriff. She had to shed half her clothing to do so.

"You're quite well toned, girl. Better than I was at your age, and I worked at it because I wanted to catch me a powerful man. All that common physical labor did you some good."

"If ever the empire falls I can work as a stonemason or swineherd. Lucky me."

"Hold still, dear."

Credence's scars were almost invisible now, being only pale dots lower than her belly button.

Mother poked each scar gently. "Do you feel anything unusual?"

"No."

Mother sat with her chin cupped in her left hand. Her left elbow rested on her left knee. She stared at Credence's belly like she was trying to see what lay inside it. "Did your sister have matching wounds?"

"I think. That's what it looked like. But when we were on those tables was the only time I actually saw anything."

"I think I know what happened, though not why. Well, maybe why, but not how your Papa intended to do it."

"Mother? You're sounding a little scary."

"With excellent reason, I suspect."

"He did something to me? What did he do?"

"He took your eggs. He took the parts of you that make the eggs. But that part only on the right side."

Credence did not understand. She knew very little about how her insides worked. Mother, though, was an expert. The study of the human body, whether quick or dead, was her grand avocation. Discards from His night sport occasionally found their ways into her hobby lair.

Mother explained the female side of the reproductive process in far more detail than Credence cared to hear.

"So why would he want our eggs?"

"Presumably in order to create more Doroteas and Credences. He could have seen himself gaining a whole crop of lovely daughters."

"But . . ."

"Did your sister have more wounds than you did? I would imagine that your Papa would have tried to recover everything he could from her."

"Maybe. I don't know. I wasn't curious right then. I was barely able to think. I had a murderous headache."

"Suppose I regress you to that moment?"

"Not going to happen, Mother. Not going to happen. That once was the last time."

Mother shrugged, mused, "One of Dorotea's eggs must have gotten loose while he was harvesting the rest. That would explain why there was one there to fertilize. It doesn't explain why the egg was healthy enough to quicken, though. Was there anything wrong with the baby?"

Credence shook her head. "Not that I could tell. But what do I know about babies? I do remember that Papa was concerned because the baby didn't cry much."

"Well, it doesn't matter now. The story will end once he reaches his natural term. Dorotea cannot persist without his support." Mother betrayed a trace of what might have been sorrow.

Amazing.

Credence left her mother soon afterward, wondering what she would do out east if ever she got the chance to go back.

She suspected that Mother might develop some eastward-leaning ambitions based on what she thought of Papa's research.

Banat Senjak had the influence and wherewithal to send out stealthy search parties.

26

Long Ago and Far Away: Generations Drift

The baby arrived within minutes of the time that Papa had predicted. The midwife, though terrified, performed perfectly.

The baby was vigorous and healthy and hungry but his mother could produce no milk.

Papa headed west immediately. While he was absent Kitten vanished, taking all of the dogs and the midwife with her.

Papa brought back three unhappy wet nurses whose own newborns would now have to share. The three understood that their family fortunes were now dependent upon Papa's goodwill. They could become fatally redundant once the preferred infant no longer needed milk.

Papa was baffled by Kitten's disappearance. He would not believe that she had run away. Misfortune must have befallen her somehow while he was not around to protect her. He made a number of search forays, flying over the nearby wilderness. He did not go farther because he did not want to tempt the mercy of his wet nurses.

He found no trace of Kitten.

Papa began weaving protective webs like those with which he had surrounded his old place. He had delayed their creation for far too long. Sad that it took the loss of a daughter to get him moving.

Laissa did not age. Papa did, despite efforts to beat time by having Laissa and the slave women put him through the rites gleaned from that lost daughter whose name he could no longer remember.

Laissa could not remember her sister's name, either. That made her sad. She did remember that she had loved that girl.

The rites helped but only slowed time. Papa was just over two hundred when, weeping because he had to leave Laissa, he passed into the darkness.

Papa never gave his son a name. He referred to him as "the boy," and, when addressing him directly, just called him, "Boy."

Laissa called him Precious Pearl, having overheard the captive women gossiping about a mythic sword of that name. She thought the name sounded auspicious for someone destined to shake the world.

Laissa's mind was working its best when she made that name choice.

The wet nurses had brought their little ones with them. Papa had the hard will to drag the women away from their husbands but not the wicked will to make them abandon their babies.

Papa collected other serving folk over the years, all women. He never molested or abused a one. That temptation never troubled him.

Laissa did not age but her need for warmth grew more insistent. Papa's ability to provide that warmth declined. Though he hated doing so he brought in several young men to help. Their advent precipitated a population explosion. They did not confine their attentions to Laissa.

Strange years followed, strange decades, and strange centuries. Precious suffered Papa's interpretation of the Blessing, which took far better with him than it had with his father.

Precious appeared to be about thirty when Papa passed.

Precious hated hearing it but he was a lot like Papa, over toward the necromancer end of the spectrum. He looked a lot like his father, too—what Papa had looked like when Laissa first wakened in the old house near Dusk.

Precious's mind was better anchored than his father's. He lost memories seldom and always recalled who everyone was. He did not drift off into imaginary realities.

From his toddler years onward Precious was a presence in Papa's lab. He watched. He learned. He became Papa's assistant, then Papa's partner, and then the man himself after Papa crossed over.

Papa was never comfortable with his son. Mostly he tolerated Precious because any failure to do so would have troubled Laissa. He did, however, ensure that the boy was as well-educated as he could be while living two steps beyond the edge of the world.

Precious took Papa's place because he knew no other way to go. His reality only vaguely extended beyond the castle wall. Never had he been so far away that he was out of sight of the place. He was barely aware that a broader world existed. He had no curiosity about it and lacked any inclination to explore it.

Papa's flying carpet leaned against a wall in a room that harbored nothing else, gathering dust and spiders.

Laissa gently declined and forgot that there was a world outside the castle. Servant generations came and went and, in time, only owned hand-me-down tales of a time when their ancestors had lived somewhere other than in a fortress without a name.

Vast changes swept the broader world. Comets crawled the skies. Fires devoured civilizations. Plagues consumed whole peoples. Empires crumbled.

Precious finally successfully fulfilled his father's grand ambition by creating a new Laissa.

A serving woman carried the baby, not voluntarily.

In time Precious would bring forth seven more infants using materials that Papa had harvested. Three would be copies of his mother. The others, although they resembled Laissa, would have black hair and a more pronounced figure once they matured. Unlike Laissa, they would be quick of wit. None would be pleased with their situation. Those with black hair would develop a psychic connection. The Laissa copies would not be fertile but would be able to carry an implanted embryo. The black-haired girls would be fertile, but not often.

Precious was not fertile. He created his children in his laboratory.

Precious was long-lived and cursed with his father's bent toward obsession. He learned a great deal that would have been valued enormously in the wider world, but that possibility never occurred to him.

Papa had been gone a hundred years when a gang of adventurous castle children found an antique wooden box in Papa's bedchamber. Hardly anyone had been in there since Papa's passing. Kids thought the room was haunted. The one who found the box only went in on a dare. She was one of the dark-haired fatherless girls. Those girls were all remarkably bold.

Precious's creations grew up alongside the rest of the castle kids.

The discovered box contained Papa's journals, seven volumes recorded in a tiny, precise hand.

Precious had been unaware that his father kept a journal. He read those volumes repeatedly. In truth, he had little else to do.

Papa started keeping journals long before he came to the Ghost Country. They recalled countless memories that Papa had sloughed unwillingly, and some so ugly that he must have wanted them lost.

The seven volumes were recorded and structured scattershot, scatterbrained, with no particular focus. The journalist could ramble endlessly about minutiae while largely ignoring something that might be of critical interest to a later investigator. Papa had meant to write down anything that he feared that he would forget. That was mostly family stuff, about not only Laissa and someone called Kitten, but also other, earlier "daughters," some collected not already conveniently deceased.

Papa had kept at his journal until the last hour.

Papa had become as obsessed with recording his story as he had become obsessed with Laissa. Work on his journal became his main reason for barring Laissa from his laboratory.

Precious found a worn playing card tipped into the last volume, where Papa's hand had become too shaky to read. Or the card could have come from a fortune-teller's deck. It was hand-painted. It was oversize. It seemed slippery and vibrant when held. Could it be a keepsake?

No! It had to be the key used to manage Papa's flying carpet.

Precious usually paid the carpet no heed, though it might be useful in an emergency. Had it deteriorated? Could he activate it? He should find out.

Reading Papa's journals, reviewing his early disappointments, Precious realized that his father had meant him to see all this long ago, hoping that the son could complete the task that the father had not been able to complete.

Belatedly, Precious felt honored. Papa always had trouble communicating with anyone other than Laissa, while Laissa never needed much from Papa but his comforting presence. Precious was an emotionally constipated reflection of his father—who did truly care for his Papa.

Precious started his own journal once he grasped the vision that Papa had had for him, though that vision could never be fully his own.

27

In Modern Times: Twisting Fate

The twins never acted up but they were not happy. I told the Old Man, "They do behave but I don't know why. Their mom hasn't been remotely motherly."

He eyed me like he wondered what was wrong with me—which got me wondering what was wrong with me? All this girly fussing just was not Croaker.

Was I being crafted into some sort of candy-ass?

"I am Croaker, sir. I promise you that."

"But?"

"Exactly. But. Between you and her . . ."

"Let me offer an innovative notion. Back the fuck off. Stop fussing. Do your job. Set bones. Sew people up. Cure the clap. Write down what you have to write down but let the rest take care of itself. Because it always does, in the end."

Not bad advice, actually. "You're right, boss. That makes practical sense. That's how we should do it. What's wrong with me lately? How come I obsess about crap that don't have nothing to do with the Company?"

"That one is easy, boyo. You went to the Tower. You fell in love. But then She turned you loose."

The Old Man was neither angry nor stressed, nor was he pleased by having gotten in a dig. He was rehearsing the facts as he saw them.

Again I was overlooking the fact that I was the Annals-writing mushroom man best kept shielded from operational and strategic details. The Captain might know why our employer wanted the first Tides Elba forgotten. He might even know why she insisted on ignoring my kids.

Only . . . !

"You're a mushroom man, too!" It was a lightning strike. If I left off feeling sorry for Croaker and raised my eyes I could see that I was no more shut out than was the first among us. I was but a single constituent of a battalion of mushroom men.

The Old Man pretended because we all counted on him to know.

"You evil bastard."

"Croaker?"

"Never mind. It's crystal, now. Every mother's son among us is being fried in the same black pan. Nobody knows what's going on. Anything that we think we know is almost certainly not true. You don't know anything more than I do. And now I'm beginning to think that maybe even the Taken is without a clue." Our mistress was known for playing lives-long games that only she could fathom. That was how she had become the Lady.

The Captain deployed his ingenuous smile, neither denying nor confirming, just suggesting that he knew something that would remain a mystery to everyone else.

I did not buy in. "That won't work . . . What the hell is that?" A huge racket had started up outside.

"How would I know? Being just another mushroom man? Maybe you could take a look and report back."

The brouhaha surrounded Buzzard Neck and Elmo, now arriving with treasures that included a passel of pretty girls. Even worn out and covered with road grime those lassies were easy on the eye. Several hundred brothers made time to come get their eyes eased and their fantasies inspired.

Sergeant Nwynn took custody and hustled the girls into the safety of the dormitory.

I did note that Elmo had come in with sixteen girls instead of twelve.

Pretties must be springing up like weeds out in the wilderness.

Turned out that the extras had been winkled out by our Tower-trained sister hunters, who looked even more exhausted than did Elmo's troopers.

The entire compound began to suffer an increasing bleakness of spirit almost as soon as those girls arrived.

Where was Tides Elba? We *had* to dispose of another kitty clutch before the emotional climate turned totally filthy!

Even the hunter girls felt it, though they had been trained to handle it. If even they were not immune to the synch . . . But we were supposed to be safe from the worst for another month!

I fussed constantly. I worried like me doing something useful was the only possible cure.

Firefly said, "You're being ridiculous, Dad. You aren't even close to being the heart of it. You're just somebody who lives in the neighborhood. Most of this stuff has nothing to do with you."

So. Croaker's ego deftly eviscerated by a six-year-old. Or maybe seven. The twins had been underfoot for a long time.

Baku sounded very Captain when she said, "Just do what you're supposed to do. Sew them up. Set their bones. Give them medicine. Nag them about taking better care of themselves. And when you don't have anything else to do try to make life more interesting for your kids."

Which was pure self-service with a life-lesson touch.

I tried doing what everyone said I should, while fearing that I would end up stuck with children forever.

The Company has little use for camp followers. They are dead weight, operationally. They complicate the tactical situation when a real fight develops. A soldier needs to concentrate on the threat in front of him, not on that to the woman and kids behind him.

. . .

I suffered through another fine supper. The meal was gloomy for me and the kids but there was merriment aplenty in the kitchen. The town girls laughed and squealed and teased one another about boys. Town boys, I hoped. We did not need the drama that could come of them getting involved with anyone from the Company.

Speaking of town boys. "Anybody seen Gurdlief Speak lately? He used to be underfoot all the time—especially at mealtime."

The kids avoided my gaze. Both looked like they were caught up in an internal debate. I snapped, "Tell me!"

Firefly took a deep breath, held it a moment, then set it free. "I can't say for absolute, but I'm pretty sure he stowed away on the carpet last time Tides Elba headed for the Tower."

The sheer audacious stupidity of that bludgeoned me mute. Eventually, I managed to squeak, "Really?"

Shin said, "Really. Ninety percent sure."

"And you think so why?"

"Because Gurdlief never stopped asking about the Tower. It never scared him like it does normal people. Whenever there was nobody but us around, the Tower was all he wanted to talk about."

"And then he disappeared," Shin said. "I looked everywhere that I could reach. No Gurdlief, nowhere, nohow, not anymore. Him trying to sneak into the Tower was the only logical conclusion."

Six years old. Or maybe seven, with no reason to make anything up.

"That's insane." Nobody goes to the Tower voluntarily.

"He's just curious, Dad. And you're the one that made him that way."

"Oh, yeah, sure. Blame it all on Croaker. El, darling! Can you stop giggling long enough to light the lamps in the mistress's bedroom?" I asked the kids, "What *are* those girls on about, anyway?"

Firefly shrugged. Shin exchanged looks with her, his face abnormally blank. Ankou materialized from nowhere obvious and stared at me as though to ask, "Are you sure about what you're planning, boss?"

"Of course I'm not sure. But I have to do something."

I was getting agitated again. A moment of reflection would have convinced me that Gurdlief was in no real peril. They would not mistreat him in the Tower, though he might never be allowed to leave. Mischievous Rain would speak up for him.

Still . . .

"Thank you, El. What are you girls up to with all that racket?"

She reddened, studied the floor. "Just joking around, sir." She scooted away so she would not have to deal with follow-up questions.

I was officially an old-fart grown-up, not to be trusted.

I said so aloud.

Firefly observed, "Was there ever any doubt? You have to be at least a hundred years old, Dad."

"I nurture a fantasy wherein I am the second-most-important thug in this gang because I read and write and pay attention to what's going on."

Nobody disagreed. Which meant squat.

Firefly said, "You think you have something to report that Mom can't figure out for herself? Then you better get on in there and jabber."

So. The little monster thought I might be wasting someone's time. Not mine, though. Nobody but Croaker ever thinks that Croaker's time can be wasted.

Cheeks still pink, El came back to make sure that she had done the lamps right, and to snuff them if I changed my mind.

Blessed Baku and I headed into the bedroom. Beloved Shin and Ankou tagged along.

Little good it did them.

Little good the exercise did anyone.

I rambled through the protocol briskly, excited, but got no reaction, not even a chirp of a wind chime.

I tried again because it was not reasonable to expect someone out west to be waiting around in case the folks in Aloe started barking.

My second try got the same nothing, at which point my oldest daughter dazzled me with, "What the hell are those morons out there doing?"

Baku exercised the protocol twice herself. Her results matched mine, whereupon she launched an inspired spate of improvisational and age-inappropriate verbal artifice.

Shin took a shot, smugly confident that Baku and I must be massive screwups. He would show us how it was done.

The boy never lacked confidence.

Moments later he looked like he had had been handed a surprise whipping.

I asked the devil cat, "You want to take a whack?"

Ankou had his third eye open and seemed seriously troubled, like there should have been some response unless a major disaster had befallen Charm.

Collective disappointment devoured a third of an hour. Sweet soul El stood by all the while, mainly being nosy but also staying handy in case we needed something. The girl did understand that although it was neither flashy nor stinky, we were involved in serious sorcery. She stood her ground despite being scared stiff.

As we abandoned the bedroom I told El that I was impressed by her courage. Were I a bit younger I would ask her to marry me.

I suffered from some weird notion that I could tease the girl.

Her courage remained unbroken. "You have a wife already, sir, who is much stronger and far more beautiful than me."

Firefly burst into laughter. "Ha! She told you, Dad!"

"I wasn't . . . I was teasing . . . El, I was teasing. Really. I would never try anything inappropriate with you girls."

"I know that, sir. I do. If you wanted a younger girl you would find a way to get past Sergeant Nwynn or you would go out in the country to catch one of the wild girls." My goofy look sapped her courage, but only for a moment. "The whole world can see that only one woman . . . interests you, sir, although she comes in a hundred age flavors."

Firefly got a real kick out of watching me writhe. "Oh! Ouch! And every single one of them is too young for you, Dad! You're stuck with me and Mom." Which made no sense.

She made a gesture, either to her brother or to El. Shin joined El in the bedroom, helping extinguish lamps. Firefly asked me, "Why don't we go visit the Dark Horse, Dad? You probably need to get yourself outside a couple gallons of beer."

How old was she? "Not going to happen, kiddo. . . ."

The other town girls arrived as a crowd. Sana announced, "There's something weird going on outside, sir. There's noises."

"Isn't it your turn to go home for the night, Sana? You want me to have someone escort you?"

"Dad, shut your pork pie hole and listen to what she's saying."

That from my son. It was the first time he called me Dad. I suspected that he had a crush on Sana, though Sana lacked Flora's outstanding assets. Sana had her own special allure. She treated Shin better than he deserved.

"Sana?"

The girl had nothing to add.

So. Weird noises. And the source of the weirdness made itself manifest shortly, without the courtesy of knocking.

Firefly shrieked, "Mom!"

"Hey, Bug."

Shin was a scant second behind his twin in a hug assault on Mischievous Rain, the version with scarlet streaks in her hair. The version that suited Croaker far better than did the cranky redhead.

Even Ankou bounded toward her.

Croaker did not bound. That would have been undignified. Croaker hovered outside the cluster hug and grumbled, "About damned time you came home, woman."

Holiday time.

I got a night off. I went to bed in my own room. But I did not sleep well.

My heart and mind would not let me forget, for even long enough to nap, that *that* woman was just barely thirty feet away, overhead. The woman who was the template for every dark-haired beauty our guys had caught. The one that El said . . .

Mischievous Rain had dropped out of the twilight without warning. She had hugged her children, petted her cat, held her husband's hand for three seconds—then had ordered that husband to get some rest because they had serious business to attend to in the morning. The children got sent to their beds, then the town girls likewise.

The Taken was readying herself for bed before her husband left the floor.

Seldom do I drink anything more potent than Markeg Zhorab's brews, and those only in moderation—where moderation can be defined as Croaker made it back to the compound without passing out before he got there.

I gave up my town place right after I came down with a crippling case of the families.

Blackhearts in Aloe had discovered the wonders of distilled spirits. The worst villains triple-distilled, then added anise to create a potation that masqueraded as licorice-flavored water. It was so tasty! So good! I kept some in the infirmary for medicinal use. I did not touch it, normally. But that night I needed a little something to help me fall asleep.

It took Blessed Baku, Beloved Shin, and all the king's horses to drag me out for breakfast. But I had gotten me seven hours of pure unconsciousness.

I was one tortured mess once it ended, though.

A devil had homesteaded the top of my head. She owned a brace of long-handle hammers that she used to pound my temples like my noodle was a big bass drum.

This hangover was epic. I could have suffered worse only in a previous life.

Exaggeration? Maybe. But I was for sure not in fighting form.

Sana produced a marvelous breakfast. That did not help. What little I did get down kept threatening to come back up.

Mischievous Rain saw me first so was the first to ask, "What the hell did you do to yourself?"

"I had trouble falling asleep. So I sipped me some uzok. The first mug was so good that I decided to have me another one. And that one was so good that I went ahead and finished the bottle. Then I broke out another bottle."

I was not allowed to do anything more hygienic than change my underwear. Mischievous Rain wanted to get to work *now.*

I self-medicated liberally. That helped only a little. It did not end the shakes. It did not keep my purported wife from becoming ferociously exasperated. The blind could see that Croaker would never participate productively in anything today.

Baku and Shin flanked me. I was on my knees, anticipating the return of breakfast. Self-medication had overcome the worst pain but now I was suffering a whole nother level of blitzedness.

It would be an age before I was fit to be useful.

Mischievous Rain put the operational part of her scheme on hold. The twins received instructions to make sure that I did not drown myself in my own barf. They herded me back to my quarters. They changed my bed. They made me drink water. Mischievous Rain did not check on me but others did, none failing to mention delays that were all my fault. And the kids made me drink more water.

Why did she not just get on with it without me?

The water helped, some. By noon I feared that I might survive. I began to think, which meant that I began to question.

Really, why had she let my stupid behavior hold her up?

So there I was, recovered enough to indulge in shame while being chaperoned mercilessly by unforgiving children, when two of my least favorite people, Two Dead and Buzzard Neck, turned up. They confiscated anything that they thought I might be tempted to use to help me sleep, ever again. They came with the Old Man's blessing, after he had been vigorously encouraged by Mischievous Rain.

That woman, my wife, had plenty she wanted to say but never said a word. She did not acknowledge my existence once I dragged myself together enough to fake an interest in developments.

Again she ordered the twins to stay on me, tight, but Shin skated out this time, leaving me to the mercy of his sister.

I could have whined and blamed my condition on Mischievous Rain but I held back. Although I might have been provoked, I was the guy who had chosen to take himself two miles past being totally messed up. Sober, Croaker loathed excuse-making when other idiots painted themselves as victims. I would not make an exception for myself.

Firefly told me, "If I could do this my way you wouldn't get any pain medicine at all, Dad. We can't fix stupid but we can sure as hell let stupid treat itself to a world of hurt."

I did not get mad. I must have had me a case of battered-wife syndrome, feeling like maybe I deserved the abuse.

Enough self-indulgence. There was no way to dress this pig and make her pretty. I held up operations for a day, so, naturally, folks were unhappy. *I* was not happy. But still I wondered why it all got set back because one moron had a hangover.

So, a day late, Mischievous Rain loaded her carpet and headed east. With her were her kids, her cat, her husband, two sister-hunter girls, and the Company's entire corps of wizards. The Annalist was on his knees beside the Taken, clutching frame wood with white-knuckled hands. The Taken was not speaking to him yet. In time, though, his wondrous personal charm would weasel its way through her resolve.

Mischievous Rain did not indulge her usual hell-bent approach to flight. She proceeded at a sedate aerial amble, presumably toward the Resurrectionist site that Elmo and Buzz had destroyed.

Once my charm did win through, she asked, "What became of the son of the girl who had a baby?"

"He stayed at the temple where we found his mother, I think. He wasn't walking yet."

Her jaw clenched. She was not pleased.

I turned, asked, "Which one of you guys had field duty the time we found the girl that had a baby?"

Nobody remembered. I told Mischievous Rain, "We're all having bad memory problems lately, I figure on account of the synch."

She grunted and muttered, "Be careful what you wish for," not speaking to me. Then she touched me on the temple and snapped an order in a language that I did not understand.

My world went dark. And then I was wide awake again, with a

knuckle-cracking grip on the carpet frame, more ferocious than ever before. The Taken had us sweeping through a tight left turn.

I squeaked, "The girl is sixteen, she went to Charm, and I know that only because Sergeant Nwynn told me. Nwynn might know about the baby. You should talk to her."

"Thank you. *You* will talk to her when we get back."

"I have a copy of her . . . Right. When we get back."

She eyed me directly, her tattoos showing bold and busy. Her usual good humor was absent. The wind chimes, silent since her return, sang now, but neither musically nor merrily. The midnight yukata had become a fathomless darkness calling hungrily. "You people," she declared, "are supposed to be the toughest, brightest, most cynical and most ruthless agents of the empire. Having met most of its other operators I stipulate that that may be true—which is a sad truth because the very best men of an elite battalion, specifically engaged to prevent a Resurrectionist exploitation of the Port of Shadows, have failed utterly to show any interest in a male child produced by a girl fully qualified to be the Port of Shadows."

"Ah, shit!" I muttered, understanding despite her convolution.

The gang of wizards agreed.

I grumbled, "It never occurred to any of you that the coupling might have happened already? Stupid! Stupid! Stupid! Why were we fixated on keeping it from happening down the road?"

More calmly, the Taken said, "That's probably my fault. I have been too preoccupied with other troubles even to pay attention to my children." Just loudly enough for me to hear, she added, "I suffered from that exact forward-focused mind-set until the pregnant girl came to the Tower and I heard Colonel Chodroze and Tides Elba wondering why amongst so many pretty girls only two ever got knocked up."

Amongst us all *somebody* ought to have thunk it.

Turned out that the Third had but he had kept his mouth shut because he figured Goblin and One-Eye would mock him.

I would not bet a moldy lump of hardtack that he was wrong about that, either.

. . .

I clung to the leading edge of the carpet frame, on the Taken's right. Firefly and Ankou were close by, Firefly to my right and so near that she could whisper translations of her mother's angry mutterings.

Mischievous Rain was unhappy with everyone and everything.

Firefly seemed more sympathetic to me than to her mother.

I asked, "What are we looking for?" Only the master of the carpet knew.

The Company sorcerers had been impressed to provide whatever magical artillery support she desired.

Firefly was not beyond the occasional seditious act if she thought she was being pinched between unreasonable viewpoints. Or, perhaps more precisely, between an unreasonable viewpoint and one owned by a gormless sort who stood around slack-jawed with no clue as to what was happening.

She whispered, "A year from now you won't remember this. And I'll cry. But that's how it's got to be." She squeezed my right arm. "You'll forget me and Shin and Ankou, except maybe in nightmares. And we might not be allowed to remember you, either. But I really do wish that you could. Remember us."

I gave her a one-arm hug. "No worries, kiddo. No way I could ever forget you." I owned a secret memory device.

The Taken ignored us. She was fully focused on something else.

We hit some turbulence. One-Eye started moaning about how we were all going to die.

Turbulence or the whine, something stuck a pin in the Taken. She seemed irked because that something had cost her her concentration.

The turbulence persisted. This soldier's breakfast tried to come back to the light but with ferociously manful grit I kept from humiliating myself.

One-Eye failed to follow my example.

Meantime, the hunter girls strolled around the carpet trying to calm the old men. The wobble and bounce did not bother them even when the bottom fell out and we plunged about six miles, or maybe really a hundred feet, before we smacked into solid air. The carpet frame creaked and groaned. I was sure it was going to come apart.

Firefly said, "That weasel Goblin is . . ."

He was, yes, milking it, having noted that the hunter pretties would comfort an anxious old man. But his hand roamed a bit too freely. He got a head-rocking slap for his trouble.

The crack of that blow killed One-Eye's terror. The little turd lapsed into a laughing fit. He never let up on Goblin after that.

I muttered, "The babies are the grown-ups, here."

We left the troubled air. The transition was a universal smack. Everybody felt it. Everybody relaxed. Wisecrack duels commenced.

Firefly murmured, "We are about to discover the source of the carpet that Slapback saw."

I had forgotten that, but remembered, now. And immediately wondered why we were headed east instead of north.

Had to have been Whisper, right? "What do you mean?"

Baku did not care if the Taken was listening. "Mom knows all the carpets. She knows where they were and what their riders were doing when Slapback saw what he saw, so she knows that no empire carpet was anywhere near Aloe that day."

I was tempted to mention that Slapback was a huge drunk and hardly a reliable witness but stifled my treacherous mouth this one time.

Slapback had been sober. I had checked.

Firefly said, "Whisper's carpet should have been the closest when that happened but on that day she was at the Tower getting reamed because of her crippled campaign strategy." Seven years old. "And the Limper was exactly where he was supposed to be."

No. He was not. He was still breathing.

So. Slapback must have treated himself to *something* that made him see things. Only . . .

Only my baby girl was sneaking up on an ugly alternate explanation.

If Slapback really saw a flying carpet, that meant that there was a carpet out there that was not a gift of the Lady. Which ought to be completely impossible.

Mischievous Rain's focus, so determined that she failed to follow the chatter around her, suggested that a rogue carpet did indeed exist. Which meant that a really powerful sorcerer was running around loose, a situation that the Lady would not tolerate.

I got me a case of the chills so harsh that I could not stop shivering. My convictions about the way the world ought to be structured were about to be swept away.

Any flying carpet operating outside the Lady's grace brayed the existence of an independent power so strong that our worries about the Port of Shadows became of secondary import because a possible opening of the Port might not be our most immediate existential threat.

Firefly snuggled closer. She looked so seriously sad that I choked up despite the horrors rampaging inside my noggin. She could not stop shaking.

I told her, "Slapback is a big drunk. He must've been seeing things."

"Bullshit. He saw what he said he saw."

How could I weasel out of that? "How do you know?"

"I told you we're looking for where that carpet came from." Stated without enthusiasm.

This long adventure, begun as a hunt for a supposed Rebel commander named Tides Elba—who had turned out to be dangerous only because she was so godsdamned attractive—kept writhing in hand like a big-ass shape-shifting snake. Nothing was what it looked like. Nothing stayed the same. Nothing went the way that it should.

Hey, Croaker! Slap a glass-half-full face on it. Focus on the plusses.

Big plus Number One: The Limper was not trying to kill you.

Big plus Number Two: Ditto, Whisper.

For now the Company was golden.

Word had gone out from the Tower, inscribed on hot iron: Do not fuck with the Black Company!

So Two Dead promised, in a private aside, insisting that the Lady had issued that order.

I studied Mischievous Rain from the edge of my eye. She was determined to pursue this search despite her emotional ambivalence.

I am quite familiar with having to get on with what I have to do despite hating having to do it.

I squeezed Firefly closer. She squeaked.

All right. Maybe she was my kid. Maybe she was an old evil pretending. No matter, right now she was somebody I cared about and feared that I might lose, in accordance with her prediction.

The wizards were restless. We were way east of the site of Elmo and Buzz's triumph. Virgin forest sprawled beneath us, vast, wild, and uninhabited. We were not likely to find any girls out here.

The girl-hunter girls were with us, though, so, maybe. If some of their kind had gone feral.

This was unknown country, the region its neighbors knew as the Ghost Country. The popular belief was that no rational being ever went there, though why not was never clear. According to Gurdlief Speak the Ghost Country had gotten its reputation more than a thousand years ago. Even the Domination had let it be—though that could have been because the Domination had not quite reached it before the White Rose's advent.

Where were we going? It was taking forever to get there.

The forest below became green fur on baby mountains. The mountains got taller. And still we flew on, the sun descending behind us.

The Taken abandoned straight flight, put on speed, began making long sweeps north and south, looking for something.

We got no heads-up as to what.

Firefly stayed snuggled against me, hanging on with both hands. Ankou and Beloved Shin crowded in behind me, part of the cluster hug.

Daylight began to fail. Mischievous Rain dropped into a meadow beside a rushing creek. Majestic pines crowded that on three sides. Poplars and birches skirted the creek. We had not been grounded five minutes before Firefly shouted, "I found some ripe blackberries! Tons of them!"

We made camp, nobody saying much, the labor divvying up without argument. We saw no sign of any human presence, nor did we see anything to support this being called the Ghost Country.

A doe ambled into the meadow, froze, stared, croggled, once she noticed us.

The Taken said, "Leave her be," before anyone suggested that we have venison for supper.

The meadow seemed idyllic but I suspected that it might be an islet of good cheer lost in a sea of unhappily not.

The wizards were anxious, excepting maybe the Third, who was too raw to be worried about what he could neither see nor smell.

Firefly picked berries. Shin roamed with a lug of shadow pots. Ankou vanished, presumably gone scouting. The Annalist and girl-hunter girls, being otherwise useless, collected the driest deadwood from alongside the creek. We should produce the least smoke possible.

As the light faded it felt ever more like we were in enemy territory.

We would have been more troubled had we not had methodical Shin and his amazing pots. The boy even waded the creek to make sure that we were protected from that direction.

Come morning he would get cold and wet all over again when he recovered his toys.

One-Eye grumbled, "There ain't nothing alive out here."

Goblin said, "There was that deer."

"But not nothing else. This here is a desert with trees."

He was not wrong. There were animals about, but surprisingly few, and those few were very quiet. Night should have become raucous with frogs and crickets and mosquitoes. I got bit once. I heard one owl hoot one time, way off in the distance. No wolves bothered to declare their presence.

The quiet made everyone nervous. The Ghost Country just plain lacked the kind of background noises that go unnoticed until they are not there.

That night the kids snuggled in so tight that I could not toss and turn. Ankou stayed missing. The Taken, that clever witch, slept aboard her carpet, probably the better to make a quick getaway.

She had herself blankets and a pillow but at no time had ever suggested that the rest of us might maybe provide such comforts for ourselves. That did not feed her popularity, not even with her own family.

The discomfort level soared next morning. Shin could not find one of his pots.

He led me and the Taken to the site. There was a dent in the soil where the pot had been, in amongst some pine saplings, near the corpse of a huge tree that had been down for decades. Some saplings were smashed, uprooted, or broken, but nobody on night watch had heard anything.

"It's not broken," Shin said of his pot. "It's gone. That's never happened before."

The Taken tasted the air, studied the broken saplings, examined a spot where something massive had slammed into the fallen tree. She plucked something out of the decaying wood.

"That a scale?" I asked.

"A hard scale. An armor scale, not just a skin scale."

And a big scale.

I considered Shin. "You didn't . . . ?"

"I slept all night. I felt nothing."

The Taken asked, "The other pots weren't disturbed?"

"They were not."

Hmm. Maybe I needed to rethink my take on those pots.

Neither Shin nor Baku had been involved in whatever had happened. But how about Ankou? Ankou was not big but he came with a major ration of tomcat nasty.

The Taken said, "Whatever happened, it's over now. The sun is up. We're all alive and we're all still healthy. Let's take this as evidence that we have to stay alert. Let's go get breakfast."

Somehow, without having been seen doing so, Blessed Baku produced eggs and sausages and the impedimenta needed to prepare them, along with ample quantities of wicked good tea. I had seen none of that aboard the carpet.

Maybe those kids could stash stuff in shadows and drag it out as it was needed.

Firefly just produced the food. She did not do any actual cooking.

The ever-observant Annalist did note, on that particular morning, in that meadow and in its surrounding forest, and down alongside the gurgling trace, that his world was awash in shadows. Tens of thousands of shadows.

And said Annalist really began to understand, deep down, that with the Taken and her sprats around the noise and sorcery was going to reach levels beyond the imagination of any Company sorcerer.

Shadows. Always shadows. Shadows always. My children were shadow spawn.

I lacked the imagination to encompass what my wife and kids could weave from shadow—which was all like mythical stuff, anyway. Like folklore, not like anything that you could encounter in real life.

Mischievous Rain, Blessed Baku, Beloved Shin, demon cat Ankou, they were all intrusions into my reality, conjured by the Lady in the Tower—perhaps as an abiding curse.

After checking out the missing shadow pot Mischievous Rain turned introspective and inert. Midmorning arrived before she decided to go aloft. I settled into my station, Firefly beside me. Mischievous Rain muttered, "We aren't going to find what I was hoping." And, moments later, "It's twisting out of control." She turned to the wizards piling aboard. "Change of plan, gentlemen. I need to take a look from as high as I can get. I need to minimize weight. You all need to get back off. Baku and Shin, you too. You'll be their hostages guaranteeing that I won't abandon them."

That was a joke. I think.

She poked me. "You stay. You'll be my spotter. And you, Kuroneko, Shironeko," indicating the hunter girls. "Watch out behind and to the sides."

Those girls were slight but they were heavier than Shin and Baku.

The wizards cleared off, per instructions. Shin went peacefully, too, but Firefly resisted. "I want to stay with Dad."

"That may be. But you'll stay with your brother instead."

Firefly put on a championship pout but she left the carpet.

The hunter girls were scared. The coming adventure might get ugly. And they were little more than kids themselves.

I was scared, too. Why was I being isolated?

Ankou bounded aboard as we lifted off, landing between the girls. He eyed me like he wondered why I was aboard, and maybe even why I kept on breathing.

So I asked, "Why am I here? Really."

"I don't know. I just have a feeling that you should be. Make your eyes useful while I keep us from crashing."

"Did you do something to them guys?"

"What guys?"

"The wizards. They haven't been talking. Not even Goblin and One-Eye, and they won't hardly shut up if their lives depend on it."

"I did nothing. But you're right. I should've noticed. However, I have been distracted." The how and why of that she did not explain.

Before I could ask anything more she said, "Ankou, talk to me."

She and the cat stared one another in the eye. I heard nothing. The carpet kept rising. The air got cold, and then it got colder. The face of the earth dwindled until it looked like a detailed map, parts of which were obscured by clouds and haze. I wanted to shut my eyes and pray till the Taken returned to earth, but I lacked my beads and I was a thousand leagues and more away from anywhere afflicted by the gods of my youth. They would not hear my screams.

Air currents toyed with us. We drifted. The carpet began a slow rotation. The Taken paid no heed.

Granite hills lay somewhat to the right of our direction of drift. They slipped in and out of focus, masked by a shimmer and possibly some thin smoke. I saw what I did because the sun was so blistering bright that it ripped right through the haze, the shimmer, and the smoke.

Straining, I managed to poke the Taken's biceps, then pointed. "Those hills."

"You're right. Somewhere there." Said with no enthusiasm.

She did not want to do whatever we were doing now.

Bless me, I could understand hoping for failure. I have been there, but with that hope disappointed more often than not.

The hunter girls produced startled squeaks. They began chirruping at one another and the Taken too fast to follow, in TelleKurre, which was a language that no modern girl ought to know.

Mischievous Rain nodded but looked like she was suffering from severe sudden-onset constipation. What was moving her?

I had no idea yet why she wanted me here.

There must be a reason. She did not act on impulse. Was it personal?

Something about the kids? It must be something that she did not want to share with my fellow thugs.

I did not think that I would learn anything now, with the hunter girls all excited and Ankou around to eavesdrop.

And there could be other witnesses. Shin's jars were amongst the junk that had not been cleared away before we took off. If I had even one ball I could creep back there, shift the girl sitting on the box, and see if the jar lids were all in place.

The sun was too bright. It slew the idea of shadow, for now.

No matter. Mischievous Rain had gotten focused again. She took us down until we floated below the taller treetops.

"What the hell?" I was seeing something that could not be. We were too far from civilization. "You couldn't build that without about a thousand workers." Which undertaking would have left tracks all over the legends of this end of the world.

We had found a castle smack-dab in the middle of a supposedly haunted, accursed, uninhabited wilderness. Well-tended fields, being worked as we watched, lay between us and the granite upthrust on which the fortress perched. It was built of dressed granite blocks, mostly in the common gray color but with some blocks black and even a few in the rare shade called rose. Some effort had gone into their arrangement but I did not recognize the resulting design.

"That must have taken generations to build. Damn! Is it for real?"

The castle had a sketchy, miragelike quality. It became invisible whenever a cloud masked the sun.

"It's real," the Taken said. "Written in stone."

"How did they ever build it?" I could not get past that.

"They used sorcery."

Of course. And that meant that there must be some real badasses over yonder. Or there would have been some back when the shack got thrown up. "Is that what you've been looking for?"

"It is. But it's not what I expected to find."

"Meaning?"

"Meaning that it's an order of magnitude more dangerous than I expected."

"So what did you expect? And why is this worse?"

Her response was imprecise and not directed toward me. "The wrong people are in control, now. How did they ever get in?"

Though ofttimes I am dim, and I understood that I was missing plenty here, I did not doubt that fierce danger lurked over yonder, wicked enough to intimidate one of the Taken.

I was way out of my element now. I could not fathom what was going on. Or was not going on yet but was poised like a viper to go.

Ankou left us after another eye-on-eye session with Mischievous Rain, whose tattoos now seethed. Her skin crawled like maggots in an old corpse.

She said something. I did not catch it.

Pale and scared, the hunter girls took jars from Shin's box. Really children still, they looked even younger than they were when they left the carpet.

They took a few steps and faded, going invisible. Definitely a useful skill for recon types.

I turned to ask the Taken about that—and decided not to trouble her.

She had become a suggestion of a hominid shape inside a boiling cloud of designs tattooed on the air itself.

Riding inches off the ground, the carpet drifted backward until it snagged on some brush.

The hunter girls returned, amazed that they had survived but totally pleased to have done so. They said nothing, just nodded in response to an inquiring look from Mischievous Rain. Both sprawled on the carpet, shaking.

Mischievous Rain withdrew, staying below the treetops. Ankou was not with us. I did not mention that. The Taken would know. And I wanted her focused on keeping us moving away from . . . an unknown something that scared me shitless.

She was shaken, too, but pulled herself together quickly. Soon we were headed west so fast that I was afraid I might lose what hair I had left.

So. We had found what Mischievous Rain had wanted to find. But that was not what she had hoped it would be.

We returned to the meadow camp, the kids, and all those grumbling wizards. Mischievous Rain cut her kids out of the herd. They whispered together for a while. Then she barked orders and went airborne again, this time with the wizards and Shin but without me, Firefly, the hunter girls, or the shadow pots.

Anyone who knew what was going on did not clue me in.

Firefly did suggest that us left-behinds ought to make preparations for a quick getaway.

Loud stuff happened off in the direction of the granite fortress. Then the Taken returned with all of our people still healthy, though she was mighty unhappy.

She had us load up while the hunter girls set out more shadow pots.

Because of Firefly's suggestion we were aloft and headed west in minutes. I was in my usual spot, sufficiently animated by an urge toward survival that I smushed down all inclination to distract the Taken by pestering her with questions.

She was in a mood to rip out livers and eat them raw, anyway.

A quick survey of the sorcerer crew convinced me that even Buzzard Neck and Two Dead were more cowed than I was. They were better educated. They better understood what we were running from.

Twice we grounded for self-relief opportunities. Shadow pots vanished from Shin's box each time.

The boy had three left when we got home and was whining about being expected to make more.

The kid was bone lazy.

28

Once Upon a Time: Shambling Toward Oblivion

Decades passed. Precious lived on. The children he created lived on, too. A few produced children of their own. Laissa lived on as well, ever in slow decline, indifferent as a mother and no grandmother at all. In time she stabilized at the functional level of a slow four-year-old. She could communicate and perform small chores but was useless otherwise. She lost all interest in keeping warm. Precious considered that a chicken-or-egg conundrum in relation to her decline.

Sometimes Laissa confused Precious with Papa. Usually Precious played along to avoid confusion-inspired temper tantrums.

Laissa knew that once she had been more than what she was now, but she could recall no specifics. Except when . . .

Randomly, unpredictably, never obviously triggered by anything, Laissa would suffer seizures of complete lucidity. The fog would clear. She would be as bright as ever she had been, fully aware of herself, her surroundings, and her plight. But those spells never lasted more than twenty minutes. They could happen hours apart or years, and when they did it seemed that a different soul possessed her, a soul that remembered every moment since her resurrection.

Souls, the existence of, were of special interest to Precious. Could his mother still possess one, having spent so many hours dead? Could his artificially created daughters have souls? Were those girls, narrowly speaking, even human?

Laissa's seizures always ended with Precious in tears because he could find no way to prolong those precious moments. Only then could he see the woman as she had been before he was born. Only then would she remember her sister. She asked when Kitten was coming home, every time.

She never confused the dark-haired fatherless girls with her sister. That amazed Precious. Those girls were exact copies of Kitten, who had, almost certainly, found death in the wilderness when he was only hours old.

Precious was an emotional boy who remained a boy emotionally because he had little chance to develop socially within his tiny community. The servant population dwindled with time. The remaining few became ever more inbred.

Thirty people populated the castle. Sixteen were Laissa, Precious, and his artificially created daughters. The only children were two dark-haired copy girls. They, as each of their sisters had, would receive the Blessing when they turned seventeen. They were the last youngsters Precious planned to create, though he could produce hundreds more. He had the process figured to perfection. He had no more need to experiment.

Too, nowadays he had no one to carry the fetuses but older copy girls. The serving women were all too old.

Precious spent decades trying to restore his mother's mind. He failed and failed again, never finding the faintest glimmer of hope. Laissa had been too long dead before Papa reanimated her.

Had Papa known then all that he and Precious would later discover, Laissa's story would have been less sad. She could have been restored so thoroughly that only a master necromancer might recognize that she had lain down with Death for a time.

. . .

Precious differed from his father in one respect. He had no interest in girls as girls, be those girls dead or be they alive, be they young or be they grown. He did experiment enough to discover that he would never be a natural father, and that he had no interest in the procreative act for its own sake. He found that all unpleasantly messy.

Most of the copy girls were not interested, either.

There were times when he thought the whole situation kind of sad.

Papa's line would end with him, and his mother's, too, perhaps.

Papa's journals told the tale. Precious was his only child, a miracle that could not be explained and that should never have been.

Decades rolled. Precious ran out of ways to busy himself. He cared for his mother, helped improve the fields and herds that supported the castle, and added, thread by thread, to the spells protecting and concealing the fortress. And, despite regular decisions to quit, he produced the occasional copy girl because everyone loved having little scampers around the house.

The Ghost Country had remained quiescent for centuries. That began to change. The "ghosts" began to stir, provoked from without.

In an age so long gone that it was recalled only vaguely in the early scriptures of Occupoa, what became the Ghost Country was the scene of a terrible sorcerers' war, horrible beyond modern imagination. The scriptures recalled it as a war for control of Heaven. The fighting was so savage, and the combatants so obdurate, that entire nations perished in seas of molten stone, were crushed by stars called down from the firmament, or were consumed by dreadful plagues.

The battlefield in time became the graveyard of the olden horrors. They buried one another way down deep. Most passed on along the normal path of corruption and extinction, but some became the hateful entities that gave the region its name. Others refused to accept nature and became the walking dead. Some had not been fully dead when they were interred and insisted on never dying. And the most powerful, the champions, full of life, too strong to be killed, got buried alive, deeper than any others, entangled in chains of sorcery so weighty that, in time, those cruel beings would abandon their struggles and resign themselves to eternal sleep.

Who did that to them? They did it to one another, one captive at a time. So Occupoa's book seemed to say.

That war had not been one strictly of sides and ideology but a last-man-standing tournament with divine supremacy as the winner's crown.

The imprisoning chains were not eternal. They yielded slowly to deep time atrophy. After a millennium all that kept the buried down was the fact that they had given up. The worst, the most terrible, the deepest buried, dreamed an endless dream in an endless sleep.

Their world had changed beyond recognition. Their magic had dwindled, had become depleted, consumed as later men appropriated the resource. Those ancient monsters would today be infants compared to what they had been—yet they would be fiercely lethal if wakened to the fact that their chains had rotted away.

Lesser olden liches had created the Ghost Country's reputation. Their chains had been weaker. They had been considered supernatural mosquitoes, though they could be deadly for any normal mortal who strayed too near their graves.

Their chains were gone but still they could not reach out far from their bones.

Those old spirits had no quarrel with the granite castle, Papa, nor any of Papa's people. Why was not clear. Papa's journals left Precious suspecting that his father had known the Ghost Country well before he emigrated to Dusk.

Papa never illuminated the mysteries of his earlier years.

There would be a grand story there, surely.

Precious experimented with Papa's carpet. He invested countless hours in careful trial and error, making short practice flights, always with copy girls accompanying him. The girls loved flying. Every one of the silly witches was ready to go whenever he was.

He caught one or another of them trying to manage the carpet herself on several occasions.

He kept the truth of the spell card to himself.

The girls were good spotters. They discovered several encampments just inside the western verge of the forest. Precious would have overlooked them because he had to concentrate on managing the carpet.

He kept away from the outsiders. He wondered why they would dare enter the Ghost Country but would not go close enough to find out.

One of his girls volunteered to go spy on foot.

"No way. That would be much too dangerous." He knew the world beyond the granite castle only through Papa's journals. In those the outside was a realm of truly awful men.

One of his girls reminded him, "You're a necromancer. This is the Ghost Country. Send a ghost to spy on them."

"That might work." Only, he had little experience with that kind of thing. Once he had tried to raise Papa's ghost. That had not worked out. Papa would not come back.

There were no ghosts in the castle. Never had been. No one ever laid a dead man, or a dead anything, down on barren granite. Precious had to find his ghost somewhere else. But where? And how?

He would have to search the forest. The protective spells close in were so dense and deep that no spirit, drow, or revenant, malign or benign, nor even anything alive, could get close or could get through. But those countless spells did nothing to keep anyone or anything in, and that sometimes led to wandering-livestock emergencies.

Properly prepared, anyone could come and go without difficulty.

No one had left since Laissa's sister deserted. No one had come in for a century before Papa passed. The rest of the world avoided the Ghost Country religiously. Or had until now.

"We should mind our own business," Precious said. "They haven't bothered us. And there's no reason that they would." No one would ever reach the heart of the Ghost Country.

The copy girls were not pleased. They had become excited, were anticipating adventures, were hoping for a break in the endless sameness of castle life.

Those sweet, pretty darlings had no concept of painful mortality.

Even Laissa's look-alikes were disinclined to remain passive, though the pro-action clique was that only relatively. Castle decisions were deliberate because time meant so little to its people. Seasons passed before a plan matured.

Precious did yield to the copy girls' desires but proceeded with extreme caution. Papa's journals had nothing good to report about the world outside, a realm of human predators for whom no evil was too black. Papa himself may have been one of the worst when he was young.

During the long preparation Precious drew closer to the fatherless girls—who were never really that, he had to admit. He might not be their parent biologically but, feeble though he was, he was the father they knew. They should more properly be called motherless copy girls.

The youngest did call him Daddy and melted his most stubborn resolve by calling him that while showing him big puppy-dog eyes.

His intercourse with the outside began with reconnaissance flights. His girls were bold and impatient but did remain rigorously cautious. He took four with him every time. They found several more outsider camps, all just within the western edge of the forest. The camps were occupied almost exclusively by ugly-looking and ugly-behaving men. Not one spoke a recognizable language. Their dress was alien, too, but Precious did not notice that. He had no standard by which to compare.

The outsiders were fugitives and brigands desperate enough to hide in the Ghost Country. Their camps featured wards against baneful spirits. How effective those might be Precious could only conjecture—but, he suspected, a practical test would not be long in coming.

The olden fallen were stirring. Soon they would leave their graves and barrows to hunt.

Precious and his girls never interacted with the haunts and revenants but sometimes they did spy a lonely lich considering their castle by moonlight, sadly, longingly, not at all in hatred.

Precious recalled a copy girl reminding him, "You're a necromancer."

Could he really do that?

Precious took some girls out and put them down near the camps. They scattered and scouted and learned nothing more useful than numbers and descriptions. They could not understand a word the outsiders said.

Those men were just barely surviving . . . and were more horrible than imagination had made them.

They caught one of the girls. They could not get her to say anything that they understood. They abused her until she died. She was just fourteen. Her trial left her sisters with a diminished hunger for adventure.

Precious restrained his lust for revenge. Instead, he pursued the course suggested by his girls.

He started in a meadow outside the fortress's protective spells. The girls helped. They meant to waken a few terrors and send them to play with the outsiders.

They succeeded.

Up from deep time rose spirits, specters, ghosts, liches, terrors in platoons. They went hunting outsiders. They hated everything living.

Precious never understood that he and his girls were not alive in the estimation of the undead.

A few invaders commanded sorceries adequate to deal with the Ghost Country's spawn. They were worshippers of the Domination, hiding from a terrible doom seeking them from out west, whence they had fled.

The Ghost Country demonstrated its wrath haphazardly and randomly, creating carnage without actually eliminating the outsiders or even driving them away. The survivors paid attention, gathered intelligence, and came to an interesting conclusion.

A truly heavyweight power must be resident at the heart of the Ghost Country, a power that had its own flying carpet.

The good guys sometimes fail to understand that the bad guys (interchangeable or arguable depending on where the observer stands) are as clever as they are.

In the centuries between the creation of the Barrowland and its breaking, and across the decades since, western peoples separated into factions like disparate lobes of a mutant four-leaf clover. Some tied their fortunes to the revenant Lady. More chose to resist her. A few maintained the struggle to free her husband, the great evil, the Dominator, from his Barrowland grave. But the outsize lobe, greater than the others together, were the folks who just wanted their kingdoms, their principalities, their free city-states, to be left the hell alone. That had been the way of the world since the Domination's fall, and just a lot of people wanted that to continue.

The interplay between factions made for a kaleidoscopically shifting political landscape.

The Lady lost battles all the time. She never lost a war. Her sway was a stain ever expanding upon the continental map. Kings, princes, prelates and syndics, all bent the knee eventually, or they perished.

The Lady's partisans strove ferociously to exterminate those of her husband, with all of their wives and children, all of their cousins and parents. They meant to expunge even the idea of resurrection.

Rebel and Resurrectionist alike suffered terribly during the Battle at Charm. Tens of thousands, even more than a hundred thousand, perished. The odor of putrefaction would persist for generations.

But there were survivors.

There are always survivors, be they ever so few.

Those who had fled beyond the Plain of Fear after the Domination's fall were the First Wave. The Second Wave were Resurrectionists who ran when the Lady emerged from the Barrowland. The Third Wave were the survivors from Charm. Few of those retained any will to fight.

The first two waves squabbled constantly. They were welcome nowhere. Most became brigands. They had no other way to support themselves.

Although they would resist the Lady later the native peoples entertained no sympathy for the Resurrectionist cause. Their cultures retained collective memories of the horrors of the Domination's brief rule, ages gone.

The supernatural skirmishing in the Ghost Country began decades before the Battle at Charm. Terrible things delivered terrible deaths to numerous unwelcome outsiders—who then sometimes returned as allies of their murderers.

Therein lay the core horror of the Ghost Country. There were numerous bits of folklore, come down from ages past, about finding friends or family among the relentless dead.

The uncommitted fled or dropped out of sight, not just of their enemies but of fanatical friends who would stalk traitors even while they themselves were being exterminated by the unrelenting dead.

The Ghost Country conflict was never one-sided. There were agile and accomplished sorcerers among the invaders, driven by a compulsion to raise up their own undead master. Remote descendants of long-dead servants of the Dominator, they disdained the ugly stories about the old days, though their dreams were haunted by whispers from afar, by tastes of the nightmares of him that they wanted to bring back.

Their effort to cleanse the Ghost Country did not go well. Their numbers dwindled to a few score. The survivors soldiered on, sure that capture of the granite fortress would guarantee ultimate success.

They knew the granite castle existed because they spent innumerable lives finding out what the Ghost Country was protecting. They spent many more lives trying to attain the castle, until they were down to those final few, most of whom were old men who considered themselves too important to be risked in the direct struggle.

Then a dark miracle happened—so it would seem.

The Resurrectionists kept records haphazardly, never reliably, never in detail, always ideologically blighted. Those began soon after the Domination's collapse and continued until the near extinction in the Ghost Country. At that time, apparently, there was no one left to keep records, even of the tainted sort found in the captured Earth Spirit facility.

There was no record of how, nor any echo in oral history, but the granite castle changed hands.

Most probably Precious did something ill-advised and got caught by enemies who forced him to take them through the castle's defenses.

Or possibly some copy girl managed to compromise Precious's control of the carpet, took it out and got caught.

Or perhaps . . .

History becomes its most problematic at exactly its most critical moments.

29

In Modern Times: No Peace, No Rest

No rest for the wicked? I lend that saying little credit, yet it is a fact of life, in a sense. A natural law. Even the good guys have to run to keep from losing ground.

I did not see much of my kids once we got back to the compound. I saw my wife not at all. She disappeared into her quarters, where she did this and that and whatever else for days on end, then at oh dark thirty one morning she piled her carpet with pretties and Two Dead and headed west.

Meantime, I consulted Sergeant Nwynn about the only child thus far produced by one of the Tides Elba girls. Nwynn did know where the kid was. Silent took a gang to collect him.

The child *was* a him. Of course. And, blessed be, he was right where he was supposed to be when Silent got there.

It did not take long to find out what the Taken had been up to during her shut-in time. She had been gone barely two hours when Whisper arrived, her carpet straining under the weight of her staff sorcerer crew. Never known for her beauty, her charm, or her winning smile, the woman looked way more grim than usual. Hell, she looked flat-out scared. Her companions were equally shaky. They were disinclined to fraternize so it took a while for word to spread.

There had been a come-to-god conversation between Whisper and the Lady, with the Lady doing all the talking. As a result Whisper would be the empire's most exemplary subject for a while, and her people would strive to outshine her.

Elmo and I shared grumbled hopes that the rest of the Taken had gotten the same word, though we had no problems with any but the Limper.

Whisper spent the night, then headed west with a girl posse and Buzzard Neck along as wrangler. That seemed sketchy, considering, despite Beloved Shin's guarantee that Whisper would cease to exist if she stuck her tongue out at Buzz.

During a rainy, blustery day two days later the Limper slipped his carpet into his usual place beside Admin. The damp brought the little shit's horrific ripeness fully to life.

Hagop told me, "It don't look like he got him a fresh ride." Snickering.

True, that. With pieces and parts tied and glued together, with webs of crude stitching keeping the ragged fabric fixed, Limper's carpet was the punch line to a very bad joke. He would have had to collect every fragment and fit them back together while keeping the monsters of the Plain of Fear at bay.

"I reckon that's to remind him that he's in this pickle because of his own behavioral choices."

Hagop and I saw the Limper early but within minutes every swinging dick in the compound came for a look and a chuckle.

Meantime, Limper vanished into some shadow space that the Old Man had set aside.

Like Whisper, Limper was on his best behavior.

So. The situation smelled nastier by the hour.

Did we now face an existential crisis *not* focused on pretty girls but on a pile of granite in the Ghost Country instead?

Could be. Could be.

Even idiots like Goblin and One-Eye soon lost the ability to remain upbeat.

Evidently we did not need clowders of pretty girls synching to spin us off into despair's darker deeps.

Every Taken blessed with a carpet found his, her, or its way to us before Whisper and Mischievous Rain came back from the Tower. Mischievous Rain showed up looking so dour that the kids and I decided not to welcome her.

Being a mushroom man I got no word at all as to why those dreadful people were all so grim.

The other mushroom men knew nothing, either.

I theorized that the Company remained involved only to provide logistical support for an operation that would involve most every sorcerer serving the empire.

So, hey, Annalist boy. You figure that granite pile out yonder might interest the Lady?

Silent brought the baby boy in—and the brat barely got a glance. He was just your ordinary, workaday love child, a biological misfortune with no significance in the grand mad scheme to resurrect an insane tyrant of old.

Sad and amazing. Or amazing and sad.

The boy moved on to the temple of Occupoa, of no interest now to anyone but himself. Poor tyke.

There is no excess of empathy in this world. When it does raise its head it is usually seen as a deadly weakness.

Elmo told me, "Stop whining. You know that if we didn't scoop him up he would've been the one."

"That would be the way it works."

The Taken swarm and their henchfolk were busy bees, round the clock doing stuff that none of them bothered to explain. The Company remained uninvolved, and, as mushroom men, had no need to know.

The twins kept mum, too. Beloved Shin did inform me that, "When Mom wants you to know she'll tell you."

The good news, sort of, came when Firefly told me, "You don't need to worry about Gurdlief. He's doing great at the Tower."

Good to hear, although I was not entirely reassured.

The Old Man kept our guys out of mischief by burying them in agricultural and civil engineering work, by having the horses and oxen exercised, and, finally, by having the fields and pastures that would begin serving the compound prepped for future planting.

Aloe was going to become a permanent imperial outpost.

Because of an improbable castle in the Ghost Country?

The Rebel was almost extinct in our province. Those still breathing had burrowed deeper than seventeen-year locusts or had run.

Markeg Zhorab said most of the survivors had abandoned their ideology and would not take up arms again. They had had enough.

I glanced at his scars. Perhaps he knew whereof he spoke.

I treated no battle casualties, just agricultural injuries. Hardly anyone, Company, townie, or even any of the reinforcements camped on our fallow ground, got sick, either. So I had time free for mischief. I used it to study on how we had gotten ourselves into our current predicament.

Something was not right. Something smelled. Maybe it was something so big that I just could not see it, something that might swallow us whole and never so much as burp.

I reread the Annals starting with the day that we got orders to move to Aloe. I reviewed my medical logs and other random scribblings. I discovered that I had done so several times before. I did not remember having done that.

What I read felt like it belonged to a life lived by somebody else.

I began to entertain paranoid fantasies that did not entertain me.

I became skittish around shadows. I could not shake the feeling that I was being watched, though the kids were not so much underfoot lately and I had not seen Ankou in an age.

I conscripted the Third and several literate troopers, put them to work making copies. "It don't have to be calligraphy, boys, it just has to be legible. Fast is more important than pretty."

Somebody delivered the inevitable wisecrack about somebody else being a champion at too soon and too ugly.

"Don't waste time on cut-lows, gentlemen. At least be copying while you're running your mouths. And, listen! Company privilege. This is top secret. Don't talk about it. Somebody keeps making us forget stuff somehow. We don't want them to know that we're trying to outfox them."

Oh, damn me! I should not have said that. Now every damned one of those bastards would put on a show of "I've got a secret!"

Too late. But I had to push on. Whatever we were into would loom large in Company history—a history that somebody wanted to take away.

I had a suspicion who but hardly a notion why.

I finished my reread in just more than a day. I started over immediately. I was amazed by the changes I had undergone in a single year. I had become focused almost entirely upon myself. I had stopped being an objective reporter. I had become a self-indulgent whiner lacking all interest in anything that did not feature me.

All right. It might not be quite that bad but it was true that my recent writing was not objective.

Whatever, my conscripts copied quickly, making severe time sacrifices and enduring hand cramps. The moment we had a complete copy I hustled off to the Dark Horse and engaged Markeg Zhorab to have his forger acquaintance produce more copies and hide them.

"How many do you want?

"Keep going until I yell 'Stop!'"

"Secret stuff in there?"

"No. Just stuff that I don't want us to forget. It's in Forsberger so he'll only be able to copy it, not to read it."

I lied. I do not use Forsberger to record these Annals.

I handed him some silver harvested during Elmo's great raid, enough to keep his associate scribbling for a month. His eyes got big. He nodded, then nodded some more, then followed up with a shallow bow.

The bastard was sure to skim. He had a Companyless future to worry about.

I did not let him see that naive Croaker had calculated corruption into the equation.

Taken came and Taken went randomly and desultorily, not a one pleased to be a guest of the Company. I had to give up my new apartment so important guests could be housed in the best quarters available.

Shin and Firefly migrated to my old digs with me. Shin remained grimly silent. His sister was never reserved about making rude comments concerning her mother and the Lady's senior henchmen, all couched in language she ought not yet to find familiar.

I tended to agree with her, though. Quietly.

Firefly enjoyed roughing it in my old shack so, naturally, Shin insisted that he was suffering the ultimate in disrespect and degradation.

I visited Sergeant Nwynn, indifferent to the pretty girls and their children. I talked. Nwynn listened. She nodded. She agreed. It might be useful to make secret copies of her records, too.

Whisper returned within the week and made a pain in the ass of herself, spinning off unwelcome orders like she had a right to tell the Company what to do. The Old Man put on a strained smile and nodded enough that the cranky witch never bloated up any worse. But then she called a meeting of the hierarchy of the Company and its sorcerers, people she had brought out with her, and a few folks from Aloe and the temple. She launched a rant that made everybody wonder if she had not fallen off the edge.

Then, like hitting a wall, she went stone silent and bug-eyed. Stroke? Could she possibly be that overheated?

A tiny golden sun formed a yard in front of her. It floated there for several seconds, then expanded into a light wreath with a woman's face inside.

Not *a* woman, not *any* woman, but *the* woman, insofar as all of us were concerned, the Lady herself. She gave Whisper a sad, disappointed look, like a mother might give a daughter acting out in public. Then she spoke.

I do not recall what she said other than suggesting that I carry on with my routine. After talking to others I concluded that she had done the same with everyone individually. Few could recall what she had said.

The Lady spoke, then she faded away, leaving us all in a more positive mood. A lot of self-important do-littles turned frenetically active, preparing us for war—while never giving up their whining and complaining. Happy soldiers, happy soldiers, every swinging dick and split-tail getting ready to go on campaign.

Whisper left without a word soon after the Lady faded away. Turned out she went to get the rest of the Eastern Army headed toward the Ghost Country.

All the Taken left us. Firefly said they were off to collect the rest of the empire's sorcerers and deliver them just outside the Ghost Country. The nearest human habitation was a hamlet called Amos. Amos would matter in no history whatsoever, ever.

I did what I could to prepare. Edmous Black pitched in valiantly, grumbling because he expected to have to do all the hospital setup work at the other end. "You get to ride out there with the Taken."

"I sure hope so. I might marry her for real just so I don't have to walk anywhere anymore."

I heard a noise. I turned, saw nothing but shadows.

Maybe I ought to watch my mouth even where there were no obvious eavesdroppers.

Black shook his head. "You're getting old, boss, if you can't think of something better to do with that than mooch a ride."

Shadow conscious, I eschewed any banter objectifying Mischievous Rain. But I could think it. Had been thinking it plenty, lately. But that was only a warm daydream. I would never find the courage.

I should not mention that even here. Too dangerous.

My fake marriage keeps intruding on real life. I do not go drinking anymore. I have not enjoyed a game of tonk in months. I do not often bullshit with anybody because I am never more than yards from one of my kids, usually Firefly.

The kids remain stubbornly unforthcoming about what is going on now. But I can do the sums. We are going to whack the Ghost Country with the biggest stick that the Lady can conjure. Only, why such a dramatic approach?

The kids insist that they know nothing. Firefly may be telling the truth. Shin, who knows? The boy spends his time pot hopping. He only turns up when it is time for supper.

So here I am, lord of the clueless, prince of the mushroom men.

The hunt for pretty girls, in its institutionally approved phase, has gone on hiatus, but my tribe keeps at it freelance. Those sweet things might still be the gateway through which an all-time asshole can snake his way back into our beautiful world.

What could be more important than stopping that?

Mischievous Rain came back as the locals were getting ready for the harvest. The Company command staff had become preoccupied with that, despite the continuous stream of imperial troops headed east.

The Taken was not pleased that the Company was engaged with agriculture rather than with getting trained up for magical warfare.

The Old Man was unapologetic. "We have to eat," he told her. "The soldiers tromping through here are like locusts. Their commanders have no concept of managed logistics. And, as an aside, I would remark that at no time were we advised to prepare for action." A dark glance my way silently suggested that I never mention that Edmous and I had been ready to roll for weeks. "We like to think that we're the best of the best but our skills don't include divining the unspoken intent of our employers. If you want something you have to tell us what it is. Otherwise, we'll execute our most recent set of instructions, which, in this case, would be to protect the locals and hunt for younger versions of yourself."

He had him some balls, the Old Man did.

Protection had to do with discouraging foragers, which made us unpopular with some of the guys headed east.

The Captain said, "Your people can't just steal stuff. That's how you get Rebels to begin with. We haven't had an incident here in almost a year. They like us. We brought peace. We're good for the economy. These people's big complaint is that we took you away and messed up their religious cycle."

This conversation happened in Admin with the Old Man forted up behind his big-ass table. The Taken faced Aloe's direction. "Yes. Sad. How soon forgotten."

I was there because that day the Taken had me tagging along everywhere like a big, goofy hound. I suspected that she wanted every little twist recorded.

Had she begun to forget, too?

I reread some of the Annals every day, now. If I let it slide the memories begin to fade.

Even so, Firefly is seldom far away. Is she just watching? Or is she under a compulsion? Could it be both? For sure she would understand why I insisted on doing so much reading. Had she reported that?

Gurdlief Speak came back with the Taken. He had had himself a great adventure. He could not stop babbling about it although, really, he had nothing new to report. He had uncovered no secrets. Shin and Baku quickly tired of his relentless enthusiasm for all things Charm. Shin told him, "I lived there! It's a corner of Hell. I don't want to hear any more! Go away!"

Gurdlief appealed to Baku. His future wife let him know that she had had a change of heart. "What Shin said, only doubled."

Gurdlief shrugged, not too bothered because the rest of us were tired of his enthusiasm.

Firefly told Shin, "They did something to him."

Shin grunted. "Probably." But he did not care. He had shadow-walking on the brain.

I should keep an eye on Gurdlief. He might be a spy, now, for the woman who rules the world from a prison of her own device.

I told Gurdlief to go back to town.

He looked hurt but he went.

Firefly told me, "That was the right move, Dad. That boy was special before but I don't have any use for him now that he's here to spy."

So. I guessed right even though familial espionage made no sense. But nothing made sense anymore, nor had done for months. Everything kept twisting crazier.

From then on we saw even less of Shin, and I became more concerned each time I did see him. He was exhausted, scared, and wanted to shed the demands being made of him. But, before I challenged his mother for risking his health, I reminded myself that, whatever Shin looked like, he was not human. Even I, his accused but still skeptical father, knew that. That stipulated, though, the boy was not a tool to be used until it broke, and then discarded.

My place within subsequent events was that of a lost boy. A totally lost boy. I never gained any grasp of what was really happening.

The last eastbound battalions passed by. Rich and poor Aloen landowners alike were happy. They had enjoyed a profitable season.

All the Taken but one, and all the empire's sorcerers but the Company's, had gone east, leaving us Company folks relieved. The outsiders were out of our hair, out of our quarters, out of our compound at last. But we did not get to celebrate.

Mischievous Rain collected the usual suspects and told the Captain to maintain the empire's interests everywhere east of the Plain of Fear, be those governance, justice, or military. He was not to be gentle when responding to problems presented by the governed.

My reaction, carefully hidden, was, "No godsdamned way!" There were eight hundred thirty-six of us now, the majority still spring green. The eastern provinces spanned hundreds of miles where we had no presence—and we were expected to be logistical monkeys for the Ghost Country operation, too.

A fierce reputation can carry you only so far.

Mischievous Rain stared me straight in the eye, her beautiful lips showing a ghost of a smirk. She knew what I was thinking. "You won't have to worry about it, dear. You'll be with me." She winked.

She what? She *flirted?*

She turned to the Captain and the Lieutenant. "The task should be less onerous than you expect. Something Whisper does well is tame a territory once she occupies it, however much she lacks enthusiasm for moving in the first place. You see her only through a veil of prejudice."

The Old Man grumbled, "Things trend that way once somebody tries to murder you."

I had no idea what she was thinking, really. Only she did. The prejudice remark might have been a joke. The Captain's response was not.

Me being me, I hatched a brood of questions. The rest of existence being the rest of existence, I got no chance to ask any of them. Important stuff needed discussing, stuff that trumped my curiosity. I went along without a whisper, pretending to be content with things the way they were.

Mischievous Rain's carpet lifted off loaded much as it had been for our previous trip to the Ghost Country, with added tents and blankets. The lady's husband knelt beside her, exercising his grip on the carpet frame. Their children were within touching distance but their cat was absent. Ankou had not been seen since our last venture eastward.

The hunter girls were with us, of course. Kuroneko and Shironeko were always nearby, now. They had become family. They never had much to say. They were sad girls, hard to tell apart when they chose to dress alike. They were only fourteen or fifteen.

The dark-haired girls, Mischievous Rain included, were identical but for their ages. It took a committed eye to discern the subtle differences between the two who were close in age.

Part of me would have loved to round up a dozen girls, in varying stages of ripeness, and hie us off somewhere like the Ghost Country, where I could found me my own special kingdom. Especially if I could do it all about ten years younger than I was now.

I was no conventional husband but I could not help thinking that it might be nice to enjoy some of marriage's more special blessings.

Firefly told me, "You're starting to turn creepy, Dad."

Having the kid point it out quelled the lateral drift.

Mischievous Rain's sidelong look and enigmatic challenge had an additional purgative effect.

We reached that same meadow with plenty of daylight left, the Taken having wasted no time this trip. The meadow was an idyll no longer. It had become an operational base. The greensward was gone. The turf had been taken up and carried off to become the base for a wall. Not one wildflower remained to remind us that not all the world was ugly.

Men were felling trees wherever there was room to swing an ax. They were building a palisade, with watchtowers, atop turf ramparts already put in place. They were building barracks to replace the current tents. They had completed a bridge across the creek and had cleared the creek's banks so sentries had an unobstructed view in that direction. A construction battalion was out there beyond, cutting a road back to the world. Another battalion was building a road toward the granite castle. You could tell where road construction was under way because a Taken circled overhead, ready to provide support.

Whisper was waiting when we touched down. She was accompanied by the special young men always found nearby when she was with her own command. They helped us unload, then led our sorcerers to a log cabin already set up for them. Some folks are special.

I stuck with Mischievous Rain. So did the kids and the hunter girls. Whisper was not pleased but deferred without demur. That surprised me. But, almost immediately, it became clear that Mischievous Rain was senior here. The Taken not on duty all turned up to show their respects.

Curious. My Aloen honey really must have clicked big-time with my Tower at Charm honey. She was Mama's clear favorite—for the moment.

Several pits had been dug to groundwater level in the middle of the meadow. Massive wooden cages surrounded those. Pits and cages contained captured things. Most were as foul as a monster ought to be.

Mischievous Rain examined each one while listening to the story of its capture.

Whisper said, "They're only shadows of what they were in their prime, but they're still a challenge."

"Have you tried communicating?"

"I have. We have no language in common."

"I see. Shin. Find Ankou."

"Yes, Mother."

I glanced at Firefly. "What was that?" The boy had been a perfect little gentleman.

Baku just smirked.

Mischievous Rain snapped, "Stay back, Shiroko!"

The hunter girl was studying a bearlike thing in a cage.

Whisper said, "You get too close, girl, you'll be dead. That thing is fast." She added, "We lost three men to that one. It calls you somehow."

Shironeko was bright enough to back away.

The bear thing was the biggest of almost fifty supernatural and necromantic double-ugly captives.

Mischievous Rain asked, "Can they be destroyed?"

"We did eliminate those that refused to surrender. They do burn, if slowly. Limper can give you better information about that. He's been experimenting."

"Where would he be now?"

"Flying cover for the men building the road to the castle. That's where we've had the most trouble. Come."

She led us to a pit where a dozen normal humans sat or stood in a foot of muddy water.

"Resurrectionists?"

"To a man."

"Have they been questioned?"

"They have been. Extensively."

"Did they have anything interesting to say?"

"No. They all claim to be spear carriers. Most are probably telling the truth."

"Pick three that may not be. Bring them to me after supper," said within hearing of the prisoners, in two languages. "The rest can become martyrs to a cause that's already lost."

She considered the captive monsters. "The same for those things, but not till after I talk to the Limper."

There are always survivors. My dearly beloved meant those, here, to be men or monsters flexible enough to shift allegiances.

I whispered to Firefly, "Mom is getting scary, isn't she?"

The kid showed me a wicked grin. "Come, O Darkness, and make me whole again."

"What?"

"It's from a poem that Mom wrote. She writes poems when she's depressed."

The kid knew about depression.

What a family I have.

Most of the men in the pits owned consciences flexible enough to let them take service with the Lady of the Tower, for the time being.

Mischievous Rain said, "We'll need lots of firewood. Have the men working construction save the waste." She gestured at the bear thing. "That might not die easily but I'm sure that it can be destroyed. We just need to make the special effort. Cut off an arm. Burn it to ash. Cut off a leg and burn that. And once the limbs are gone we can go for the head."

I flashed back to a harsh winter night when we burned some badgerlike things infested with absurdly aggressive poisonous beetles. "Damn! I wish Two Dead was here." Why was I remembering this?

Mischievous Rain said, "Yes?"

"We had an incident last winter." I told the story, remembering it all.

"I see. Your suspicion might be valid. That could have been a test attack."

"Maybe the people in that castle were pulling Rebel strings all along."

"Not in any major way. Too many logistical difficulties. But they could've influenced the establishing of Rebel priorities."

My wife, the onetime temple orphan, still only barely twenty-one, sounded like a humorless antique general who was a serious hard-ass. She started talking about us burning our way through the Ghost Country by sheer brute force, leaving nothing unfriendly or even neutral at all able to move.

Hard to love that girl while she was in cannibal mode.

Beloved Shin turned up suddenly, presumably having leapt out of a handy shadow. Ankou accompanied him. Ankou looked the worse for wear. He was missing several patches of fur. He had an ugly purple wound healing on his right haunch. He might have been missing a chunk of tail, too, though I could not be sure. His tail never stopped lashing.

Ankou and Mischievous Rain indulged in eye contact for several minutes, then the cat limped off toward the monster cages.

Shin said, "We need to hide the shadow pots better."

"Meaning what?" his mother asked.

"Two went missing. Six more were smashed."

How many pots did we leave up here?

Oh. He probably hauled more in during his nighttime adventures.

Ankou approached a cage containing a gryphon thing. It cringed despite being twenty times Ankou's size.

I said, "Those things have been here for over a thousand years? I can't get my mind around that kind of time." I could remember my grandfather telling stories about his grandfather's youthful adventures. That was as far a reach in time as I could make despite my fixation on old Company lore. I could go no farther than my kids in the other direction.

But old Company lore was my religion. Sort of. Was it not?

Mischievous Rain said, "They go back a lot farther than that. There isn't much we can do right now. Let's go get settled in and have supper." After which she would torture some people.

She slipped an arm around Shin, pulled him in against her left hip, then grabbed my left hand with her right. Firefly ducked in under my right arm. We all headed back toward where we had landed.

The hunter girls followed close behind. Whisper's men paused to ogle my wife and her little sisters. I might not appreciate their lust but I understood it. The lot were totally lustworthy, even in field apparel.

Whisper's jaw did drop because of our show of intimacy, though I was too stunned to do anything but go along. Whisper's soldiers paid me no heed. They did not know who I was and probably did not know Mischievous Rain, either, other than as a delicious alternative to their boss.

My wife said, "I like this. It's nice to be human once in a while."

For the next six days I was chief medical officer for the Ghost Country expedition. Despite spending my nonwork time with Mischievous Rain and despite bunking in the same cabin, I slid back into mushroom man mode, becoming the prince of the profoundly uninformed. I had no idea what was going on, or why it was going.

In some fashion, via Ankou, Mischievous Rain managed to communicate with the captive monsters. A few shifted allegiance to the Lady. Most did not.

Their pyres burned day and night.

Firefly stuck like my shadow. She said, "Those that choose the fire just want it all to end. Mostly."

Did she sound a bit yearning herself?

"No," she told me, divining my thoughts with a glance. "I have stuff to look forward to." A flash of devilish smile. "You want to play with your grandchildren, don't you?"

My answering smile was forced. That might be nice but she had promised me already that I would not remember her a year from now.

Accident-prone members of the Eastern Army had weeded themselves out long ago. There was not much work for the medical staff. Near as I could tell, we had it much easier than the other thousands, who put in sixteen-hour days between working construction and doing watch duty.

The biggest reason that I had nothing to do was that the troops were meeting no normal resistance. The Taken and their associates had scoured the forest of human foes. The Taken had no trouble discerning revenants on the move, either. They tracked those from above until overwhelming magical force could be collected to eliminate them.

Mischievous Rain's strategy was straightforward industrial. She was totally thorough, by the numbers, a step at a time. She would not hurry. She exterminated the lesser monsters before she focused on the big ones, the groggy ancients that were still not yet fully wakened.

Her approach to those, who in their prime might have been stronger than the Dominator, was industrial, too. Detect something. Identify it. Isolate it. Hit it with all the power of every adept available. Rest, then repeat with the next one.

I have heard that the light of those burns was visible two hundred miles away and the thunder could be heard for a hundred.

The Ghost Country became pimpled by upwells of molten earth

once again. Nobody called down a star but probably only because nobody had any idea how.

Molten earth proved sufficient unto every modern challenge.

Suppertime. The whole family was there, including Ankou, Kuroneko, and Shironeko. Everyone was bushed but me and Firefly. My wife said, "I am *wiped*. And we're doing eight more of them tomorrow."

"I wish I could contribute something."

"You do what's needed just by being here when I get home from work."

Firefly snickered. "Great riff, Mom."

"Maybe. But I mean it."

I said, "I was thinking, maybe the Lady could use the same tactics to fix it so we don't ever have to worry about a Port of Shadows."

The Taken, my wife, looked thoughtful. "I see problems that we don't face out here."

"Like what?"

"Like He hasn't been in the ground long enough. He's still awake. He's still scheming. An attack like what we're using here would break His bonds seconds before it could get to Him. We would set His tail feathers on fire but He would get away." She chewed a few mouthfuls before adding, "But it's worth consideration. There might be an angle. Good thinking, love."

"I don't have much to do but think. You don't let me ride along."

"No. I don't. And that isn't going to change."

Firefly said, "Hahh! You're too precious to lose, Dad."

The Taken said, "Blessed Baku! You are an imp."

"I can't help it, can I? Look who my mom and pop were."

Really? What was happening? This was the kind of silly shit that went on inside real families, or so I was inclined to imagine. It had gone on inside mine when I was Firefly's age, before the shit commenced its pitiless rain. There were few good days, then, however determined we were.

Mischievous Rain asked, "You just remembered something sad?"

"I did. From when I was little." I was uncomfortable. All those eyes looking at me. "You share a knack with our mistress's sister, Soulcatcher. She always made me feel like she was reading my mind, too."

"I'm sorry, dear. That's never been my intention. And I really don't know what you're thinking. Which is probably for the best."

Firefly giggled. "Here's an idea, Dad. Don't think thoughts that will get you in trouble."

"Baku, you're not funny," Mischievous Rain said. "*You* would be in deep trouble if I really could read minds, wouldn't you?"

"So it's not funny when Firefly says it but it is when you do?"

"Exactly. I'm a special case, dear."

Shin scowled. Firefly cackled and muttered something about perverted thoughts. I kept my big mouth shut.

Whatever verbal reassurance she offered, Mischievous Rain's smirk made me think that she knew exactly what horndoggery had been going on inside my noodle lately. But she was young. Maybe she was still too innocent to smell that out.

"In your dreams, Dad," Firefly said, meaning I know not what.

I never thought that *she* could read my mind.

Shironeko told me, "You're getting all creepy again." And she was six years younger than my wife. Then she said, "Shin, hand me another lamb kabob."

It was good to be tight with the top Taken. Carpets not out hunting or on air-support duty stayed busy moving supplies, of which there were always never enough—although there were always enough for some.

I was lucky in another way, too. Other than the wizards, who stayed too damned busy to spy on me, there were no Black Company witnesses to my brief season of favor.

Still, the riding would get seriously annoying someday—if I was not lucky enough to get killed.

Might as well savor the moment. Life is too profoundly harsh not to snag any treat or happy chance, however brief or small.

One thing I have learned for sure about life is, there will be changes for the badder. No matter how fair or foul the present, it can turn uglier in a blink.

. . .

We received doses of deep ugly the following week, starting when the troops awakened something millennially horrible. Something Dominator-scale horrible, or worse. Had every swinging dick not been anticipating something of the sort, had not every sorcerer not instantly run *toward* the fire, the more mundane thousands of the Eastern Army would have been well and truly butchered.

Even so, Croaker finally had him some real work. Too much work.

The forest bearding the Ghost Country suffered more than did Whisper's army. Vast tracts got smashed. Pines, firs, and spruces centuries old got shattered into kindling, then burned. Our sorcerers had no time to fight those fires because they had to focus on killing monsters so that they could stay alive. For a while it looked like we might have to run for it just to escape the fires.

A naughty weather god thought it would be fun to intervene.

It rained.

It rained every bit as savagely as it had that time when the summer storm came down on Aloe from the north. It pounded away for three days. The Taken and sorcerers stayed in the fight while the rest of us cowered inside leaking log houses, trying without much luck to stay warm and dry while water levels inside the camp rose because Whisper's engineers had not foreseen any need for catastrophic-monsoon-scale drainage.

The creek rose and rose. It swept the bridge away, and that a stoutly built bridge. Floodwater gnawed at the turf wall on the creek side of camp.

The good news was that the forest fires died.

The further good news was that the thing responsible for the fires disliked the rain more than the fires themselves did. If that makes sense to anyone who was not there.

There was a stunning magazine of lightning in that storm, and several vicious cyclones. One of the new Taken had claimed the departed Stormbringer's knack for managing violent weather, at least insofar as being able to direct the lightning.

That mostly smashed down on the revenant, down and through. Soon the lesser sorcerers were able to get in close and hack off chunks.

Pieces of the last and greatest monster went into sealed boxes. Once the world dried out and bonfires again became practical those boxes would get toasted, roasted, and charred into ash that could be scattered on the wind or the racing creek.

The lightning tried to make sweet love to the granite castle.

Every bolt was a hammer blow that powdered an infinitesimal fraction off its protection. The strikes never stopped. Once the storm moved along they continued using directed sorcery. Mischievous Rain was smug about her industrial strategy. The spell nets abraded steadily, slowly, like an edifice of salt assailed by a relentless rain.

After the storm we survivors suffered a wealth of sunshine and humidity and, uncharacteristic for the Ghost Country, mosquitoes. But old campaigner Limper turned out to own a spell for noxious bugs and he was willing to share.

Even the worst among us occasionally does something good.

My dearly beloved never lost her concentration. Once the rain stopped it took her just hours to determine that no further revenant threat would emerge. There was no reason for anyone, from herself to the youngest and lowliest apprentice farrier, to worry about anything but getting on after our main objective.

Damn, was it ever obvious why the woman in the Tower was invested in my special girl.

Mischievous Rain might be an incarnate animation of the Lady's will.

"You can come along this time," she told me. We had just finished breakfast. The family had collected around her flying carpet. It was an incredible autumn morning. Mischievous Rain squeezed my right hand. Firefly was on my left, clinging, maybe scared. Her mother, on the other hand, was relaxed and confident. "This will begin the wrap-up. I want you to be there."

Really? That did not start the happy sparks flying. It felt like she had a secret need for her deeds to be remembered, which left me thinking that she might be as unoptimistic about the long term as our daughter was.

I assumed my usual position on the carpet, full cloaked in abiding, nonspecific sorrow. Firefly stayed clingy. Shin was more sullenly silent than ever. Mischievous Rain mumbled constantly. I caught only disjointed snatches of something gloomy, utterly sad mutters.

But sadly sounds and moody bleaks soon abandoned us. The day would not sustain them.

It was an amazing morning, perfection, halfway between sunrise and noon. Nothing threatening lurked anywhere nearby. Much of the Ghost Country no longer existed. Vast tracts had been burnt barren. We had attained total success against the olden moldies and their modern allies. Only the granite castle now defied the Lady we loved.

Mischievous Rain took us to where she and I and the girls had studied the fortress before. She hovered where Ankou had left us, and where Kuroneko and Shironeko had demonstrated their aptitude for remaining unseen while they planted shadow pots.

The rustic charm was gone. Except for charred stumps and trunks the land had gone nude right up to the razor-slash line marking the boundary of the castle's protection.

The ground was black and turned to glass in spots. There should have been drifts of ash but that had washed away in the storm.

We had not improved the beauty of the province.

Mischievous Rain paraphrased an old saying: "We make a desert and call it victory."

Mischievous Rain then said, "Amazing, isn't it?" Not being specific about what she meant.

To me the amazing had to do with her approach to taming the Ghost Country. Her side, our side, had suffered inconsequently compared to our opposition. She had achieved absolute dominion over the second-most-problematic prefecture of the modern world. I did not doubt that she could crack the granite castle. I could see her taming the Plain of Fear using the same strategy, if she so chose. If our mistress at Charm so chose, although I could not imagine any reason for her to make that choice.

To be truthful, I had no idea what this ferocious campaign was all about. Well, yes, there were Rebels and Resurrectionists in need of butchering out here. Hints from the wife and kids suggested a possible connection to the Port of Shadows business, but . . . I could not help suspecting that something more was afoot.

. . .

We floated fifteen feet off the ground. The other Taken joined us. Not much got said. We stared across partially harvested fields. The rain had not fallen heavily there. The protective spells were even proof against the fury of nature. Damn!

There had been people in those fields last time. There was no sign of human life today. No animals were visible, either. I had seen sheep, cattle, goats, and swine before. "They've totally hunkered down."

Mischievous Rain said, "Yes. I had hoped that they would talk."

Firefly blurted, "After what you did to the rest of the Ghost Country?"

"Perhaps you're right." She said something in the language of the Domination. Flying carpets scattered, the Taken going off to check the shielding spells for vulnerabilities.

The protection should have suffered a serious weakening. Gone were the shimmers, the hazes, and the fogs that sometimes formed little patches at the boundary.

Mischievous Rain took us so close that the spells made my teeth ache. We traced the boundary upward.

Taken rejoined us, delivering reports in the old language.

Firefly hugged me harder and closer.

Ankou jumped overboard, undismayed by our altitude. He slid down the face of the invisible dome, growing as he went. He hit the ground still long and lean and black but now twice the size of the biggest, fiercest tiger that ever lived.

So. That explained why Whisper's caged monsters had been afraid of a little three-eyed kitty.

Ankou was one brutally terrifying apparition in this form.

I hoped my kids would not pull a similar stunt. I did not need to add them to my nightmares.

Mischievous Rain said something loudly but calmly, in TelleKurre. Clever Croaker recognized a few nouns, which let him know what language was being spoken but not much else. He had no idea what was actually said.

Swirling insanity followed. Carpets scattered again, after dropping off all not-Taken passengers, which included me, my kids, their hunter-girl aunties, and every associate sorcerer ever conscripted for the Ghost Country campaign.

Those guys had them a mission, though. Apparently.

Mushroom man Croaker had no clue before he saw the direct action. And what he saw then had little to do with what actually was going on.

He saw only what Mischievous Rain wanted the denizens of the granite castle to see. But those people did not care what she showed them.

The Taken found no weak points. They did determine that the barrier was more robust than Mischievous Rain had imagined.

From the mouth of a babe, Shironeko fetchingly wondered, "How come those people aren't making any effort to reinforce their protection?"

Firefly whispered, "Dad, stop with the creepy face."

Mischievous Rain said, "That's an interesting question, Shiroko. You would expect them to try to replace what we've ground away, wouldn't you?"

"Are they that confident in what they have in place already?"

Kuroneko chimed in, "They *want* you to do what you're doing."

The Black Company Annalist achieved a slow epiphany. "It's about exhaustion."

Our sorcerers had been dragging since the storm. They worked longer hours than did the soldiers with their axes and shovels. And sorcery drained not just the body but the soul. Even the Taken had been unmerciful with themselves during the life-or-death struggle with those absurdly powerful ancient monsters and revenants.

The barrier looked like just a little more furious effort would destroy it, yet the Taken declared it deceptively solid.

I said, "Darling, you are doing what they want, which is to wear yourself out. What if there's another barrier behind this one and it's just as strong?" I went on, "Those people are Resurrectionists or Rebels, right?"

"Resurrectionists. So we hear from prisoners."

Some of those had bought their lives and now made their livings doing scutwork around our camp.

"Did any of them know how they made such a wild and weird and marvelously invulnerable . . ."

"No!" Snapped with startling ferocity, so angrily that I did not need Firefly's warning nudge to put any further questions on hold.

Damn! What?

Minutes later, having calmed herself, my wife announced a suspension of offensive operations. She would not continue to do anything that our enemies might want her to do.

"We have time," she said. "I will not rush in and commit an error in haste."

It occurred to me that having the Lady's champions and sorcerers concentrated here already offered the rest of the world a serious temptation to indulge in bad behavior. I said nothing. Life went smoother when I kept my mouth shut.

Mischievous Rain left two Taken to orbit the castle slowly, low enough not to stand out against the sky.

Ankou stayed, too.

Everyone else got the rest of the day off.

Mischievous Rain declared herself a period of solitude. No one was allowed to interrupt her brooding.

I have reached a time of life where I need to make water during the night. Firefly sometimes snuggled in with me, when she chose not to go roaming with her brother, evidently feeling safer when she was there with me. I thought she was getting a little old for it but no one else seemed bothered. Normally I was careful not to disturb her when I got up. . . . She was there this time but she was not the only one. My wife was with us, too, making half a Croaker fantasy come true.

I dealt with my business, came back to see that I had not been dreaming, settled in, whispered, "Are you awake? And if you are, how come you're here with us?"

"Relax. Hold us. We need that. And go back to sleep."

I wrote it down next morning as soon as I could get to pen and ink. When I finished I was no longer sure that all that actually happened. It might have been wishful thinking.

Anyway, nothing more serious than spooning happened, in the real world or in that of the dream.

"Are there any ghost or revenant survivors?" Mischievous Rain pointed at me. "I know your mantra. But I'm asking about things that were dead already, now."

It did seem probable that plenty of spooks still haunted the Ghost Country. We had not been making war on them. But did they matter anymore?

Mischievous Rain said, "My husband is thinking that there are always survivors. I want to find a few that will bear witness to Ghost Country history back to the time of the coming of the first refugees from the fall of the Domination."

All of the Taken and several score senior sorcerers were on hand for this strategy session. They all heard her statement about our relationship. The Taken were all aghast, with Whisper either dreadfully distraught or deeply apoplectic. Limper had him some kind of shaking, sputtering fit. My dearly beloved pretended not to notice any of that.

The un-Taken sorcerers were indifferent, however—excepting those from the Black Company: Buzzard Neck Tesch, Two Dead Chodroze, and Silent. They were croggled. Two Dead was prostrate with amazement.

Oh, I was going to take me some shit somewhen down the road.

Mischievous Rain said, "Those of you with necromantic skills should look for a ghost, a fetch, a revenant, or any similar entity that might be able to offer a peek into the minutiae of the last few centuries."

She did not explain, though even the numb of skull could get that she wanted to know something about some particular past event. Something, no doubt, that had to do with that unlikely fortress.

She must have concluded that the castle's true weak point must be hidden inside its history.

She would not tell anyone what she was after. That would be an anonymous flake of gold hidden in a bucket of pyrite chips.

Was her reticence a control thing? Or could a bit of specific revelation put her at risk somehow? Or might the suggestion of a hunt for something specific blind any hunters to some alternate windfall?

Could it be all those things and something more?

One thing for certain. Mischievous Rain's approach told the other Taken that there was something worthwhile to be found.

The gathering broke up without anyone having said much more.

I never ceased being amazed by the fact that all those people just did whatever they were told, never offering suggestions unless they were asked.

Mischievous Rain's final remarks were, "Spread out. Check every acre of the Ghost Country. Whatever you find, I want to see it right away. Or be told about it if you can't bring it to me. Now go. Now hunt."

That drew further attention to the chance that there might be something more precious than gold concealed inside Ghost Country history.

Deliberate false trail?

I would ride that pony and see. I would learn nothing from my wife.

Firefly muttered, "She's playing with fire now," thinking out loud. She followed up by giving me a worried look.

I pretended not to have heard. She for sure could not read my mind. She decided that she had gotten away with something.

Mischievous Rain called in the Taken orbiting the granite fortress. Baku, Shin, and Ankou replaced them. Shadow walkers could deliver information faster than the fastest carpet rider.

This gets more difficult not just by the day but by the hour. How long before I lose everything that I do not record instantly and reread daily? I would suspect early-onset senility were I alone in my forgetfulness, but lately even some of the Taken have been struggling.

I wish that I had brought Sana along to remember for me.

Why did I write that?

Why am I not more focused, especially where the future is concerned? I am here to record my wife's . . . ah . . . what?

What, indeed? I have no idea what I am supposed to be doing. Certainly not patching anybody up. Nobody ever needs patching.

It is all scary and confusing. If it was not for my daughter's unwavering love and support I would not be . . . I would have no notion . . .

Any supernatural survivors were disinclined to be sucked into the maelstrom of today's power contests. "They're out there but they don't want to be found," my wife confided during supper. "But they *will* be found and they *will* be questioned. And they *will* tell us what we want to know."

My woman just stating the facts.

In a bold moment I observed, "And four centuries from now some megalomaniac will call up our shades so he can force us to do something for him. Or for her." Said entity might be the megalomaniac who had initiated our invasion of the Ghost Country, backed by a new generation of henchfolk.

Mischievous Rain cast a speculative eye my way, her expression less than affable.

It was in such moments that Firefly normally came up with some wiseass crack. Or Kuroneko offered some pithy and not quite apropos comment. Neither said a word now. So. Maybe I had stepped in it again.

I did not care. I was wasted physically and exhausted emotionally. The stress that began when Mischievous Rain named me her husband in public would not let up, though I did know that it was stupid to obsess about it.

After an extended silence, during which nobody met anyone's eye, Mischievous Rain said, "Darling, you and I will be going for a long walk after supper."

"If that is what you wish."

"Oh, it is, my love. It is. Be afraid. Be very afraid."

Shit! Oh, hell yes! I was afraid! I was, I was. Very afraid. There might be a painful do-it-yourself divorce coming up.

. . .

My woman and I strolled up to the pits. Those now lacked tenants. They were filled with water from the storm. The cages were gone. They had been broken up for firewood.

Mischievous Rain said nothing during our walk but once we arrived she stunned me by grasping my left hand with her right.

She stared into a flooded pit. I thought confused thoughts. I was absurdly conscious of her touch.

My apprehension began to fade.

She felt me relax. She edged closer, till we were in contact at hip and shoulder. I succumbed to a whole new set of insecurities.

What the hell was she doing?

I was about to melt like a slug freshly blessed with a shower of salt.

She said, "I laid awake all night thinking." There followed a ten-second eternity during which I could have gone into cardiac arrest but did not, then she continued, "The geology of the Ghost Country is all wrong."

Huh? Fut the wuck?

"There are all those granite hills, some of them baby mountains. But granite country isn't usually dense evergreen forest country, let alone hardwood forest country. Right?"

"If you say so." I had no idea.

"Granite country anywhere else is mostly bare rock and poor soil. Thin, rocky soil when the ground is relatively level. Vegetation usually consists of scraggly pines and scragglier brush. Hardly like most of this. Parts of this forest are plain lush. Parts of it are hardwood. And a granite country forest shouldn't have open meadows where you can dig sod blocks from black soil that goes down fifteen feet or more, either, guaranteed."

I had no idea what she was on about or how I ought to respond. Trying to be clever, I said nothing, just stood there looking expectant.

"In real granite country a clearing in the forest is there because the rock under the soil is so near the surface that trees can't put down decent roots."

That might be true. I did not know. If you asked me I would guess that trees did not grow where they could not get the nutrients they needed to get on about their tree business.

My beloved sniffed at that and let most of it slide on past. She was not interested in trees. She was interested in that unlikely fortress.

Somehow, someway, the boy child of shadow and the cat of shadow had found the truth that my love so earnestly wanted to claim. But it would be a while before the mushroom man learned about that.

It would be a while before anyone did.

30

In Modern Times: Dayfall

Another family breakfast. My kids were present. The hunter girls were, too. Mischievous Rain sat beside me, in touching distance. My left knee and her right were, in fact, in contact. Firefly was on my right and gloomy, like she had contracted old man grumbly and that would break out publicly at any moment. My wife smoldered, pervy, like she was inclined to rape me but was holding back because there were too many witnesses.

I do have me a lively imagination.

I was no more optimistic than my daughter was. How could I be? I was oppressed by a sense that we were drifting into our personal end of days.

And then I found myself wondering what the hell was I thinking when I imagined that? How did that even make any sense?

Whatever else, we had us a castle to reduce.

. . .

Somebody located a ghost for my darling. I did not get to audit their conversation. I was, in fact, invited to take myself far away. Not one but two Taken got told off to make sure that I complied.

How come?

The Taken, thankfully, did not include Whisper or the Limper. Feather and Journey still pretended to be human. They were young, as Taken go, and did not yet fully revel in their badassery.

With them babysitting, neither Ankou, Shin, nor Blessed Baku had to stay to wrangle me. Kuroneko and Shironeko did come along with, though probably to support the Taken if I went bugfuck or made a break for it. Unless they were along to keep an eye on the Taken, on the off chance that those two had caught a case of the unfriendlies from Whisper and Limper.

This was as close as ever I had been to those two Taken. They were not chatty. And I did not have what it took to focus and get a read on them as people. I learned nothing that was not general knowledge: they were young, male, female, lovers, that both before and after their Taking.

My head evidently had room only for Mischievous Rain and her captive ghost, and my kids. In particular.

Knowing what they must be, intellectually, did not keep me from wanting to shield them from horrible reality.

And I felt ridiculous whenever I caught myself thinking that way.

My banishment did not last long, though a subjective age passed before my reprieve came through.

Mischievous Rain told the assembly of heavyweights, "The call for the dead was successful. I confirmed the suspicion that I developed based on the odd geology of the Ghost Country, which, I now know, is a legacy of the conflict that took place here in ancient times."

She sounded a little pedantic but also excited behind an effort to appear calm. Which, if *I* could see that, had to be screamingly obvious to the other Taken.

"They tunneled under the bottom of the protective dome!"

They? Who they? What was she talking about?

"And the tunnel is still there. It saw occasional use until maybe twelve years ago. The storm flooded it and caused a couple of small collapses but we should be able to restore it and use it exactly the way the Resurrectionists did. Although, by now, they may have remembered their solution to conquering the barrier and be worried that we might work it out ourselves."

I wanted to squeal and shriek. What the hell was she yammering about? If Resurrectionists did not build that place, who the hell did? Who got that castle taken away from them?

Blessed Baku settled beside me and snuggled up while her mother was talking. I whispered, "What is she talking about?"

I did not expect an answer. None of them ever answered that kind of question.

So Firefly surprised me, but only by telling me what I had figured out for myself. "The Resurrectionists didn't build the castle, Dad. They took it away from the people who did."

So then I just sat there with my mouth open, wondering if I had known that before but had forgotten. My memory problems worsened by the hour. I strove desperately to record everything as soon as I could.

Maybe I should record everything in present tense, to get happening stuff down before it surrenders to the fade.

Firefly squeezed my arm and wiggled closer. "It's all right, Dad. You don't need to worry about it."

She seemed sad.

Mischievous Rain said, "Let's go!"

My wife's command turned out to be something less than a call for immediate action. Eight days passed. Nobody did much that was obvious. My wife started taking me along on her aerial travels, which consisted mostly of inspection tours along the roads to the world and to the granite castle. The former was complete and being proved up. The latter was good enough to let two men, shoulder to shoulder, march up to the castle's protective barrier without them having to clamber over anything or having to deal with brambles or obnoxious underbrush.

The hunter girls accompanied us everywhere. They were warming, some, to the old man who hung out with their boss. Firefly tagged along most of the time, too, looking like the hunter girls' little sister.

We kept doing nothing in particular and nothing spectacular, except that my wife ordered a half-ass resumption of demonstrations against the castle's shields. It did not seem likely that the people inside would take those attacks seriously.

They were not busywork, though. Taken who were able worked day and night hauling supplies in if they had no other obligation. The attacks must have tactical value.

I told Firefly, "Those people in there have got to figure that we're up to something."

"Well, duh."

We sat side by side on a rotten log in a chunk of Ghost Country that had not been damaged during the recent disturbances. Men from one of Whisper's battalions were entertaining us with their efforts to reopen the tunnel that Mischievous Rain had uncovered.

That was not an enjoyable or exciting show.

The kid added, "They'd never believe that we just packed up and left. They probably figure that we'll come at them exactly the way that we are. You think about it, it's really the only way."

"All right. Yeah. Probably. Hey! We know who's in there now but not who was in there before. Who built that place?"

She shrugged. "I don't know. And I don't really care."

Her attitude was not unusual. It was, in fact, almost universal. None of our people cared enough to ask why about almost anything. They just got on with doing whatever they were told to do.

I, of course, belonged to a gang whose calling it was to stomp on people who demanded answers and explanations.

The mine head for the tunnel lay a half mile outside the castle barrier, behind a hummock crowned with lightly singed trees and brush. The original miners had chosen the site because it could not be seen from the castle. It remained masked now but with so much nearby cover burned away I reckoned the castle folks would see enough activity to understand what was happening.

The work for the soldiers was nasty. They had to clear out mud and water and tangles of roots while installing supports to keep the tunnel from collapsing. They got filthy fast. I was so glad that I did not have to participate. I got rocky just thinking about having to creep through so much tight and cold, damp and darkness.

The soldiers worked in short rotations. After those they enjoyed hot baths and ate better than the other troops. That kept the complaints down.

Me being on the scene and handy to fix up anybody who got hurt boosted morale, too.

The fighting was over. The roads had been completed. There was very little work for the mass of the men to do—though Mischievous Rain did have busywork projects going on out in the wilderness, projects that I was not allowed to audit.

Mischievous Rain was in a quandary. She wanted to return several regiments to their home bases but at the same time she feared that she might need every sword and spear after she passed the castle's barrier. Logically, there could not be many enemies in there but we had no intelligence to that effect. None of our prisoners had ever visited the castle. They considered the insiders a separate tribe who had as little to do with other Resurrectionists as was possible. The prisoners were convinced that the Port of Shadows would be found in there, and might have been already. And even possibly opened.

That chance ignited no urgency in Mischievous Rain or Charm. Near as I could tell, the Lady had lost interest in the Ghost Country, being confident that her satraps could handle the denouement.

I grumbled, "I wish there was a way to know what's happening in there."

"Inside the castle? You and everybody else, Dad. But the barrier is too strong. You can't even do divinations about what's inside. Mom is actually excited about that."

Yes. She had mentioned that it would be absolutely dandy to know how to build such a masterpiece of a barrier.

I said, "I just had an idea. Remind me to tell Mom."

"Uhm?"

"She keeps fussing about having the soldiers all stay here. I just figured out why we don't need to."

"Uhm?"

"Those people in there haven't done anything to make the barrier stronger. That has to mean that they don't want us to see how weak they really are."

"No, Dad, what it means is, they don't know how to make it stronger because they didn't create it."

"Oh." Did I feel dumb. That was so obvious.

Silent sat down on the log on the other side of Firefly. My daughter signed, "Hello, Uncle. How are you today?"

Silent signed back, "I am doing well. You signed that perfectly."

My kid grinned, pleased. Her father shivered.

Evidently Baku had been learning sign from "Uncle" Silent.

I should keep that in mind. It was one more way that the kid could keep an eye on me.

I said, "The original miners definitely wanted to make sure that they wouldn't get found out early, starting from way out here."

Silent signed, "They could not know what awaited them. There were few of them left when they started."

Most of them, I supposed, stayed busy holding off the hungry spooks of the Ghost Country. I said, "A surprise attack. Makes sense. But there are plenty of us now. Why don't we just cut a trench underneath?"

Silent frowned slightly, like he wondered if hanging around with the hotties had broiled my brain. He signed, "That would offer them a point defense opportunity, though that would not be needed because the barrier would sag into the trench as the diggers removed the earth." He made a downward push motion with his right hand.

"No matter how deep?"

A nod. Exactly. "A mine is the only way."

"That sucks." I pointed. "No way am I looking forward to going through that."

Silent sneered, signed, "Pussy." There is nothing wrong with his hearing. He caught the note of panic.

I confessed, "I am a bit claustrophobic. And I'm no fan of wet feet or of having cold water drip down the back of my neck."

Silent's sneer expanded. His opinion was that it was time for Croaker to man up.

Firefly leaned back against a branch as thick as she was, stared at the heavens. "You have to remember that you aren't all that special, Dad." Then, before I could take offense, she added, "What you've got going, big-time, is that Mom has a massive thing for you, which baffles not only her but all the rest of creation, in every dimension that matters."

She stopped.

That was plenty too much for me already, too.

Silent seconds dribbled away into the ocean of eternity. Then Firefly sat up straight, scooted over, leaned against my arm and grabbed hold. "But I understand."

And then she cried.

And I found myself inclined to do the same, if only out of frustration because I did not have a clue as to what was happening.

Silent looked confused, too.

Sisters and whores.

Suppertime. Mischievous Rain was so close that I feared I might melt from the heat of her proximity. Kuro and Shiro smirked, surely thinking mocking thoughts. A certain old Company physician considered drowning himself because he might be turning into the kind of madman who begins believing that his fantasies have become objective reality.

Still, something might be going on. Unable to take a swim through the latest Annals, I could not know what had happened more than a few days ago. Only . . . My memories of life before we came east did remain clean and sharp.

And that left me terrified. Lost and terrified.

Why was I losing my life today?

Still, part of me was content with the loss if the payoff was that I got to be Mischievous Rain's consort, however disgruntled I might be because I never got to enjoy the full fruits of marriage.

. . .

There were comings and goings amongst the Taken even though it was midnight and there was only a sliver of moon for light. That did not bother me. I did not need the light. I was the mushroom man, entirely in the dark again.

Small units had been slipping away since nightfall. The logical suspicion was that the tunnel was set to go—only, those men were not moving to the tunnel head. They went off into the wilderness like maybe Mischievous Rain wanted the castle surrounded so nobody could get away after the final hammer came down. Which suspicion gained credence because the Limper got sent to hover above the granite fortress.

Last order delivered, Mischievous Rain came to me where I waited with Kuroneko and Shironeko.

The hunters girls were nervous in the extreme. Not terror nervous but like first-time-for-sex nervous.

My honey told us all, "Time to go."

Kuroneko said, "Yes, ma'am." Both girls headed for her carpet.

Mischievous Rain asked me, "Have you put down roots, then, husband? Do you want to miss it all?"

"Uh . . . No. All right."

We were fifty feet above the tallest surviving trees and headed toward the granite castle when I thought to ask, "What about the kids? Where are the kids?"

"They're working."

Shadow walking, then.

Mischievous Rain halted so near the barrier that it made everyone uncomfortable. A single light shone feebly high up in the castle. It looked like nobody over there was concerned about any possible attack.

I could see nothing but what was happening right where I was watching.

Out there somewhere Taken and soldiers were moving, the former darting hither and yon to keep one another informed. . . .

"Here it comes!" Mischievous Rain murmured. "Cover your eyes! Three . . . two . . . and now!"

A blast of white light ruined my night vision even though I had a hand over my eyes.

One of the hunter girls cursed. Amazing in itself, that.

"It begins," my love said.

The light blast was the signal.

The earth erupted a hundred yards behind the barrier. Venomous crimson light welled up, turning the world all red and black. The light totally betrayed preparations made to greet invaders.

What emerged from the earth was no band of soldiers. It was Ankou in demon form, fast and violent and spinning off shadow pots, murdering ambushers wholesale.

I saw that in moments only, unclearly, because so much other stuff was happening, like further explosions at other points that opened the way for other invading gangs.

Mushroom man was as surprised as was any defender of the granite fortress. He had not caught any hint that there might be supplementary tunnels.

In six minutes everything inside the barrier, excepting the granite castle itself, had become a prefecture of the Lady's empire, controlled by her legate, Mischievous Rain. Several formidable Resurrectionist sorcerers got transitioned on to the next world because they were unprepared for what befell them.

I saw no fine details from my vantage point but I needed no close-up to see that my wife had executed another coup, this one far more important than Honnoh.

"Excellent," she whispered, I think to herself. "Most excellent indeed."

She moved the carpet sideways, downward, away from the barrier. In minutes I was chin-to-chin with the nightmare that I had known was coming for days.

We settled at the head of the tunnel that I had been watching. Mischievous Rain left the carpet. Kuro and Shiro followed her. All three turned to wait on me.

All right. Those girls were barely adolescents but neither was scared of a little darkness and stinky muck. My wife did not think the passage would be any big deal, either. So who was the whiny little girl in this picture?

Croaker dared not even *think* of wimping out.

Well, he could think of it, plenty, but he could not act on what he thought. If he did he would hear about it every damned day for the next thousand years, or at least until he passed into the hands of Outsweeper.

Croaker sucked it up and stormed the filthy dark.

Swear to the gods, crickets were barking when I dragged my grubby ass up out of the ground. For several seconds I was so surprised that I forgot to turn and help the girls. I forgot that I was covered in filth and slime. This was not cricket season.

There were no seasons inside the castle's protective dome. That made for a gigantic greenhouse wherein it was always a growing season.

Amazing, yes, but the passage under the earth still had me by the imagination. I needed time to notice that nothing much was happening. My wife was surrounded by our cat and kids. I did not try to understand what that meant. I barely noticed Kuro and Shiro pointing at the castle while babbling in that language that no modern kid ought to recognize let alone speak.

I wanted a bath. Oh, so badly, I wanted me a good long soak in steaming hot water. Only . . . The only way to get that would require another slither through that tunnel. Unless . . .

"Honey, why don't you and me and the kids just retire here? It's a great place, out of the way, and nobody would ever bother us." A claim unlikely to fly because we ourselves were right now hard at it bothering the crap out of the current tenants.

Instead of chuckles or snide comments I got odd looks from Mischievous Rain and the hunter girls, like I had rubbed up against something without noticing.

Then I sat down and went to sleep, wet, dirty, and instantly.

I might have had help from an outside agency.

The eastern sky showed traces of orange when I wakened. Day was on its way. We would soon get a better look at what we had captured.

We would now move on the granite castle. Formidable as that looked, there on its granite peak, I did not doubt that Mischievous Rain could crack it.

So. While I had napped Ankou had clambered up the outside of the castle with a sack of shadow pots that he deposited in hidden places.

Meantime, Feather and Journey brought their disassembled carpets in through one of the tunnels and were reassembling them when I awakened.

Mischievous Rain gathered her favorites. "Several strong sorcerers await us in there. We should capture them if we can. There'll be other people in there, too. They aren't our enemies. Anyone who doesn't resist is not to be treated cruelly. So. Get set. We start when Feather and Journey are ready."

She beckoned me, then. I joined her where the hunter girls, clearly agitated, were helping Firefly produce a rough breakfast.

Some poor schlub had had to drag the fixings through one of the tunnels. Maybe a gang of schlubs since our whole mob was tucking in.

Firefly seemed distracted.

Everybody had something nagging them.

I asked Mischievous Rain, "What's bugging the kids?"

"Kuroko and Shiroko? They're about to see where they were born. They might even meet their mothers. Firefly is just aggravated because she can't get her own way." She laughed. "I pray to the gods that I don't smell as bad as you do. But I suspect that my prayer will be in vain."

This was where a guy should get all chivalrous. I went curmudgeonly instead, though I did retain sense enough to say nothing out loud.

Anyway, I was distracted by the suggestion that the hunter girls might be about to meet their mothers.

Was this strange castle where the copy girls originated?

Would that not mean that this was where my beautiful wife first saw light herself?

She did the mind-reading thing. "No. I was not born here."

I believed her without understanding why I believed. Somebody inside that place was mass-producing Mischievous Rains and Tides Elbas, then scattering them wherever orphans were welcome. Looked like the frog-eggs-laying strategy. Lay enough, some will survive and reproduce.

I took Mischievous Rain's right hand with my left, then Shironeko's left with my right, checking their pulses. My wife was excited. Shiro's heart was pounding so hard that I feared for her health. Kuroneko appeared to be equally stressed.

The sun cleared the horizon.

A boundary between light and shadow began to descend the castle's east face. Once it touched the castle's foundations my honey pointed and shouted what sounded like an order in that old language she favored lately.

Several granite blocks extracted themselves from the wall. The loving call of gravity brought a dozen more tumbling after, but the rest stood firm.

Kuro said, "There is our way inside."

I told her, "You girls be careful. The rest might not be stable."

My beloved mumbled on as the noise and dust settled, apparently proud of herself while, at the same time, being irked by some obscure failure.

She grumbled at two nearby Taken, then turned to me. "Have you seen the children, dear?"

"I thought you had them working."

"So I did. But I expected them to be back by now. Well. Whatever. Let's go on up there and see what's what." She said something more to Whisper, who nodded unhappily.

Whisper went off and collected the rest of the Taken, spoke to them briefly. Then they all got busy forming up the troops.

Nothing made sense but I kept quiet. This was no time for Croaker's big mouth. It was time for Croaker to shut the fuck up and try to remember so he could get stuff written down before it faded.

Going on up there meant climbing a lot of granite steps built at an odd pitch, taller than most stair steps are. We got to the breach, still forty feet below the regular entrance. My calves ached. Obviously sorcery had been needed to build the castle and to maintain and supply it once it had been built.

I did survive the climb, fourth in the procession. And although I was hurting I could not fail to notice the sweet fundaments waggling in front of me. And I did not feel embarrassed or guilty about noticing them.

It was all their fault. Those girls did not have to be so screaming desirable.

Sisters and whores.

Beloved Shin and Blessed Baku were nowhere to be seen, nor had Ankou been in evidence for some time. I suspected that there were shadows by the thousand up inside that rock pile, some of which had been seeded with stoneware jars. And now Feather and Journey circled the fortress, daring a response, probably serving as a diversion.

The rest of the Taken remained on the flat ground with the troops, all drawn up in neat formations.

The Limper, however, remained outside the barrier, overhead, waiting.

Mischievous Rain paused at the breach, leaned in for a look. From where I stood there was nothing to see but darkness.

She was about to step into that darkness when Firefly called down from above, "Come on up, Mom. The door's open. It's all settled inside."

"More climbing," I grumbled.

Mischievous Rain chuckled. "You can use the exercise, love. And look on the bright side. This way you won't have to do it in the darkness down here." She climbed several steps, then turned to ask, "Should I have Kuroko and Shiroko get behind you and push?"

"I'm not quite that far gone. Yet."

The normal entrance to the castle was ten feet tall and five feet wide. It opened by lying down to create a bridge over an eight-foot-wide dry moat, which here was just a long fall. The spire the stair climbed to the bridge point was clever but looked like it had not been part of any determined defensive design.

Whoever built the granite castle had not anticipated having to face real enemies. The place was someone's fantasy that was, only accidentally, hard to crack.

Firefly was excited. She did an excellent imitation of the pee-pee dance while she waited on us.

Mischievous Rain said, "I will lead when we go in." Behind her, Kuro and Shiro did their own pee-pee dance. Those two had no desire whatsoever to go into the granite castle but they were convinced that they *had* to do so, compelled by their very existence.

Firefly stuck with me, behind everyone else. She clung to my left arm, shivering, I think not because she was excited.

Mischievous Rain beckoned Feather, then told the rest of us, "I just had a thought. Something to check. I'll be back in a minute."

Feather eased her carpet in flush with the bridge and granite pillar. Mischievous Rain stepped aboard. Feather drifted away, climbed, then made a lazy circuit of the castle.

I presumed that Mischievous Rain's real purpose was to deliver fresh instructions.

Once my honey rejoined us Feather swooped down to the troops and other Taken, who then began getting ready to evacuate.

Why not wait till we took the barrier down?

Oh. Got it. Mischievous Rain had concluded that it could not be taken down.

Shit. That guaranteed me another slither through the dark and flavorful muck.

All of my recent whining about the sad course of my life had begun to seem justified.

Firefly did say, "We'll have to leave the way that we came in."

"Don't think you can trick me with that rat poop, kiddo. This guy can't walk through the shadows."

"So you got me there, Dad. But even so, you don't have to put on all the drama."

"If I don't do it, who will?" But she did have a point.

My posing was, likely, yet another symptom of my narrowing focus. Less and less was I able to see anything that did not center on me.

Mischievous Rain spent what seemed an age staring into that doorway. The surface of her yukata crawled. Her tattoos did the same. The stripes in her hair writhed. Then she said, "Here we go."

So. She was no more eager than the hunter girls now that she was where she wanted to be.

The entrance led into a storage area for cured foods and vegetables that had been carefully stowed: garlic, onions, potatoes, and turnips. Military necessity never entered the mind of whoever set this up. This was designed for the comfort of the lazy.

There were lights. They were not torches. They were not magical. They were weak blue flames in fixed sconces. I wished I had time to study them but Mischievous Rain wanted to keep moving.

Firefly told me, "Those lights are everywhere here. They're weird. They're always burning and they don't smell like oil or tallow."

We were falling behind. I whispered, "Does Mom seem like she's nervous?"

"Oh, yeah. She's scared. But don't ask me why." Then she added, "Maybe she *should* be scared."

"Why?"

"Because it's really, really, really weird in there. You'll see."

It was really, really, really weird in there. Really.

As I followed her it struck me that Mischievous Rain knew where she was going. She led rather than have Baku show us the way. We left the storage area, headed upstairs through fallow kitchens and on to what in any normal castle would be the great hall.

We arrived there on a platform three feet above the main floor, an architectural choice that made no sense whatsoever. The platform was twelve feet wide, a half-moon in shape, and had descending steps all round.

Mischievous Rain was one step down when Baku and I reached the platform. Kuro and Shiro were crowded up behind the Taken, holding hands and shaking. All three women seemed mesmerized.

I could not blame them.

The great hall was illuminated by dozens of pale blue flames. Only a scatter of tall, narrow, heavily glazed windows let any natural light infiltrate the fortress.

The hall was not huge. It was eighty feet broad and about fifty feet deep. A straight wall with one door sealed off some space opposite where we stood. Furnishings were sparse. Stairs at either side of the hall climbed on up to higher levels. There should be quite a few of those.

The human element provided the odd part, the really, really, truly weird.

There were a lot of people crowded into that hall, certainly more than a hundred. And they were really, really . . . and so forth.

Shin and Ankou, the latter back in kitty form, had them seated on the floor or furniture. The Resurrectionists stood out because they were all men and were all injured or dead. The three that remained healthy enough to pay attention stared at us in aghast horror.

Firefly murmured, in TelleKurre, "And they see their doom come upon them."

That had to be a quotation of some sort. It did not concern me much. What did, some, was that I understood her.

I counted nine men, eight of them obviously Resurrectionists.

The rest were all female, scores of them, all but two dead ringers for Mischievous Rain at varying ages, from clearly older than Kuro and Shiro down to a few months. Several older girls were obviously pregnant. Others might be without having yet begun to show.

The Resurrectionists may have been less considerate than had we of the Company.

I felt my woman's rage blossom.

Their doom come upon them, oh yes.

So. I now knew why the hunter girls had reacted so strongly when first we scouted the castle. A hundred of their sisters lived here.

Some of the older ones, I suspected, had been brought back once the Company began collecting Mischievous Rain look-alikes.

So many eyes looking our way.

Shadows danced around Mischievous Rain like those cast by breeze-tainted candles. Stars swarmed the surface and deeps of her yukata. Her tattoos remained as busy as a bushel of snakes.

All those girls looking at us were agape. Astonished. Dumbfounded.

I saw no fear, great or small.

I checked an islet of difference, two women in Tides Elba guise, one old, the other maybe the age of Kuro and Shiro. Hard to tell. The difference was more a feeling than anything definitive. They flanked an old, stooped man who looked like a duskier, gaunt version of them.

The only sound in the place came from people shuffling and breathing. Nobody had anything to say. The freeze stretched and stretched while everyone waited for the next thing to happen.

The mushroom man turned to stone. He wanted to be overlooked. He wanted to get everything firmly committed to memory, so it would stay fixed in his mind long enough to get committed to ink.

The elder Tides Elba suffered a sudden metamorphosis, going from total slumped disinterest to spear-shaft straight and absolutely focused. She stared at Mischievous Rain, mouth open wide. She produced a wild wide grin, then shrieked, "Koneko! You came back! You finally came back!"

She charged us.

Well, she charged Mischievous Rain.

Mischievous Rain stepped down to the floor, swept the old, old teenager into a big bear hug. "Laissa! Laissa! Yes. I did come back. I finally did."

The two sort of danced without moving their feet while hugging. The redhead said, "Papa died, Kitten. I cried a lot. That man over there is my son, Precious Pearl. The bad men forced us to make more of me and you."

"That's over now, Laissa. You're safe, now. No one will ever trouble you again."

Their conversation was in TelleKurre but I understood every word. Something had been done to me. Why? It for sure would not last. I wished that I had pen and paper in my pockets now, because this was something that my wife would not want remembered—even if she wanted it witnessed.

Stuff just went right on not making sense.

Somewhere, somehow, some woman was using some man to somehow validate something that neither he nor she understood in their hearts. And that somewhere was here in the heart of a castle that should not be.

"Firefly, do you know what's going on?"

"Not really. Mom doesn't tell us much about stuff that she doesn't tell you about. But I think that's her sister."

Really? A sister who had been a prisoner for ages out here while Mischievous Rain still had not yet turned twenty-one?

No. Wait. That would be Tides Elba . . . would it not?

Firefly clung to my arm like my touch was her last hope of life, crying quietly. She murmured something like, "It's almost over," in Telle-Kurre.

The thin man and the younger Tides Elba approached us. The elder Tides Elba repeated, "This is my son. He was just born when you went away."

"I remember. I see a lot of Papa in him."

The thin man bowed. "Aunt Koneko. Mother says many good things about you during those rare moments when she's lucid."

His mother said, "I forget things, Kitten. I even forget to be me, sometimes, for years. It probably won't be long before I forget again now."

The one called Precious Pearl said, "Because Papa did not start her treatment soon enough."

"I am a lost soul again, Kitten, like I was when you came to our old house . . ."

Laissa froze. She frowned. Her expression turned decidedly puzzled, like she had just lost complete grasp of her thoughts. Then a light seemed to overcome her.

"Kitten! I remember! When you came to our old house. When Papa had to go out into the storm . . . He wrote about it in his journal but even then I couldn't remember. But I remember now!"

Like every woman in the great hall this one wore heavy peasant homespun, crudely sewn. She added a pocketed leather apron over her floor-sweeping brown skirts. "Koneko! Your rings! I saved them for you but I forgot about them forever until now! I always treasured them, even when my mind was dark and I couldn't remember why."

Precious said, "Mother gets really excited when her mind works right. She tries to crowd as much into the time she has as she can. I think that she would last longer if we could keep her from getting overly agitated."

He seemed very sad about that, whatever it meant.

I caught only a glimpse of several black and silver rings that Mischievous Rain made disappear inside her yukata. I noted her considering me considering them and suspected that she was not pleased with my attention.

Those were some ugly rings. I had seen their repugnant like before but could not recall where.

Firefly's grip was so fierce that it hurt. And, somehow while I was focused on my wife and her sister, Ankou and Beloved Shin had joined us. The cat was at my feet, ready to do cat stuff and trip me. Shin had taken station in close on my right side.

My daughter's cheeks were wet with tears. My son eyed the gallery with emotions grimly stifled.

I could not help a growing sense of imminence.

Despite all, I surveyed those many sad-eyed dark-haired girls, some with infants in arms, and guessed that none of their babies were male.

So. For one insane moment I felt total triumph. We had won. The Port of Shadows would never open . . . unless one of those fat bellies there contained a boy. But that was all under control now, was it not?

Firefly whispered, "I love you, Dad. I really do. So does Shin, even if he can't say it. I'm sorry. We're both sorry. I think even Mom is sorry. But what has got to be has got to be."

Her grip on my arm tightened further.

I glanced down at Shin. He had teared up, too.

Mischievous Rain half turned, looked up, met my eye. Her tattoos swarmed. She said, "Laissa, this is my beloved husband . . ." and she spoke a name that I had not used since long before I met any of her kind. Not since a time when I knew only sisters. A name that no one in the Company knew, not even the Captain himself.

THE LAST

In Modern Times: Croaker in the Vertiginous Shade

The darkness began to fray. I heard distant voices, as if filtered through living water, discussing me. I had been drawn way far away, beloved of death, but then had eluded its embrace. Clever me, I slithered back to the living side of the boundary.

As my mind reconstructed shape and depth I strove desperately to reclaim my dreams. Without exception they slipped away. I salvaged only abiding sorrow and a vague recollection of a little girl crying. I did not know why she cried, though the core of me believed the incident to have been existentially important. The recovering everyday me was just baffled, wondering who the hell that kid was.

There was something in there about a boy and a cat, too, turned even more obscure.

None of my people shed any light. Head of the roster to its foot, wall to wall, every man of the Company had endured severe intellectual impairment, and every woman, too.

Dreams. Nightmares, perhaps. Everyone suffered colorful and detailed dreams that could not be recalled once the sun came up.

I tried to get Goblin, One-Eye, and Silent to study on that. Their efforts produced nothing. They just fumbled and stumbled, too.

A communicable insanity had claimed us all.

Edmous Black told me, "I've done everything that I can, boss. You couldn't be more set. But I'm not going with you. I'm staying here. If the Company was gonna stay, I'd stick. But there's no way that I'm gonna leave Aloe, love you guys or not."

"I understand." I did not understand. Not that, not much of anything else anymore. I was on a slide into madness. I woke up at night weeping, in flight from dreams so genuine that I could smell and taste stuff that must once have been real . . . though I found nothing in the Annals to support my convictions . . . which ever faded like morning dew.

A stroll around the compound took me past structures that no one could recall our reasons for building. The builders themselves could not remember why we had hired them. I could wander through a women's barracks big enough for a hundred troopers and never guess why we had needed the space when the Company had only nine female members, most of them married to Company men. My near nemesis Chiba Vinh Nwynn was more baffled than I was. She was convinced that something terrible had been done to her mind. She retained ghost memories of a time when the barracks she managed had been overcrowded.

Almost nine hundred people make up today's Company. All of those who belonged a year ago are now cursed with confused, distorted, evaporating recollections . . . of something. From the Old Man down to the Third and local kid Gurdlief Speak, folks keep asking me for news they need to make sense of a time that no surviving memories make sensible. I cannot help them. My own memories have been compromised worse than anyone else's. The Annals that might explain have all disappeared as though they never ever were.

The Old Man, the Lieutenant, Candy, those guys are not even a little stupid. They can winkle out truths just by staring down things that are not there when other people look at them. But they do not know now, either.

I suppose even a moron would conclude, based on the evidence, that the Black Company must have been smacked with a widespread, savage, and utterly, angrily deliberate memory assault.

Our top echelons are now preoccupied because we have received warning orders. The Company is to move on to a province named Tally, where the Rebel has been making a mighty comeback. When the need for preparation does not consume us we gang up and try to weave feeble recollections into a trusty portrait of what we had survived and then lost to an insidious thief.

Between us we can recall maybe ten names of people who are not now with the Company but who never graduated into Outsweeper's keeping.

Foremost, recalled by most everyone: Mischievous Rain, hauntingly beautiful. My heart, whom I shall love forever.

Secondarily, Two Dead Shoré Chodroze, possibly a will-o'-the-wisp Taken, though I cannot quite connect with that notion myself, and, then, Tides Elba.

Names I sometimes dream include: Ankou, Beloved Shin, Blessed Baku, Koneko, Kuroneko, Shironeko, Firefly . . . But I do not have the least notion what those names mean. Are they people? Places? Things?

My heart wants them to be people that once I loved.

Those names surfaced in the dreamtimes and evaporated quickly once I wakened. I kept pen, paper, and ink close by my bed. I got misty-eyed during the recording, every time.

I never developed a convincing theory of why.

Sometimes I find myself missing a pet cat that I never had. More often I find myself totally, insanely paranoid, shying away from every damned shadow when there is no way that shadows can hurt me.

So there I was, ready to head out to Tally, totally confident that I was insane and almost equally confident that sanity no longer mattered.

Silent invited himself into my kingdom of crazy.

He signed, "The truth cannot be lost, Croaker. Not even your children will be able to ferret out every copy . . ."

He stopped, stricken by the sudden realization that I had no idea what he was talking about.

He signed, "Even I will forget, of course, but, still, there will be a few who do not."

Sana. Of course.

Sana? That had to be somebody's name. But whose?

I said, "I'm lost. I'm drenched in ghostly dreams of things that cannot possibly have been. I'm drowning in dreams about people and events that can't possibly be real. And every dream totally fades within moments after I wake up. The only rational explanation is that I have gone completely mad."

And I was not entirely uncomfortable with that.

Silent signed, "Indeed you have, but not in any way that you or I will long be able to imagine."

I remember him signing that but do not recall why his opinion mattered, nor why he came to me to express it.

He no longer recalls the incident himself. As he had foreseen.

So what I have now is a sketchbook wherein I record any fragment that surfaces, like a bone chip working its way to the light. Scores once contributed bits but now no one bothers to report in. The forgetting is almost complete. Even I no longer jump out of bed in the night to attack my sketchbook with some sudden, unexpected recollection.

It will not be long, now.

Even the conviction that I might have lost something infinitely precious steadily grows more pale.

POSTSCRIPT

In This Age of Shadow-Soaked Days

The foregoing history was created using manuscript fragments found while Aloe strove to resurrect itself after having been devastated by a cyclone twenty-eight years after the latest events described. The most complete manuscript came from a chest that belonged to Sora Zhorab, spinster daughter of the Markeg Zhorab featured in the record. Oral history suggests that Sora never got over one of the men of the Black Company.

The testimony of Sana Ans, who actually remembers everything, corroborates what Croaker recorded.

The Company left Aloe a year or two after the subjugation of the Ghost Country. Imperial forces abandoned the Aloe facility a decade later, during a general withdrawal westward, once the Lady's empire began to tear itself apart with wars amongst the Taken.

Scholars generally concede that what Croaker recorded was what he witnessed, within the limits of tainted memory. The man never showed any will to deceive.

However, anything that he based upon secondary sources, to be maximally generous, *must* be accounted unreliable. Anything concerning the Senjak family, whatever the source, must, in the vernacular, be considered utter bullshit.

None of the Senjak sisters were described accurately. None of them were identified by their correct names. Laissa could not possibly have been Dorotea Senjak because Dorotea Senjak is almost certainly the Senjak sister who became the Taken Soulcatcher.

Most scholars are skeptical about the whole death and resurrection scenario, too, preferring to believe that to be a cover story for an elopement in defiance of the Senjak family elders.

Modern thought agrees that the Bathdek of the manuscript, supposedly Credence Senjak, sometimes referred to as Kitten or Koneko, has to be the sister who became the Lady. Her time as Kitten would influence her forever after, gifting a fierce sociopath with rudimentary empathy and a ghost of a conscience that would compel her, *in extremis,* to make unlikely choices when the welfare of the world trumped her personal ambitions.

The manuscript delivered several other likely accurate surprises. The pedophilic proclivities of the Dominator were traditionally reckoned to be just mud flung in hatred. And the likelihood that many of the original Ten Who Were Taken were related to one another, and were Senjak family outliers, unraveled several long-standing mysteries.

The modern events described by Croaker are supported by witness testimony, though not always in exactly the way that he reports them. The Black Company's interactions with the Limper are attested nowhere else, although a copy of the imperial rescript that Croaker references is amongst the Sora Zhorab papers.

Edmous Black, Gurdlief Speak, and Sana Ans, all still living, believe the Limper stories to be true.

However, all of those three do allow that Croaker was never above adding drama when he described events, nor did he disdain to portray himself as more heroic and central to events than he actually was, despite his literary inclination toward self-deprecation.

Today's fiercest debate revolves around the identity of Mischievous Rain. Who was she, really?

Most scholars believe that she was the Lady herself, while a minority argue that she must be one of the earliest copy girls sent to the Tower, especially trained for the Mischievous Rain role. That argument fails upon a quick skim of Croaker's work. He reports that Mischievous Rain's first visit to Aloe took place before any copy girls were found and relayed to the Tower.

Determined conspiracy theorists counterargue that, yes, indeed, that Mischievous Rain might have been the Lady herself, but the Mischievous Rain who came next time, who directed the campaign to cleanse the Ghost Country, had to be a different and more naive woman because she became so thoroughly infatuated with the Annalist.

A common belief at that time was that the Lady could not leave the Tower at Charm without weakening her supreme powers. That belief was, almost certainly, created through the deliberate spread of disinformation. During and after the Battle at Charm the Lady did exactly that, accompanied by Croaker himself, when she went out to hunt her sister Soulcatcher. That particular adventure did not cost her, nor did she lose her powers when later she visited the Barrowland.

Croaker is vague about the Taken of this time. He names Limper, Whisper, Feather, and Journey, and Mischievous Rain, who may not have been Taken at all. But there were others at that time, perhaps as many as five more, all of whom supposedly participated in the shriving of the Ghost Country. Some, surely, as with Whisper, Feather, and Journey, would have been recycled Rebel magic users who had been captured at Charm.

Few of the original Ten survived that battle.

But what of Tides Elba? The real, original, ginger-haired Tides Elba who came and went and in no reasonable man's mind could have been an actual avatar of Mischievous Rain?

Clearly, Tides Elba did not participate in the Ghost Country campaign, nor would she be mentioned again, under that name, in any recorded recollection of the Lady's empire. She ceased to be, disappeared. Perhaps she and all the copy girls, of whichever sort, joined the cat Ankou and the twins when they went wherever they went, never to be heard from again. Perhaps Buzzard Neck Tesch accompanied them. He was heard from no more forever as well.

The granite castle remains, damaged, empty, its fields gone feral. No one lives there anymore.

The most reliable information about the late empire is not reliable at all. It, too, is consensus guesswork woven from untrustworthy fragmentary records and hand-me-down oral histories. The memory problems suffered by the Black Company were not unique to them. The Company was just most intensely targeted. Nowhere in the Annals captured after Queen's Bridge is there any mention of the Company's time in Aloe. There is a grand blank there, and it spans almost four full years.

Bottom line, someone in the Tower felt existentially threatened by something hidden in plain sight within the record of the everyday facts of the Black Company's Aloen sojourn. Certainly they tied up loose ends by the hundred.

So, weigh what has been recovered, consider the sources, form your conclusions, then come to the discussion prepared to argue.

ABOUT THE AUTHOR

GLEN COOK is the author of dozens of novels of fantasy and science fiction, including the Black Company series, the Garrett Files, and the Instrumentalities of the Night. Cook was born in 1944 in New York City. He attended the Clarion Writers Workshop in 1970, where he met his wife, Carol. He lives in St. Louis, Missouri.